W9-CDA-082

Readers love Anna Jacobs:

'It's been quite a while since I found an author whose books I have trouble putting down. Keep up the GOOD WORK!!' A reader, Windham, Maine, USA

'I wanted to write to you to tell you how much I am enjoying your books. I have just finished reading *Beyond the Sunset* which I read in a day because I couldn't put it down. I get such a lot of happiness out of them. Thank you so much.'
A reader, Hampshire, England

'Just to say how much I enjoy your books and to thank you for transporting me into another world! I can easily lose track of time when indulging myself with a good read. Long may you continue to enthrall your readers.'
A reader, Tipton, West Midlands, England

'I would like to say thank you for your brilliant novels, of which I have become an avid reader. I have now completed 27, it would be difficult to say which was my favourite as I have enjoyed all of them equally.'
A reader, Bath, England

'Just wanted to say a huge THANK YOU for *Beyond the Sunset* which I absolutely could not put down!!! Only trouble was, I wanted it to be 640 pages not 340!! Can't wait to catch up with "the girls" again.' A reader, Victoria, Australia

'I'm twenty-one years old and just wanted to drop you an email to tell you that I love your books. I intend on keeping your books for a long time and hopefully pass them down to my children who I hope will love them as much as me. You are by far my favourite author.' A reader, Lincolnshire, England

'I have just finished reading one of your books, the first one I have read of yours actually, called *Our Lizzie*. Absolutely brilliant, one of the best books I have read in many years. I felt like I could actually see these people and felt Lizzie's pain. Fantastic. Thank you.' A reader, Ajax, Ontario, Canada

ANNA JACOBS

The Trader's Wife

HODDER

First published in Great Britain in 2011 by Hodder & Stoughton
An Hachette UK company

First published in paperback in 2012

8

A CIP catalogue record for this title is available from the British Library.

ISBN 978 1 444 71126 4

Typeset in Plantin Light by Palimpsest Book Production Ltd,
Falkirk, Stirlingshire

Printed and bound by CPI Group
(UK) Ltd, Croydon, CR0 4YY

Hodder & Stoughton policy is to use papers that are natural,
renewable and recyclable products and made from wood grown in
sustainable forests. The logging and manufacturing processes are expected
to conform to the environmental regulations of the country of origin.

Hodder & Stoughton Ltd
338 Euston Road
London NW1 3BH

www.hodder.co.uk

To David Boris, our delightful grandson,
with all my love. At age 4 he already loves books,
which shows he's an intelligent lad.

ACKNOWLEDGEMENTS

Once again, I have to thank the Australian library system, which is wonderfully helpful about research.

I'm also grateful again to Eric Hare, who is always there to help me with matters nautical.

PROLOGUE

Singapore, April 1865

The steamy heat of Singapore wrapped itself round Isabella Saunders like a warm blanket as she walked to the interview. She'd been applying for positions for three weeks now: governess, nursery governess, companion, lady's secretary, anything she saw advertised in the *Straits Times*. Most of the people to whom she'd written hadn't even bothered to see her, had merely sent a one-line response saying the position was filled.

But this employer had sent her a pleasant note inviting her to take tea. Surely that meant she had a chance? Because if it didn't . . . she shuddered to think what she would do then.

She knocked on the door and was shown into a very comfortable house. She smiled as children's voices echoed from upstairs. She liked children. They were so honest about life.

The maid left her in the hall, then went to tell her mistress. When she returned, she showed Isabella to a small room at the rear.

Mrs Wallace stood up and stared at her in dismay. 'Oh, dear!'

Isabella stiffened. 'Is something wrong?'

'You're much younger than I'd expected.'

'I'm twenty-nine, Mrs Wallace.'

'You look younger.'

The door opened suddenly and a young man put his head round it. 'Mama, I—'

He broke off to stare at Isabella, smiling, and her heart sank. The last thing she wanted was a son of the household showing an interest in her. She glanced quickly back at Mrs Wallace and saw that the woman's face had gone rigid.

'I'm busy, James. Come back later.'

He lingered for another stare at Isabella then left, his whistling echoing back down the corridor.

'I'm afraid you won't suit, Miss Saunders.' Mrs Wallace took a folded, lace-edged handkerchief and patted the sweat off her upper lip in an automatic gesture.

This was the bluntest and quickest rejection Isabella had yet had. 'Why not? You haven't even asked me about my experience or knowledge.'

'It must be obvious why not. I have an impressionable son at just the wrong age to have someone like you in the house. I *never* employ young and pretty governesses.'

'But I wouldn't—'

Mrs Wallace held up one hand. '*You* might not do anything wrong, but he is young enough to act foolishly. I'm sorry.' Her voice softened a little and she pushed a coin across the table. 'This is to pay you for your time and trouble in coming here. I really am sorry.'

Isabella would have liked to shove the coin back across the table, but she couldn't afford to be proud. She forced herself to say, 'Thank you for your kindness, ma'am. And if you hear of any other position where I might suit . . .'

'I'll let you know.'

She managed to get out of the house before the tears overflowed and stood for a moment fighting to regain control. When she had banished the tendency to weep, she set off back to the lodgings she had shared with her mother until the latter's death the previous month.

She crossed the Elgin Bridge, a long iron structure, heading south towards the native area of town, specifically the Chinese district, weaving her way in and out of the bustling crowd. Children ran past shrieking and calling, sturdy matrons gave ground to no one and coolies with bare chests and baggy, knee-length trousers trotted along, carrying loads of this and that, sometimes balanced on the ends of a pole.

None of them seemed affected by the steamy heat, but most Europeans found it trying and took their exercise very early in the morning. Isabella was used to it now. Sometimes, though, she longed quite desperately for the cool, invigorating breezes of England.

Below her, tied up round the edges of the water, were rows of small vessels, on many of which whole families lived. She slowed down because she never tired of watching them, envying the way they had lots of other people to turn to. They watched her too, because European women didn't usually walk out unaccompanied.

She was alone in every way now that her parents were both dead, and in the slow, dark hours of the night that terrified her.

Her father had been a clerk, working for the East India Company, and her mother a parson's daughter, who'd married beneath her. At first they'd all enjoyed living in Singapore, where servants were so cheap. Her father had brought them here with high hopes of making a fortune in the East, but instead he'd started smoking opium and gambling, gradually losing everything, even his life.

Now, with everyone gone, Singapore felt more like a prison to Isabella and she grew more afraid for her future with each day that passed. She had no money to pay for her passage back to England, no friends to turn to, either here or back in England, not even a language in common with most of the people she passed.

Her cousin Alice, who was more like a younger sister, had lived with them for several years. Then three years ago, her stupidly naïve cousin had believed the lies told her by Nicholas Renington and when forbidden to associate with him, had run off to marry him. Of course he hadn't married her! That sort of man never did.

A few months later another woman had moved in with him and no one seemed to know or care what had happened to her cousin. Isabella had stopped Renington in the street one day to ask him and he'd shrugged, saying Alice had run away from him and he didn't know where she was now, or who she was living with. He'd stared at Isabella's body in such an offensive way as he spoke that she'd hurried off, blushing.

She often thought about her cousin and wished she at least knew that she was safe. Alice had been lazy and not at all clever, but she'd also been affectionate and fun. They'd been close because they'd had no one else – until Renington. After that episode, Isabella's mother forbade her to have anything more to do with her cousin if she ever came back, or even speak to her in the street.

She shook her head. Why was she dwelling on that? It was over and done with. Alice was gone.

Once she left the crowded bridge, Isabella walked more briskly, eager to get home. She felt a surge of relief as she turned into a narrow side street where fewer people stared at her, because they'd grown used to her presence. Why should they bother about her? She wasn't a rich Englishwoman, accompanied by servants, or a European man striding out as if he owned the world. She was almost as poor as most of them.

What was she going to do if she didn't find employment? There were no lowly maids' jobs, because the natives worked so much more cheaply. She didn't have the skills to become a lady's personal maid, nor, if truth be told, the inclination to fiddle with another woman's hair and body. She preferred to use her brain, but that was as suspect as her appearance. No one trusted a clever woman, especially if she was reasonably pretty as well.

And although she was a competent needlewoman, she didn't have her mother's skill at creating gowns or altering old ones to look new. For plain sewing and mending, once again the native women were far cheaper. Anyway, she couldn't have lived on what they were paid.

When her lodgings came in view she gasped in shock at the sight of her possessions piled up anyhow outside the house. As she ran forward, her landlady's son used a stick to drive away a ragged Malay who was trying to steal her hatbox.

'What's happened?' she asked, knowing he spoke some English.

'Mother find new lodger. Pay more. You go away.'

'But I have nowhere to go! And I paid my rent till the end of the week.'

He shrugged and turned back towards the door.

'Missy.'

She spun round. A man stood to one side, taller than most Chinese, but still shorter than her. He seemed neither old nor young, and had a calm, confident expression. When he spoke to her in his own language, a few slow words, she wondered if she'd understood correctly. There were so many languages here, because there were Malays, Babas and Chinese – and the latter meant several languages since people came from various regions of China. She understood a few words here and there because of needing to shop at the markets, but that was all.

The man waited for a moment then repeated what he'd said. It sounded as if – no, surely he wasn't offering her a room?

When he took a step forward she shrank back, afraid

of what kind of price she would have to pay for a room, as well as surprised by his offer. The élite of the various races living in Singapore mingled at social functions, she knew, but although this man was decently dressed, he didn't look rich enough to attend those.

Did he think she would sell her body for a room?

He studied her face, then as she took another step backwards, he shook his head, as if reproving her, and with a slight smile, beckoned someone forward, a much older woman. She was dressed in dark baggy trousers and a tunic, and she had an extremely disapproving expression on her face. He put one hand on the woman's shoulder and said simply, 'Mother.' He waited, cocking his head to make sure Isabella understood.

She nodded and repeated the word.

He pointed to her. 'You – sister – room.' He repeated the last two words.

She guessed he was trying to tell her that she would be safe with him, and would either be sharing a room with his sister or be like a sister to him, but she wasn't completely certain which. And she didn't understand why he would offer this anyway. He must want something from her in return. What? She sought in vain to ask this in one of the local languages and failed to find a word, so said it in English, 'Why?' spreading her hands and trying to show she was puzzled.

He nodded as if he understood her question and pointed to himself. 'Spik Englis.' He gestured to his own mouth, said something in his language, then shook his head, frowned and said again, 'Spik Englis.'

'You want me to teach you to speak English?'

He nodded several times, looking as if he understood what she'd said. Well, people often did understand more than they could say in a foreign language.

If she'd understood him correctly, if it was a genuine offer, it might solve her problems, temporarily at least. But did she dare trust him? She didn't even know his name.

Just as she was about to ask, an Englishman walked along the street, moving arrogantly and forcing people to get out of his way. That man was the last person she wanted to see her like this.

He stopped beside them and stared from her belongings to her face, then eyed her body as he always did. Renington, the man who had ruined her cousin Alice.

'Trouble, Miss Saunders?'

'None of your business.'

'Looks to me as if you've been thrown out of your lodgings. I wonder why that happened?'

As he pretended to rub two coins together, she realised in sick horror that he must have bribed her landlady to throw her out.

'What did you do to upset the respectable people in this street?' His predatory smile made her shudder.

'What I do is none of your business,' she repeated, moving away from him. And if that brought her closer to the Chinese couple, she infinitely preferred them to him.

'Perhaps we can discuss my proposition again? I can offer you a home and bed.' Renington winked. 'I'll treat you well, give you money, buy you pretty clothes.'

She drew herself up to her full height. 'I've already said no and nothing has changed.'

'Oh, I think it has. Where are you going to sleep tonight? My young friend Wallace said you didn't get the job with his mother.'

How had Renington found that out so quickly? He was like a spider, spinning a web to trap her. That thought made up her mind. Turning to the couple waiting patiently to one side, she said, 'Yes, I'll teach you to speak English.' She tapped her chest. 'Like sister.'

The man bowed his head as if in acceptance and said something to his mother, who nodded. He clicked his fingers and two coolies came forward from an alley. They were strong, well-built men and moved forward so determinedly that Renington fell back before them.

She watched as they began sorting out her luggage and possessions, but it was soon clear there was too much for them to carry, so one said something to her companion then ran off.

The Englishman stared at her in shock. 'You're going off with *him*? A native?'

'I'm going off with this Chinese gentleman and his *mother*. He wants to learn English. I need a roof over my head. I've been looking for a job as a governess. Now I've found one.' She prayed she'd understood the offer correctly, but at least she had some hope if she went away with the two Chinese. She'd have no hope whatsoever if she went with Renington. He'd destroyed her cousin Alice's life and now he wanted to destroy hers.

One reason she thought there was a better chance

that her new employer didn't have designs on her virtue was because he hadn't looked at her in *that way*. The European residents considered that she and her mother had 'gone native' since her father died, which was not approved of at all. When her mother died and she continued to live alone in the native quarter, the European women treated her very frostily and their menfolk sometimes made remarks she considered insulting as they passed her in the street. All she could do was ignore them.

The Chinese and Malays muttered when she passed at the markets, but didn't say anything to her, nor did they touch her or pester her. From the bits she could understand, they were fascinated by her red hair and white skin, though some seemed amused by her feet, which were much bigger than most of the Chinese women's, especially those hobbling along with bound feet. She hated to see that.

'Missy!' The Chinese man beckoned.

She suddenly realised she didn't know what he was called. 'Your name, please?'

'Lee Kar Ho.'

She knew the Chinese put their family name first, so presumed Kar Ho was his given name. 'My name is Isabella Saunders.' She pointed to herself and repeated the name, 'Isabella Saunders.'

'Isaberra Saunda,' he repeated, speaking slowly.

His mother repeated her name too, though less accurately and it came out as 'Is-beh'.

Isabella wondered how much he had understood of her exchange with Renington, but there was something more important to do before she left with him. She pointed to her old lodgings and pulled a coin out of her pocket. 'They owe me money.'

He frowned and she tried to work out how to explain that they owned her four days' rent money. She took some small change out of her pocket, indicated the pile of possessions in the handcart and pointed to the house, miming paying them money, then miming holding out her hand as if waiting to be given something.

'Ah.' He walked to the door, where her landlady and son were standing watching. They bobbed their heads to him respectfully and after a rapid exchange of words, the woman scowled at Isabella and fumbled in her pocket, counting out some coins.

He brought them back to Isabella and offered them on his palm. She nodded at the amount and he took her hand and tipped them into it.

For some reason this exchange had his mother nodding approval at her.

When Mr Lee beckoned again, Isabella cast herself into the arms of fate and turned to follow him. His mother fell in beside her, not beside him.

'Whore!' Renington yelled after her. 'Chinese whore!'

Tears came into her eyes and she tried to wipe them away surreptitiously, but the old woman noticed and called something to her son.

He stopped dead, turned round and stared at Renington. He said nothing, but his expression was somehow threatening and the Englishman was the first to look away. Then he walked off quickly without so much as glancing back.

Mr Lee looked at Isabella. 'Name?' He pointed to Renington.

'Nicholas Renington.'

He repeated it twice and frowned, knowing he'd got it wrong, so she said it again slowly, and this time he got it near enough correct, nodding and saying it again, as if to seal it in his memory.

His mother muttered something and they continued walking.

Isabella could see the cart with her possessions bobbing ahead of them, could sense the people they passed staring at her. A lazy breeze stirred the hot air briefly, blowing in the same direction they were taking. I'm following the wind, she thought. I don't even know where I'm going. But I know where I'm *not* going, at least.

Holding her head high, she walked in silence. Whatever came, she would face it with the best courage she could summon up.

This might be her last chance at making a decent life for herself, earning enough money to go back to England and hunt for Alice. Surely her cousin would be there somewhere? Where else would she have gone from here?

Please let it not be a mistake to take this job.

Mr Lee led her to another part of the Chinese quarter, turning into a better street than the one where she'd been living. It contained neat rows of shophouses, built in brick and tile, three storeys high, with the shop itself on the ground floor. She'd occasionally visited shops like these with her mother or cousin, walking along the verandas which ran along the front of each row, gazing at the wares, buying something for one of her mother's clients, material or trimmings, rarely anything for herself.

The verandas were about two paces wide and food hawkers or other street sellers were offering their wares there, so as usual in this quarter, you couldn't walk quickly but had to thread your way in and out of the obstacles. Her mouth watered and she sniffed appreciatively as a man offered her a tray of skewered meat.

The old woman gave her a sharp look, as if she'd guessed her companion was hungry. Isabella looked away quickly. She'd been subsisting on one meal a day, usually fried vegetables and rice, with a little plain rice in the mornings.

To her surprise, they stopped at a shop selling beautiful materials. Lengths of vivid silk were suspended from rods near the ceiling, the colours arranged harmoniously but to catch the eye, with other pieces neatly folded on the shelves which covered the side walls and rear of the shop. A young woman, immaculately dressed in dark trousers and red tunic, was serving a customer, and she kept her attention on that until the woman had bowed herself out of the shop. Then she turned to smile at them.

'Sister,' Mr Lee said to Isabella, then said something in his own language to the young woman, who smiled and nodded to the newcomer.

He led the way through a narrow corridor to the back of the building. Goods were piled neatly in the rooms they passed, and only at the very rear was there a large room devoted to daily living.

Two young girls were in attendance there. They wore shabby clothing and Isabella guessed they were servants. One was working in a cooking area, where a huge metal pan sat on a hole above a beehive-shaped clay oven with glowing charcoal inside it.

The room also contained a table and chairs, shelves of crockery, smaller cooking utensils and blue and white crockery containers which might hold food and spices, as well as some smaller glass jars. On one shelf was a stack of bowls of the sort people ate out of, a jar containing chopsticks, a broader jar with some stubby pottery spoons sticking out, and one or two larger platters. Everything was immaculately clean.

Mrs Lee spoke to her son and when he nodded, she gave some instructions to the girls, one of whom left the room and pattered up the stairs that led up from the corridor. He went to the back door and called something to the coolies who'd taken Isabella's luggage. They were waiting patiently in a narrow rear area between their row of houses and the next.

They brought in her trunk and portmanteau first. Mr Lee beckoned to her and without waiting, led the way out of the kitchen and up the narrow stairs they'd passed earlier. He climbed the stairs so quickly she had trouble keeping up and he had to wait for her at the top of the second flight of stairs. This led to a row of narrow, open-ended cubicles, some with sleeping mats, others filled with goods.

There was a vacant cubicle next to the end, which the servant had just finished sweeping. A few items were standing in the corridor nearby. He pointed to Isabella and gestured to it.

Was this narrow little cell her new abode? When she hesitated, he pointed to the two cubicles at the darker end and to the servant. The next two looked slightly larger and as he pointed he said 'Mother', 'Sister'. Finally they came back to the bare cubicle and he pointed to her.

What could she do but bob her head in agreement?

The coolies brought up the trunk and Mr Lee looked at her then at her cubicle, as if to ask where they should put it.

She pulled herself together and indicated a spot near the open end. One by one they brought up the few pieces of furniture she'd managed to keep, including her mother's small table, which she used for writing letters. There were too many to fit in as well as leave space to sleep.

Mr Lee frowned and indicated the next cubicle. The servant hastened to make room in it for some of her furniture. Stepping back, he let the coolies position the chest of drawers where she indicated in her cubicle and other things next door. Finally they dropped the bundle of bedlinen and her rolled sleeping pad. Other people might be able to sleep on straw mats on the hard ground; she found it too uncomfortable.

Even with some things next door, her possessions were crammed so tightly into the small cubicle that she only had enough room for the sleeping pad, which would be rolled up during the day.

Mr Lee looked at her, studying her face. When he reached out towards her, her heart skittered and she jerked back. Had she made a mistake about what he wanted? But he shook his head, smiled gently and pointed to her mouth and then to his own. Beckoning her to follow, he led the way downstairs again.

Relief made her feel weak and she stumbled on the stairs. His arm was there to steady her, but he let go immediately and continued on his way.

In the kitchen one girl was cooking something which smelled delicious and the other was setting out bowls. Mrs Lee indicated a place for Isabella at the end of a wooden bench, and the cooking girl carried a huge bowl of steaming white rice to the centre of the table. The other carried two bowls, one containing some sort of meat, not a lot and sliced very thinly, the other containing vegetables in a sauce. Then both the servants sat down at the end of the table.

Mrs Lee began to spoon rice into the bowls, passing one to her son first, then to the others.

Although she was ravenous, Isabella waited to start eating, worried that she didn't know anything about correct table manners. She was relieved that she'd waited when everyone looked at Mr Lee and he looked at his mother, who picked up her chopsticks and took a mouthful of plain rice. Everyone else did the same, so Isabella followed suit.

She'd learned to eat with chopsticks but was not nearly as skilled as they were. They all took a little meat, and a bigger helping of vegetables, but the rice was the main thing they were eating, even Mr Lee. She couldn't help contrasting this with the huge meals the Europeans ate, the large helpings of meat.

The food was delicious and when her bowl was empty, Mrs Lee gestured to the container of rice. Isabella hesitated, not wanting to appear greedy, but the old woman looked at her shrewdly, grasped her thin wrist in one hand and shook her head, making a tutting sound.

It was that almost motherly concern for her health which made Isabella feel truly safe here. Swallowing the lump in her throat, she bowed her head gratefully and accepted another bowl of food. When it was finished, she offered her first English lesson, which Mr Lee was quick to accept.

'Bowl, chopsticks, table . . .'

She was so exhausted she was ready to go to bed at nightfall, which was about six o'clock in this part of the world, with only the smallest variation, because of being just about on the Equator. Sometimes she missed the long summer evenings of England, the soft, cool air, the filmy, clinging rain and oh, the crispness of an autumn morning! Here, it often poured down in the afternoons and the air was hot and humid all year round.

Only when Mrs Lee and her daughter led the way upstairs did she get her wish. They showed her how to deal with her bodily needs, the servants brought her a jug of water for the morning, then everyone settled down to sleep.

Isabella felt exhausted. Lying on her mat, covered only by a sheet for decency, she allowed a few tears to fall, tears of relief as well as unhappiness.

But following behind them came a tiny warm thread of hope. She hadn't felt this safe for a long time, hadn't eaten so well, either. Perhaps things would be better for her now.

I

April 1867

Bram Deagan stood at the stern of the *Bonny Mary*, staring back towards a glorious sunset as they sailed away from Galle in Ceylon. He'd travelled to Australia with his boyhood friend Ronan, and then come back to Galle. But from here onwards, his friend would be travelling back to Ireland and Bram would be going to Singapore. He doubted the two of them would ever meet again.

It was painful to think he'd never be able to go back, never see his family. He'd been dismissed and if he'd refused to leave the village, his family would have lost home and jobs.

His friend had never cared that he was gentry and Bram only a groom, and had assured him there was always a place in Australia for a man who was good with horses. But it was Bram's own choice to go to Singapore, which was to the north of Western Australia, right on the equator.

Sure, at the rate he was travelling, Bram might even find one of those fabled lands he'd read about, marked on the old maps 'Here Be Dragons'.

He'd have to rely on his new friend Dougal, the captain of this schooner, to show him round Singapore, because Dougal had traded there before.

Bram couldn't see his new path in life clearly yet, but after sailing halfway round the world and meeting new types of people on the ship, he'd begun to think differently about his future. Hearing their stories, seeing places like Alexandria and Suez, had set a flame burning inside him – just a small flame at first, but one which burned brighter and higher as it took hold.

When he first asked himself in the quiet reaches of the night whether he could be more than a groom, he'd been terrified by the daring of that thought. But it wouldn't go away, creeping into his mind again and again. Other people had made their fortunes in Australia, why not him?

Could he make a success of his new life? Could he really do that? He knew he wasn't stupid, but did he have the talent to make money? He looked down at himself with a wry grin. Nothing special about a medium height body, rather on the scrawny side, because he'd never had enough to eat when he was growing up. The food had seemed very lavish on the ship to Australia. It might have been plain, but he'd had as much as he could eat and more at every single meal, for the first time in his life.

He was by no means a weakling, because hard physical work in the stables built muscles, but it was his brain he needed to use now if he was to make money, and he worried that he wouldn't know enough. He wasn't stupid, had learned to read easily in the village school and continued his meagre education after he started work at ten by reading any book he could lay his hands on. His employers hadn't approved of that and he'd quickly learned to keep the books out of sight of the head groom.

You could learn a lot from books. He'd brought one with him on this voyage, about accounting it was, and a dry old thing too, but still – if he earned any money, he must learn to manage it carefully. Fools were easily parted from their gold, and he didn't intend to be taken for a fool. There had been other books available on the ship, and long hours of leisure in which to read them or simply chat to the other passengers.

If Dougal was right, in Singapore Bram would be able to buy trading goods cheaply to sell at a good profit when he went back to the Swan River Colony. He could also sell the rest of the contents of Ronan's mother's trunk. She'd died on the voyage to Australia and Ronan, grief-stricken, had said to throw her trunk overboard.

The waste of it! Why, the clothes and trinkets it contained would bring in enough to give Bram a modest start. So he'd spoken out, ignoring the disapproval in his friend's eyes, and got the trunk for himself. He'd sold several things from it on the ship and more in Fremantle, so now had a few coins to jingle in his pocket – if he were the sort to jingle his money for others to hear, which he wasn't.

I'll open a shop, he'd told everyone, seizing the first idea that came into his mind. But he wasn't sure he wanted to be shut up inside a shop all day every day.

No, he wasn't at all sure about that. All he was sure about was that he wanted to make money, was hungry for it.

He suddenly found himself praying, something he hadn't done in a good long while. *Please let me succeed, Lord. I won't be greedy, won't forget those struggling to fill their bellies each day. And I'll look after my family, bring them out to Australia, if I can. Please, Lord . . .*

Now there was a fine dream: to give his mother and father an easier time, and buy his sisters pretty clothes.

He stayed by the rail looking back along their wake, lost in thought, until Dougal came to join him.

'Let's hope we won't have such bad weather this time.'

Bram grimaced. 'I'm not fond of being seasick, I must admit.'

'Some people gradually get over it.'

Unfortunately Bram soon found he wasn't one of the lucky ones. The minute the weather turned brisk, he was again sick as a dog. Brisk! What a word for seas like mountains. 'This is the last time I come on a damned ship,' he said in between bouts of heaving over the rail or into a bucket in his cabin. It was the same vow he'd made when he arrived in Australia.

But what choice did he have? He needed to make contacts in Singapore, find people he could trust, people who could supply him regularly with the right sort of trading goods, things he could sell for a profit.

While staying in Dougal's house, he'd found an old copy of *The Straits Calendar and Directory*, which contained a list of goods traded in Singapore, but most of them weren't suitable for a small shopkeeper. He turned to the list again, trying to take his mind off his roiling stomach.

'Anchors, arrack, beeswax,' he muttered, running his finger down the page. 'Brandy – might be possible – brass wire, canes, china – what sort of china? – cloves, coffee, gutta-percha, mother-of-pearl, mace, nutmegs – yes, spices were a good possibility – piece goods, whatever that meant, rice, silk, tea, window glass, wine.' What sort of wine would you find in Singapore? Did the Orientals make wine? The family at the big house had got their wine from France.

He was woefully ignorant of the world, had never even tasted wine till Ronan shared a bottle with him in London. The colour had been pretty but he hadn't thought much of the taste. Give him a glass of porter any day!

Then he forgot everything else as he snatched up the bucket again.

Standing behind Mr Lee, Isabella kept a careful eye on the clerk in charge of releasing the cargo. He was speaking more loudly than usual, as some English people did when dealing with foreigners. What a fool! Mr Lee had already spoken to him in clear English!

To her relief, it didn't take long for her employer to finish his business and they began to walk home, side by side now because Mr Lee liked to chat about the things they saw and practise his English skills. There was always something new to see in Singapore, for her at least.

Today he was quieter than usual and she didn't break the silence, thinking about what she wanted to say to him. She intended to choose her moment carefully, however. She'd been feeling restless lately, hadn't enough to occupy herself, if truth be told.

A lazy movement of hot air, too slight to be called a breeze, wafted the street smells around, some of them good, some of them bad enough to make her hold her breath for a few paces. It reminded her of the faint breeze that had accompanied her on her momentous walk to the Lee family home over two years ago.

As they passed a display of durian fruit, she wrinkled her nose in disgust. It might taste wonderful, but the huge, lumpy green fruit smelled so bad she could never bring herself to eat it. The Lee family laughed at her for that, but in a kindly way. Once she'd proved that she was a hard worker, they'd accepted her as part of the family and been very good to her. They'd even told her to address Mr Lee as Ah Sok when they were at home, which was more like 'uncle'. And she called his mother Ah Yee, which meant an older auntie.

That night Isabella waited until they'd finished their evening meal before asking, 'Can we discuss my future, please, Lee-Sang?' Today she addressed him more formally, using the Chinese word for Mister.

His mother looked at Isabella sharply. Mr Lee gave her one of his bland looks, followed by a slight inclination of the head, as if to tell her to continue.

She felt nervous but knew she couldn't continue living like this. 'I've done the job you asked me to when we first met. Your English is now good and you don't really need me any longer. All I do is write a few letters in English and help Xiu Mei in the shop sometimes. Any clerk could do the letters for you and it'd be easy to find someone to help in the shop.'

He stared at her thoughtfully, giving nothing of his thoughts away.

It was his mother who asked in her jerky English, 'What you want do?'

'Go back to England, Ah Yee, to look for my cousin.'

'Not know if cousin is in England.'

'She must have returned there. Where else would she go?' Surely she couldn't be dead? Not lively, pretty Alice!

They'd had this discussion several times. Isabella looked pleadingly at Mr Lee, who was very much the master of this household – and of her. 'I've got to find out what's happened to her, Lee-Sang, and how can I do that if I stay here? Alice is the only close relative I have left. I'm grateful to you for all you've done for me. Very grateful indeed. But I'm not *needed* now.'

'You have roof over head. No need spend money. Good to save more. You safe here.'

He hadn't spoken sharply, which gave her hope. 'That's what you always say. And I'm grateful that you keep me safe. But I need to keep busy, to use my brain.' Not fill her free time with housework and plain sewing, or putting things into packages, under his mother's eagle eye.

He looked at her thoughtfully. 'Yes. Got good brain. So . . . I ask about Alice.' He still couldn't pronounce 'L' easily, so it came out as Arris, just as she was Isaberra. 'Be patient, little sister.'

He called her that sometimes and it made her wish she really was part of his family. 'But—'

'No benefit to me if you leave now. I do no business with England and if you go there, I not able help. And you need be safe.'

She felt touched by this evidence of his concern. He never said anything he didn't mean. She had been so lucky that day when she met him. 'But—'

'I find something better. Be patient.' He made a chopping movement with one hand, which meant the subject was closed, and she knew better than to try to pursue the matter. He was honest, kind to his family and careful with his dependants – but also ruthless if crossed, or if someone tried to cheat or steal from him, and a very sharp businessman.

She saw that he was still looking at her, so bowed her head in acquiescence. It would be wiser to leave Singapore with his blessing. And anyway, she'd want to come back one day to see them, if fate let her.

From what she'd overheard in his chats with his mother and sister, Lee Kar Ho had been a farmhand, who had come to Singapore years ago, like so many others, because there were more opportunities for a young man with ambition in a city that had only been founded in its present form a few decades ago. He'd worked as a coolie at first, but unlike most of the other coolies, he'd used the money he made to make more. He was now quite rich by local standards and getting richer, though he still lived in a shophouse. She admired him and his family very much.

He'd done this partly with his mother's help. Bo Jun

was a hard-working woman and shrewd with it. She ran the house economically, and was in charge of the day-to-day affairs of a small but exclusive shop on the ground floor.

But it was her daughter Xiu Mei who did most of the selling these days, who loved the beautiful silk and the other materials. She was not only good with customers but good at selecting fabrics to sell, and she'd shared her skills with Isabella.

The shop was only one of Lee Kar Ho's many business interests. Isabella had helped with the English paperwork for several others, the ones where he dealt with cargoes from incoming European ships or shipped goods to other ports. He had other interests, too, but kept the details of those mainly to himself.

Where would she be now if she'd been part of a family as hard-working as this one? It was a secret grief, not having any family of her own at all. But even when her mother and father were alive, they'd not made the most of their opportunities here. Her mother might be able to make beautiful clothes for ladies, but she'd done nothing else well, especially not cook or manage money. After her husband's death, she'd have been lost without her clever daughter to manage her life.

At a signal from Mrs Lee, the maid cleared the table and after everything was cleaned and put away, the women of the family sought their beds.

Isabella wasn't certain where Mr Lee was going tonight, but he went out several times a week after dark. Perhaps to a meeting of the secret society to which he, like many others round here, belonged. Perhaps to visit his concubine. She'd been shocked when Xiu Mei first told her about the concubine, but his mother and sister seemed to accept that as a necessity for a man still young and virile.

He visited singing rooms too sometimes, for these were very popular with the Chinese. For all she'd been living with the family for two years, Isabella had never been out after dark on her own. And his mother and sister stayed quietly at home, too.

Well, she thought as she unrolled her sleeping pad, she'd done all she could now to change her future and could only wait. Mr Lee had promised to look into Alice's disappearance, and he always kept his promises. But he'd do it in his own good time and use the information for his own purposes as well as to help her.

She felt she needed Mr Lee's help because Renington still stared at her in the street sometimes with that hot, loose-lipped gaze she loathed. The man always seemed to have plenty of money and without a protector like her employer, she'd have lost her battle to stay respectable long ago, she was sure.

Would she ever be free again? Was there such a thing as freedom, especially for a woman on her own? She didn't know, but she still hoped to make a better life for herself, perhaps even go back to England eventually. She knelt on her bed mat to pray, as she had so many times before.

Please let Alice be alive. Please let me not be alone in the world. Please, if it's not too late, let me have a family of my own one day.

The last wish was a forlorn one. She was thirty-one,

well past the age by which women usually married. But you could dream, couldn't you? That cost nothing, except a few tears and sighs.

Bram leaned over the rail of the *Bonny Mary*, watching the crew finish mooring the schooner in the Boat Harbour at Singapore.

'Coming ashore?' Dougal asked a short time later. 'Got to get everything in order before we can start trading. Official stuff first, then unofficial.'

Bram nodded. Unofficial meant bribes, he'd found out. He hated the thought of paying to ensure favours, but Dougal said it was normal here.

What Bram really wanted was to stroll the streets and stare at this amazing new world. Even the moist warmth of the air had surprised him, though his friend had tried to warn him about that.

The two men walked at a moderate pace, Dougal perspiring and cursing the heat, Bram saving his energy. He'd stopped wearing his merino undervest days ago and was wearing cotton drawers instead of the woollen ones he'd used in Ireland. So stupid to keep wearing woollen clothing in hot climates!

He remembered all the times he'd been cold or wet, and longed to be warm. Here, it was the other way round, you'd long for crisp, cool air – or at least you might if you knew such a thing existed. Was there such a thing as winter here? Dougal said it was the same all the year round – hot, and often with short storms in the afternoons.

An elbow jabbed into his ribs. 'Don't stare! It's considered very rude.'

So Bram tried to walk without staring, just letting the images slip into his brain: oriental faces everywhere, different types of clothes, women in trousers, men clad only in knee-length breeches, carrying bundles on the two ends of long poles. Little children were shrieking and running, older children seemed more serious, going on errands, perhaps, or walking respectfully behind an older person.

In the distance he saw a European woman. She stood out among the crowds of Orientals, not only because she was taller than most of them, but because she had red hair. She wasn't beautiful, but she was striking. She was strolling along with a Chinese man and the two of them were talking earnestly. Bram was sorry when she disappeared from view. He'd enjoyed watching her expressive face as she gesticulated and chatted.

He could have walked round all day, filling his eyes with the sights, but Dougal wanted only to get back to the ship, insisting it was cooler on the water. That was doubtful, but if he believed it, no doubt he felt better there.

Duty calls paid, Dougal stayed on the ship, waiting for certain men he knew and traded with to come to him. 'I don't trade with only one person. Not wise, that. Gives them too much control over you.'

Two days later, Dougal lay in his bunk, looking wan, disinclined to do anything, because he'd eaten something that disagreed with him the previous day. Bram stayed on deck for a while, bored, then decided to go into town on his own.

'Take a guide,' his friend insisted. 'You think you'll

remember your way back, but you won't. And remember, tonight we're going out for dinner at the Wallaces. He's a relative on my mother's side, pretty distant, but it's nice to have somewhere to go in the evenings. I'm certainly not going to a wayang theatre again – you never heard such caterwauling in your life as that Chinese opera.'

So Bram allowed a crew member to haggle for the services of a guide who spoke some English, then set off to wander round the streets. His guide took him to the European area, which had wider streets and pleasant villas in one part, larger houses in another area, and he had difficulty convincing the man this wasn't what he wanted to see.

They went next to Raffles Place on the south side of the river. He was confused at first because his guide sometimes called it Commercial Square, its previous name.

Afterwards Bram made the man understand that what he really wanted to see were the native quarters, also south of the river.

It was as he and his guide were walking down a side street that led off an area of water filled with rows of small vessels – sampans, he thought his guide had called them – that he saw the red-haired woman again and stopped to admire her. 'Do you know who she is?' he asked.

'Work for Lee Kar Ho. Teach English. Not know name.'

Bram felt disappointed. Surely a European woman wouldn't work for a Chinese? Even in the short time he'd been here, he'd gathered that this was not considered respectable. Yet she didn't look immoral, not with that clear, intelligent gaze.

On an impulse Bram followed her along the street, hoping for a chance encounter, which was foolish, but there you were. He wanted to meet her.

As she was passing a narrow gap between two rows of houses, two Chinese men darted out and grabbed her, dragging her back into the alley. It was done so quickly, without her even having a chance to scream before a hand covered her mouth, that if he hadn't been watching her specifically, he'd not have noticed.

He set off running, followed by his guide, bumping into people and not stopping to apologise. When he got to the end of the alley, he saw the men dragging her along it. She was struggling like a wild cat he'd once seen, clawing and scratching, trying to get free of the hand that prevented her from screaming. At the end of the alley a man was watching, a European man, making no attempt to help her and smiling as if he was enjoying the sight.

'Hoy! Stop that! Let her go!' Bram rushed forward.

Behind him his guide was calling out, but Bram was intent on getting to her before she was harmed or taken away, so he ran on alone. Anger lent him strength and speed, and he punched the nearest man before the fellow could defend himself. That freed her to struggle against the one holding her from behind.

Men were rushing into the alley from the street now and his guide called out that help had arrived. The white man vanished round the corner.

The two attackers let go and tried to run away too, but Bram was still furious and wanted more than just to drive them away. He intended to find out why they'd done this and who the European man was, because if they'd attack her so openly once, they might try it again. He grabbed the man he'd thumped as he tried to flee, and swung him into the wall as hard as he could.

Suddenly hands were there to help him and the man was secured, so Bram turned to the woman.

She was panting, her upper clothing torn. He slipped off his coat, which had also suffered a little, and swung it round her shoulders.

'Thank you.'

'What was all that about?'

'I'm not sure.' She moved forward and spoke to the man they'd captured in Chinese. Bram's guide shouted at him and he cringed back.

Then another man came into the alley and the bystanders fell back. He spoke to the woman then looked at the man and said something sharp, with a growling undertone to his voice.

The attacker now looked terrified.

The woman came quietly back to Bram's side.

'What's happening?'

'They're taking him to my employer, who's an important man. Mr Lee will deal with the matter.'

'No police?'

'The tongs will manage this, since it's an affront to my employer. We keep our own law and order here.' She hesitated, looking down at the jacket she was still holding round herself to hide her torn clothing. 'Would you let me borrow this till I get home? You should come with me anyway. My employer will want to thank you.'

'I'm at your service, Miss—?'

'Saunders.'

'I'm Bram Deagan.' He waited but she didn't offer her first name.

'You're Irish.' It wasn't a question but it seemed to him that she didn't have a scornful look in her eyes as she said the word. In both England and Australia he'd found to his surprise that some people despised the Irish, just because they were Irish.

She led the way out of the alley, moving slowly because she had to respond to the bowing of heads as she passed. 'It isn't far.'

But before they'd moved more than a few steps, a rickshaw pulled up beside them and the man pulling it gestured to her.

She held a short conversation and another rickshaw seemed to materialise from nowhere. 'Please get in, Mr Deagan. We'll make sure you get back safely afterwards, so you won't need your guide.'

So he paid and dismissed the man, then clambered into the rickshaw. He felt sorry for the scrawny man pulling him along.

They pulled up outside what his guide had called a shophouse when they passed some earlier. This was one of the larger sort. Miss Saunders led the way into the interior.

A beautiful Chinese girl gaped at the sight of her torn clothing and shot a quick question at her before turning back to her customer.

They went through the rear door of the shop and he found himself in a corridor that led past several rooms to what seemed to be a kitchen. A man was waiting for them there and as she explained in Chinese what had happened, his expression turned grim. He was the same man she'd been walking with two days ago.

She turned back to Bram. 'This is my employer, Mr Lee. Lee-Sang, this is the man who saved me, Mr Bram Deagan.'

Bram bowed his head, because that was what people seemed to do here and the other man did the same, surprising him by addressing him in English.

'Most grateful for your help, Mr Deagan. Please take seat.'

An older woman came forward and Bram waited to sit down, looking at Miss Saunders enquiringly.

'This is Mr Lee's mother. You should call her by her full name, Lee Bo Jun.'

So Bram bowed his head again and hoped he'd pronounced the words correctly. 'I'm pleased to meet you.'

The woman barely spared him a glance, however, because as the jacket slipped, she saw how badly Miss Saunders' clothes were torn. Making sounds of distress which you didn't need words to understand, she pushed the younger woman out of the room and he heard them going up some wooden stairs.

'Please take seat, Mr Deagan. Excuse our humble room.'

He sat down, not allowing himself to stare round. It

didn't look humble to him, but large and comfortably furnished.

'Could you please tell me what happen? People come running, say Isabella was attacked and a white man saved her.'

Bram explained. He could see the anger deepen on Mr Lee's face and wondered once again if Miss Saunders was his mistress. But a man didn't usually keep his mistress in the same house as his mother, and surely the Chinese were no different in this respect?

'I'm grateful to you, Mr Deagan. Very grateful. Isabella is like family now.'

'I was happy to help. May I say that you speak excellent English.'

'I employ her as my teacher.' A quick sideways glance, then, 'Only as teacher. It's better to understand what trading partners say. I speak several languages.'

'I've never had the chance to learn anything except English and even that, I speak with an Irish accent.'

'Isabella explain Irish, also Scottish and Welsh. When my mother and Isabella come back, we hope you drink tea with us. Please honour us by staying.'

'I'd like to do that, to make sure Miss Saunders is all right. She's a brave woman, fought back like a fury.'

Mr Lee smiled. 'Very brave. She work for me when her own people offer her nothing. First time you visit Singapore?'

'It is. I've only been here three days, but it's fascinating.'

'And the heat? Most Europeans not enjoy that.'

'I prefer it cooler, I must admit, but it wouldn't be Singapore without the heat, I suppose.'

'You here to do business?'

'A little. I'm just getting my start, trying to learn as much as I can.'

'Good to learn.'

They continued talking and by the time he heard footsteps coming down the stairs again, Bram realised he'd told Mr Lee exactly what had brought him here and how little money he had to make his start with. Which surprised him. He wasn't usually so free with information.

His host smiled. 'I think you do well in business, Mr Deagan.'

Then it was a flurry of hospitality, with Miss Saunders guiding him in a low voice as to what to do so that he didn't offend. Isabella, he thought. She's called Isabella. Such a pretty name.

A very refreshing pale tea without milk was drunk out of tiny bowls, which were refilled frequently. They were so pretty he couldn't resist running a fingertip over the flowers that graced one side. Then he sneaked another glance at her beautiful hair. Of course she was a lady – he could tell that from the way she spoke – and far above him, but still, a man could admire her, couldn't he?

Miss Saunders was dressed now in a plain gown. She didn't wear the huge hooped skirts wealthy English ladies favoured. The colour was subtle, a greenish grey, and it flattered her. The material was surely silk and he loved the way it gleamed as she moved.

The old lady presided at the table, firing off the occasional English remark at him as she refilled his bowl with tea. Sometimes he found it hard to understand her, because she spoke in a jerky way and didn't always pronounce the ends of words.

It all felt very unreal. What was he doing here? he wondered. He'd been a groom back in Ireland, came from a dirt poor family, was a man who had yet to make his mark on the world, while Mr Lee had an aura of power about him that was quite unmistakable. Anyone who was fooled by these humble surroundings was an idiot.

'You not eaten yet, Mr Deagan?' Mr Lee asked.

'Not for a while.'

The old lady spoke and Miss Saunders translated.

'Ah Yee asks if you would join us for a meal. It's an honour to be invited, but the food will be different.'

'I'd be happy to accept the invitation, but you'll have to tell me how to eat, because I'm sure I can't manage with only those little sticks.'

'It takes practice. We'll get you a spoon.'

It was a pottery spoon, stubby and broader than was comfortable.

'Let Ah Yee eat first, then you eat a mouthful of plain rice,' Miss Saunders whispered. 'Watch what I do.'

He did as she told him and at least he managed to get food into his mouth without spilling it down himself.

The meal took a while. Several courses, two or three dishes in each, but not much meat. He found it delicious. Some courses were cooked by a young maid, others were brought in when, at her mistress's nod, the maid went to call out of the back door. As those coming in were still hot, they must have come from nearby. He prayed he'd not get an upset stomach from the food, but if he did, it'd be worth it.

'I don't think I've ever had such a wonderful meal,' he said at last.

Mr Lee translated this for his mother, who gave him a satisfied nod.

After the table had been cleared, Mr Lee stood up. 'I walk back to ship with you, Mr Deagan.'

'I don't like to trouble you.'

His host smiled. 'No trouble. Good for you to be seen with me. You not only safer but find it easier to do business.'

Bram looked at Miss Saunders, who gave him a quick smile and lowered her eyes. He took his leave of Mrs Lee and bowed to the daughter as they passed through the shop. There were two customers there this time, both looking affluent. What was it about people that showed so clearly that they were not short of money? He wondered if poor and hungry was stamped on his own face.

On the way back to the ship, Mr Lee took the time to explain some of the things they saw and Bram listened with interest, asking questions.

When they arrived, he said, 'It's not a large ship and we can't match your hospitality, but you'd be welcome aboard, sir.'

'Very honoured to visit another time.'

Before he turned away, Bram said hastily, 'May I visit you again, to see how Miss Saunders is?'

Mr Lee studied him, head on one side, then nodded. 'I send invitation to tea, you and captain too? I also help with business if you like.'

Bram didn't hesitate. 'I'd be very grateful, very grateful indeed.'

As Mr Lee turned and strolled away. Bram noticed two men following him and called out, 'Wait!' He ran after him, keeping an eye on them. 'There are men following you.'

His companion smiled. 'My own men. But thank you for warning.' Then he strolled off again.

Dougal was on deck by then, looking better. 'Who was that?'

So Bram had to tell his tale all over again.

'She must be pretty,' Dougal said.

'What do you mean?'

'From the tone of your voice when you speak of her and the look in your eyes, she must be pretty.'

He hesitated, then admitted, 'Not pretty, no. But striking. Handsome, perhaps. And intelligent.'

'Strange things to admire in a woman. I like them soft and pretty myself, with no troublesome thoughts in their little heads.'

'Then we've very different tastes in women.'

As soon as he could, Bram sought his tiny cabin, to lie there thinking about the encounter. His main conclusion was that he must see her again. '*Isabella.*' He mouthed the name. He'd never met a woman like her.

Was he an idiot to think of her as a man thinks of a woman? She was a lady and he was . . . nothing yet.

Could he help thinking of her? He smiled and shook his head. No, he couldn't get her out of his mind.

When Mr Deagan had gone, Mrs Lee gave Isabella a strange look. 'Good man. Save you. Get hurt.' She touched her chin in the place where Mr Deagan was now sporting a bruise.

Isabella found herself flushing and jumped to her feet, not wanting to face an interrogation yet from a woman who would never stop questioning until she'd found out exactly what she wanted to know. 'I'd better change out of this dress. I don't know why you wanted me to wear my best one around the house.'

Mrs Lee smiled in a knowing way but said nothing.

In her tiny cubicle of a bedroom, Isabella changed her dress, hanging the skirt up carefully on the two hooks placed in the wall to hold the loops of material sewed into the top of her skirt, then folding the bodice carefully over a rail. The upper storey of the house was stiflingly hot at this time of day, so she dipped a cloth into the washing water jar and wiped her face and armpits, then got dressed in an everyday outfit.

She never wore the layers of petticoats that made the European ladies' skirts balloon out, which the Chinese thought ridiculous. But she couldn't bring herself to wear the more practical garb of trousers and tunic that Mrs Lee and Xiu Mei wore, either, though she owned a few sets for sleeping in, it being more respectable in a cubicle without a door. Not that Mr Lee ever came to this end of the upper storey after dark. This part was for the women of his household only.

Why had those men tried to abduct her? That was what she didn't understand. She'd been wondering ever since it happened. She'd seen Renington standing at the end of the alley, but surely he knew he'd be in serious trouble with Mr Lee for this? Why had he expected to get away with it? That thought worried her.

Would she not be safe going out on her own from now on? Or would Mr Lee do something to prevent it happening again? Surely he would?

She hoped she'd see Mr Deagan again. She'd enjoyed talking to him. He had a smile that lit up his whole face. You couldn't call him good-looking, but he was certainly charming and courteous. Even Mrs Lee had liked him.

After he'd left Bram at the ship, Kar Ho strolled on, pleased that the Irishman had tried to protect him just now. Not that he'd needed it, but it showed an honest heart and a loyalty to friends. He went on to one of his warehouses, where he spoke to the man who had been captured. His bodyguard had to treat the fellow roughly because at first he refused to speak.

What Kar Ho found out had him grim-faced, and he sent the man off to work in a very unpleasant job in a mine, from which he'd find it hard to escape.

Others might have killed the man, but Kar Ho liked to turn everything to a benefit for himself, his family and even for the woman who had taught him English. Isabella worked uncomplainingly with his mother and sister, doing anything they asked, and he now counted her as one of the family.

What he had not yet worked out was: how best to achieve the benefit from letting her go off to search for her cousin? But he would, because she was set on it. And family was important, he agreed.

That evening Bram dressed up in his best to go to dinner at the Wallaces, glad that the afternoon thunderstorm had cleared the air. He was nowhere near as well turned out as his friend, though.

Dougal studied him. 'You'll need to get yourself some smarter clothes. Better do it here. They're far cheaper and those tailors can copy anything. I have clothes made here regularly.'

'I'll think about it.' Bram would rather save his money for trade goods than waste it on clothes he'd never use again. 'Had I better not go tonight? You could tell them I'm ill, that I ate something bad.'

'No. They like to meet new people and they hold open house for Europeans. I'll say you lost some of your luggage.'

'And will they believe that?'

'They'll pretend to.'

Mr Wallace was plump and red-faced, sweating profusely in spite of overhead fans being used to waft the hot air about. 'That's a nasty-looking bruise. Get into a fight, did you, Deagan?'

Bram shrugged. 'Two Chinese were attacking an Englishwoman. I helped drive them off.'

Wallace frowned. 'I've not heard about that and I usually hear all the gossip. Who was she?'

'Miss Saunders.'

'Oh, that one.'

Bram stiffened. 'Why do you say her name in that tone?'

'She's gone native, lives with the Chinese.'

'I know where she lives. I took her home afterwards.'

'Just a minute.' Wallace beckoned to his wife. 'She'll want to hear this. Dorothea, my dear, this is Bram Deagan. He rescued that Saunders woman today and escorted her home.'

'Pleased to meet you, Mr Deagan.' She leaned forward slightly, her eyes avid. 'What was it like at the house? I still can't believe she's living with that man.'

Bram stiffened, feeling like walking straight out at this way of speaking about Miss Saunders. But it would do neither of them any good, so he said quietly, 'She's not living there in the way I think you mean. It's all very respectable. His mother runs the household, a stern old lady, and his sister lives there. I met them both and I'm absolutely certain that Miss Saunders is living in very respectable circumstances.'

'Oh.'

There was a faint trace of disappointment in her voice, which angered him further, but he kept his temper under control and added, 'I stayed for a meal with them.'

Her eyes gleamed. 'You did? And how was the food?'

'Excellent, though I can't be managing with those chopsticks, so they had to give me a spoon. The meal was served by a maid and there was another maid helping. They're not without money.'

'Oh. Well, I'm glad to hear that Miss Saunders is

not – er, in any trouble. I did think of employing her as a governess myself, but she's too pretty and I have a son at an impressionable age.'

Wallace spoke. 'This Lee fellow has his finger in a lot of pies. They live modestly now, but people say he'll be very rich one day, even by European standards.'

'That wouldn't surprise me. I found him very intelligent, speaking quite good English, as a result of Miss Saunders' efforts. His mother and sister speak some English too.'

Bram managed to change the subject after that, but other guests kept bringing it up and each time he had to repeat his assurances as to Miss Saunders' respectability.

He was glad when Dougal signalled that it was time to leave.

His friend was grinning as they walked away from the house. 'Well, you've put the cat among the pigeons. They'd all decided your young lady was living in sin.'

'Well, she's not. A less sinful household it'd be hard to find, as you'll discover when you come there with me for a meal.'

'I'll look forward to it. He'd be a good man for a trader to have on his side.'

2

That evening Mr Lee didn't go out. He sat and chatted to his mother and sister, then turned to Isabella. 'I like young man.'

She wondered where this was leading, because he didn't speak for no purpose. 'Mr Deagan? Yes, he seems pleasant enough.'

'We owe him debt for saving you. Shall I help him get started as trader?'

'That's up to you, but I certainly wish him well.'

'You must decide too, Isabella.'

'I don't understand.'

He answered obliquely, as he often did. 'Have men watch docks all time. Renington left Singapore on ship this evening. Going to Calcutta then England. Not dare stay after attack you. I think he want take you with him. He stare at you many time.'

She wondered what this twist in the conversation had to do with Deagan. 'If Renington's gone, that's good, surely? I shall be safe here now.'

'Not safe if go back to England alone.'

'It's a big country. Many people. I'd never see him. And if Alice is there . . .'

He steepled his fingers togehter and stared down at

them. 'Man saw Alice leave before, with another man. Not Renington. Ship not go to England. Go to Australia.'

Isabella closed her eyes for a moment, feeling tears of relief trickle down her cheeks. 'She's alive, then.'

'Was alive. Not certain now. I tell you many time. Never certain until prove.'

'It's likely, then.' She knew she could be too impulsive. Mr Lee never was.

'The man's name was – how you say it? – B-e-a-u-fort.'

'I think that's pronounced Bo-fot.'

'Ah. Is easy to say.'

'Are you sure Alice went with him?'

'Yes. Got married in church first.'

'*She's married*? What sort of a man was he? Did he have money? Was he honest? Surely he wasn't another like Renington?'

'Was foolish man. No good with money. Family send him away to Australia. He visit friends here first. Servants like him, though. Treat them well.'

'And he definitely married my cousin?'

'Ah. Then they take ship to Sydney.'

'I can go and look for her there, then.'

He hesitated, looking worried, which was unlike him. She waited patiently.

'You not go look for her alone. Young woman on own is in great danger – like today. Need family to look after young woman. You have no family, but we look after you now.'

She felt tears rise in her eyes at this simple statement of their concern for her. She owed them so much.

Another pause. His mother snapped something in Chinese and he nodded, then turned back to Isabella. 'We look after you, search for Alice and find benefit for me.'

She was completely baffled by how they would do all this. 'How?'

'With Mr Deagan's help.'

'If we help him in with his trading, he may help me look for my cousin? Is that what you mean?'

He laughed gently. 'That not enough to protect you.'

His mother grew impatient. 'Mr Deagan good man. Not fool. You marry him, you be safe.'

Isabella stared at her in shock, then turned to Mr Lee, who always had the final say in the family. 'You can't mean that!'

'Not marry if you dislike Mr Deagan. But I like him. My mother like him too.'

'He may be married already.'

'Not married. I ask when we walk to ship.'

'But he may be engaged to marry someone. He's not a young man.'

'I talk to him, ask if he's willing, make arrangements.' He paused and when she didn't speak, added softly, 'Then you help him with business, he help you find cousin in Australia. I send you goods. Make more money. Benefit for me and for you, too. Good wife for trader.'

Her head was spinning. She couldn't believe she was even considering it. But she was. 'I hardly know Mr Deagan.'

'Not know any man till live with him,' Ah Yee said with a chuckle.

'We ask him to visit again,' Mr Lee said in his gentle but implacable way. 'You get to know him better. I get to know him better. Then we decide.'

She didn't refuse outright, because he looked very pleased with himself and it was indeed a very practical arrangement. But Isabella was reluctant to marry a man she didn't know. That would be putting one's head right inside the lion's mouth.

Though she didn't think Mr Deagan was a lion. He seemed . . . kind . . . and not a fool.

And the idea did make sense.

No, she couldn't!

In Western Australia, Conn Largan rode up to Perth. He'd told his wife he might not be back for several days, so took his time. It was good to get away from the homestead occasionally and his head groom could be trusted to make sure the horses they bred were looked after.

He conducted some business at both the Post Office Savings Bank and the Perth Building Society. Because there had been too many banks failing in Western Australia, he didn't keep all his money in one place.

After that he went to look at some young horses a broker had written to him about, but rejected them all. It upset him when he saw how hard some people had been on animals, not giving them a chance to grow to maturity before they used them for hard work.

Since he'd offered to help finance Bram's business, he took a fancy to visit Fremantle next and perhaps see if he could find a piece of land for sale. There might be more scope for a new shop in the port than in Perth, and better access to goods coming into the colony, as well. They had to find somewhere to build the shop and he could help with that.

He felt quite sure Bram would succeed. When they'd been growing up together Bram had stood out among the other village lads, not only quicker to learn but also good at thinking of different ways to tackle everyday jobs.

When he left Perth, Conn took the ferry across to the south side of the Swan River and rode in a leisurely way to Fremantle, the port for the capital city. He hadn't yet ridden to Fremantle along the north bank and must do so one day. This had only just become convenient because of the new bridge across the river at the port, built by convicts. He looked at the huge structure as he rode past it, made of pieces of timber criss-crossing and building up several storeys to allow the road across and ships to go underneath. How much wood had it taken to build that monstrosity? He much preferred the elegant stone bridges in Ireland to this.

As he came to the lunatic asylum, he shuddered and averted his eyes. His first wife had died here. He still felt bitter about the way his father had forced him to marry her for her dowry, concealing her slow wits and strange behaviour. When Conn had tried to have the marriage annulled, his father had faked evidence to have him convicted of treason, which was why he'd been transported to Australia.

He gave himself a mental shake. No use dwelling on that now. His father was dead, the conviction was in the process of being overturned, thanks to his eldest brother in Ireland, and he had a second wife, a wonderful woman. Maia and his son Karsten were the lights of his life.

He smiled as he rode. The fact that his name was in the process of being cleared and that this was becoming known in the colony, gave him the confidence to go out in public more frequently.

He didn't want his wife and children growing up buried in the countryside. Nowhere had such isolated farms as Western Australia, he was sure, places where you might see no one pass by for weeks on end. That was all right for a man wrongfully transported, who was seeking shelter from a hostile world, but not right for a lawyer who could hold his head up in any society.

He called first at the McBride household, which he always did when he was in Fremantle. Of course Bram and Dougal had not yet returned from their voyage to Singapore but he wanted to find out when they were expected.

'Where are you staying tonight?' Mrs McBride asked.

'I'd be happy to stay here, if that's all right. Have you a room free?'

'Yes. We only have one guest, an elderly gentleman who's come across from Sydney. He was very tired, said the coastal steamer wasn't at all comfortable. Poor fellow, he doesn't seem in good health. We're trying to feed him up.'

'I'll go and put my horse in the livery stable, then.'

She pulled a face. 'The owner of the place you

usually use died suddenly and I've heard his son isn't nearly as careful with the horses.'

Conn left his saddlebags with her and rode along to the livery stables. He didn't dismount, but sat on his horse, frowning at the place. It was showing distinct signs of neglect, and it smelled as if the horse dung had not been removed for some time, which boded ill for the care of his mare. He was about to leave and look elsewhere for stabling, when he saw a piece of wood with words burnt crudely into it hanging beside the door: LIVERY STABLE FOR SALE.

He sat there for a long time, thinking hard, until the mare grew restive and began to side-step, whinnying softly. Dismounting, he went to Gypsy's head. 'Sorry, girl. I forgot about you.'

At the sound of his voice, footsteps came shuffling to the door and George Mundy stood there, the son of the previous owner.

'Are you looking for stabling, Mr Largan?'

Since the fellow was distinctly the worse for wear, Conn said curtly, 'Not if you're drunk at this time of day. I care more for my horses than to leave them with someone in that condition. I was sorry to hear your father had died. He was a good man, knew a lot about horses.'

George scowled. 'That's all anyone says, sorry about *him*. They don't say sorry he passed the fever to my wife and son, or sorry they died soon after him. People don't say that, do they?'

Conn saw tears rolling down the man's hollow cheeks and his anger faded. 'Of course I'm sorry about that as well. I didn't know about your other losses. Why are you selling the place?'

'Because I can't stand the sight of it, that's why. Or of this cursed town. It reminds me of *her*. She liked it here, loved the sun, and what good did that do her? I'm going back to England as soon as I can get some money for my damned *inheritance*. I came here to make my fortune, not bury my wife and shovel horse shit.'

He'd heard similar sad stories before, Conn thought as he dismounted and tied up his horse. Mundy was lucky he'd come out here as a free man. Convicts didn't have the choice of going home.

He would be able to return to Ireland once his conviction was overturned, but he didn't think he'd do so, not after all that had happened there, not now that his mother was dead. When life moved you on, it changed you. Thank goodness Maia loved it here, even though she missed her twin sister desperately. 'Do you have some water for my mare?'

George slouched off and returned with a bucket.

Conn checked and found the bucket and water clean, so offered it to his mare, then put a nosebag on her. 'How much do you want for the place, George?'

'Five hundred pounds.'

'Rubbish. It's not worth anything like that.'

'I'm not giving it away. There's a bit of land with it too.'

'How much?'

'Over an acre, with the sheds and all that.'

'Show me.' Conn walked round with him, agreeably surprised at how much land there was. When the tour was over, he said, 'I'm interested, but I'm not paying a fancy price like that. And I'll need to ask around and check that the land and buildings really are yours before I can even think of making an offer. In the meantime, do you have a stable clean enough for my mare?'

Mundy nodded, suddenly very eager to co-operate. 'We've got good stabling, as you know. Dad built to last. It needs painting, that's all.'

Conn didn't comment on that.

When he got back to the McBrides' house, it was time for the evening meal and he apologised to his hostess as he joined her and her daughter at table.

'I'm considering buying Mundy's Livery Stables.'

Mrs McBride looked at him in shock. 'Are you leaving Galway House?'

'No. Well, not permanently. But I've a son who will need educating, and we'll have other children one day, I hope. I don't want to bury poor Maia in the depths of the bush for ever. Not a word to anyone, if you don't mind. I'd like to do this quietly. My name isn't yet cleared, after all.'

As the evening progressed, he felt sorry for Dougal's sister. Poor Flora seemed to be at her mother's beck and call, and looked unhappy at some of the orders, however gently phrased they were. He often felt sorry for spinster daughters tied to their mother's apron-strings by a lack of money.

The following day he went back to Perth, travelling up the river on the paddle steamer this time, because it was much quicker, and returning the same way.

When he got back, he went straight round to

Mundy's to check his mare, and found George sleeping on top of the straw bales nearby. Conn wrinkled his nostrils in disgust. Once again, the man stank of booze, but at least the mare didn't seem to have suffered from the neglect. George must have fed her and given her some fresh water before he drank himself stupid.

He heard a rustling sound in the straw. Rats? Or a cat? There should be at least one stable cat in a place like this to keep the vermin down. But this had sounded like something bigger.

On that thought he pretended to leave the stables, creeping back to listen just outside the door.

The rustling became more pronounced and a man clambered out from among the bales, brushing pieces of straw off himself before going across to talk softly to the mare.

Conn walked in again, making no attempt to keep silent, and the man spun round with a panicked expression.

'Don't I know you?'

The man's shoulders sagged and he hesitated, then nodded. 'Came out here on the same ship as you.'

'It's Les, isn't it?'

'Yes, sir. Les Harding.'

'Why were you hiding?'

'I'm supposed to be working for a man a few streets away, another livery stables. But he feeds us badly and thumps us when he's upset about something. Doesn't treat his animals much better than his men, either. I ran away a few days ago after he gave me this.' He pointed to a massive yellowing bruise on his face. 'I'll be in trouble when they catch me. I'm only on a provisional ticket of leave, and I've been in trouble before.'

'And what are you doing here?'

'Hiding. Mundy never notices and besides, the poor horses would go without food or water half the time if I wasn't here. I can't bear to see an animal badly treated.'

'Are you hungry?'

Les nodded.

Conn remembered being hungry when he was a convict, because at first he'd been unable to stomach the filthy food they gave him. 'I'll go and buy you something to eat, then we can talk.' He went out and found a baker who still had a few loaves left. After buying one, he got some ham to go with it from another shop before returning to the stables.

He found Les stroking Gypsy's nose and the mare, who was very fussy about who she let close to her, was nuzzling him contentedly.

Conn set down the bread and ham on his handkerchief on top of the bales of straw. Pulling out his pocket knife, he hacked off a chunk of bread and took a piece of ham out of the paper. He gestured to Les, whose hands were trembling as he picked them up. To his credit he didn't gobble them down, though he was clearly ravenous.

And all this time, the owner of the stables lay on the pile of straw, snoring in fits and starts, oblivious to what was going on around him.

'I need to talk to Mundy,' Conn said when Les had eaten his fill. 'Have you any idea when he'd be reasonably sober?'

'He usually wakes up in an hour or so from now and does a bit of work around the place – not much – then he goes out drinking again.'

'You seem good with horses.'

'Yes, sir. I've always liked animals. I used to work on a farm.'

'What were you transported for?'

'Stealing.'

There were some sorts of stealing that Conn found more forgivable than others. 'What sort of things did you steal?'

'Food. My kids were hungry.'

An all-too-common tale. 'Would you take a job with me?'

'I would if I was allowed, but I told you, I've run away from my master. They'll punish me for that when they catch me, probably put me back in prison.'

'If I can arrange things, will you work for me?' He knew he was being soft-hearted, but having experienced the humiliations of being a prisoner, of being at other men's mercy – often brutal men – he understood what a living hell that life could be. There were employers who took advantage of the situation to treat ticket-of-leave men badly. Besides, he owed Les for looking after Gypsy.

He went to let Mrs McBride know he'd be late for tea, then returned to the stables, losing patience with the snoring wreck of a man and shaking Mundy rudely awake.

When Mundy at last realised Conn was about to make him an offer for the livery stables, he said, 'Wait a minute.' After dunking his head in the water butt, he rubbed his dripping hair with a filthy towel. 'Better go into the house.'

'I'll want to look round it, too.'

It was just along from the stables and had a small garden behind it, protected by a rickety fence. The house was little more than a four-room cottage, and small rooms at that. He went to the front door to look up the slope at the sheds, which he hadn't gone inside.

'It wouldn't take much to bring 'em up to scratch,' Mundy said. 'The roof leaks a bit on the big one and some of the wood's fallen off the walls, but with weather-board buildings, you can just nail on another plank.'

'Hmm.' Conn followed him back into the cottage.

Someone had once loved it enough to embroider little mats to stand under the candlesticks, and arrange ornaments on the mantelpiece. The ornaments were now covered in dust and the mats were spotted with candlewax. An oil lamp stood in pieces on the window-sill, its blackened chimney lying sideways and its bulbous oil reservoir empty.

Conn took the seat he was offered and settled down to some hard bargaining. At the end of it, he had an agreement to sell. Not content to let the man get drunk again, he drew up a simple bill of sale himself, and took George along the road to the baker's to get it witnessed there and then. He paid George a deposit, again with the baker as witness, to seal the bargain.

As the two men walked back past an alehouse, George licked his lips. 'We could seal the bargain with a drink.'

'I'm not a drinking man. Now, how soon can you get out of the cottage? I'll pay you the rest of the money as soon as the premises are vacant.'

'Are you going to live here? I thought you had a place in the country.'

'I do. But I want a place in the town as well. I'll leave a man here to keep an eye on the place for me.'

'I can easy find somewhere else to live, but I want the money handing over before I move out.'

'So that you can drink it?'

George shook his head. 'No. Though I shall celebrate a bit. I hadn't any hope before. No one seemed to want to buy. Now I've got money, I'm going back to England as soon as I can find a ship.'

'You may have to go down to Albany to catch the mail steamer.'

'Good idea. You get the money for me and I'm away.'

From there, Conn went to Les's previous employer and wrung from him a written quittal of employment, in return for a small cash payment 'for inconvenience'.

When he went up to Perth the following day, it was not only to get the money from the bank, but to ask what he needed to do to get Les Harding reassigned to him.

This was more difficult than he'd expected because he encountered an official who seemed more determined to punish Les than see him in gainful employment. He didn't believe that Conn was about to get his record cleared, either. If one of the priests Conn had dealt with hadn't been passing just then and able to bear witness to the truth of his tale, he'd have got nowhere. And even so, the official persisted in calling him 'Largan' and treating him in a patronising way.

It was hard not to hope for a chance to pay back these gratuitous insults one day. He wouldn't forget this fellow.

And though Conn had hoped to leave Les as caretaker at the stables, he was not now so sure this would be a safe thing to do. Things weren't always easy to arrange in the colony, especially for an ex-convict who was not yet exonerated.

He'd not forgotten how it stung, and never would.

3

By the time his friend Dougal had sold his main cargo of sandalwood and was negotiating for a return cargo as well as buying some trading goods for himself, Bram had more or less worked out what sort of trade goods *he* could take back and sell profitably: mostly crockery, glassware and window glass this time, he thought. Perhaps a few perfumes and maybe even a few of the soft, pretty little rugs, if he could stretch his money that far.

He'd have liked to take some of the beautiful fabrics and silks he'd seen for sale, but didn't feel he knew enough about these – or about the ladies' fashions for which they'd be used. How much material did you need to make one of those huge bell-like skirts that the wealthier women wore, or a simple skirt like those of the ordinary women? He'd have to find out.

A couple of days after their encounter, Mr Lee came sauntering along the dock and stopped next to the *Bonny Mary*. The two men following stopped a short distance behind him, as they had before. Bram hurried down the gangway to greet him, feeling it quite natural now to bow his head in greeting instead of shaking hands. 'Please come on to the ship. Can I offer you a cup of tea or a glass of wine, sir?'

'No wine, but tea very nice.' He followed Bram on to the ship. 'This is not big ship.'

'No. It's a schooner. It belongs to my friend Captain Dougal McBride.'

Mr Lee inclined his head and strolled along the deck, his eyes flicking from one piece of equipment to another.

Bram suddenly realised he was studying the state of the ship. Well, he'd not find anything out of order here. Dougal insisted on every rope being carefully coiled and stowed, every inch of the ship being scrubbed and kept clean.

But Mr Lee seemed a shrewd man, and if he wanted to make sure the ship was seaworthy and well cared for, why stop him? Bram would have done the same in his place. He was glad when Dougal walked along the dock and he could hand over the gentle questioning about the ship and its cargoes to his friend while he went to supervise the tea-making.

When he came back on deck, he set the tray down carefully and called, 'Please come and get a cup while it's hot.' Even on the ship they didn't have milk to put in their tea, so that was suitable, but he wished they had a prettier cup to serve the drink in. The guest took it with a smile and sipped it with every sign of enjoyment.

When he set the cup down, Mr Lee bowed first to Bram then to Dougal. 'We offer you hospitality – have meal with us tonight or tomorrow, whichever suit you.'

'We'd be happy to accept,' Bram said at once, remembering the delicious food he'd been served last time, but more importantly, remembering Isabella Saunders.

When Mr Lee had gone, Dougal said, 'I'm not sure about this Chinese food. I've already had one upset stomach since we got here.'

'It's delicious and I didn't suffer at all afterwards.'

'But it's hard to tell what you're eating.'

'Who cares? The food I had was far better than anything I ate when I was growing up, and if they're eating it as well, it's not going to be bad for you, is it? I should think they have a better idea of what to buy than your English cousin's cook does.'

'Oh, very well. You're clearly eager to go.' Dougal grinned and nudged him. 'Eager to see Miss Saunders again too, eh? She's a fine figure of a woman. I saw her in the distance. It couldn't possibly have been anyone else, not with that hair.' He winked and went back about his business.

Bram stayed by the rail, staring down at the busy scene but not really seeing it. Even Dougal had noticed his interest in Isabella Saunders. Well, she was very attractive and such good company . . . He sighed and didn't allow himself to continue. He was in no state to start courting, with his livelihood in such an uncertain state.

And anyway, she was a lady, even if she didn't have much money. What was he but a rough Irish peasant with a little education? He was sure that difference mattered a great deal to someone like her.

But still . . . he did want to see her again.

★   ★   ★

Isabella felt nervous as she helped get ready for their guests and of course Xiu Mei noticed this as she took the brush from her hand and finished pinning up her hair for her, practising her English at the same time.

'You like this man?'

'I don't know him!'

'My brother like him.'

'Yes. But I don't intend to marry to suit your brother. Choosing a husband is too important.'

Xiu Mei gave her tinkling laugh. 'If my brother say marry, you marry.'

Isabella didn't deny this. Mr Lee was never violent, but somehow if he wanted something to happen, it did. She appreciated the feeling of security working for him had given her, but now she felt uncertain, with the feeling she was being pushed headfirst into something she wasn't at all sure about. Though she rather liked Mr Deagan. He was . . . nice.

She went through some of his good points in her mind: he had a lovely smile, seemed kind, treated the Lees with courtesy – and had rushed to save a stranger when those men attacked her. But that still wasn't enough for her to marry the man. Only – it would solve her present problems.

She wished women were not so dependent on men, wished she had an income of her own, just enough for her to live as she pleased. She wasn't greedy. But though she'd been saving hard and living frugally ever since she took this job, she only had enough to tide her over for a few months. And if she spent some of that money on a passage to Australia to look for her cousin, she would once again be in a difficult situation, short of money with nowhere to live.

She shuddered at the memory. She never wanted to feel that helpless again.

When she went down, once again wearing her best gown, Mr Lee frowned at her.

'Same clothes?'

'This is the best I have.'

'Need more clothes.' He turned to his sister and they spoke so quickly that Isabella only caught half of what they were saying. But Xiu Mei nodded and smiled as if what he was saying pleased her.

The scrawny lad keeping watch at the door of the shop, which they'd closed for the rest of the evening, came running through to tell them two huge foreign devils were walking down the street.

Mr Lee went to greet the visitors at the door and brought them through to the back room, which had had a specially thorough clean today, even though it hadn't really been dirty.

Isabella felt shy as Bram smiled at her, then got angry at herself for stuttering like an idiot, so clamped her lips shut. It was left to Mr Lee to manage the conversation, which he did with his usual gentle skill.

'You live in Swan River Colony, Captain McBride?'

'Yes. In the port of Fremantle. It's a small place, compared to Singapore, but it's the main port for the colony.'

'Sydney is bigger, Isabella say.'

'Much bigger. But I like living in the Swan River Colony.'

'You married?' Ah Yee asked with her usual bluntness.

Dougal shook his head. 'No. Too busy with my ship and earning my living by trading.'

'Need wife and children. What else work for?' She turned to Bram. 'You need marry too.'

'Not till I have some money behind me. I come from – um, peasants and have my way to make in the world.'

Isabella had to translate the word 'peasants' and both Mr Lee and his mother nodded approvingly, because that was their background, too. She turned to Mr Deagan. 'Mr Lee has also come from humble beginnings working on the land.'

'Then I admire what you've done even more, sir,' he said with obvious sincerity.

A little later Dougal turned to Xiu Mei and asked, 'Do you work in the shop with those beautiful materials?'

She nodded.

'I wonder, if I come back tomorrow, will you and Miss Saunders help me choose lengths of material to buy as presents for my mother and sister?'

Isabella had to step in and make sure her friend had understood, and they agreed to look at the materials by daylight and select suitable ones.

Ah Yee, who was like her son in always keeping an eye open for benefits, nodded in satisfaction.

'If this trip prospers,' Bram said, 'I'd like to trade in dress materials one day, especially silks. They're so beautiful.' He glanced quickly at Isabella's lustrous skirt then tore his eyes away and looked back at his host. 'Perhaps in a year or two your sister could send me a few dress lengths each time Captain McBride comes here?'

'You not come back?'

Bram shuddered. 'I'm not a good sailor. I get very sick in rough weather. I wanted to come once at least to see what I could find here, but after I get back to Fremantle, I hope not to have to sail anywhere again for a long time.'

Again, Isabella translated in a low voice for the two women, for whom Mr Deagan had been speaking too quickly, and with an Irish lilt that confused them still further.

'We discuss business tomorrow,' Mr Lee said. 'I have ideas to help you. That bring benefit to me too.'

He smiled at Isabella tranquilly and gave her a little nod, so she knew instantly that he'd decided Mr Deagan would make a good husband. She wanted to cry out to him to stop – or at least slow down – and didn't dare. She knew he was ordering her life with the very best intentions, doing what he felt best for her safety – as he would do for his own sister one day – which made it even harder to go against his wishes.

Maybe . . . just maybe, he was right.

She was attracted to Bram, but wanted to know him better before going further, only there wouldn't be time. His ship was leaving in a few days and it sounded as if he wasn't coming back to Singapore.

She was the one who'd said she was no longer needed here, the one who'd wanted to do something else with her life. But that had led to such a headlong rush into a new life that it frightened her. She wished she'd never started it. Or did she?

Oh, she didn't know what she wished.

As the two men walked back to the ship, escorted by some of Mr Lee's men, Dougal said appreciatively, 'You were right. The food was exquisite, very different from what's offered in European homes.'

'I enjoy drinking tea from those small bowls, too.'

'You only get a thimbleful each time.'

'But it's always hot and fresh. And the bowls are so pretty. I must look out for some to take back with me. I'm sure they'd sell well in the colony and I want a few for myself.'

'Well, we're going back to the shop tomorrow morning to look at the dress materials, so you can ask your new friends where to buy them.'

'I don't know why you want me to come too. What do I know about dress fabrics?'

Dougal walked along for a few paces looking thoughtful, before saying, 'It's Mr Lee who wants you to come tomorrow. He made a point of it. And if he does as he's offered and helps you with trade goods, then you should take care not to upset him. I asked my mate to find out about him and the word is that he's rich and going to be much richer before he's through.'

Once on the ship, Bram went straight to bed, even though it was still quite early by his usual standards. He lay on top of the sheets in his narrow bunk, thinking hard, sweating slightly, as you always seemed to do here. But his thoughts kept getting tangled up with memories of Isabella's face, the animation that lit her up when she forgot herself and started discussing something that interested her.

She'd been rather quiet tonight, quieter than before, and he had the feeling that she was worried about something. But it was clear she was considered part of the family and felt at home with the Lees, so she was not without help. It was nothing to do with him, really.

Life led you into some strange situations. Who'd have thought a man like him would end up in the Orient setting up as a trader?

Where would fate take him next? Would it be kind to him? Would he make a success of his life?

And why did Mr Lee want to see him again?

In the morning Isabella felt quite agitated as she tried to force some food down. Mr Lee looked at her across the breakfast table. 'We need talk.'

She didn't ask what about. She knew.

'Deagan is honest man,' he began.

'How can you be sure?'

He shrugged. 'I can tell. Is how I make money, find honest men. Work together, buy, sell.'

She looked down at her skirt, an everyday skirt this time, just a simple blue cotton. She knew what he was going to say next.

'You can marry him before he leave.'

Her hand spasmed against the material, clutching a fistful and crushing it, then she saw what she was doing and forced herself to let go. 'I'm – not sure I want to get married. Not so quickly, anyway.'

Ah Yee, who was sitting beside her, patted her hand. 'You got no family, so we arrange. Find husband for Xiu Mei soon. Is time.' She didn't say for her son as well, but the way her eyes flickered towards him said it for her.

The Lees both fell silent, waiting for her to speak but she didn't know what to say. She could see getting married might be a good thing in practical terms. But the business side wasn't the only thing you faced in a marriage. There was the day-to-day living – and this would mean living with a man who was a stranger to her – not to mention sleeping with him. She knew little of the intimacies between married people, except that some women found it distasteful, some didn't. How did you know which it would be for you? 'I'm afraid,' she admitted in a low voice. 'I don't know him.'

And Ah Yee, blunt and bossy, spoke gently for once, and even took hold of her hand. 'Family see what is needed. You trust us.'

Isabella clutched the bony little hand and for a moment it felt like a lifeline, then Ah Yee unclenched her fingers and stood up, back to her usual brisk self. 'You wait in shop. Help captain choose silk. My son talk to Mr Deagan.'

So Isabella walked along to join her friend, her stomach a churning mass of nerves.

As usual, Xiu Mei spoke in Chinese and she answered in English, both of them understanding more of the other's language than they could speak.

'Elder brother say you must choose material for new dress for your wedding. We can get it made quickly.'

Isabella stared at her in shock. 'Is he so certain the marriage will happen?'

Xiu Mei nodded and beamed at her as if this was good news. 'Look at this one.' She pulled out a length of silk, very soft and of a colour that was neither blue nor turquoise, but rather like the sky at dawn. 'Good colour for you. Not wear red.' She flicked a finger towards Isabella's head. 'Not with your hair.'

'This one is too light. It'll show the dirt.'

She laughed. 'You not be wearing it to clean the house! You wear it to get married and on special days.'

Isabella tried to distract herself by looking at other materials, but she couldn't concentrate. When she heard heavy footsteps coming along the street, the louder sound made by European shoes, her heart skipped a beat and she felt dizzy, she was so apprehensive.

What if Mr Deagan said no to the marriage?

Even more frightening, what if he said yes?

Bram saw her the minute he entered the shop, because her hair shone brightly in a shaft of sunlight as she moved. She was helping her friend roll up a piece of material, a gorgeous soft blue it was. They laid it on a shelf at the back of the shop. She'd look beautiful in such a colour, instead of the darker muted colours she'd worn so far.

He followed Dougal inside, expecting to stand and watch, but Mr Lee came out from the back to join them almost immediately and asked if he had a moment or two to discuss trading goods.

Isabella was blushing furiously. Now, why was that?

This time Bram was shown into a little room just along the corridor, which had packages piled along one wall, but also space for a table and chairs.

'I have offer for you,' Mr Lee said without any preliminaries. 'I help with trading business. Help make you better trader. You got much to learn.'

Bram sat forward eagerly. 'I know that. But how do I learn unless I start?'

'Take partner who know more than you.'

He waited, wondering why Mr Lee should make this offer.

'No family to help you. Not good, that. Can trust family more than strangers.'

Bram nodded. It was a sadness to him to be cut off from his family. 'If I make a success, I'll be bringing my family out from Ireland: my parents, brothers and sisters.'

'Good. Family important. But for now, you need a partner and a wife.'

Bram stared at him in surprise. Where was this leading? 'A wife? I can't afford to get married yet. I don't even have a house to live in.'

'Isabella need husband. My mother and I help her find one.'

If a choir of angels had suddenly flown in and started singing, Bram couldn't have been more surprised. He tried to speak but no words came out. He tried to take in the idea of Isabella as a wife. As *his* wife. And he couldn't. A lady like her wouldn't look at a man like him, surely? He must have heard wrongly. 'I . . . don't understand.'

'Isabella need husband. She good woman. Work hard. Make good wife. And she need go to Australia.'

'Why?'

'Has cousin there. Alice go to Sydney. Isabella want to find her.'

'Sydney's a long way from Perth, two weeks' sail in a coastal steamer.'

'Can send messages there?'

'Well, yes, of course.'

'Better if Isabella not go looking. Danger for woman on own.'

'Does she know you're talking to me about – this?' Bram knew the answer to that even as the question hung in the air between them. She'd been embarrassed to see him in the shop today, had flushed and avoided his eyes, staying beside her friend.

Oh, yes, she knew.

'We talk. She not sure. But she know I not let her leave here on her own. She need husband, honest man who treat her well. Good woman, Isabella.'

As Bram would have spoken, Mr Lee held up one hand to stop him. 'This help me too. I want to do business with Australia. Start trade in small way. Good for me if Isabella there. She help you, help me. I trust her.' He tapped his forehead. 'Very clever. Like my mother. Think a lot. Work hard.'

He waited and as the silence dragged, he began to frown. 'You not like her?'

'I don't know what to say, Mr Lee.'

'First say if you like Isabella.'

Bram couldn't help smiling, could feel his face

softening. 'Oh yes, I like her very much. Only . . . I have so little money. How can I afford to get married?'

'Will have money if work hard. Isabella can help.'

The silence was so fraught with possibilities, with hope and also with fear, that Bram could only sit there struck dumb, like an idiot at a fair. Did he want her, like her? Oh, so very much. Did he see the benefit of such a relationship? Definitely. There was just one thing standing in the way. He looked up. 'I can't say yes unless she truly wants this.'

Mr Lee gave a wry smile. 'She see benefit. But is big change. Is also afraid.'

That wasn't what Bram really wanted to ask. He needed to know if Isabella liked him enough as a man, if she felt she could be happy with him.

Mr Lee's mother came into the room and Bram stood up out of politeness. She nodded to him and sat down, speaking to her son in a torrent of incomprehensible sounds.

When the conversation ended, she turned to Bram. 'You marry Isabella.' It wasn't even a question. 'Good plan. For her, for you, for us.'

He was only certain of one thing. 'I want to, but I need to talk to her before I agree.'

She nodded. 'Good idea. I fetch.'

Mr Lee stood up, smiling but implacable. 'You can marry before ship leave.'

On his own in the dim little room, Bram sagged back in the chair, feeling shocked and uncertain . . . and hoping desperately that this miracle, this bright beautiful miracle, would happen.

When he heard footsteps, he stood up and watched her come in.

She looked so worried and upset, he moved forward without thinking, gentling her as he would a horse that had been startled. Her hand was soft in his and it trembled slightly as he took hold of it. 'Come and sit down, Isabella. It's all right if I call you Isabella, isn't it?'

All she did was stare at him as if she hadn't understood the words. But she did sit down. He was sorry to let go of her hand.

He couldn't think of a tactful way to say it. 'Mr Lee says we should marry.'

She nodded.

'I'd like that. Very much. But I'm doing nothing unless I'm sure you want it too, whatever Mr Lee says.' He saw her relax a little. 'Do you want it?'

'I . . . think it might be a good idea. But it's happened so fast, I can't seem to think straight.'

'I'm feeling a bit like that myself. And I need to tell you before anything else that I won't have much money left once I've bought my trade goods, or even a house to take you back to. I told Mr Lee but he said it didn't matter. I'm a hard worker, though. I *will* work hard for you. That I can promise.'

'I have a little money and I can work hard too. It's not the money, Bram.'

'It's us being nearly strangers.' He laughed suddenly. 'I've read books where the hero is tall, dark and handsome. Sure, I'm dark-haired enough, but I'm not tall and I'm not handsome, either.'

She gave him one of her lovely smiles. 'That doesn't

matter. I have red hair – and a temper to match sometimes.'

'I love your hair. It's beautiful.'

'Oh.' She began to fiddle with her dress, as if she didn't know what to say.

'I won't let them push you into anything that will make you unhappy,' he said gently.

She stared down at her tightly clasped hands as she asked, 'Would you . . . want to marry me?'

He didn't hesitate. 'Yes, I would. I'm sure it'd make me very happy indeed . . . as long as you weren't being coerced. That's what's holding me back. You're a lovely woman, Isabella. Any man would be proud to marry you.'

She relaxed a little more. He could see it in the way she held herself.

'Mr Lee said something about you looking for a cousin in Australia.'

'Alice. Yes. She's the only close relative I have left. I want very much to find her again. It's not good to be alone in the world. And I worry about her. She's not – not a very practical sort of person.'

After another silence, she added, 'If it's not you, Lee-Sang will come up with someone else for me to marry. Now he's decided, he won't let the question of finding me a husband drop. He's a very determined man when he wants something.'

'I think he's fond of you.'

'In his own way. But he thinks about the world differently. Marriage is a business matter to him. That's why he's not married. He'll find someone soon, I'm sure. After he's moved to a better house, so that he can find a wife of better status. He's much richer than he looks.'

'He says you'd not be happy to stay in the kitchen.'

'No. I'd be bored. Though I'd do what I had to.'

'I don't even have a kitchen, don't have anything except a very risky venture which may end up giving me a shop. I have one little pot of money and if I don't make it grow, I can't think what I'll do.'

'But you do want to open a shop?'

'It's the only way I can think of to make money, though what I really know about is horses.'

'Why did you think about trading, then?'

'I've talked to people, kept my ears and eyes open, and it seems to me they're short of goods in the Swan River Colony. People are starting to seek comforts for themselves and for their houses. So it's a good time to be opening a shop. Well, I think it is. Maybe an educated person would know better.'

'Educated people aren't always practical.'

That was a thought to hug to himself. He knew he was practical, given the chance. Yes, he could claim that, at least.

No one came to interrupt them and they chatted for a while longer. It was easier to talk about business than about their feelings. But in the end, he realised they were getting nowhere, were avoiding the main question, so he brought it up again, more sure of himself now.

'I'd really like to marry you, Isabella.'

She was instantly tense again. 'How can we be sure it's the right thing to do?'

'How can we be sure about anything in this life? We can't. We can only do our best. And I *will* do my best to be a good husband, if you'll be doing me the honour of marrying me. I promise you that.'

He looked at her and waited as she raised her eyes to meet his.

'And you'll help me try to find Alice?'

'If I can. I won't have much money to spare for that at first. But Mr Lee said he'd help, too. And I will try, yes. There's something I need to get clear. Later, if we make good, I'd want to bring out my family to Australia.'

'Would they come?'

'Oh, yes. Definitely. Most of them, anyway. They've not much to hope for where they are.'

'Tell me about them.'

'Da works a small plot of land, which belongs to the family in the big house. He also does jobs for them in the winter. He and Ma can't read or write but they're hard workers. Da gets angry sometimes. He worries about feeding the family, you see. I've eight brothers and sisters, some of them married, some still quite young. Those who have anything to spare give money to our parents to help raise the younger ones, because the big house doesn't pay them much. They have a little land, grow potatoes. So they get by – just.'

'What did you do back in Ireland?'

'I was a groom, and a good one, too. But I want more than that now. Much more. I was sad to leave, but I don't want to go back.' He gave her a wry smile. 'I've found hope, you see, hope of making something of myself. It's heady stuff, hope is.'

She nodded. 'What I want most is to have enough money to feel safe. My father had a job which could have made money for him, but he gambled our chances away. Do you gamble, Mr Deagan?'

Bram laughed. 'I've never had anything to gamble with. But it's a sort of gamble, me setting up as a trader. But to gamble on dice or cards, no!' He hesitated then told her about Mrs Maguire's trunk and the start it'd given him. 'I've still got it and some of the things from it. If there's anything you want from it, you'd be welcome.'

'Or if there's anything we can sell here.' She broke off to stare at him, her mouth falling open on a little intake of air that wasn't even a gasp.

But *he* noticed it. He was noticing everything about her today, like the way her hair curled more tightly near her ears, where it was shorter. He'd like to twist a strand of that richly glowing red round his fingers. But that would frighten her, so he smiled and forced himself to concentrate. 'You said "we".'

'So I did.'

He took a deep breath and said it again, 'So will you be marrying me, Isabella Saunders?'

'Yes, I will, Bram Deagan. But that's the only gamble I'm ever taking.'

He didn't try to kiss her, didn't dare, in case it broke the fragile link that was starting to build between them. But he did pick up her hand and hold it in his for a moment or two. He did allow himself that much.

And she didn't pull it away.

4

Conn wanted to leave Les in charge of the livery stable, but as an ex-convict the man might not be trusted by customers to handle money. He thought it over carefully, then mentioned it to Flora McBride, anxious to find a solution that would allow him to go home. He was sure Maia would be worrying about him being away for so long.

'*I* could manage the money side of things,' she said at once.

'You certainly won't,' her mother snapped. 'It'd not be seemly.'

Flora turned to her and it seemed to Conn that intense anger flared in her eyes for a few moments, then she said calmly, 'I can make my own decision about this, Mother.'

Mrs McBride glanced at Conn then back at her daughter, saying curtly, 'We'll discuss it later.'

Flora ignored that and continued her conversation with him. 'I could keep an eye on the livery stables for you, too, Mr Largan.'

'What do you know about horses?' Mrs McBride said scornfully.

'Not much.' After another of those resentful glances

at her mother, Flora looked pleadingly at Conn. 'But I do know about ordering food, which I do here, and it can't be all that different to check the orders for supplies and see that the place is kept clean. I do the household accounts for Mother and Dougal, so you needn't think I'll get confused about the money.'

He smiled at how eager she was and felt sorry for the way her mother was trying to put her down. Until now, he'd not paid Dougal's sister much attention on his brief visits because she was rather quiet. But perhaps that was because her mother never stopped talking. Flora was a sturdy woman, with sandy hair, prettier than her brother's. She wasn't pretty and probably never had been, but she wasn't ugly, either. Wholesome might be a good word to describe her. Her most attractive features were her hair and her low, quiet voice. Today the determined expression gave her face much more animation.

Mrs McBride clicked her tongue in exasperation. 'I've told you before not to talk about that sort of thing to gentlemen. What will people think about a lady who does accounts? I'm sure I could never add up a column to the same figure twice running. And as for working at livery stables, it's not at all the same thing as managing a house!' She turned to her guest. 'I'm sorry, Mr Largan, but she can't do it.'

'I've told you before, Mother: I'm old enough to make my own decisions.'

Caught between the two of them, Conn couldn't think what to say. He saw Mrs McBride breathe in so deeply she positively swelled up, then snap her lips together and throw her daughter a glance which said the quarrel would be continued in private.

'I can do it, Mr Largan,' Flora begged. 'I know I can. But I'd want paying.'

He saw her mother glare at her, a nasty expression that changed her from the fussy old lady he'd previously considered her. For some reason, that put him on Flora's side in this argument. 'Very well.'

A glowing smile lit her face to near prettiness and her mother's expression turned even sourer.

'Shall we say a weekly wage for your trouble and a percentage of the stable's earnings?'

Mrs McBride stood up. 'I'd like a word with you in private, if you please, Flora. In my sitting room.'

Flora waited until her mother had got to the door, to say, 'I'll join you when I've finished speaking to Mr Largan.'

The older woman hesitated, shot another furious glance at her daughter, then swept out of the room.

Conn felt it better to speak frankly. 'I don't want to cause trouble between you and your mother.'

Flora leaned forward, sounding as blunt and forthright as her brother. 'The trouble between us is already there. Years ago she wouldn't let me marry the man I wanted and I can't forgive her for that. I'd be glad to have something to fill my days and get me out of the house. Most of all, though, I want to have some money of my own.'

He was surprised by this, because usually young women were eager to get married. But Flora was past the usual age for marriage, so perhaps she'd given up hope. Though from what he'd seen, with the shortage of women in the colony, a lot of women who'd given up hope got married here. And good luck to them, too.

Well, he'd been away from his wife and child for long enough, so he wasn't going to turn down this offer from someone he trusted. 'If you're sure you want to do it, Miss McBride, and can deal with your mother, could you come to the stables with me in the morning, so that we can discuss what needs to be done in more detail?'

'I'd be happy to. Immediately after breakfast?'

'Perfect. I should mention that my main purpose is to keep the livery stables in operation until Bram Deagan gets back, then he and I can work out how to open up a shop there. Or perhaps he'll come up with some ideas of his own. He was always good at getting ideas, even when we were lads together.'

She looked at him in surprise. 'The stables are far too big for a shop, surely? Couldn't you keep them going *and* run a shop?'

'We can do anything we choose, but not till Bram's had time to look things over and think about it. I'm a minor partner only, providing money mainly.' He didn't want to keep all his money in a bank, in case it failed. 'I won't be involved in the day-to-day running of things and I trust him not to do anything stupid.'

He went up the stairs to his room and even from there, he could hear the two women arguing, the older one's voice being particularly shrill. He shook his head sadly. It wasn't wise or fair of Mrs McBride to stifle her daughter's ambitions and keep her penned up like a pet dog. He'd seen how his sister-in-law Xanthe had fretted at being confined to domestic duties and through that, he'd come to understand that not all women were made for quiet lives, whatever people said about it being a woman's natural role.

Being a convict had changed him, he knew, made him more thoughtful about others, all sorts of others, not only the gentry.

When Mr Largan had gone upstairs, Flora hesitated, but knew she couldn't avoid an argument, so decided she might as well get it over and done with. She went to the family's private sitting room and found her mother sitting bolt upright near the fire, anger radiating from her.

There was often trouble between her mother and herself when Dougal was away, though Flora didn't usually bother him with her problems. Unfortunately, her mother was always on her best behaviour when her son was there, so he might not believe any complaints. Everyone thought her mother was such a kind, friendly person, but they were wrong. Her mother was the most selfish person she'd ever met, and Flora sometimes felt like a slave not a daughter.

For a moment, her mother simply glared at her, then she screeched, 'How *dare* you defy me like that! In front of a guest, too.'

'I've told you before, I need something to keep me occupied and I need money of my own.'

'Why do you need money? You have everything you can possibly want here. *I* see that you're well dressed. Your brother supplies you with pin money.'

'It's occupation I lack, something to keep my mind occupied. I sometimes think I'll go mad shut up in this house, doing the same things day after day. So whatever you say, I'm going to do the job for Mr Largan.'

Her mother raised her hand and Flora quickly prevented the slap by pushing the raised arm away. If this weren't so serious, it'd be amusing to see the shock on her mother's face.

'Don't try to hit me again, Mother. Ever. Or I swear I'll walk out of the house and never come back.'

Her mother drew back. 'That's an empty threat. You'd never dare because you have nowhere else to go.'

And suddenly Flora knew she'd be better leaving it at that before she said something she might regret, so she moved towards the door.

'Where are you going? Come back. I've not finished.'

Flora turned to face her. 'I've said all I want to say, Mother. And I've heard all I'm willing to listen to. I'll just repeat that from now on, I intend to start living my own life. There's no need for me to be at your beck and call all day. You can run this boarding house perfectly well without me.'

'We'll see about that. You're going to regret this, my girl.'

She knew her mother would make her life very uncomfortable, but was quite sure she wouldn't regret taking a stand, should have done it years ago. She sometimes felt she would go insane as she listened to the foolish chatter of her mother, watched her playing the gracious lady with their 'guests', most of whom would rather have been left in peace.

Flora had suggested to Dougal that it wasn't necessary now to take in paying guests, as it had been when
he first sank all his money into his ship.

He'd smiled. 'Mother needs something to keep her
occupied, Flora. It might as well be taking paying guests
as anything else.'

He hadn't seemed to realise that Flora too needed
something worthwhile to do. But she'd make it plain
to him when he returned this time. Very plain.

The time had come for things to change.

As they walked together to the stables the following
morning, Flora said, 'Thank you for letting me do this,
Mr Largan. I get very bored sitting at home with my
mother and paying calls on the same ladies every week.'

'I hope you don't mind my asking, but don't you
ever wish to marry?'

She shrugged. 'It's getting a bit late for anything but
widowers and older men now. My mother wouldn't care
if the man I married had only one leg and was half-witted,
as long as he could give her the grandchildren she longs
for and be meek enough to let her boss him around. I'm
thirty now, you see, and Dougal's thirty-five. She's only
feeling desperate for grandchildren because all her friends
have some, not because she loves children.'

'A natural desire, surely?' He wished his mother had
lived long enough to see her grandson, but at least she'd
known about the baby. 'I think my wife was born to
marry and be a mother. But Maia's a companion too
and she has an excellent brain. I always value her opinion.'

Flora looked at him in surprise. 'Well, you're the first

man I've met who'd boast about his wife's intelligence. Have you got any brothers needing wives?'

His expression became sad. 'Just an older brother and he's married. I doubt I'll ever see him again.'

'It must have been hard for you being transported. Dougal told me you were innocent.'

He shrugged. He didn't like to talk about those dreadful, humiliating months of first waiting in a filthy gaol, then travelling to Australia. 'Yes, but unlike many others, I survived.'

'Is that why you took on the man you found hiding in the stables?'

'Yes. I try to help any ex-convict who seems willing to change his ways and work hard. Some of them were transported for trifling offences. He was only stealing food to feed his family, which is not the worst of crimes. Ah, here we are.'

She stopped to study the buildings. 'I hope you don't mind my bluntness. It's either hold my tongue, as I mostly do at home, or say what I think. I don't seem able to find a happy medium. This place looks rather run-down. If you want to keep it as a going concern, you should brighten up the outside a little or customers won't even come through the door.'

'I don't want to spend a lot of money on something we may close down, though you're probably right. I could maybe find a little money.'

'How much?'

Conn thought for a moment and mentioned a sum. 'Will that be enough for you to get the place thoroughly cleaned on the outside as well as the inside?'

'I think so. If you leave the money with me, I'll see what I can do. We've lived in Fremantle for a while, so I know people who'll be glad to earn some money.'

By that time Les had heard their voices and come to the door. 'Good morning, sir.'

'Good morning. Is everything all right?'

'Yes, sir. We got another horse in late last night. It's a sorry beast, but you can't tell some people how to treat their animals.'

Conn showed Flora round, and it was clear where Les had made a start on clearing things up. That showed initiative and a willingness to work hard.

When the two of them went to look at the owner's cottage, a small wooden place, they found that Mundy had taken most of his possessions and left the inside like a pigsty, with rotting food in the kitchen. Conn fumbled for another couple of sovereigns and handed them to Flora. 'Get someone in to scrub this place out, please, because Bram might want to live here. It's disgusting.'

'What about the odds and ends of furniture that are left?'

'I'll ask the baker to put the word round that if Mundy doesn't come and collect them, we'll sell them.'

'There's not much and I— Oh!' A door in the bedroom led to a cupboard full of women's clothes, with a few children's things lying there too. Her heart filled with pity. 'These must have belonged to his wife and child.'

'Yes, they died very suddenly. He mustn't have been able to face dealing with them.'

'If he doesn't want them, I could sell them to a second-hand dealer for you,' she offered. 'Most of them are hardly worn and fairly clean.'

'No, keep them. Bram thought he might deal in both new and second-hand items, so we should make the most of everything we find.'

After they'd seen everything, Conn turned to her. 'What do you think? Could you look after the stables for me and get this place cleaned out? Any items for sale can be stored in one of the big sheds behind the house.' When his inheritance from his mother came from Ireland, he'd have more money to invest, but he had to be careful now that he'd spent his spare cash on buying this place.

She beamed at him. 'I'll be happy to do that. What about the shop?'

'Bram will be back in a few weeks, so we'll wait for him to decide how he wants to organise things. I suggest I give you ten per cent of the money the stables make, in compensation for your overseeing efforts, as well as your weekly wage.'

'That's generous.'

'Well, you quarrelled with your mother for me.'

'No, I did it for me. It's more than time I stood up to her, though I hate quarrelling.' She held out her hand to him. 'It's agreed, then.'

He shook it, surprised by this masculine gesture and the firmness of her grasp.

She went home to change her clothes, so that she could make an immediate start on the cottage.

Conn felt he was within his rights to sell the things

Mundy had left, but on his way back he bumped into the man himself. Fremantle was a small place, after all. 'I thought you'd have left for Albany by now.'

Mundy shrugged. 'I'm staying with a friend.' He smirked. 'A lady friend.'

'What about your wife's clothing and the other bits and pieces you've left in the cottage?'

He scowled. 'I forgot them. Give me two guineas and they're yours. I don't need reminding of what happened to my Amy.'

After Mundy had pocketed his coins and slouched away, Conn stood in the shop doorway watching Mundy walk away.

The baker, who had seen him pay Mundy, said disapprovingly, 'That fellow will soon go through his money. I've seen his type before. Watch out he doesn't try to get back at you for more.'

'He can't. The property sale is signed and sealed, and I've registered my ownership of the house in Perth.' He was being careful, because he didn't want anyone to be able to accuse him of being dishonest. He shuddered at the mere thought of that, and people did jump to conclusions with ex-convicts.

He remembered something. 'Mundy said he was going back to England but he didn't bother to catch the last steamer to Albany, so he can't be in that much of a hurry.'

The baker shrugged. 'I see 'em come and go all the time, men like him. They want to make a fortune here but don't want to work for it. You mark my words, when his money's gone, he won't dare to go home for shame. Now, I must get back to my own work. Can I serve you with anything?'

'Yes. A loaf for my journey. I'm riding home now.'

'A currant loaf will taste nicer than a plain one.'

'Good idea.'

Although it was late afternoon, Conn decided to leave straight away, because he was longing to see Maia and his little son again. After a glance at the sky, which didn't seem to threaten rain, even though it was May, the start of the rainy winter season, he decided to set off straight away. Well, he'd set off as soon as he'd written a letter to Bram to explain about the livery stables. He could rest under a tree when he and the mare got tired, and get home easily before the end of the next day.

He went to pick up his things from the guest house, sighing in relief as he set off an hour later after a cool farewell from Mrs McBride, very different from her effusive welcome. Was the woman foolish enough to think she could keep an intelligent woman like her daughter tied to her apron strings for the rest of her life?

There would be more trouble between them in the future, he was sure, and Flora would mostly have to fight her own battles, because like all sailors Dougal spent a lot of time away from home.

Once Bram and Isabella had agreed to marry, Mr Lee took charge of the business side of the matter, leaving his mother to make preparations for the wedding.

'I shall need to discuss a few things with Isabella,' Bram protested.

'Need to discuss trading goods and prices with me,' Mr Lee said. 'Business is for the men. We leave wedding to my mother and sister.'

'But I have to arrange the ceremony and find out what Isabella wants.'

'Captain McBride can do that. Must be European marriage.'

So Bram asked his friend to help.

'You've decided to marry her, then?'

'Yes. I really want to.'

'She's a fine figure of a woman. I hope you'll be happy together.'

'It won't be my fault if we're not. Will you arrange the wedding for me?'

'Yes, of course. I shall enjoy doing that,' Dougal said enthusiastically.

'Don't forget to ask Isabella how she wants things done and where.'

His friend grinned. 'Not much choice about it here, old man. Leave it to me. I won't let you down.'

He wasn't seen again for the rest of that day, leaving his mate to supervise the loading of the first part of their cargo.

For much of the next three days, Bram found himself spending a lot of time in the small room behind the shop where Mr Lee conducted his business, going over figures and potential profits, or walking round a series of workshops and warehouses inspecting goods. It was very interesting and gave him a lot to think about. But at the same time, he was afraid Isabella might be upset by his neglect of her and change her mind.

The only time Bram saw her on her own was when they passed in the corridor one day. 'Are you all right?' he asked, concerned about the dark rings under her eyes. 'If you've changed your mind—'

'I've not changed my mind. Have you?'

'No, of course not! But you look – worried.'

'I've a lot to think about and I didn't sleep very well last night.' She sagged back against the wall. 'I'm all right. Truly. Just busy. Mrs Lee doesn't believe in wasting a second.'

'Ah, there you are!' Dougal suddenly walked in from the shop. 'I need you both to come with me to see the clergyman I've found. He's reluctant to perform the marriage without meeting you both and is concerned about its suddenness. He fussed so much I told him you'd been corresponding for a while, just to shut him up.'

So Isabella flew upstairs to change once more into her best dress and put on a demure little bonnet, which failed to hide her glorious hair. After that, the three of them walked across town to St Andrew's Cathedral, which was only a few years old.

'I'm a Catholic,' Bram muttered as they stopped to gaze at the imposing building.

'Don't, for heaven's sake, tell him that!' Dougal said. 'If you do, we'll never get you married.'

But Isabella took Bram's arm to prevent him moving. 'Does it matter to you where we marry? I'm not a Catholic and to tell you the truth, I don't have any strong beliefs, so if you'd rather marry somewhere else . . . There are Catholic churches here, too.'

He shook his head, knowing the fuss a priest might

make about him marrying a non-Catholic. 'It'll matter to my mother, but not to me. As long as it's done legally, that's all I care about.'

The clergyman was impatient, took their details and frowned at them. 'Is there any reason for this unseemly haste?' The look he gave Isabella showed what he was thinking.

Bram grew angry at his patronising tone and couldn't hold back any longer. 'Stop this!'

Everyone fell silent, staring at him in surprise.

He glared at the clergyman. 'The only reason for haste is that my ship is leaving in a day or two. If you find me a Bible, I'll swear on it here and now that I've not touched her in that way and won't till after we're married.'

Isabella blushed and Dougal coughed to hide a laugh.

The clergyman stiffened visibly. 'I apologise for any offence I may have given you, Mr Deagan, Miss Saunders. I didn't mean to insinuate that . . .' His voice tailed away.

As they walked out of the church, Bram muttered, 'That one's the last person I'd choose to marry me.'

'Shh!' Dougal took both their arms and hurried them out of the doorway and along the street, stopping to look up at the sky. 'Let's hurry back. It's going to rain soon.' He started walking again.

After a while he smiled at them. 'Whatever the weather, we'll get the marrying done decently and legally in St Andrew's and never mind who officiates. The important part of the marriage is what happens between you two afterwards.' He grinned. 'You looked frightening for a minute or two back there, Bram. I'd not want to cross you in that mood.'

He shrugged. 'Well, he had no reason to be so rude to Isabella and I won't have it. I've got a bit of a temper, I must admit, but only if I'm pushed unreasonably. I learned how to control it when I worked for the Largans back in Ireland. You couldn't get anyone more unreasonable than Mrs Kathleen. If I hadn't kept my mouth shut, I'd have lost my job. I lost it anyway in the end, on one of her stupid whims. I was bitter about that at the time, but now I'm glad.' He smiled at Isabella. The marriage and this new venture would be the making of him, he was sure. He'd work twice as hard for a woman like her.

She smiled back, then turned to their companion. 'I'm grateful to you for your help, Captain McBride. There's just one other thing, though. I want the Lees to attend the ceremony. They're as near to family as I've got now. I couldn't possibly leave them out of things.'

Dougal stopped moving again to stare at her thoughtfully. 'That won't go down well with the stuffed shirt who's officiating. I wonder how he'll react to the appearance of a Chinese family at the wedding.'

Bram let out an angry snort. 'He'll just have to accept it. It's our wedding. The Lees have been good to Isabella and I won't do anything to upset them.'

She smiled at him. 'Thank you.'

He wished she'd smile like that more often. She'd looked so worried these last few days.

They parted from Dougal, who was going straight

back to the ship and Bram escorted Isabella home to report that it was all arranged. Just as they arrived, it started to pour down and they ran down the street, laughing.

Mr Lee listened to the arrangements, smiled and nodded. 'Good, good.'

'I hope you and your family will attend the wedding service,' Bram said.

Mr Lee bowed, not seeming at all surprised by this. 'Happy to do that. Afterwards, I take you for special meal to celebrate.'

It came out more like 'celeblate'. Bram had got used to being called 'Blam' now.

'You're too kind to me, Lee-Sang,' Isabella said. 'You don't need to do that.'

'We kind to each other. Later, you rich trader and me rich native, we remember wedding.' He laughed at his own joke about himself.

It was probably the truth where Mr Lee's fortune was concerned, Bram thought. But he couldn't imagine himself ever getting rich. Comfortable was as far as his dreams would stretch, having enough to live on and a little to spare, saved for a rainy day.

Aloud he said only, 'Good! That's settled, then.' He glanced outside. 'I think it's stopped raining now, so I'm afraid I have to leave. Dougal and I've been invited to dine with his relatives again. He thinks it'll be wise to tell them about the wedding, since they've been kind enough to invite me to their house twice.'

'Invite them to wedding. Can come for meal after as well,' Mr Lee said at once.

'I'll – um, see if they're free.' There was no way they'd accept, he was quite sure of that. But some devil inside him, a devil that had been barricaded inside for most of his life, thought it'd be amusing to see their faces when he invited them.

It was dark outside now. It got dark early here. As he walked back to the ship, he was glad of the gas lighting in the main areas, so that he could avoid the puddles that still lay around. He was also glad of the man walking behind him, sent by Mr Lee to keep him safe.

The streets were almost as busy now as they had been during the daytime. When vendors offered him trays of small, highly coloured cakes, or other food items he didn't recognise, he smiled but refused. He'd no mind to risk unknown foods and be ill on his wedding day.

He stopped just before he got to the ship to look back. What a vibrant place Singapore was! He wished it wasn't quite so far away from the Swan River Colony or that he was a better sailor, because he'd love to come back here regularly.

5

The Wallaces again had several other people to dinner and Bram wondered how Mr Wallace ever got any work done if he spent so many evenings staying up late and drinking.

He was glad the Singapore tailor Dougal had taken him to had finished his new suit, while another man, a Malay this time, had made him several shirts at an incredibly cheap price. Though his suit wasn't evening dress, it was the only brand-new outfit he'd ever owned, the only one that fitted perfectly. He hadn't even owned underwear when he was growing up, none of them had, except his mother, who had a ragged petticoat and shift.

At one stage during the evening, Dougal mentioned to his cousin that Bram was getting married the following day to Miss Saunders. Everyone at the table fell silent and stared at the bridegroom in shock.

'I'm honoured that she's agreed to marry me,' Bram said into the silence. 'I hope you'll wish us well.'

'But – um, isn't she the one who's gone native?' one man exclaimed.

Bram's inner devil gave him a prod. 'What the hell do you mean by that?'

'Well, no offence, but she's been living with the

natives. Who knows what she's been doing there. Are you *sure* marrying her is a good thing to do? I mean, you're just starting up and—'

Bram didn't wait for him to finish. 'Miss Saunders has been living with a highly respected Chinese family, if that's what you mean, and they're quite well-to-do, actually. I gather she sleeps in the room next to Mr Lee's mother and sister. She doesn't go out alone at night, or associate with anyone except the family and their servants. She does help translate for her employer's business dealings with Europeans, but always in his company. So in what way is she behaving badly?'

Another silence, then Dougal chuckled. 'Ah, you can't blame a man for defending the woman he loves. I've met the Lees, too, dined with them. I can promise you they're extremely respectable people. Lee Kar Ho will be as rich as Whampoa one day, see if he isn't. Singapore seems to attract successful men of all races.'

Even Bram had heard of Whampoa, who had come to Singapore in the early days and made himself a huge fortune. That name stopped the conversation short.

'Well, I'm sure we all wish you happy,' Mrs Wallace said and changed the subject firmly.

People nearby began to chat about other matters, but since those further along the table lowered their voices and occasionally glanced at him, Bram guessed they were still discussing his shocking piece of news. He found it hard to concentrate on his food, which wasn't nearly as tasty as that served by the Lees.

He kept fairly quiet after the meal ended, too, not understanding half the things they talked about. He'd never seen an opera, or had time for reading novels or seen famous paintings or sculptures.

He was relieved when Dougal said they should leave. As he walked across the drawing room to say goodbye to his host and hostess, the noise again died down as people tried to listen to what he was saying.

There was nothing he could do except ignore their rudeness and take a polite leave of the Wallaces. It wouldn't do to set people's backs up if he intended to keep trading with people in Singapore.

He thanked his host and hostess for their hospitality, then Mrs Wallace smiled and said, 'I hope you'll accept this small gift for your wedding.'

She gestured and a servant came forward carrying an object wrapped in a quilted cloth. Bram stood with it in his hands, lost for words. It was the last thing he'd expected of her.

'Open it, you fool!' Dougal muttered.

Bram removed the cover and found an elegant clock. 'It's beautiful. I didn't expect anything, Mrs Wallace, but I promise you it'll have pride of place on our mantelpiece.' Once they had a mantelpiece.

She smiled and dabbed at her eyes. 'I always like to see young people getting married.'

'Do you? If you'd care to attend the ceremony tomorrow, we'd welcome you,' he said. 'Mr Lee is taking everyone for a special meal afterwards to celebrate. He said any other guests would be welcome to join us.' He looked round the room as he said this.

She couldn't hide her surprise and glanced at her husband for guidance.

Mr Wallace pursed his lips then nodded. 'We'll be there. Lee's a coming man, so I want to meet him.'

'I'd like to come too,' another man said.

Bram had to ask Dougal who he was. As they were walking home, he admitted, 'I don't know how to take these people. They're snobbish and yet they can be kind. Even to a man like me.'

'They like people who stand up to them – though not too fiercely. And they've an eye for men who're going to be successful. You'd better learn how to deal with them if you want to make a lot of money. It's people like them who hold commercial power in the Swan River Colony too. Maybe you'll be just as affluent as them one day. I certainly intend to be.'

But however hard he tried, Bram couldn't imagine himself living in a big house, waited upon by servants. He clutched the clock and was grateful when Dougal left him to his thoughts for the rest of the walk back.

Was he really getting married tomorrow? It was beginning to seem unreal. He wished he'd seen more of Isabella, got to know her better, wished his head wasn't crammed to bursting with thoughts of all those trade goods he'd seen and the suggestions Mr Lee had made.

His greatest fear was that she'd end up despising him because of his background.

Why was being happy never simple?

When dawn brightened the cabin, Bram stopped pretending to be asleep and got up. He went to stand at the rail, watching people moving about their business, even this early in the morning. He felt wide awake, ready for this important day, but on edge too, as he always was when he associated with affluent people. He wished these near strangers weren't coming to his wedding.

Some of the ordinary men and women he saw passing by were carrying what looked like food for sale on little trays suspended from straps round their necks. They must have got up while it was still dark to cook this. People were stopping them to buy and eat. It was simple food. One man had plain rice in a big round pot and a pile of leaves to serve it on. Maybe that was their breakfast?

Coolies were carrying loads of all shapes and sizes, the men with lighter loads moving more quickly, some even running. There were fewer children around and no Europeans at this hour. Except for him.

He'd always loved early morning and here in Singapore it was fascinating to watch the way people lived. You saw bad things as well as good. Dead dogs in the street, which no one seemed to bother about for a day or two, then the bodies would vanish. Fruit which smelled dreadful. Other fruit which smelled like rich, honeyed flowers or was star-shaped. Vegetables he didn't recognise, but which looked fresh and appetising, all shapes and sizes of greens, not just cabbage or nettles as he'd grown up with.

'You're awake early.'

He turned to see Dougal standing on deck, stretching and making growling noises, rubbing his chest through his nightshirt then rubbing his forehead. His friend had taken quite a few drinks the previous night, but since Bram had no head for ale and even less for wine, he'd contented himself with one glass and making it last, just to show willing.

'Enjoying the last of your freedom?'

Bram shook his head. 'Worrying that she'll change her mind.'

'She won't. Come on. Let's get some food into you, then we'll get dressed.'

When they were ready, they walked to St Andrew's Cathedral and Bram was relieved to see Isabella standing with Mr Lee, his mother and sister at the entrance.

She hadn't changed her mind!

She looked beautiful, in a dress he'd not seen her wearing before, though he thought he recognised the blue silk he'd admired in the shop. The dress was simple, like all her clothes, with just a little lace collar at the high neckline and lace at the edge of her sleeves. The lustrous material needed no other embellishment, but it seemed to bring out the glory of her hair under a tiny mainly lace bonnet tied under her chin.

He'd not have noticed such things before but he did now, because this was his bride.

As he moved forward, the Lees bowed and stepped back a little. Solemnly, he returned their bows and offered his arm to Isabella. Only then did he realise that he'd completely forgotten to buy her a ring and gasped, staring at her in consternation.

'What is it?' she whispered.

'We forgot about a ring?'

She smiled. 'I forgot too until this morning and I guessed you might not have remembered because you hadn't said anything or measured my finger. But I have my mother's wedding ring and it fits beautifully.' She offered it to him. 'I'd like to wear this in her memory, if you don't mind.'

'Of course. It's a good thought, but I'm still sorry I didn't talk about a ring before.'

'We've been rushing round like *eejits*,' she said, mocking his accent gently.

He smiled. 'Well, we can stop rushing now, and surely even *idiots*,' he pronounced it in the English way, 'can take the time to enjoy their own wedding.'

When they went inside the cathedral, he was surprised to find the Wallaces and two other couples waiting for them at the rear of the church.

'We felt we should come and give you our support,' Mr Wallace boomed.

Why did the man always speak so loudly, Bram wondered. Was he going deaf? 'That's very kind of you. May I present Miss Saunders, and her friends, Mr Lee, Mrs Lee and Miss Lee.'

There was a slight hesitation, then the group of Europeans acknowledged the Lees, and allowed themselves to be introduced in their turn. After that everyone moved forward to the front of the church.

'Who's giving away the bride?' Mr Wallace asked.

Isabella answered. 'Mr Lee. I've explained to him what it means, and since he and his family have been so kind to me, I can't think of anyone better to do it.'

There was another awkward silence, filled by the

clergyman bustling forward, frowning at the Lees and smiling at the Wallaces.

The ceremony itself was rapid, though the words they uttered seemed to Bram too important to be gabbled like that, so he made his responses slowly.

'And thereto I plight thee my troth.' His eyes met hers as he said those words and he hoped she realised that he was making a solemn promise which he intended to keep.

'I now pronounce you man and wife.'

He took both her hands in his, leaning forward to kiss her gently on the cheek.

The clergyman cleared his throat and once he had their attention, took them away to sign the register, after which he presented Bram with his marriage lines and said a curt goodbye.

One day, Bram vowed, people like you will not treat me so scornfully.

Then he forgot the man as they rejoined Dougal. He was talking to the Wallaces and their friends, while the Lees were standing apart. Isabella immediately went to join them and let Xiu Mei twine some red ribbons round one of her wrists 'for luck'.

She turned to explain to the Europeans, 'Red is normally the colour for brides, and it's said to bring luck, but I couldn't wear a red dress with my hair.'

Bram wouldn't have cared what colour she wore. It was Isabella he was marrying, not a dress.

Dougal smiled across at them. 'If it's all right with you, Mr Lee, we would all be happy to accept your invitation to join you for refreshments.'

'Very welcome. Honoured to have your company.'
Mr Lee bowed. After some hesitation, so did their guests.

Bram now had Isabella's arm linked in his and was
holding the hand that lay on his sleeve. He leaned closer
to her to murmur, 'They're only coming out of curiosity.
Doesn't he mind that?'

'Not at all. It won't hurt his standing to be seen with
them, or yours and mine as traders later on.'

Well, that was a practical way of looking at it, he
thought.

When they were all seated, Mr Lee held out a package
wrapped in red paper, offering it to Bram with both
hands.

Isabella again explained. 'Wedding gifts are usually
wrapped in red.'

He passed it to her. 'You open it.'

She did so, revealing some money, but pushed it
quickly back into the wrapping, turning to Mr Lee.
'You shouldn't have done this. It's too much.'

'You work hard, part of family now.'

The other guests nudged one another.

Xiu Mei held out another package, a much larger
one. 'From mother and me. Is a dress. Open corner
only.' She tugged at a loose corner.

The material was in a dark green shade and Isabella
was speechless for a moment. 'It's beautiful. I didn't
expect this.'

Mrs Lee then handed over another red paper
package containing money. 'Brides need gifts of money.'
She cast a superior glance at the Europeans. 'Is Chinese
custom.'

The two women nudged their husbands, who fumbled in their pockets and produced some sovereign coins.

Mrs Lee tutted as they would have handed them over, and took some red paper from a pouch round her waist. 'Must wrap up for luck,' she said severely.

They did this meekly and Mr Wallace winked at Isabella, which made her feel a little better. After all, the guests were going to have a wonderful meal.

The present-giving over, Mr Lee took the newly-weds across to a side room, where a photographer was waiting for them. 'Is important to remember the day,' he said with a smile.

She stopped him going. 'Could I also have a photograph of us with you, and Ah Yee and Xiu Mei?'

He inclined his head.

When the meal began. Bram and Isabella hurriedly explained the polite way to start eating and the Europeans did their best to conform, though they all asked for spoons, not chopsticks. Well, he had to use a spoon himself.

He worked his way through several courses of the most superb food he'd ever eaten, not surprised as the other Europeans were about its quality. He'd thought he wasn't hungry today, but he found differently once he tasted the food, which was much more elaborate than that they'd eaten at the Lees' house.

Isabella explained to their guests what each course was and after cautious tastes, most of them ate heartily.

Mr Lee managed to hold his own in conversations in English and his mother fired occasional staccato comments at the other ladies, showing an understanding of what she'd heard.

No one lingered after the meal, except for the main group, but their guests were very complimentary about the food.

Bram heard one woman say as they walked away, 'A wonderful meal, I must admit, but I don't know why they have to eat with those primitive little sticks.'

He frowned, thinking it rude to say this so loudly.

Mr Lee smiled as he watched the guests leave and said quietly, 'Useful to know these people and for them to know me. They don't know they rude.'

'Well, I don't like it and you don't deserve it. But I don't think they *mean* to be rude. They did enjoy the food.'

Mr Lee was still smiling. 'I know.'

'I want to thank you from the bottom of my heart for giving Isabella to me. I'll look after her, I promise you. And I shall never forget this wonderful meal.'

Bram turned to his wife. *His wife*! 'Are you ready to leave now, Isabella? Do we have to pick up your things from home?'

'No. They'll have been taken to the ship.'

'And your improved cabin awaits you,' Dougal said. 'I'll go ahead and make sure everything is all right.'

Bram whispered to her, 'He's refused to let me see it, so I have no idea what it'll be like.'

'I'm sure it'll be fine.' She turned to the Lees. 'You've been very kind to us. In so many ways. I don't know how to thank you enough.'

'Important to make good start to marriage. You come

see me tomorrow, both of you, make final arrangements about trade goods.'

When they went outside, Bram asked, 'Do you want to ride back in a rickshaw?'

She looked down at her beautiful gown. 'I'd better. I don't want to get the hem of this dirty. I'll change out of it as soon as we get back and keep it for best. The Lees have been so kind to me.'

'They're very fond of you.' He took her hand, delaying her for a moment. 'I've been waiting till we were alone. I just wanted to say – I'll do my best for you, always.'

She nodded. 'I know. As I will for you. Our situation is – a bit difficult.'

'We have no need to rush into anything until we're both ready, not tonight either.'

She shot him a glance, wondering if she'd misunderstood, but when he repeated the last phrase, she relaxed a little. 'You're a kind man, Bram.'

'I hope so. Life's hard enough without adding unkindness to the mix. Now, come on, Mrs Deagan. Let's find out what Dougal's been doing to our new cabin.'

On the deck was her pile of luggage, and a big pile it was too. A sailor was standing next to it, on guard against pilferers.

'I have a few pieces of furniture and I brought a few trade goods for myself,' she whispered. 'I hope you don't mind.'

'Why should I mind?'

The sailor smiled at them. 'Congratulations on your

marriage, sir, madam. If you'll tell me which is your cabin luggage, Mrs Deagan, I'll have the rest taken down to the hold.'

She indicated the various items she wanted to keep with her during the voyage, then waited for the sailors to clear the pile away, before Bram took her to the cabin they would share.

He stood back to let her go first, waiting in the doorway, smiling at her exclamation of pleasure. The cabin was larger than the one he'd been occupying and somehow the sailor who was also the ship's carpenter had made a double bed for them. It had a beautiful cover on it, quilted, the material a series of bright reds and pinks that seemed to glow with life and colour. It must have been made in Singapore. He'd never seen quilts like that anywhere else.

That gave him an idea, then he grew annoyed with himself for thinking of trade goods at a time like this.

The sailors had put Isabella's trunk in a corner and someone had previously gathered together Bram's things, which were piled next to them.

From behind them Dougal said, 'The bedspread is my wedding present to you. Mrs Lee helped me find it. She said it had to be red.'

Isabella turned round. 'Thank you so much. The colour's not only associated with weddings but, um, fertility.' She tried to hide her blush by looking down at her wrist. 'That's why I kept these ribbons on, because it was important to them that I wear something red.'

'You look beautiful,' Bram said, his voice soft. He

saw Dougal smile and walk away, and was glad to be left alone with her.

As he shut the cabin door, Isabella realised she was feeling nervous again. She found it difficult to breathe steadily, didn't dare look at him. Stupid really.

He took her hand, holding it as if it were very delicate. 'I said we'd not rush into anything and I meant it.'

She felt more able to look at him then. 'Silly to be so nervous, isn't it? People get married all the time.'

'You're not the only one to be nervous.' It was his turn to look embarrassed. 'I've not been married before, either.'

'But you must have – done that sort of thing.'

He shook his head. 'No, I've not. I lived in a small village, where everyone knew everyone. I worked in the big house from when I was ten. There, the female servants were kept right away from the male servants, and very strict the family were about it, too. You could be sacked for even speaking to one of the maids.' His voice took on a bitter tone. 'Old Mr Largan, though, he could do what he wanted, and what he did was so terrible, I'll not sully your ears with it. But his servants had to behave like monks and nuns.'

She was astonished, but this confession reassured her. She was glad he wasn't trying to pretend about anything, but she couldn't find appropriate words to say this, so gave his hand a squeeze, hoping he'd understand how she felt.

He smiled at her then, his lovely cheerful smile, and that lifted her spirits.

'We'd better sort out our things or we'll fall over them in the night.' She waved one hand towards the piles of luggage and bundles of who knew what.

'We'll do it together.'

They worked in harmony, stopping to drink some tea and eat cake that the ship's cook had baked especially to celebrate the wedding. The cake was a bit lopsided, but tasted fine.

'I've not had fruit cake in years,' she said, delighted. 'I'd forgotten how delicious it is.'

Only when it was time to go to bed did she feel her cheeks grow hot again. It was hard to undress in front of a stranger.

He cleared his throat. 'I'll, um, just go for a stroll round the deck while you get ready.'

She didn't pretend not to understand what he was doing. 'Thank you.'

She folded up the beautiful quilt and put it on top of her trunk, then put on one of the pretty new nightgowns she'd found in her luggage. Xiu Mei and her mother must have done that. How kind they were! How she was going to miss them.

Bram came in, carrying a bottle of wine. 'Dougal says we should have a drink, but to tell you the truth, I'm not much of a drinker.'

'I'm not, either. We'll keep it for another time, shall we?'

When he started to get undressed, she closed her eyes, then grew curious and peeped out through her lashes. He had a wiry body, and he moved easily and gracefully. It was a hard-working body, not carrying an ounce of fat. Good. She couldn't have borne to marry a lazy man like her father.

When Bram slipped into bed, clad in a nightshirt, he sighed wearily. 'I'm not pretending, Isabella, or trying to avoid you, but I hardly slept last night and I'm exhausted. Not a good time to be trying out new things, eh?'

'You're right.'

'But I would like to hold you.' He reached out to take her in his arms and she wriggled till she was comfortable in the crook of his arm.

'It's nice to have this again,' he said in a slurred, sleepy voice as they lay quietly together.

'What?' Hadn't he said he'd not had a woman before?

'Not being alone in bed. I always shared with my brothers till I left home. We talked a lot in the dark. You can say things in the dark that you can't in daylight. I missed that.'

She heard him yawn, his hand slackened in hers then he was asleep, as quickly as that.

She smiled in the darkness. Not a frightening man, her husband. She'd been a fool to get so het up about it all. She was sure now that he'd deal gently with her. In every way.

In the morning, Isabella woke early, but Bram was awake before her, lying on his side smiling at her. He must have been watching her.

'I fell asleep on you without even a good night. What a poor excuse for a bridegroom I am.'

'I wasn't far behind you. I was exhausted, too.' She

looked at the new clock, sitting on the floor beside the bed, because they hadn't found anywhere to tie it down yet. 'We should get up. Mr Lee starts work early and we have a lot to talk to him about.'

'We need to count the money before we go to see him, the wedding presents, I mean. I didn't want to start doing that without you. We could maybe buy some extra trading goods with part of it. What do you think?'

'I agree. But we should keep some for emergencies and setting up the shop.'

He got out of bed. 'Let's get something to eat first. I think better on a full stomach.'

To her relief he made no attempt to touch her and looked away as she got up. She had a quick wash and dressed.

She did the same for him, pretending to sort out some clothes that were already neatly arranged while he got ready. She wondered how long it would take for them to grow comfortable with one another.

After a simple breakfast of boiled eggs with huge chunks of bread, they went back to the cabin and counted their gifts.

Her eyes filled with tears. 'He's been so generous.'

Bram was silent for a few moments. In one day he'd trebled his capital, thanks to Mr Lee. He'd never forget what he owed the man, never. He saw her looking at him, a question in her eyes. 'Yes, very generous. And we've even received a pile of sovereigns from the wedding guests.' He laughed softly. 'Very practical people, the Chinese. The Europeans were shamed into giving us presents, I know, but I'm not handing the money back. They're not short and we are.'

'We should spend the Chinese money here on trade goods and keep the sovereigns for Australia, don't you think?' she suggested.

'That's a good idea. And . . . will you help me choose the trade goods? I know very little about what women like to buy. Do we choose things which are pretty or things which are useful?'

'Some of both, I should think.'

They strolled across to Mr Lee's house, not needing rickshaws because she was wearing her dark, practical clothes once more. He was wearing his shabby everyday things too. She felt more comfortable with him when they weren't dressed up, more comfortable with herself, too.

She was determined to help him in every way she could, determined to make as much money as possible. That way they would not only have a better life, but she'd be able to afford to look for Alice. Surely she'd find her cousin one day?

Xiu Mei looked up with a smile as they entered the shop. 'He's waiting for you.'

They walked along the corridor and found Mr Lee in his room.

'Lee-Sang,' she said by way of greeting, bowing slightly.

He inclined his head to her then to her husband. 'You look well.'

'We'd both like to thank you for your generous gifts,'

Bram said. 'Isabella and I've discussed it and we thought we should spend some of the money on trade goods, but perhaps we could change some of it into English money so that we have something to work with when we reach Australia. Is that possible?'

Isabella felt warm inside at this further sign that he was treating her publicly as an equal. That meant a lot to her.

At the end of a busy day shopping for trade goods, they followed the coolies who were carrying their packages back to the ship, packages which contained dress materials, two rugs and some quilts as well as a great many smaller items.

Dougal was sitting on deck, looking relaxed. He waved to his mate to oversee the new goods being stowed in the hold. 'It looks as if you've been busy. Come and sit down, Mrs Deagan.'

'Call me Isabella,' she said. 'I'm not used to Mrs Deagan yet.'

'And I'm Dougal. What have you bought today?'

'So many things, I don't know where to begin.'

He seemed genuinely interested so she went through some of them and answered his questions about prices, in turn asking what prices they could expect for these goods in Australia. The answers made her blink and exchange quick glances with Bram. No wonder some traders got rich.

They had a pleasant, relaxed evening and it wasn't until they got to the cabin and she bumped into Bram in the confined space that she remembered they hadn't yet consummated their marriage. She could feel herself growing stiffer.

He sensed it at once and took her hands. 'Don't be afraid of me, Isabella. Never. I'll not touch you in that way until we're both ready.'

She swallowed and tried to summon up a smile, but couldn't.

When they were lying in bed, he again wanted to cuddle and reached to pull her close.

She was getting to like lying in his arms, enjoyed being able to chat and was sorry when he turned away from her with a murmured, 'Go to sleep now, wife!'

She lay in the darkness, hearing his breathing slow down, wondering at him. Did he not want her? Or was he as considerate as he seemed?

Did she want him?

Not yet, she admitted. Not until she knew him much better.

How long would he hold back, though? She wished she understood this side of men better.

6

Alice Beaufort sighed as she looked at the clock. Parker was late again. He had no idea of time and it drove her mad sometimes, trying to make sure he was home for meals, and that he didn't bring noisy friends back late at night and wake their little daughter. This was a very small house in a terrace of similar dwellings. Luckily, at two, Louisa was too young to understand a lot of what was going on, but Alice worried about how the child would be affected by their quarrels as she grew older.

When she heard footsteps outside she didn't rush to open the front door and throw herself into his arms, as she had when they were first married. She waited, foot tapping, praying he'd be alone.

He was, but when he smiled at her owlishly, his lips loose, his body swaying, her spirits sank.

'You've been drinking again. Oh, Parker, you promised me you'd come straight home with the money. And you said you'd never get drunk again!'

'I'm not drunk. I jus' had a few drinks with my good frien's.'

'What about the money? Did you get it? Did your family send any extra this time?'

He came across and pulled her to him for a crushing kiss, but she shoved him away, hating the smell of rum on his breath. 'The money, Parker! I need money to buy food.'

She hadn't understood when she married him what a remittance man was, but she understood all too clearly now. His family had grown tired of his debts and his embarrassing attempts to prove himself an artist, so had sent him as far away as they could: to Australia. They now paid him a fixed amount every year to remain there. They were ashamed of him, wanted nothing more to do with him, but they didn't want him to starve.

They no doubt understood, and she did too now, that Parker was never likely to make a living by his own efforts. And they understood his carelessness, as well. The money was paid quarterly, she guessed because they knew they couldn't trust him to make it last out for a whole year.

She'd fallen in love with him because he was handsome, gentle and kind, unlike Renington. And because he didn't care about her past. Not many men would marry another fellow's mistress. But she soon found out that Parker was totally impractical. It had been a rude awakening for her, because she was more used to letting others take care of her, but she'd managed to find them a house and keep the rent paid, at least.

His family were merchants and sounded to be rich, but she'd never be able to meet them, or introduce them to their granddaughter, because if Parker went back to England they'd stop paying his money. 'Well?' she asked even more sharply.

He pulled a face but turned out his pockets and she saw with dismay that he'd spent quite a bit of the money already. 'Is that all you have left?'

He fumbled in his pockets again and found one more sovereign, then patted his clothing and nodded.

She counted the money and quickly stuffed it into the hanging pocket under her skirt.

He tried to grab it back. 'You've not left any for me.'

'This has to last us three months. Three whole months, Parker. Or do you want your child to go hungry?'

'Of course I don't.'

'You've spent nearly half your allowance tonight. *In one night!*' That caught his attention.

'I can't have.'

She burst into tears suddenly. 'You have. I don't know how I'm to manage.'

He sat down, shoulders drooping. 'But I only bought a few drinks.'

'Then someone must have picked your pocket.'

'No! They're my friends. They'd not steal from me.'

'They do steal from you. Every time they come near you. They stole from me, too, till I forbade them to come here again. Look at me! I haven't had a new dress for two years. Everything I own is shabby.' She continued to sob and though she leaned against him when he put his arms round her, it didn't mean she'd forgiven him.

When she'd wept herself dry, she sat up and said firmly, 'There's only one thing for it, Parker. Next quarter, I'm coming to the lawyer's with you and I'm taking charge of the money straight away.'

He flushed. 'How will that look? As if I can't be trusted to handle money.'

'You can't. And I don't care how it'll look.' She played her trump card, knowing how much he loved their little daughter. 'Do you want Louisa to go hungry and be dressed in rags? She's growing all the time, needs new clothes regularly.'

He shook his head, looking miserable. 'I can't believe that's all there is left. Show me.'

She counted the money again carefully, in case she'd made a mistake. But she hadn't. She put it back into her pocket, fielding off his hand. 'No, you're not to take any, Parker. You can't *afford* to go out drinking any more.'

'But even if I don't drink, I'll still need to buy paints.'

'I'll buy them for you. It'll be better that way, really it will. You always run out of money before the quarter ends and have to wait to buy new paints. This way, I'll make sure you don't run out.'

His face brightened a little. 'That's all right, then. I'd better get ready for work tomorrow, hadn't I? I have an idea for a new painting. I'm sure this one will sell and we shan't have to worry about money any more.'

He put on his stained painting smock and went up to the attic to prepare a canvas for a new picture. He loved what he called his 'work', but there was something not quite right about his pictures. She'd tried to figure out what it was, the composition or the colours, but the reason eluded her. He was best at sketching and made money from time to time by sketching rich people's children or pets in charcoal – something he despised doing and would only undertake when they were down to their last few shillings. Yet it was there his small talent really lay.

She sighed as their daughter woke up and began to call out for her. Life hadn't gone as she wished. But she was here now and had to make the best of it.

Alice wondered as she gave her daughter something to eat whether her cousin still thought about her. Was Isabella married? Did she have children? Was she happy?

Would they ever meet again?

She was quite sure Isabella wasn't stupid enough to run away with a handsome scoundrel, who wasn't able to keep his promise to marry her because he was already married. Nor would Isabella fall in love with a man who couldn't support her, however much he loved her.

But at least Parker had married her, given her respectability again. And he'd written to his family about her. They hadn't written back, though. And they hadn't increased his money, not even after Louisa was born. She'd get him to write again, and make him do it the very next day, before he started work. They couldn't ignore their grandchild, surely?

And if that didn't move them to send more money, she'd write herself, explaining her background and asking if they'd consider sending money for Louisa direct to her.

She had learned the hard way to be tenacious when she needed something.

Flora decided to scrub out the little house next to the livery stables herself and keep the money Conn had given her for that purpose. It was a dirty job, but the two guineas would be a nice addition to her savings.

She hadn't told anyone how much money she'd got squirrelled away, because her mother would want to 'look after it' for her. She'd already seen signs that someone had been searching her room. As if she'd be foolish enough to leave her money where it could easily be found! As if she didn't know that her mother went through her things.

If her mother got hold of it, she'd just spend it on the house. She always had some justification for the 'improvements' she made, even when they weren't necessary, and she discarded furniture as other women discarded out-of-fashion clothing.

Only it wasn't their mother's house; it was Dougal's. He'd worked hard for it and been generous with them, but their mother wouldn't be in charge of it for ever. Of course, even if he married, he'd always provide a home for them, Flora was sure. But that wasn't the same. You were then a guest in the wife's house and had no choice about how things were organised.

Just as Flora had no choice about how her mother organised things.

She had a friend in a similar position, and had seen Jeanie weep at the small insults she had to endure when her sister-in-law was in a bad mood. Well, Flora had no intention of becoming Dougal's poor spinster sister after he married, even if his wife turned out to be a wonderful woman. Nor did she intend to marry a man she didn't respect in order to get her own home, whatever her mother said.

As she worked, she looked round the little house. Once it was all sparkling clean, she sighed enviously. She'd love to live in a place like this – on her own. But that would shock her mother and cause a furore in their family. She wasn't even sure Dougal would allow her to live alone because that wasn't *respectable* for an unmarried woman. But she was over thirty and answerable to no one legally.

It was lack of money that kept her with her mother.

She'd used up all the hot water and the fire in the stove was dying down, so she decided to wait to have a proper wash when she got home – she hoped before her mother saw her. Rubbing her grimy hands on a damp cloth, she pinned up her hair again anyhow and began to gather her cleaning materials together.

Before she left, she went to check on Les Harding, finding him hard at work, whistling cheerfully as he whitewashed another of the stalls. The place had been filthy and was taking a long time to clean out properly, with only one man to do it and a need to keep most of the stalls available for horses. Les was a good worker. She'd give him that. But as an ex-convict, he'd have to prove himself trustworthy over a length of time. She intended to make sure he didn't cheat Conn and Bram.

Going out to the street, she stopped to study the front of the livery stables. The men she'd hired had washed down the outside, which was of painted wood, but it was peeling here and there and Conn hadn't given her enough money to have it fully repainted. Maybe she could get the white paint on the window frames and doors touched up and a better sign made.

Conn hadn't said what name the stables should have. His name or Bram's? She shrugged. That was easy. She'd just have a sign made saying 'Livery Stables' and have room left underneath it for the proprietor's name. It needed a bigger sign, one that people could see from a distance.

As she was about to pick up the bucket and cleaning rags she'd brought from home, a man rode up on a weary-looking horse. He tipped his hat to her and studied the stables. 'Is Mundy around?'

The way he said it sounded as if he didn't like the former owner. 'The stables have new owners now, Mr Largan and Mr Deagan. I don't know where Mr Mundy is, but you could try looking in the alehouses.'

'But the livery stables are still open for business?'

'Oh, yes. I'm helping the new owner to brighten things up a little. He's a friend of my brother's.'

'Is there room for me to stable my horse here tonight?' He patted the animal's neck. 'I've worked her hard, I'm afraid, and she deserves some cosseting.'

'I'm sure they'll be able to accommodate you. Shall I fetch the man who's running it for the new owner?'

'Thank you. I'd appreciate that.' He got down stiffly, stretching and easing his shoulders, then removed his saddlebags, slinging them over one arm.

'Les!' she called. 'We have a customer.' She turned back to the stranger. 'I handle the money and accounts, so you'll be paying me.'

To his credit, he didn't quibble at paying a woman, but handed over a florin on account.

Les came hurrying out just then – she approved of

him bustling to serve a customer. You should show willing. He took the horse's bridle, listened to instructions and murmured to the animal, promising to give it a good feed then leading it away.

'He's certainly got a way with horses,' Flora said, thinking aloud.

'Yes, you can't fake that. I wonder, do you know somewhere decent that lets rooms near here? The place I stayed in last time wasn't up to much.'

She studied him. He seemed respectable and clean enough, an educated man from the way he spoke, the sort her mother allowed to rent one of their rooms. 'My family does, actually, and we've no one staying at the moment. I'm walking back now if you want me to show you the way.'

'Thank you. I'd appreciate that. Let me carry that bucket for you. I'm Mitchell Nash, by the way.'

'Miss McBride.' Flora picked up the rest of her cleaning equipment, glad not to have to make two journeys.

Mr Nash didn't say much as they walked the short distance to her home but she stole a few sideways glances, wondering about him. He had a tightly closed and unhappy look, one she'd seen before, usually on ex-convicts' faces. Only if he'd been transported, she'd guess it was like Conn Largan, for political reasons, which wasn't the same thing. There seemed to be nothing shifty about his expression or bearing. You couldn't always tell, of course, but she liked to guess about strangers.

Her mother offered Mr Nash the usual over-warm welcome, which seemed to make him feel uneasy.

After he had vanished into his room, her mother turned to her and said icily, 'I don't know what you've been doing to get yourself into such a disgraceful mess, but kindly have a wash and change your clothes before you come down to dinner.'

Flora inclined her head. She'd not meant for her mother to see her like this and no doubt there would be more arguments and recriminations later about it.

Mr Nash didn't emerge from his room until the gong went for the evening meal. He seemed a little surprised to find he'd be eating with the family, but snapped his mouth shut on a comment and sat down, standing up again out of politeness when Flora left to fetch the tureen of soup.

Normally her mother could get anyone talking, but not this man. As the meal progressed, Flora hid a smile and kept almost as quiet as he did. She knew her mother wouldn't question her about how she had got into such a state in front of anyone, so concentrated on enjoying her food.

At the end of the meal, Mr Nash asked quietly, 'If I decide to stay in Fremantle, Mrs McBride, could I take a room for a longer period of time? Perhaps you have a weekly rate?'

'Of course you can. We'd be happy to have you as our guest.'

Flora stifled an impatient sigh. Her mother treated people who stayed as if they were friends of the family, but she felt it was better to make the position absolutely clear. 'As long as you pay on time and keep your room reasonably tidy, Mr Nash.'

His smile seemed to surprise him as much as it did her, as if it'd escaped his control. 'Of course.' He turned to her mother again. 'The food was excellent. I enjoyed the meal.'

'I'm glad. And you're welcome to sit in here in the evenings. Our guests use it as a sitting room.' She waved one hand towards a sofa, armchair and small writing desk at the other side of the room.

His face became expressionless again. 'Thank you. But I'm rather tired, so I'll go straight up to my room.'

'Will you want a cup of tea and piece of cake before you go to sleep? The maid can easily bring one up when we have our supper.'

'Not tonight, thank you. I'm too tired to stay awake.'

When he'd left the room, Mrs McBride looked at her daughter. 'Someone's upset that man.'

'Yes, he does look unhappy.' She stood up. 'I'll just clear the table then I'll—'

'Lally can do that. Come and explain what you've been doing today. You didn't leave a message to tell me where you were going and now you look tired out. What's more, when you got back this afternoon, your skirt was stained and damp. How on earth did it get into that condition? I don't know what Mr Nash must have thought of you.'

'It doesn't matter what Mr Nash thinks of me.'

'It always matters what a gentleman thinks, especially an unmarried one.'

'You don't know that Mr Nash is unmarried.'

'He might be.'

Flora didn't let herself sigh. Like their guest she

would have preferred to go straight to bed. She felt exhausted and not in the mood to be carped at and criticised. But she went into her mother's little parlour, to get it over with.

'Well, how did you come to be in that disgraceful condition? Did you fall over?'

'No, I cleaned out the cottage.'

'*You did what?*'

'I cleaned out the cottage.'

'Why?'

She was fed up with lying. 'Because I wanted the money.'

'We've discussed this before. You don't *need* money, and you certainly shouldn't be working at menial tasks. Why do you need it so badly?'

'Because I have none of my own.'

'You do not – *need* – money!'

Her mother yelled so loudly, Flora knew she'd seriously upset her, but she wasn't giving way and saying she'd been in the wrong, so she just stood and waited for the tirade to end.

'And you are *not* taking that job.'

'I've already taken it and Mr Largan has left the stables in my charge. He's relying on me and I won't let him down.'

'A lady shouldn't soil her hands with such menial work.'

'I'll be doing the accounts and ordering hay and feed, not mucking out the stables.'

'You'll be alone with a man, a convict too.'

'He's a very polite, respectful man.'

'I forbid it, Flora.'

'I'm sorry to upset you, but I'm going to do it and there's no way you can prevent me.'

Her mother went on and on, repeating herself – as if that'd make any difference – and trying to forbid her to do it. Flora was exhausted and suddenly lost the last shred of patience. 'I'm going to bed now.'

'I haven't finished.'

'Well, I have. And I won't change my mind.'

She hurried up the stairs, ignoring her mother's 'Come back this minute!'

Locking the bedroom door, she sagged against it for a moment, relieved to be on her own. She listened but as she'd expected her mother didn't follow her upstairs. No doubt she was taking a 'restorative', which meant a glass of brandy.

Pulling herself together, Flora took the jar in which she kept her savings from its hiding place under a loose floorboard, which was itself under the bed. She was happy to add the money she'd earned, keeping the rest of Conn's money in an old purse.

She now had thirty-seven pounds and two shillings, a tidy sum but not nearly enough to allow her to start a new life. The only plan she could devise for the future was to open a boarding house, for which she'd need furniture and bedding, kitchen equipment, all sorts of things. Goodness knew, she'd had plenty of experience in letting rooms. But she'd do it so differently from her mother and would make far more profit out of her guests, while still giving them good service.

She and her friend Jeanie had discussed going into

business together, because they were both spinsters and dependent on their families. But Jeanie at least had a small private income, not enough to live on, but enough to make a difference if she went into business. The trouble was, both of them were reluctant to upset their relatives.

You didn't make a lot of money running a boarding house, but you could make enough. Flora didn't mind working hard, but she felt annoyed sometimes that she wasn't able to do the jobs a man could undertake, the jobs that brought in the decent money. Why could she not have been a lawyer or an architect? She had a good brain, better than many men.

Well, once she'd set up her boarding house, she'd keep her eyes open. Surely there was some way for her to earn more than a pittance?

Conn arrived home late in the afternoon to find a smiling wife and rosy child waiting for him. Karsten lay cooing on a blanket, kicking his feet madly. After he'd cuddled his baby son, Conn pulled Maia into his arms and held her close for a few moments, blessing the fate that had brought them together. No man could have a more loving wife and helpmate. As always, the world seemed a better place the minute she was beside him.

'Has our boy behaved himself and allowed you to sleep at night?'

'He's been a little angel. I never heard of a sunnier-natured child. Are you hungry, Conn?'

'Only to be with you, my darling. But I'd love to

share a pot of tea, then eat our meal a little later, after Karsten's gone to bed.'

'I'll tell Nancy.'

Maia came back and sat beside him, nestling her head against him. 'Tell me everything you did while you were away. I noticed you didn't bring back any more horses. What else kept you away?'

'I didn't find any horses good enough for breeding stock, not if we're to build a reputation for excellence.'

He broke off as Nancy brought in the tea tray and Maia poured him a cup, then he continued his recital of everything he'd done, knowing how Maia loved to hear the small details about other people. It was that which made him think she'd welcome a less isolated lifestyle.

'I'd like to see the livery stables and meet Flora,' she said when he'd finished. 'She sounds to be a hard-working woman.'

'I've been wondering . . . Perhaps once I've got my conviction quashed we can buy a house in Perth or Fremantle, and spend time there as well as here.' He held his breath, waiting for her answer.

'Is that what you want?'

He nodded. 'Yes. I think I've been hiding away. It's such a shameful thing to be a convict.'

She gave him one of her glorious smiles. 'It didn't stop me falling in love with you, my darling.'

'Or me falling in love with you.'

'If you want to go and live on the moon, I'll come with you. You know that, Conn. But yes, it would be good to be closer to people.'

'I'm the luckiest man on earth.' He took her hand and raised it to his lips, his eyes promising much more once they were alone in their bedroom, promising and knowing his slightest caress was welcome to her.

Mitchell Nash fell straight asleep, but woke in the middle of the night, something which had been happening all too frequently lately. He'd spent weeks following another trail that led nowhere, because travelling outside Perth was restricted to horseback. No railways here. No real roads even, just sandy tracks most of which wound round trees rather than going straight.

How his wife had managed to disappear so completely once she arrived in Australia baffled him. It must be the doing of the scoundrel she'd run away with, because Betsy wasn't a clever woman.

Now that she'd proved herself unfaithful, the fellow was welcome to her – but not to Mitchell's son. Never that. If he had to search for years, he would, and one day he'd find Christopher again.

He hadn't seen his son for over a year now, which was a long time in a six-year-old's life – no, seven-year-old now. Every time he thought of how she'd stolen their son from him, fury boiled up inside him – except during the night, when it was anguish, and sometimes tears. Until he lost his son, he hadn't wept since he was a child.

All he'd been able to find out was that she'd landed in the Swan River Colony – or a woman who called herself Mrs Foyle had, with her husband and small son Charles. He'd shown people the *carte de visite* which bore their photographic likeness and they'd been certain it was her.

Though he remained wakeful, Mitchell didn't get up because he couldn't wander round a strange house in the dark. He could only lie there going over what he had to do next. He would have to wait for the coastal steamer to come in from the eastern seaboard of Australia and show the captain and crew the image of Betsy and Christopher he carried everywhere with him. Surely someone from the ship would recognise them?

This was the only way by which they could have left the colony. He was sure now that they weren't anywhere in Western Australia – unless they'd grown wings and flown away.

7

Isabella stood by the rail, watching Singapore dwindle to a misty line on the horizon and then vanish completely.

'Are you sad?' Bram asked quietly.

'Yes. I'll miss a lot of things and I don't like leaving my parents' graves there in the British cemetery, with no one to tend them.'

He put one arm round her. 'We could come back for a visit one day.'

'If fate wills it.'

He didn't try to object to that caveat, because fate could decide some powerful things for you. It had carried him off to Australia, then to the Orient, given him an unexpected ambition to better himself and brought him an educated and lovely lady wife like Isabella.

After standing for a while beside her, feeling comfortable with the silence, he added, 'Dougal hopes to make a swift journey back to Perth, not much more than two weeks if the wind and weather are on our side. He says he's been away longer than he'd intended and his family might be worrying about him.'

They looked up to where crew members were busy

balancing and trimming the sails. They were carrying a full complement of sail today, eight pieces in all, and the captain kept issuing orders to keep them well trimmed, which the sailors hurried to obey. Dougal the Captain was a very different man from Dougal the friend, Bram had found.

He turned his gaze to the water creaming and curling past the ship's side. 'I thought we'd stay with the McBrides for a few days till we get our bearings – if they have a room free, that is. His mother and sister rent out rooms, though I daresay they'll not be doing that for much longer, since Dougal's doing pretty well for himself. We'll have to look for somewhere to rent, preferably with space for a shop and living quarters, though that won't be easy to find.'

'Do you have enough money?'

'I think so. Our wedding gifts have made a big difference. And last time I saw him, Conn Largan offered to invest money in my business, suggested he might even help us buy a place if somewhere suitable came up. It'd be better if the building was ours, I think, then we could add on rooms, if we had to. It's quite easy to do that here with wooden houses. I'll have to ask him if he's still willing.' He was amazed at himself. Fancy thinking of owning your own house. No one from his family or village had ever been that rich, and even most farmers usually rented from the landowner.

'What's Fremantle like?'

'It's a small town, still, but it's beginning to get better buildings and look more – I don't know, permanent would be a good word for it, perhaps. The whole of the Swan River Colony has been built piecemeal, from the looks of it, with occasional grand buildings, like the Cathedral in Perth, and brick and stone residences. The main street of Fremantle has some shops, but there are a lot of small wooden houses outside the main area, some of them looking as if the next storm will blow them down.'

He smiled at her. 'So what I'm trying to say is, don't be expecting to live in anything as big as Mr Lee's shophouse.'

They stood in a companionable silence for a few minutes, then he started telling her about the western part of Australia. 'It's huge, bigger than England and Ireland put together. It takes days to sail up it from Perth to the north. But very few people have settled anywhere except for the south-west corner and, I think, a place called Geraldton further north, so a lot of the land's unoccupied, except for the natives.'

'If they're there, it's not unoccupied,' she pointed out.

'No one pays much attention to them. They don't farm it or mine it or anything like that, just wander round.'

'None of the British pay much attention to the Chinese and Malays in Singapore, either – unless they want something. It's very strange how they think theirs is the only way to live. I've learned differently. I admire the Lees, who work hard, live decently, and have been very kind to me. Is the rest of the land in the Swan River Colony not usable?'

'Some of it's desert, but other parts are suitable for

stock rearing. On the ship coming from England, I was talking to a man whose family were among the first settlers east of York – you can learn a lot talking to people. He told me some people are starting to make good money from sheep and cattle farming. Wool's always needed, isn't it?'

'Do you want to stay in the Swan River Colony, Bram?'

'Yes, definitely. Well, unless you hate it.'

'I doubt I shall. It's a home I want, and I don't really mind where it is.'

'I know what you mean. I'm the same. I didn't really want to come to Australia, but I love the warmth in summer and the friendliness I've found among the ordinary people, who're more independent than in the village where I grew up. And when I see or hear of people who've made a fortune, well, it gives me hope that I can at least make a decent living. I'm even more determined to make money now I'm a married man.'

'We'll work together to do that,' she said softly. 'I'm sure I'll be able to help you.'

He didn't answer because a wave of nausea had suddenly afflicted him and he had to concentrate on controlling it.

A short time later, she said, 'You've gone very pale. Are you all right?'

'Not really. I'm sorry, Isabella, but I get seasick, even in fine weather, and I'm starting to feel bad.' He couldn't hold back a sour-tasting hiccup. 'I don't know whether to go back to the cabin and lie down, or stay on deck and make a public spectacle of myself.'

'You poor thing! But you may be better in the fresh air. When I've been locked down on ships in stormy weather, it's always made me feel worse. And the crew will understand, surely, if you're unwell?'

He managed a smile. 'Oh, they'll be expecting it. They've seen me like this a few times before. I was sick going to Galle, then on the journey to Singapore. But at least I know better than to vomit into the wind like one poor woman did on the ship coming to Australia.'

He fell quiet, trying to control his nausea. He hated her seeing him like this.

Isabella found somewhere for them to sit and continued to chat to Bram, trying to take his mind off his seasickness. But he was quiet and listless, very unlike his usual lively self, so she was left mainly to her own thoughts. These were still in a muddle as she tried to sort out her feelings and prepare herself mentally for a new life.

'I vowed when I first arrived in Australia,' he said suddenly, 'that I'd never go on a ship again, and look at me, been back to Galle and then to Singapore!'

'You had to find out for yourself if it was worth making a trading connection there.'

He took hold of her hand. 'Worth it in many ways, not least in finding you. I hope you'll be happy as a trader's wife.'

She didn't know what to say to that, so said nothing, but she let him keep hold of her hand, enjoying the unspoken message of support that offered. She wasn't used to having someone touch her because her mother hadn't been very demonstrative, but she liked it. It made her feel less . . . alone. They hadn't yet taken the step that made them truly man and wife, but Bram kept saying such charming things she was beginning to believe he really was glad to have married her, which was a good start, surely?

Why had he not tried to make love to her that first night, then? Most men would have done, from what she'd heard other women say. Most men seemed to want to do it more often than their wives did.

Isabella still felt nervous about sharing a cabin, wondering if this was going to be the night Bram would consummate their marriage. Then she smiled. As if a man who was seasick would feel like loving her!

Oh, he did look dreadful, poor dear!

She, on the other hand, found the movement of the ship soothing and was enjoying the fresh salty breezes after the humidity of Singapore.

One day some new people moved into the house next to the Beauforts and Alice couldn't resist standing at the window to watch them. Neighbours could make such a difference to your life. The previous ones had been loud, prone to fighting and drunken shouting. They'd moved out secretly in the middle of one night, leaving rent unpaid.

The new woman was pretty or would have been if she hadn't looked so tired. The little boy looked cowed and the man looked . . . She searched her mind for a word to describe him and at first thought of grumpy, but that wasn't strong enough. Threatening, perhaps?

He was well-dressed and looked very respectable, but still, she'd rather have her own Parker than him any day, for all his faults.

She waited till the next day to go and introduce herself.

The man opened the door and looked at her in such a way that she faltered to a halt.

'I'm pleased to meet you, Mrs Beaufort, but my wife and I like to keep ourselves to ourselves.'

He shut the door in her face and she stormed back to tell Parker what he was like.

'Mmm.'

She watched Parker dab at his canvas. It was a big one and would cost them a lot in paint. And it was no better than his other paintings. The woman's head looked too big for her body and the colours were muddy, but Alice didn't dare say that because the one thing that made Parker angry was criticism of his paintings.

She went downstairs again, wishing she could make friends with someone. But it was hard to make friends when you couldn't afford to invite another woman to tea and didn't have a decent dress to wear when you went calling on them.

She heard a sudden outcry next door, a man's voice shouting loudly, and rushed to the kitchen window at the back to see the boy climb over the fence and hide behind her wood pile. He looked terrified, poor thing. She stood back so that he wouldn't know he was being observed.

A short time later there was a knock on the door

and she opened it to see the man next door standing there.

'Mrs Beaufort, I wonder if—'

She interrupted him, putting on her loftiest expression and speaking coolly. 'I thought you kept yourselves to yourselves.'

He glared at her so fiercely she took a step backwards, tempted to slam the door in his face.

'I just wanted to—'

'If you wish to be on speaking terms with my husband and myself, you'll need to tell us your name at least.'

'Gresham.'

'I'm pleased to meet you, Mr Gresham.' She nearly held out her hand but at the last minute changed her mind because for some reason she didn't want to touch him. 'How may I help you?'

'Have you seen my stepson? He's run away and I think he might have come over your fence, because the back gate's locked. It was yours or the other neighbour's.'

She didn't even hesitate to lie to him. 'He didn't come over our fence. I was working in the kitchen and I'd have seen him.'

He inclined his head. 'Thank you.'

She watched him walk away, feeling sorry for that poor boy.

Later, she went out to the woodpile and picked up some pieces of wood, saying in a low voice, 'I know you're there and I won't give you away. You can hide there any time.'

There was silence, then some rustling, then a wobbly

young voice said, 'Thank you, ma'am.' She heard a sound suspiciously like a sob as she walked back inside with the wood, but didn't dare stay out any longer in case her neighbour was looking out of the window.

She didn't tell Parker about the boy because he could never keep a secret and would blurt out whatever came into his head.

Later, she watched the young intruder sneak out from behind the woodpile and slip into the alley that ran down the back of the row of terraced houses.

She knew when he came back, because the walls were thin. Mr Gresham yelled at him and beat him – she could hear the cane whistling. Then a woman began to scream and beg him to stop.

After that, the arguments and sounds of violence stopped in the daytime and she guessed Mr Gresham must have found a job because he went out every morning, neatly dressed, and returned at the same time each evening. The lad went out later, at the time other children went to school, looking equally neatly dressed.

Two days later she met Mrs Gresham at the shops and stopped to say, 'I believe we're neighbours.'

The woman looked flustered. 'Yes. I'm, um, pleased to meet you, Mrs Beaufort.'

'I know your husband doesn't want to associate with the neighbours, but I heard how he treated your son and I just wanted to say the lad can take refuge in our garden any time he likes.'

The woman's eyes filled with tears. 'Thank you. I wish—' She shook her head blindly, repeated, 'Thank you!' and hurried off.

The poor creature was terrified of disobeying her husband, even when he wasn't there, Alice decided. How dreadful!

She looked round at the food and sighed. She hated cooking, was always burning things, and when she could, she got only bread and ham for tea, with perhaps a piece of fruit. Thank goodness Parker never seemed to care what he ate.

Life had been easier in Singapore because servants were cheap and her cousin Isabella was a very capable housewife.

Alice hadn't expected married life to be such hard work, or that she'd have to manage without a maid.

The only thing she did enjoy was the bed play. Parker was a fine husband in that regard.

The ship made excellent time on the journey to Fremantle and Bram watched with some jealousy as Isabella seemed to thrive. Dougal remained in the best of spirits, ruddy-faced, bursting with health, damn him. He said they'd been blessed with favourable winds, but the voyage still seemed to take a long time to Bram, who couldn't wait to walk on something that didn't bob about and move every which way beneath your feet.

Thanks to the fine weather, he'd only succumbed to his nausea now and then, and made it to the rail each time, thank goodness. But he felt queasy nearly all the time, certainly not in the mood to make love to his new wife – not even in the mood to regret that.

He was cutting a sorry figure, he was sure, and yet

she was blessedly patient with him. She'd consulted the cook and got him to prepare food that went down easily and sometimes even stayed down. Bram looked at himself, holding out one arm. He'd grown even thinner in the past few days, because even with her coaxing, he couldn't force much down.

When he saw the island of Rottnest on the horizon, lying just offshore from Fremantle, and then watched the pilot come on board, Bram breathed a prayer of thankfulness. For safety's sake pilots who knew the coast were sent out from the port to guide the ship into Gage Roads, the anchorage near Fremantle.

Dougal had already offered to store their trade goods with his, as well as Isabella's few pieces of furniture, so it was only their personal luggage that needed to be unloaded once they'd been cleared to disembark at the port. Most of the luggage was Isabella's, however, because the Lees had given her some garments and household linen before she left Singapore.

She'd told him what they'd said about these gifts, even remembering the exact words because she'd been so touched.

'Wear to remember us,' Ah Yee had told her.

'Wear to show off our beautiful silks,' Mr Lee had said. 'One day you buy plenty from me to sell in Australia.'

'Wear to be pretty for new husband,' from Xiu Mei.

The ship dropped anchor some way from the land in Gage Roads. Apparently the water wasn't deep enough for a larger ship to berth against the short South Jetty at Fremantle.

'What sort of port is this,' Isabella asked, 'when the ships can't dock properly?'

'The only one we've got.' Bram pointed out some of the landmarks, which included the prison and the lunatic asylum.

She started to laugh.

'What's the matter?'

'I do hope you're not expecting us to stay in either of those!'

He laughed with her, then pointed out the Anglican, Catholic and Wesleyan places of worship, which were more imposing buildings than most.

'Isn't there a railway station?'

'No railways in the colony, though I heard they're thinking of building one down to Albany on the south coast. The mail steamers from Europe dock there, because they have a much better harbour. Here the goods have to be offloaded on to lighters and then transported across a neck of land to the river jetty, where they have to be reloaded for the journey up to Perth.'

'Can they not deepen the river channel?'

'They ought to, but Dougal told me some people were against it, in case the lighters took the trade straight past Fremantle to Perth.'

'How do people get ashore?'

He hesitated. He'd not mentioned it before because he didn't want to upset her. 'In a small boat. It comes alongside.'

'You mean – I'll have to climb down the side of the ship?'

'I'm afraid so. If you don't feel right about climbing down, they can rig up a sling, instead.'

She shuddered. 'I'd prefer to climb down and remain in charge of myself, not dangle in mid-air under someone else's control, thank you very much.'

Her voice was sharp, but he didn't blame her. The port's facilities were very poor and it worried him to think of bringing trade goods in by this inefficient route, especially ones arriving during the winter, with its storms.

A short time later he watched, heart in his mouth as his wife clambered slowly down the heavy rope netting slung over the ship's side to act as a ladder. She looked beautiful with her cheeks flushed from sun and wind, and strands of hair blowing loose around her face. When her skirts flew about in the breeze, even though she'd tried to tie them down, he caught tantalising glimpses of a trim ankle and neatly rounded calf, and felt a stab of desire, also annoyance that other men were seeing this.

He was definitely feeling better. The mere thought of getting back on dry land had cheered him up and settled his stomach.

When they got to the jetty, they climbed out of the small boat and had to cling together, laughing at the way they staggered when they tried to move. After a while, their bodies got used to solid, unmoving land, but they still had to wait for the rest of their personal effects to be lowered into a lighter and brought to shore. They turned to look at their future home.

'The town's much smaller than I expected,' she said at last.

'I told you it wasn't big. It's growing rapidly, though.'

Dougal couldn't leave the ship yet, but lads with handcarts came to carry their luggage, assuring them that they knew the way to the captain's home. What would the world do without such lads? Bram wondered. They were everywhere in the colony with their roughly made handcarts, ready to earn a coin or two, and he'd seen a lot of them in London.

They followed the lads up Cliff Street, with its big warehouses. It was a short street and was paved only along one side. 'Dougal told me they didn't have enough paving stones to do both sides of the various streets,' Bram told her, 'so the Town Trust decided to pave one side only, then they could do more streets.'

'Which is all right unless you want to cross the road.'

Cliff Street led them to High Street, where they stopped for a moment to look back at the Round House, the original prison for the colony.

Clouds were building up, but it was still intermittently sunny and when the sun shone, the buildings seemed dazzlingly bright because many of them were made of limestone, not brick.

Isabella blinked and shaded her eyes. 'I could do with smoked glass spectacles to look through, it's so bright. And look at all this sand!' The shops had swept it away from their entrances, but simply left it lying nearby in piles and as the wind rose, it was blowing about again, twisting wisps being whirled to and fro.

Isabella was glad when they got to Dougal's house, because she was out of practice at walking so far. It was a commodious residence, built of the limestone that all the better buildings seemed to use. Two storeys high, it had wooden balconies on both the ground and upper floors.

'It's not at all like English houses, is it?' she said.

'Not like the ones I saw in London or before we sailed from Southampton,' he agreed. 'Not like Irish houses, either.'

The door opened and he whispered, 'Mrs McBride,' as a plump matron came hurrying out to greet them. She was followed by a young woman who was surely Dougal's sister, she looked so like him, sturdy and with a similar colour of hair, strands of which had escaped from its pins.

'Hello again, Mrs McBride, Miss McBride,' Bram said cheerfully. 'It's glad I am to see you. I'd like to introduce my wife. Isabella and I were married in Singapore.'

She gaped at them for a moment. 'Goodness me, I can't believe it! But how delightful. Welcome to Fremantle, Mrs Deagan. I hope you'll be happy here.' She looked up as drops of rain began to fall. 'You'd better get that luggage inside before it's soaked. You are staying with us, aren't you?'

'If that's all right. Just till we find a house to rent.' Bram grimaced as the rain began to fall more heavily. 'I've been telling Isabella how beautifully sunny it is here in the colony and look at this for a greeting.'

'June and July are our coolest months and winter is our rainy season, Mrs Deagan,' Flora McBride said. 'You were here in summer and autumn before, Mr Deagan. It's not really cold, though, and we never gets frosts, though they say that happens occasionally in the hills beyond Perth.'

Isabella liked her on sight. The no-nonsense way of talking reminded her of the Lees, whom she was missing. She hadn't taken to the fussy older woman, though.

A man was coming down the stairs as they were about to be shown up to their room, so as he reached the hall, Flora introduced them. 'Mr Nash has been staying with us for a while. Did you have a successful day's business, Mr Nash?'

He shook his head, looking grim, and she wondered if she'd offended him by showing an interest. Most people liked to talk about what they were doing and ask advice of those who lived in Fremantle.

'Perhaps my brother will be able to help now he's back,' she said lightly.

'Yes. I'll ask him.' He nodded to the newcomers and left the house.

'He's a man of few words,' Flora said. 'Now, this bedroom should suit you. It has a lovely view of the ocean and there's plenty of room for your trunks and bags. When you're ready, come down for some refreshments.'

The room was spacious, but by the time the lads had puffed up the stairs with their trunks and luggage, it looked very cluttered.

'Let's unpack later,' Bram said. 'I'm suddenly feeling hungry.'

'I'm glad to hear that.'

He smiled at her. 'It was grand introducing *my wife*. I hope you're not too ashamed of me.'

She was startled by this, but he'd turned to lead the way out, so she didn't pursue the matter.

Oh dear, she didn't want him to feel she looked down on him, because she didn't. He was charming and kind and hard-working – and already she was enjoying his company, his clever comments about the world and its vagaries, the way he never seemed to forget anything.

8

The boy next door took refuge in the Beauforts' back yard regularly. He went to school in the mornings, neat and tidy, but often came home looking as if he'd got into a scrap. The damage to his clothes seemed to be landing him in a lot of the trouble.

If Alice had been his mother, she'd have protected him, though, not let *that man* beat him so often.

Inevitably, Parker noticed the lad's presence, so Alice had to tell him what was happening.

He frowned. 'You shouldn't interfere between husband and wife, or between father and son.'

'Oh? Would you let Mr Gresham beat that poor boy senseless every few days, then?'

'It's not that bad, surely?'

'It is. He uses a cane *and* sometimes a strap. I hear it. That poor lad is a mass of bruises. You can see them on his arms and legs.' Her voice wobbled. 'If anything happened to you, I'd not marry a man who beat Louisa.'

Parker opened his mouth, looked down at their little daughter, and closed it again, absent-mindedly reaching out to stroke her hair. 'Are you sure the boy doesn't deserve it? If he's naughty . . .'

'No child deserves to be beaten so severely, however

naughty he is. But I don't think Christopher is naughty. He's too scared for that.'

Parker pulled her to him. 'I'm very glad my daughter has you for a mother.'

She wished she could say she was glad Louisa had him for a father, but she wasn't. She'd chosen to give herself to two unsuitable men now. One had been a disgusting cheat. She couldn't think of Renington without feeling sick that she'd been taken in by him.

But although Parker had married her and made her respectable again, he was weak and a poor provider, and that wasn't very nice to live with, either. On that thought, she said firmly, 'You'll need to do some of your sketches. We don't have enough money to last us until the end of the quarter.'

He looked at her in dismay. 'I told you last time I wasn't doing that again.'

'Then you shouldn't have spent our money, should you? It's either do some of your sketches or go without food and paints.'

'Surely it can't be that bad?'

'It is. I had to pick up spoiled fruit from the ground at the markets today, I was so desperate for something to eat.'

'Oh.'

He went upstairs and she heard him getting out his sketching materials. She wept a little, then told herself not to be foolish and tried to make them a nourishing stew from some bits and pieces she'd bought at the market, the cheapest cut of meat, one onion and a lot of potatoes. It turned out pale and unappetising, but at least she didn't burn it today.

When Bram and Isabella went down to the dining room, where guests usually sat in the evenings, Mrs McBride heard them coming and insisted on them joining her and Flora in the family's private parlour. Isabella pinned a smile to her face and endured the fussing. She didn't like Dougal's mother, nor did she like the way she snapped at her daughter. She'd not put up with that from anyone and wondered why Flora did.

It was such a fussily furnished room that they had to move carefully round the furniture. Isabella was glad she wasn't wearing a crinoline like Mrs McBride. She accepted a cup of tea and a piece of cake, glad to see Bram eating heartily for a change.

'I was going to wait until Dougal arrived, but I doubt he'll be here until nightfall,' Flora said. 'So I suppose I'd better tell you about the premises Conn's found and give you the letter he left for you.'

'He's rented us a shop?' Bram looked delighted.

'Not rented, bought. The livery stables you used when you came up from the country were for sale, so he bought them. They're very central and have about an acre of land, plus a small cottage next to the stables and some sheds.'

Bram beamed at her. 'I remember them clearly. But surely the stables are too big for a shop.'

'He thought you might keep them going as livery stables for the time being, to keep the money coming in. He's hired a man to look after them and I've been keeping an eye on things.'

'Which is not a suitable occupation for a young lady,' Mrs McBride put in disapprovingly.

Flora cast a look of dislike at her mother. 'I enjoy doing it.'

When Bram looked at her speculatively, Isabella guessed what he was thinking. 'You want to go and see the place right now, don't you?'

Rain pattered against the windowpanes and Mrs McBride said, 'Surely it can wait till tomorrow? That rain looks to have set in for the rest of the day.'

'I can just nip along the road and have a quick look,' he said. 'I don't mind if I get wet.'

'I'm coming too.' Isabella intended to start as she meant to continue, as a full partner.

'You look tired.'

'So do you. And you've not been well.'

'I'll be the better for some fresh air.' He grinned at her. 'And anyway, I always was impatient.'

'I'll come with you, as well,' Flora offered. 'It's not far and we have several umbrellas.'

Mrs McBride shot her daughter an angry glance. 'You're all very foolish. You don't want to get drenched and catch a chill. You're doing too much, Flora.'

'Ah, we'll not melt,' Bram said but even his charming smile didn't draw an answering smile from her this time.

'I'll go and find the umbrellas,' Flora said.

So they set off again, each holding an umbrella.

It wasn't far to walk and Isabella found herself

enjoying Flora's company. She thought the Lees would have liked her, too, but not her mother. They had no time for people who fussed like that and often laughed at the ways of European ladies. She sighed, missing them yet again.

'Are you too tired for this?' Bram asked. 'We can take you back if you'd rather.'

'What? Oh, no. I was just thinking of the Lees.'

'Ah. You'll be missing them.' He explained to Flora who they were.

'What an interesting life you've led, Mrs Deagan. You must tell me more about Singapore another time. My brother goes to all sorts of interesting places while I have to stay at home and . . .' She stopped and pointed. 'This is it.'

The livery stables were a decent size but looked rather shabby, Isabella thought.

'We did our best to spruce them up,' Flora said, 'but Conn wasn't sure what we'd be doing with the place, so didn't want to spend too much of his money.' She looked up as lightning slashed across the sky then thunder boomed in the distance. 'Come inside quickly.'

After she'd introduced them to Les, the two men began talking about the livery stables.

Isabella whispered to Flora, 'I'd like to see the cottage.'

'It's pouring down.'

'Oh, never mind that. We can run and our umbrellas will keep off most of it.'

The two women dashed across the muddy space, and arrived at the front door of the cottage laughing. Flora unlocked it quickly and led the way inside.

Isabella walked round it thoughtfully.

'It's small,' Flora said.

'All I've had to call my own for the past two years was a sleeping cubicle. It'll seem like luxury to me to have privacy and four rooms. Will Mr Largan really let us live here?'

'I think he was expecting Bram to do so.'

'Good.'

'My mother will say it's too small,' Flora said. 'She's not very tactful, I'm afraid.'

'I shan't take offence. My mother would have been thankful for any roof over our heads. We had some hard times after my father died.' Isabella went to try the pump in the kitchen and found the water that came out to be reasonably clean, though she'd boil it to be sure before they drank it, as they had in Singapore. She opened and shut the doors of the two cupboards on either side of the fireplace. 'Plenty of shelves, anyway.'

The door opened and Bram joined them in a whoosh of damp air and a flurry of raindrops. 'It's still pouring down,' he said unnecessarily, shaking his umbrella and folding it, before standing it next to theirs in the hall.

After he'd been shown round the cottage, he asked, 'What about Conn's letter?'

'It's at home. Sorry. I meant to give it you. I wanted to get out of the house before my mother thought of some way to stop me.'

'Well, we'll see what he says when we get back.' Bram went to peer out of the kitchen window. 'What's that building up the slope there? Is it part of this block of land?'

Flora joined him at the window to stare at a huge ramshackle shed. 'Yes. It's just an old shed I told you about, or rather several old sheds built, one against the other. I don't know what they were for. I peeped inside and the whole place seems more or less weatherproof, but I had enough to do with the rest so I didn't go back. There seem to be quite a few bits and pieces of wood and junk stored there.'

'I'll inspect the sheds another time. First thing is to make sure the stables are running properly. Les seems to know his job, though. He says Conn hired him.'

'Yes. Les was hiding in the hayloft but he'd been secretly caring for the horses because the owner kept getting drunk. Shall you keep Les on? I know he's worried about that. He may be an ex-convict but he's a hard worker.'

'I'll be happy to give him a trial.' Bram looked out of the window. 'I think it's easing off, but there are some more dark clouds over the sea. Perhaps we should hurry back.'

At the house Flora went to find the letter and gave it to them, then left them to read it in private.

Bram led the way up to their room.

Dear Bram,
    You'll need somewhere for your shop and I thought the livery stables were a good bargain. I hope you agree. Since I'm not sure when you're returning, I'm going home, but if you write to me once you're back, the local post office will see it gets to me quickly.

*You could maybe live in the cottage and get a
woman in to do your washing and cleaning. What
do you think?*
Sort the rest out as you see fit.
Yours in haste,
Conn

Bram passed the letter to Isabella and went to sprawl
beside her on the bed as she read it.

'He doesn't say much about the business side of
things,' she said thoughtfully. 'We must have everything
made clear before we start, to ensure that we can't
easily be kicked out. We should draw up a contract,
really.'

'I don't need that with Conn. I've known him since
we were lads and I trust him absolutely.'

'And if he died suddenly? Do you know his heirs
and trust them?'

'It's just his wife and child.'

'She could remarry. No, Bram, I've been trained by
a very astute man, and Mr Lee wouldn't enter into any
business arrangement without knowing exactly where
he stood.'

He threw up his hands. 'All right. You take charge
of that side of things. What do I know about contracts?'

He fell silent as Isabella began getting ready for the
evening meal, half-lying on the bed now and looking
white with exhaustion.

She watched him in the mirror. 'You've done enough
for today,' she said firmly. 'You need to recover from
your seasickness and get some proper meals down you.'

He smiled and got up, pulling her to him for a hug. 'You sounded very wifely then.'

She could feel herself blushing. 'Did I?'

'Yes.' He planted a kiss on her cheek, looked her in the eyes, and then kissed her properly on the lips.

The kiss was different from his others and made her senses reel. When he drew away, she felt so breathless she couldn't speak. She hadn't known a kiss could do that to you.

'Very wifely,' he teased, running one finger down her cheek and making her react with a gasp.

The spell was broken as the front door slammed below and Dougal yelled, 'I'm back!'

Bram smiled. 'This is not the time to be kissing and cuddling.' He went to wash his hands and face in cold water from the ewer, but she noticed that he continued to smile as he got ready for the evening meal.

She found herself smiling too, and blushing as she met his eyes. She wished the kiss had not been interrupted. That augured well for them – didn't it?

Mitchell heard the voice calling and assumed it was the captain back from his travels. And a good thing, too, because he'd just spent another fruitless day asking questions and showing people his precious *carte de visite*. Who would have thought when Betsy persuaded him to have a series of likenesses taken of the three of them, that the one of her and Christopher which he'd kept for himself would have been so useful? And so painful.

The edges of the small card were roughened now

from being handled, but the image still showed clearly. It was hard to keep up one's hopes after so many disappointments, but he had only to look at the face of his son to feel a surge of determination to find Christopher again.

He got ready, hoping he'd not be asked to dine on his own tonight, because he was desperate to enlist the captain's help in speaking to the officers and crew of the coastal steamer. Surely this time he would find some clue to where she'd gone? It had been a hard journey to Australia then there had been some tiring journeys into the countryside. His hopes had been dashed several times already. He was weary of the search, so very weary.

His wife must have left the Swan River Colony and could only have done that by coastal steamer, because he'd followed the other two possible couples to the country and proved for himself that the woman wasn't Betsy.

When the dinner gong rang, Mitchell waited for the Deagans to go down and followed them shortly afterwards, hesitating in the doorway of the dining room. They were all there, looking so much a family party his own loneliness struck him like a hammer blow.

'Do come and sit down, Mr Nash,' Mrs McBride called.

For once, he was glad of her fussing. 'If I'm intruding, I could eat in my room.'

'Nonsense! We treat our guests as part of the family here. This is my son, Dougal, just back from Singapore.'

Mitchell nodded. 'Captain.'

He sat down, finding himself next to Miss McBride and opposite her brother. She passed him a bowl of soup with her usual calm efficiency. What a restful woman she was, so different from her fluttery, fussy mother.

As he ate, he listened, trying to work out what the newcomers were like. The Deagans seemed a bit uncertain with one another at times, which surprised him until he found out they'd only recently got married just before they left Singapore.

Under Mrs McBride's questioning, Mrs Deagan described the wedding. Mitchell found it interesting to hear about the Chinese food and customs, and at any other time would have asked several more questions.

'You didn't tell us yesterday exactly what you're doing in the colony, Mr Nash,' the old lady said.

He hesitated, not sure that he could face revealing his problems to strangers.

'Perhaps Mr Nash would prefer to keep such information to himself, Mother,' Flora put in quickly, throwing him an apologetic glance at the same time.

Mitchell was touched by her attempt to shield him and came to a sudden decision. 'It's all right. I need to tell people or I'll get nowhere. I'm searching for my wife and child. She ran away from home in England with another man. They came to the Swan River Colony, that's the only thing I'm certain of. I don't want her back, but I do want my son. He was only six when they left. He'll be seven now.'

'Oh, my dear Mr Nash, how dreadful for you! You must—'

'It seems a strange place to come to if you're running away,' the captain said. 'The population is so small, it's hard to hide.'

'They might not have known that. She definitely came here but I don't know what name she's using now. His real name is Gresham. I've checked the passenger list and there were three couples with a son that age. I've checked two of them, which leaves a Mr and Mrs Foyle. Only, I can't find any signs of anyone here with that name.'

'They may have travelled on to Melbourne or Sydney once they found out what a small place Perth is,' the captain said. 'A lot of people do. And in that case, they'd have had to take a coastal steamer.'

'That's the conclusion I came to. There's another steamer due in soon and it's the one she probably left on. I have a *carte de visite* with my wife and son's likeness. It's not easy to conceal a lively child like Christopher, even if they changed their names again. He had blond hair and blue eyes, was tall for his age and—' His voice broke and he had to pause for a moment to pull himself together.

'If you like, once the steamer comes in, I'll help you ask around,' the captain said. 'I'm bound to make better progress than you ever could on your own.'

'I'd be immensely grateful.'

There was silence, then to Mitchell's relief, Deagan changed the subject and began talking about the trade goods they'd brough back and the possibility of opening a shop at the livery stables.

While the others were chatting, Miss McBride said

quietly, 'I'd like to look at the photo of your wife and child, if you don't mind, Mr Nash. I'm out and about in Fremantle all the time and I have an excellent memory for faces.'

'You're very kind.'

'If I had a son,' she added, suddenly sounding fierce, 'I'd hunt for him to the ends of the earth, too.'

He saw her flush and guessed that her lack of a husband and family was a source of pain to her. Who would have guessed that from her quiet demeanour and calm common sense way of talking? She was a plain woman, though not ugly. His damned wife had been pretty and had used that to get her own way in life. He'd grown tired of Betsy's foolish ways but at least she'd given him a son. She had trouble entertaining herself and had complained bitterly about the uninteresting life they led and the long hours he worked in the timber yard he'd inherited from his father.

As he was about to light his candle and go up to bed, Miss McBride came into the hall. 'Do you have the *carte de visite* with you?'

'Always.' He pulled it out of his inside jacket pocket and unfolded the paper that protected it.

'Come into the kitchen. We have oil lamps there and I'll be able to see more clearly.'

He followed her into the rear of the house where a little maid was just finishing clearing up in the adjoining scullery.

'You can go to bed now, Linny. You've worked hard today.'

'Thank you, miss.'

Mitchell followed Miss McBride across to the lamp and held the likeness so that the figures showed clearly. He knew it was an illusion, but Christopher always seemed to be looking directly at him.

'Your wife's pretty.'

'I've come to see the sense of the saying, *Handsome is as handsome does*,' he replied, hearing how sharp his own voice sounded. Well, and should a man not be sharp when his wife had run off with another man?

'And your son's a fine little fellow.' She frowned at the photograph. 'He looks familiar, for some reason.'

Mitchell looked at her in disbelief. Was she pretending? 'How can you possibly remember one face seen a few months ago?'

She looked at him calmly, not taking offence. 'I know I've seen him, but I can't remember any details. If I try to pin down when or where, it'll not come back to me. Best if I sleep on it and look at the likeness again tomorrow.'

'Are you sure?'

She gave him one of her direct looks. 'I'm sure I've seen him. Not sure of anything beyond that. But I *am* good at remembering faces, and this isn't a large town, after all. There are only about three thousand people in and around Fremantle, very few more in Perth itself.'

He didn't dare hope, but he did allow himself to give her the chance to prove what she claimed. 'I'd be extremely grateful if you could remember anything – anything at all.'

'I'll do my best. And Dougal will be a big help in your search, I'm sure. My brother knows most of the nautical community.' She nodded and stepped back. 'I'll see you in the morning, then, Mr Nash.'

'Yes. Thank you.'

He went upstairs, expecting another disturbed night, but to his surprise he slept soundly. Perhaps when you became as weary as he'd felt today, your body overrode your mind and insisted on getting some sleep?

Or perhaps it was the tiny thread of hope Miss McBride had offered. He was quite sure she'd not have said anything unless she meant it.

Was it possible she'd seen Christopher? Oh please, God, let it be possible!

When the brother and sister were alone after everyone else had gone to bed, Dougal said abruptly, 'What do you think of our guest?'

'Mr Nash? I think he's a very unhappy man, and who can blame him? He sounds to love his son dearly, doesn't he?'

'Yes. What a terrible thing for his wife to do.'

'He showed me a *carte de visite* of them. He touched his son's face with one fingertip and said Christopher was so good about sitting perfectly still for over a minute while the likeness was being taken.'

'And did you recognise them?'

'I think I've seen the child, but I don't remember the woman.'

He looked at her in surprise. 'Are you sure? It must have been a while ago.'

'You know I never forget a face. It'll come back to me.'

'How have things been?'

She sighed. 'Mother's very happy to have her favourite child back. Perhaps she'll be in a better temper now.'

'Has she been difficult?'

'Very. Worse than usual.'

'I don't know about better temper. She's been on at me already to find a "nice girl to marry". She's desperate to get us married off.'

'Get you married, you mean. She's given up hope of me.'

'Have *you* given up hope, Flora?'

'Yes.' She changed the subject. 'Seeing Mr Nash's *carte de visite* made me think that we should find someone to take our photo as a family. We're none of us getting any younger.'

He grinned. 'If you're thinking of Mother, she'll live to be ninety and still be nagging us as she lies on her deathbed.'

She shuddered at the thought and that casual remark made her even more certain that she had to break away soon. The thought of spending another thirty years at the beck and call of her mother was not to be borne. Let Dougal make other arrangements for looking after her. He was away often enough to see their mother mainly as an amusing figure.

Flora had long since lost her ability to laugh at her mother's ways.

When Bram and Isabella went up to their bedroom, he took her in his arms as soon as the door had closed.

'I've been remembering our last kiss all evening and wanting to repeat it.'

She didn't pull away because she'd been thinking about it, too. It was, after all, what marriage was for, bringing a man and woman together, making children. When she enjoyed his caresses so much, why was she making such a fearsome mountain out of the rest of it?

The kiss was as softly beguiling as the earlier one had been. 'I didn't know a kiss could make you feel like this,' she murmured, sorry when he moved his head away.

'I don't think it always does, but we seem to be rather good at it.' He ran his fingertip down her cheek, used it to tilt her chin and kissed her again. The world blurred, reduced to Bram and her, just the two of them, just . . .

To her surprise she found herself lying on the bed, without the slightest memory of how she got there.

'Shh now,' he murmured. 'Let me love you. We'll go gently and I'll not be doing anything you don't like.'

His voice sounded more Irish than usual, soft and lilting, curling around her like a silk ribbon of sound.

He seemed to sense her agreement, blew out the candles and came back to the bed, helping her out of her clothes in the cosy darkness. It was as if they were alone in the world and everything they'd said and done had led up to this moment.

It was impossible to be afraid with a man so gentle, though she was surprised and shocked by the way he touched her – and her own responses to that touching.

Then she lost the ability to think as he took over her body . . .

Afterwards, they lay entwined and he chuckled. 'We didn't do badly for a pair of ignorant beginners, did we?'

'Not badly at all. I was – surprised.'

'Why?'

'People said it hurt the first time.'

'It doesn't have to.'

'Are you sure this was your first time?'

'Oh, yes. But I've heard other men talk about it and I remembered what they said pleased women most.' He pulled the covers up and held her close. 'Let's not move. Let's just slip into sleep together.'

'But we're still naked!'

He chuckled again. 'So we are. Lovely, isn't it?'

She didn't want to spoil the moment by making a fuss, and anyway, what did it matter whether she was wearing her nightdress or not after what they'd just done? She had always thought she preferred sleeping alone, but she'd grown to enjoy cuddling up against a warm body.

Bram was soon breathing deeply and steadily, and she found it comforting that his arms were still round her. She was growing fond of him, too, this husband of hers, hadn't expected that. But it was . . . very nice . . .

9

The following day Flora was in charge of the break-fast table, because her mother had slept badly and decided to stay in bed for an extra hour or two. Dougal had eaten and left for his ship at dawn.

'That was an excellent breakfast. Thank you,' Bram said once he'd finished eating a heroic amount of food. 'Now, I need to send off a letter to Conn, so I'll have to go out and buy some writing paper and a pen, if you'll tell me where they're sold.'

'I've got some notepaper but it's packed away some-where,' Isabella said. 'I thought I'd remember where everything was, but I don't.'

'There's some in the drawer of the table over there.' Flora pointed to the chairs and table set out at the rear of the dining room. 'You can use that.'

'Thank you. You're very kind.' Bram turned to his wife. 'Come and help me write the letter.'

Flora watched them smile at one another and sit down together. They seemed more comfortable with one another this morning. Perhaps they'd been tired yesterday. She banished the feeling of envy and turned to Mr Nash, about to tell him she hadn't remembered where she'd seen his son. Then he put up his chin and stared at her as if expecting the worst and the memories came tumbling back to her – of a little boy running through the streets with a man pursuing him, a very angry man.

Of course he'd caught the child. The boy had jutted out his chin, mouth in a pinched line, and looked at him just as Mitchell was doing to her now. The man had clouted him about the ears good and hard. She caught her breath, remembering how obvious it had been that no love was lost between the two of them.

She'd felt sorry for the boy, because the man cuffed him again as they set off walking, not caring that he was humiliating him in public. And the boy still hadn't cried, young as he was, had continued to stare at his tormenter defiantly.

She closed her eyes for a moment then looked at Mr Nash. 'I've remembered. Perhaps we can go somewhere quiet and I'll tell you. Come into the sitting room.'

He was silent as she related what she'd seen, his expression becoming even grimmer. 'When I find them, I'll teach that fellow not to ill-treat *my* son.'

'Dougal said he was going to come back mid-morning to help you.'

'That's very kind of him.'

'I'll show you where I saw the child, if you like, and we could go in the direction they took. If we come to any lodging houses, we can ask if they remember your son. He was such a good-looking lad, easy to remember even without the *carte de visite.*'

'I've been to them all. Every single lodging house I could find in Fremantle and Perth.'

She pursed her lips, thinking for a moment. 'Would your wife know that you'd pursue her?'

'Oh, yes.'

'Then they must have tried to hide all traces of their passing. Perhaps people will talk to me more than they did to you, the ones who know me, at least?'

His unhappy expression lightened just a little. 'You're very kind.'

She glanced at the clock. Her mother would be down soon. 'Let's go straight away so that we can get back by mid-morning.'

Mr Nash offered her his arm and it felt strange to set off walking beside him. Except for Dougal, she rarely had a male escort, was most often out and about on her own.

She showed him where the incident had taken place, then they went in the direction the man had taken. She knew which lodging houses catered for ordinary people and which for the better class of person.

They knocked on two doors of the latter type and got no response except, 'I told you last time, sir. I've never seen them.'

Then they arrived at a third lodging house. 'I know the woman who lives here.' She knocked on the door. 'Good morning, Mrs Kennedy. I wonder if I can have a word.'

But the woman looked at the man beside her and shrank back. 'I don't know anything.'

Flora touched his arm. 'Would you wait for me further down the street, Mr Nash?'

After a moment's hesitation, he walked away, casting an anxious glance over his shoulder.

She turned back to find Mrs Kennedy about to shut

the door. 'You've seen them, haven't you? The people whose likeness he showed you?'

'No. No, I haven't. My husband told him that before. I don't know why he's come back.'

'Because he's a man whose son has been stolen from him, a decent man who is grieving for his lost child. And because I saw the other man beating the child.'

A voice called from inside the house. 'Callie! Stop gossiping at the door.'

'I have to go. My husband needs me.'

Flora prevented her from closing the door for just a few seconds more, whispering, 'You know where I live. Search your heart, Mrs Kennedy.'

She rejoined Mr Nash in the street and told him she suspected his wife and son had stayed there.

'I've got to go back, then, persuade her to tell me about them.'

'No. Her husband's not a kind man. He'll not let you see her and he'll not speak to you. If we do it my way, there's a chance she'll come and see me without telling him. I've helped her back from the markets with her shopping a time or two. I think she trusts me.'

But there was no sign of Mrs Kennedy as Flora sat chatting to Mr Nash, waiting for her brother to return. She'd seen how her revelation had upset him. The memory upset her too. She didn't like to see children being beaten.

Bram and his wife walked slowly along the street. 'It's nice to see a fine day, isn't it?'

'Delightful.' He didn't comment or say anything else,

just smiled. But she knew what he was thinking and blushed.

They stopped to post the letter to Conn and found the post office tiny, more suited to a village than a port.

As they passed another shop which sold stationery, he stopped. 'Will we buy some writing materials? We'll be needing to make lists. We can't keep taking the McBrides' paper.'

They found not only paper, but pencils and even a rubber.

'The village schoolteacher used to call rubbers lead eaters,' Bram said as they walked on. 'He had one for his own drawing – that man loved to draw and was good at it. But he'd not let us children use it, because it had cost him three shillings for just a small square of rubber, only about half an inch across, it was. They're a lot cheaper nowadays.'

'My grandfather called them lead eaters, too. He said they used bread to rub out pencil marks before but it didn't work nearly as well. Ah, here we are.'

They stopped by mutual accord to study the stables and cottage from the outside, then went to say hello to Les, who was clearing out another stall, working so hard he didn't hear them coming.

Isabella waited patiently as Bram chatted to him, then they went into the cottage to explore every inch again and work out exactly what furniture they needed to move in.

She smiled at him. 'It's a long time since I've had a whole house to live in. How soon can we move here?'

'As soon as we have enough furniture.'

They paced out the rooms and were still working on the list of what they needed to move in when there was a knock on the door.

Bram opened it to find Dougal standing there.

'I thought I'd find you here. Will you show me the house?'

When they'd finished, he said, 'Well, you'll not need much furniture, but you can't use this house as a shop, can you? The rooms are far too small. What's in that big shed at the top of the slope?'

They went to explore it and found it far bigger than they'd expected. The low, rambling structure seemed to have been built in several stages.

'Needs quite a bit of work,' Dougal said. 'How about I get the ship's carpenter to make sure it's waterproof and not likely to fall down on you? Though I think it's more strongly built than it looks from outside.'

'We can't do anything till we hear from Conn, surely? And we can't let you—'

'He'll approve it, I'm sure.' Dougal looked at them both and said more gently, 'It's not charity I'm offering. You can pay for the materials he uses and I'll pay for his labour. Once it's more secure, I'll pay you for storing my own goods here and I'm sure you'll charge me less than that warehouse owner does.'

Bram hesitated, then took another risk. 'I'll accept your offer, so I will. But don't ask him to do anything fancy. We've not got a lot of money to spare.'

'Good.' Dougal pulled out his pocket watch. 'I'd better get home now and see if I can help Mr Nash.'

He got to the door, snapped his fingers as he remembered something and turned back. 'Look, we've got a few pieces of furniture stored in the attic. Old stuff we were going to throw out, much of it broken and I don't know why we've kept it. You're welcome to any of it that you can mend. You'll be saving us the trouble of getting rid of it. My mother's such a hoarder.'

When Dougal had left, Isabella looked at Bram with tears in her eyes. 'People are being so kind.'

She looked so soft and tearful, he had to give her a hug and a kiss to be going on with. Oh, but it felt good to have someone to love, someone who was family to him. He wasn't a man made to live alone. His father had been cold with his children, but his mother had been loving, and he and his brothers and sisters took after her. They might fight one another but let anyone else hurt one of them and they united to defend one another. He was hoping desperately that some of them would come out here to join him one day. He didn't think his parents would easily be persuaded to move, though, especially his father.

But he felt how stiff she was in his arms and guessed that she wasn't used to casual hugs, so forced himself to pull away.

She was as skittish as a mare he'd once had the care of back in Ireland. Gently does it, he told himself. Go slowly and win her round, just as you did that mare.

He wanted very much to make her happy and for them to have a good marriage. He wanted so many things these days. Was he asking too much of fate? He was prepared to work hard for it, every hour he could stand upright if necessary. And would share any good fortune with those in need.

Mitchell kept glancing at the clock in the dining room, because the captain was later getting back than he'd expected. He couldn't sit still, so began pacing up and down the room.

Flora came in carrying a heavy tea tray with a large teapot on it, as well as the other paraphernalia. He hurried to take from her and set it down where she indicated.

'My brother will be here soon,' she said in a soothing tone.

'I know. But I can't help being impatient. I've been searching for so long. And what if others refuse to talk, as that Mrs Kennedy did?'

'Then we'll think of another way to find your son. Here. You hardly ate any breakfast.' She passed him a cup of tea and cut him a generous piece of fruit cake.

The front door banged open.

'That's my brother. He can never come into a place quietly.' She raised her voice. 'We're in here, Dougal. Are you ready for a cup of tea?'

He came striding in, beaming at her. 'Always. And a piece of cake, too.'

Mitchell tried to wait patiently as Dougal demolished his piece of cake in a few huge bites.

'Put the poor man out of his misery,' Flora said suddenly.

Dougal grinned at them and drained his cup, holding it out for a refill. 'I know the captain of the coastal steamer that came in this morning. We'll go and see him later today, but it'll be better to give him time to get his passengers and luggage off the ship first.'

'We have some news, too,' she said. 'I remembered where I'd seen Mr Nash's son and we called at some of the lodging houses nearby. I think the Kennedys know something, but Callie was terrified to admit that.'

Dougal's ready smile faded. 'Was she now? Maybe I should go and speak to her husband. I know the man he works for.'

'Give her a few hours. I hinted that she should come and tell me quietly. It's better if her husband doesn't know, or he might thump her.' Flora turned to Mitchell. 'I'm sorry you have to wait and wait. It must be dreadful for you.'

He shrugged. 'I've been waiting for nearly a year. I'm used to it. At least now I know for certain that Christopher was alive a few months ago.' But he didn't like the waiting. And now he wasn't worrying about whether his son had forgotten him and was calling another man 'Father' but about whether his son was being beaten.

What did Christopher look like now? How much had he grown? Mitchell had so many questions and so few answers.

When Bram and Isabella got back to their lodgings, they found that Dougal had gone back to his ship, so they explained to Flora what he'd offered them.

'It's only old stuff,' she said dubiously, 'but Mother will insist on keeping it "in case". Still, it'd be good to have the attic cleared out. Have you got time to have a look now? Right, then. I'll show you where the things are and leave you to poke around. If you want something, take it. I'll probably throw out the rest. We've no possible use for it.'

Bram said what Isabella was thinking. 'We can take it all, if you like, and sell it for you. We'd keep a percentage for our effort and give you the rest.'

Flora stared at him, mouth open. 'Offer that again after you've seen the things. They're old and some of them broken. They can't be worth much.'

'I grew up too poor to throw away anything that'd bring in a penny or two,' he said grimly. 'Every single penny helps, every halfpenny even, and I'll never grow careless with money.'

'And I've learned to be just as frugal over the past few years.' Isabella exchanged smiles of mutual approval with her husband.

The attics were musty and cold, with a small window at each end.

'We need oil lamps,' Flora said briskly. 'I'd forgotten how dark it is up here. Perhaps you could help me carry some lamps up, Mr Deagan?'

Left alone, Isabella started poking around. There were chairs with one broken leg or cross-piece. Surely the pieces of wood could have been glued together again? There were dusty old curtains, vases, ornaments, old clothes, all sorts of things.

Footsteps and a glow in the stairwell heralded the return of Bram and Flora, so she turned to wait for them to hang the lamps on wall brackets.

'That's better,' she said. 'What we need is someone who can repair things.'

'I can do some of it,' Bram said. 'And we'll find other help, if we need it.'

'You think . . . we can make money from these?' Flora's voice wobbled a little.

They looked at her in puzzlement, wondering what had upset her.

'Yes. Definitely.'

She swallowed hard and looked close to tears. 'Then take off the cost of the repairs and give me half of what you make. I'm saving to open my own boarding house, you see, only don't tell Mother or she'll have a fit of hysterics.'

Isabella could sympathise with that. 'We won't say a thing to anyone, not even your brother. I do understand your feelings. It's not easy to live in someone else's house, even with a person who means you well.'

'I don't know why I've told you about my plans.' Flora mopped her eyes. 'I've not told anyone else except for one friend.'

'We're honoured by that,' Isabella said. 'And if we can help you in any way, we will.'

When Flora had left, Isabella went across to thread her arm in Bram's and say, 'I don't know whether you understand how hard life can be for a woman on her own, if she has no money behind her – whether she was born a lady or not. If you live with a relative, you're a "poor relation" and you're at their beck and call.'

'Oh, I do understand what it's like,' he said quietly. 'I've seen it, and in two-room hovels, too. It's even harder there.'

She rested her head on his shoulder for a minute, then straightened up, ready to start work.

'Here's a chance for us to make a bit more money,' he said with some relish.

'But what sort of shop will it be with second-hand goods and new ones all mixed up? It'll look . . . strange.'

He beamed at her. 'It came to me as we started poking around up here today. It won't be a shop at all, it'll be a – I don't know the name for it, but a place where people can leave stuff for us to sell, a place where you can find all sorts of oddments, like a small market. It's an eastern word. It'll come back to me.'

'A Bazaar, do you mean?'

'That's it. Deagan's Bazaar.' He plonked a kiss on one of her soft cheeks then couldn't resist kissing the other before forcing his attention back to practicalities. 'Come on. More lists to make. Where's that pencil?'

'Do we need to make lists? Don't we just need to get that old shed repaired and then take everything they don't want – and sort it out once it's there and we've space to lay it out? Otherwise we'll be doing the work twice.'

'You're right, so we do. Ah, Isabella, I'll make you proud of me yet. You won't always have to work so hard.'

She looked at him in surprise. 'What would I do with myself if I'd no work to keep me occupied?'

'I don't know. Whatever other ladies do. Sit and embroider.'

She laughed at him. 'I'm no idle lady, don't want to be. And I've always hated embroidery.'

But he wanted to give her the moon. And he would, too, one day.

10

Flora went to sit in the small parlour, where she started mending a torn petticoat, sure that Bram and Isabella would do better ferreting round the attic on their own. Her mother was out visiting, so for once she was able to sit and work in peace.

Just before two o'clock, Linny came in. 'There's a woman to see you, miss. She's in the kitchen and she looks very nervous. She won't give her name, but I'm sure I've seen her at the market.'

'I'll come and speak to her. If Mr Nash is around, ask him to wait outside the kitchen in the passage and listen to what we're saying, but tell him to leave it to me. And don't come back to the kitchen yourself till my visitor has gone.'

Linny looked surprised but hurried away.

Flora went into the kitchen. 'Callie, I'm so glad you've come.'

The visitor looked over her shoulder, as if expecting to be pursued. 'I can't stay and I want your promise that you won't say anything about me coming, not to anyone. If my husband found out I was here . . . Only I can't abide to see people ill-treat children, so that's why I came.'

'You saw the boy in the photograph, didn't you?'

'Yes. And his mother. The family stayed with us. The Barwells, they called themselves, but she had an "N" embroidered on some of her things, so I thought it must be a second marriage and perhaps the child was from her first husband. I don't pry, but you can't help seeing things. They called the lad Charlie. They paid us extra not to tell anyone who came looking for them that they'd been in Fremantle, made my husband swear it on the Bible. But I didn't swear it and anyway . . . He was a nice lad, that one, didn't deserve slapping around. I've never forgotten how brave he was, how he hardly ever cried.'

Flora murmured encouragingly and waited.

'They sailed on the steamer – oh, six months ago now, it'd be – and I heard them talking about going to Sydney.' She stood up. 'And that's all I can tell you. I have to go before my husband gets back.'

The poor woman was so skittish Flora didn't attempt to keep her longer, but saw her to the door and then went to find Mr Nash. He was waiting in the corridor outside the kitchen, standing as rigidly as a sentry on duty.

'You heard?'

He looked at her in anguish. 'Yes. She said they'd been ill-treating him regularly and *you* saw that man hitting Christopher. I have to find my son as quickly as I can. And if he's been badly hurt, I won't be answerable for what I do to Mr Humphrey Gresham, damn the fellow.'

When Dougal came back, he found Nash pacing up and down the dining room. Flora joined them and once they'd explained what they'd found out, he said, 'Leave it to me.'

'But surely you want me to come with you to see the captain?' Mitchell said.

'Not this time. Give me the likeness. I'll take great care of it, I promise.'

He left almost immediately, returning just after they'd started dinner, with their other guests, not that Mitchell had much appetite.

When Dougal came into the dining room, his mother pulled a face. 'You've been drinking again. I do wish you wouldn't.'

He grinned. 'It oils the tongue, a little drink does, and I've oiled a certain captain's tongue to some purpose today. Mr Nash, the people you're looking for did leave on that ship, and went to Sydney. The lady was ill for most of the journey and kept the lad with her in the cabin.'

Mitchell stared at him, hardly daring to believe that his search in the Swan River Colony had at last yielded fruit. 'He was certain they were the people I'm looking for?'

'Absolutely certain, said he'd stake his life on it.' Dougal gave him back the *carte de visite*. 'I've booked you a place on the steamer. It's leaving the day after tomorrow. You'll be in Sydney in just over two weeks.'

Mitchell stood up and went to shake his host's hand, then left the room hurriedly, looking distressed.

Flora explained quickly to her mother what was going on and Dougal took a place at the table.

'That poor man,' Mrs McBride said, her eyes full

of ready tears. 'How I feel for him! Now, would you like another helping, Mr Deagan?'

Flora felt sorry when Mr Nash left, because he'd been better company than most of their guests.

Once the Deagans had taken the furniture they needed for their cottage, she plunged into the work of clearing the rest of the attic, promising to send anything not needed to them for sale. There were a lot of pieces she'd be able to use to set up her boarding house, which would save her a great deal of money.

She had trouble keeping her mother at bay, but luckily an elderly lady came to ask for a room for a few days and the two women got on so well that Mrs McBride spent most of her spare time with her new guest.

Flora enlisted the help of a lad down the street to move the bigger items to one side, paying him with a good midday meal and a shilling. As Bram had said, every penny counted when you were short of money.

It was surprising what turned up in the attic, perfectly good items which her mother had discarded simply because they were a little shabby.

Dougal came up one day and found her tugging a small table across to 'her' side. 'Here, let me take that.' He stared at the pile of things. 'What are you doing with this lot? We're never going to use them. You know how Mother hates shabby furniture. I thought we were giving them to the Deagans.'

She hesitated and was lost.

He chanted as he had when they were children, 'What are you hiding from me, Flora-McDora?'

She could never lie to him. 'I don't want to spend my life waiting on Mother and I don't like being dependent on you. So . . . I'm going to open a boarding house of my own, like we run here.'

'Do I make you feel as if you're a burden to me? You're not and never could be.'

He sounded hurt so she took his hand. 'No, of course you don't. But I'm always at Mother's beck and call and she isn't easy – and I can't go on like this. She's too demanding. I've no life of my own. She's different when you're away, Dougal, quite horrible sometimes.'

He looked at her in consternation.

'I'm not likely to get married, not at my age, but surely I can have my independence, live a life of my own choosing? The world is changing and ladies are doing all sorts of things they never did before, especially in the colonies, where they've had to do the menial work, for lack of maids and other help.'

He was silent for so long, she was afraid she'd upset him, afraid he'd forbid her even to think of it.

'Poor Flora,' he said at last. 'I hadn't thought – but I can see your point, truly I can.'

'You ought to think of your own future, too. Your wife won't want Mother living here, I can promise you that.'

'Well, I'm not getting married yet. When do I ever have time to meet suitable women?'

'Mother would be delighted to find you someone.'

He grimaced. 'If the men she introduced to you were anything to go by, I'm not letting her near me when I start looking for a wife. I was glad you had the sense to refuse those dull creatures.'

'You do intend to marry, though?'

'Of course I do. In the next year or two, perhaps, before it's too late to enjoy my children. But let's get back to you. I'll help you in any way I can to set up your boarding house. Indeed, if my voyages continue successful, I could buy you a house and you could pay me rent. I'd trust you not to skip out on me, so it'd be a good investment for me.'

'Oh, Dougal!' She flung herself into her big brother's arms, as she hadn't done for many years. 'I've been so afraid of telling you about my plans.'

He hugged her close. 'Never be afraid of talking to me, Flora. But I agree with you about not telling Mother. She can't help interfering. I'd already decided that once I marry, I'll need to find her a little house of her own.'

Flora looked at him in dismay. 'If you do, she'll expect me to go and live with her. It's what unmarried daughters are supposed to do.'

'We'll find her someone else, put an advert in the newspaper for a lady's companion.' He saw that Flora was unconvinced and added, 'You stick to your guns about your independence and I'll support you, I promise.'

She went back to sorting out the attic with renewed vigour – and hope. Such a tender new shoot of hope that she watered with her tears that night. She didn't know why she was crying, but she'd waited so long, held her emotions in check for so long, that she couldn't help letting them out now.

Since the ship needed little work doing on it this time, the ship's carpenter was still working on the rambling old shed when the things from the McBrides' attics started arriving there. He told Bram which part of the shed was likely to be most waterproof and goods began to pile up there.

By this time Bram and Isabella were able to move into the little house. They hired a scrubbing woman whom Flora found for them to come three times a week. Mrs McBride was horrified that they were going to manage without a maid as well, but there were few maids to be had in the colony and anyway, they didn't want to share the house with anyone.

On the day they moved in, Isabella burst into tears of joy as they closed the front door on the world.

Bram held her close, understanding how she felt, only men weren't supposed to weep. He'd never had a home of his own, either.

When her sobs had subsided, he wiped her eyes with his handkerchief, pretending to polish her nose afterwards. 'Come on. Let's put our things away, then we'll go shopping for food.'

'That's not a man's job.'

'Who's going to carry your baskets?'

'A delivery boy will bring such a big order, I'm sure. Get out to that shed and make a start there!' she ordered with mock ferocity. 'I'll join you when I've done the shopping.'

She made the acquaintance of a nearby baker, a grocer and was told about a man who brought fresh vegetables and fruit into town to sell on Tuesdays and Fridays.

It was bliss to go to bed together that night, their

own bed, in their own house, with no one to hear what they were doing.

Bram was so tender with her, she found herself looking forward to the nights, which she hadn't expected.

In fact, everything was so wonderful she was terrified something might spoil it.

Conn turned up at the livery stables a few days later, leading a young stallion he'd bought in Perth. He stopped in surprise at what he found. It looked so much neater, a going concern rather than a run-down business.

As he dismounted, a man came hurrying out.

'Can I help you, sir? Oh! Sorry, Mr Largan. I didn't recognise you at first, with the sun behind you.'

'Good afternoon. How are things going?'

Les who looked a different man from the one Conn had left in charge, grinned cheerfully at him. 'It's going really well, sir. We're full some nights now – but Mr Deagan will tell you about that.' He stared at the horse being led. 'He's a fine young fellow, isn't he?'

'Yes. I've been trying to buy one from this line for a while.' He didn't say that it was the Governor's support and acknowledgement that he had been unjustly convicted that had turned the trick and made the owner willing to deal with him. 'Look after him carefully for me.'

'I shall, sir. It'll be a real pleasure.'

'Where can I find Mr Deagan?'

'He's moved into the cottage, went across a few minutes ago to have afternoon tea with his wife. Shall I take your horses?'

'Yes, please, I'll come for my saddlebags later.'

'I'll keep them safe in the tack room, sir.'

Conn strolled across to the cottage, which had also undergone a metamorphosis, and used the shining brass knocker.

The door opened and now it was Bram's turn to beam at him. 'Conn! Come in and meet my wife. You'll have a cup of tea with us?'

So Conn sat and chatted to them, finding the new Mrs Deagan a very pleasant lady. After a while he glanced at the clock on the mantelpiece. 'I must see if the McBrides have a room for me.'

They looked at one another and Isabella said, 'If you'd like to stay here, Mr Largan, we have a spare bedroom and a bed in it, though not much else. After all, this is your property.'

'If you're sure it's not too much trouble? I'd like to stay near that horse. He's very valuable. And do call me Conn.'

'Then I'm Isabella.'

He turned back to Bram. 'We must have an agreement drawn up about the property and the business. You need to know exactly where you stand. After all, you're putting in the trading goods *and* the hard daily work.' He paused and grinned at them. 'Did I do the right thing buying this place, Bram?'

'Exactly the right thing. And we've even acquired some stock, as well as the goods we brought from Singapore. Will we go up and look round the shed? If we make that our shop, we can keep the stables going, which will keep bringing in money. Isabella, you'll join us, won't you?'

Conn looked at him in surprise.

'My wife is a full partner in the business and I'd like that to be in the contract, too.' Bram grinned. 'She knows more about trading and selling than I do, that's for sure.'

'Then she must certainly join us.'

Chatting about their plans, they walked up the gentle slope to the sheds, where Conn approved what had been done. 'This gives you a stake in the property and we should reflect that in our contract.'

'I'm grateful for your support.'

Conn smiled. 'Oh, I think you're going to make me a lot of money, or I'd not have considered it.'

Bram stared at him. 'Do you now?'

'Yes. I've got complete faith in you. You've a way with people, you see. And now that you have a wife like Isabella, I'm even more certain you'll make your fortune. Some people prosper greatly in the colony and we're going to be among them.

'Next time I visit, I'll see if I can bring my wife with me. It's about time Maia got out and about a bit more.'

11

Sydney

Mitchell was glad to arrive in Sydney. He'd been on edge during the whole journey, hardly daring to hope that this time he'd find his son.

He asked the captain's advice about where to start his search.

'Try the post office. They've moved it to Wynyard Street, but they're going to build a proper new one. The man you're looking for may collect his mail there or they may know where he lives. If not, try the sort of areas where a man of his means might live. I can't advise you there.'

So Mitchell left the steamer and went out into the bustle of Sydney. He was dismayed at how much bigger it was than Fremantle or Perth, how many people there were in the streets, not to mention vehicles, carts and carriages, even bullock carts, which surely didn't belong in a city centre. How would he ever find someone here without having some clue as to where to start?

If the fellow wasn't using his real name now, it'd be hopeless.

He stopped to heft his carpet bag to his other hand.

It contained all he'd brought because he'd left the rest of his luggage in Fremantle in the McBrides' attic, trusting that he'd be able to return there if – no, *when* he'd found his son.

A cab driver stopped beside him. 'Take you somewhere, sir?'

'Yes. I'm looking for some lodgings for a few days, possibly even a week or two. A decent place, with a room to myself.' He'd found out the hard way over the past year that he needed to specify that when seeking lodgings.

'I know just the place, sir.'

'It must be central.'

'It is, sir. Couldn't be more convenient. It's run by a cousin of mine.' The driver waited for him to settle into the cab, then told his horse to walk on, threading through the busy traffic with the ease of long practice.

The lodgings were in a terraced house of three storeys. The room was small but clean but the landlady was a dour sort. Her only welcome was to hand him a handwritten list of rules glued to a piece of card.

'Since you're not a regular, sir, I'd be obliged if you'd fit in with the others. It's all written down.'

'Of course.' He arranged to have breakfast and an evening meal, paid her for two days on account, and asked directions to the General Post Office.

He set off walking, glad to stretch his legs, interested in what he saw. As he got to George Street, he slowed down to avoid hawkers, shoppers, couples promenading arm-in-arm without much regard for other pedestrians, and ladies in huge crinolines, which were surely the most ridiculous garments ever invented.

Inside the post office, he pretended he was trying to find a friend who'd moved house, but the man behind the counter refused to divulge Gresham's address, though he did go so far as to admit that a few men by that name collected mail there.

As Mitchell walked slowly away from the counter, an old man sweeping the floor came alongside him and whispered as he passed, 'Might be able to find out about your friend for you, sir.'

'I'd happily pay you for your trouble. I'm trying to find a man called Gresham. I think his first name is Humphrey.'

The man slowed down and took out a handkerchief to wipe his brow. 'Any idea where he lives, sir?'

'No, but it'll be a decent area. He usually works as a clerk.'

'Come back in two days about six o'clock, sir, and I'll see if I can find out. I'll meet you outside.' He carried on sweeping and stopped to chat to another customer before finishing his task.

Mitchell decided to take a walk round the central city streets. A faint smell of burning led him to a place where a huge building had collapsed. A passer-by told him that it had been St Mary's Cathedral until it burned down recently. He stared at it, horrified at the destruction a fire could cause.

By the time he got back to his lodgings, he was exhausted and after the evening meal he didn't linger to chat in the sitting room. When he went up to his room, he read the list of rules to find out what time breakfast was served and when hot water was brought up for shaving.

Getting into bed, he composed himself for sleep. But his mind wouldn't settle. Questions and worries kept nudging him awake. And hopes. Surely he'd find his son here? Surely fate wouldn't keep them apart much longer?

Alice walked slowly back from the local market, holding her little daughter's hand. Her basket was lighter than she'd have wished because she hadn't been able to afford much beyond a four-pound loaf, a cabbage and a few thin slices of ham. She hated living from hand to mouth like this, and was tired of eating dry bread or plain boiled potatoes and cabbage without even butter on them. She longed for fresh vegetables, fruit and a juicy piece of roast beef.

A tall man crossing the street caught her eye and for a moment she thought it was Renington! She ducked into a nearby alley and peered out, feeling foolish when she saw it wasn't him. Why would he be here in Sydney, for goodness' sake?

Once she'd have sat down and wept when she got home at how cheerless and miserable the house was. Two storeys, with two rooms on each floor, and a scullery at the back on the ground floor. There was a narrow porch at the front and a narrow balcony above it. But the balcony was unsafe, the wood rotten in places, so she didn't dare go out to sit on it.

She didn't weep any more at such things, had learned

the hard way how useless tears were. All they did was make her look ugly and frighten her child.

When Parker came in, she asked, 'Did you earn any money today?'

'I did two charcoal portraits. There's a new man at the shop and he says he can find me other people wanting their children's likeness sketched. Here. I had to buy some more paints for my real work, but I've got some money left for you.'

'You bought paints when your daughter's going hungry?'

He flushed. 'I didn't spend it all.'

'Give me what's left.'

After turning out his pockets, he gave her nearly two guineas. Yet he usually earned five guineas for each charcoal portrait. She smelled the drink on his breath but didn't say anything. What was the use? He never seemed to learn when it came to money.

She used to be foolish about money too. You couldn't be foolish about it when you didn't have any, though, when your stomach was growling with hunger. The only thing she did make sure she could afford was the Godfrey's Cordial she gave to Louisa. That mixture was a godsend to many parents, keeping a child calm and sleepy, instead of naughty and tiring. She called the bottle her 'nursemaid'.

And since Parker wouldn't do it, she wrote to his family and begged them to send her a little money each quarter, for the child's sake. She suggested they ask the lawyer to give it directly to her, so that she could feed and clothe their grandchild. Surely they'd do something when she told them how desperate her situation was.

She'd given Louisa some wooden bricks to play with while she wrote the letter, but the child had fallen asleep. The cordial did that to her.

She turned back to the letter. She'd leave it at the lawyer's office the next day because she hadn't the money to pay for postage to England. He could verify that what she'd said was true because when they arrived in Sydney, Parker had shown him their marriage lines. Surely he'd have to forward a letter addressed to his clients?

She wondered what to do with herself now and decided to follow her little daughter's example and have a rest. She was feeling exhausted because they couldn't afford a maid and she had to do nearly every-thing herself, except washing the sheets and larger items.

Parker had once suggested she tidy up his 'studio' – a fancy name for the attic – but she'd told him in no uncertain terms that if he wanted it cleaned, he must find the money to pay someone. She was spending all the money he gave her on food and clothing, and had no energy to spare after keeping the rest of the house clean.

He hadn't mentioned it since.

Every now and then, out of sheer necessity, she went upstairs to fetch cups and plates he'd taken up and forgotten to bring down again, or to throw away anything that smelled bad, taking it down to the end of the alley behind their little row of houses where people dumped rubbish and left it in piles until the authorities cleared it up.

She sighed. She didn't know what she'd do if Parker's family refused to help his child. And herself. Her clothes were nearly in rags now and Louisa kept growing all the time.

Alice's neighbour Betsy was worrying too that evening. Her husband was acting strangely and had been for a while, but in the past two days, he'd been worse than ever.

If she had anywhere to run to, she would. Only she didn't know anyone in Sydney because he didn't like her making friends, or even speaking to the neighbours.

She wished she'd not let him persuade her to leave Mitchell and come to Australia. It would be better to be bored than afraid like this. Humphrey might be good-looking, but he was cruel and violent.

Worst of all was the way he seemed to have taken a dislike to her son. He'd been kind to Christopher at first and she couldn't understand why he'd changed. Christopher was such a good child, so uncomplaining, though he led a dreadful life now.

She wished she hadn't brought him with her when she ran away. She'd not wanted to give him up, but now she realised only too clearly that she should have left him with his father. He'd have been safe there.

It couldn't go on like this. There had to be some way to stop Humphrey. But if she intervened in the beatings, he would beat her instead of the child. He'd done that a few times now and hurt her so badly last time, she'd had to stay in bed for several days, because her ribs hurt too much when she moved.

He'd said he was sorry, didn't know what had come over him, but she'd seen his face when he was beating her. He'd enjoyed it, enjoyed hurting her. It was the same when he hit her son.

Mitchell might have been grumpy and mean about money, but he'd never laid a finger on her, or their son.

She feared for her son's life now. And her own.

Mitchell spent the day walking round Sydney, staring at everyone he passed. At one stage he saw a sign for the North Shore Ferry Company and on an impulse, took a ride across the harbour to the northern shore and back again. The man he was standing next to at the rail told him this ferry service had only been running since 1861, and it was a godsend.

This was a magnificent site for a city, but it must be very inconvenient for those living on the other side to have to cross the water to go to work each day, Mitchell decided as he got off after an equally pleasant return journey.

He found a shop selling maps of the city and bought one. He'd mark it out and visit every single house, if necessary. Nothing and no one was going to keep him from rescuing his son.

The next evening he went to the General Post Office at six o'clock and the old man he'd seen before walked past him and muttered, 'Follow me.'

Once they were round the corner, his companion stopped and smiled at him. 'I found two Greshams in respectable areas. Couldn't see their Christian names on the lists, had to do it in a hurry.' He pulled a grubby piece of paper out of his pocket.

Mitchell fumbled in his pocket and came up with five shillings, which seemed to please the fellow, judging by the gleam in his eye.

After he'd walked away, he stopped to glance down at the paper again, memorising the addresses in case it got lost.

It was getting dark now. Strange to have winter in July. Stopping at a street stand, he treated himself to one of the few remaining copies of the *Sydney Morning Herald* newspaper and made his way back to his lodgings. He hoped the meal would be better than last night's stodgy food, but didn't feel optimistic.

Filling was the word for the soup served with hunks of bread, the plain boiled potatoes with a little, a very little, stewed beef and gravy, and the jam roly-poly pudding with thin white sauce that needed more sugar in it. He sighed, remembering the food at the McBrides' house.

Never mind, tomorrow he'd be able to continue his quest. That was the main thing.

The following morning Mitchell set off early, asking directions and walking to the first address. People hurried past him, presumably on their way to work. When he found a small market on a piece of spare ground, he stopped for a cup of tea at a hawker's stand. It was strong and hot, far better than that offered at his lodgings, and he was able to check that he was moving in the right direction from the man who served him.

As he stood sipping the last of the tea, he saw a woman walking round the little market with a small child, looking carefully at the goods on each of the stalls. Having finished the cup of tea, he followed her example, thinking to buy a couple of pieces of fruit. He watched her feel the fruit and vegetables, making her choices very carefully. Short of money, he guessed, even though from her speech she sounded like a lady.

When he set off for the first of the addresses, he saw her ahead of him, walking slowly because of the little child.

Then suddenly a man stepped out from an alley and grabbed her, trying to snatch her purse, from where it was hanging inside her skirt. As she screamed and fought back, the child began to wail and the man kicked her out of the way.

Mitchell began running and reached the struggling pair before the thief realised it. No one else from the market had made any attempt to intervene.

The man drew back his elbow for a punch and Mitchell nearly laughed aloud at his amateur way of fighting. He dodged easily enough and landed a blow to the man's jaw.

The thief reeled back, stared at him for a moment, and mustn't have liked what he saw, because he ran away.

Mitchell turned to the woman to see if she needed any help. She was trying to comfort the child, who must have been hurt as she was kicked aside. The shopping was scattered around, so he collected it and put it into the basket, waiting till she'd soothed the child.

He held out the basket. 'I think I have everything here, ma'am.'

'Thank you for coming to my aid. I don't know what I'd have done if he'd taken my purse.'

The child was still sobbing and the woman looked so slight that he'd offered to help before he could stop himself. 'Shall I carry her home for you? She's a bit heavy for you on your own.'

She looked at him doubtfully, then nodded. 'Thank you. You've been so kind. I'm Mrs Beaufort.'

'I'm Mitchell Nash, a visitor to Sydney. I've only been here a couple of days.'

'I wish there were more newcomers like you, then. The gold rush brought in a lot of undesirable people and sometimes they get desperate enough to attack in broad daylight.'

'Can the police not do anything?'

She shrugged. 'I haven't the time or energy to walk into the city centre and report this. And anyway, the thief is long gone.'

They arrived at a crossroad and she smiled at the child. 'You must get down and walk now, Louisa. Say thank you to the kind gentleman for carrying you.'

But the child just stared at him then yawned and put a thumb in her mouth, so he set her down gently. She didn't seem badly hurt, was probably just bruised, poor little thing.

'I'm looking for Aswin Street, Mrs Beaufort. I believe it's round here somewhere. Could you direct me?'

'Oh, yes. It's easy to find.'

She was right. He followed her directions and found the street easily enough, but when he knocked on the door of the house, the elderly man who answered proved to be a Mr Robert Gresham who didn't have any relatives in the city. He was unfriendly enough to close the door in the stranger's face at that point in the conversation without so much as a goodbye.

Another dead end, Mitchell thought. How many more would he have to follow?

He had to hope the second address would yield the correct man, or he'd have wasted his five shillings.

A sudden downpour reminded him that he'd not got an umbrella and soon water began to cascade from the brim of his hat. By the time he'd found a shop and bought an umbrella, he was soaked to the skin and shivering. You might not need heavy overcoats in an Australian winter, but you did need protection against the weather.

As the rain continued to pound down, he decided to go back to his lodgings and spend a peaceful evening with a newspaper. Tomorrow was another day and he'd be no use to his son if he neglected his own health and died of pneumonia.

What he'd really have liked would be a hot bath, but when he suggested that to his landlady, she refused point blank. She did produce a pot hot-water bottle and a piece of faded flannel to wrap it in, which was a minor comfort, at least.

His fellow lodgers were a quiet bunch, who didn't

seem interested in him or even in chatting, so he went back to his room again. It seemed a long evening.

It was pouring with rain. Betsy stared out of the window, willing it to stop. Humphrey was like a cat, absolutely hated getting wet, and this weather was bound to put him in a bad mood. She shivered at the thought.

She turned to the stove, giving the stew a stir. She must concentrate when she was cooking and not burn the evening meal again. It sent Humphrey wild when she did that. But the wood stove in this house was so hard to manage and went out sometimes for no reason, or flared up just as inexplicably. She'd begged him to complain to the landlord and ask him to fix it, but he wouldn't. He said it was her fault and she was too stupid even to cook a decent meal.

This week Humphrey hadn't left for work as early as usual, which she couldn't understand. And a couple of evenings he'd come home early, taking her by surprise. He said he'd finished all his work so quickly they'd been pleased with him and had let him finish early. He must be doing really well at work, but if so, why was he looking angry all the time? Why did he keep saying nasty things about his employers and the chief clerk?

She'd given up trying to understand him.

With a sigh she looked at the clock. He'd be home soon. She must have everything neat and tidy.

But of course while she was tidying up, the stew burned and she couldn't help sitting down and weeping in fear.

Christopher was in his room, because Humphrey didn't like him playing out, said it was better to keep an eye on a lad of that age. Poor child, he spent a lot of time staring wistfully out of the window, watching other children play in the street. Oh dear, she was doing it again, calling him by his proper name. 'Charles,' she muttered. She had to call him Charles.

The door banged open and Humphrey called, 'I'm back.'

He came into the kitchen and stared at the stove, wrinkling his nose and sniffing. 'You've burned it again.'

'I'm sorry. The wood was damp and then it must have flared up suddenly. There's something wrong with this stove, truly there is.'

He slapped her so hard she went flying across the room and as he moved across after her, she began screaming, terrified by the expression on his face. He hit her again and again, till she was too weak to scream and the world turned black.

When they heard the screaming start in the next house, Alice went to find Parker. 'What do you suppose he's doing to her?'

He shook his head. 'Beating her again, I suppose.'

'She's never screamed like this before. Can't we do something?'

'How can we intervene between husband and wife? The law allows a man to chastise his wife.'

'That's not chastisement, it's a brutal beating.' She let out a scornful sniff. 'Well, if you ever lay a finger on me, I'll do a lot more than scream, I promise you.'

'As if I would.' He tried to pull her close for a cuddle, but she knew where that led and pulled away. 'Stop that. You know we can't afford another child, Parker.'

'You're my wife.'

'And your daughter is below, waiting to be fed.' She ignored his sulky expression.

But a few minutes later, she saw the child from next door, looking utterly terrified, sneak into their yard again and hide behind the wood pile, in spite of the heavy rain cascading down on him. She couldn't bear to see him shivering so pitifully. Keeping an eye on the next house, she opened the back door and beckoned to him to come in.

He stared back at her, shivering so hard he was shaking all over.

She beckoned again and with a quick look to his own house, he ran across the yard. 'You'll be safe here, and you can stay the night, if you like.' She shut the door behind him and locked it, gasping in shock as she saw his bruised face from close to. That monster wasn't going to beat this child again today, she vowed. Usually their neighbour's temper seemed to die down the day following a beating, as if he'd got it out of his system for a while. Let the mother who couldn't protect her child take the brunt of her husband's rage this time.

Water was dripping on to the floor. 'Get out of those clothes, Charles. You'll catch your death of cold if you don't. I'll go and find you a blanket to wrap yourself in.'

He nodded, starting to unbutton a jacket that was far too small for him. She ran upstairs to the attic.

'Parker, I've let the boy from next door come into the house. He was soaked to the skin and he's terrified.'

'Poor little thing.'

'Don't you dare send him back.'

'Why would I do that? Look, Alice, don't you think this one is coming on well?'

She didn't even glance at his painting, which was just like the others . . . not nearly good enough to sell. Grabbing a blanket and towel, she ran back down to the kitchen and found the lad half-undressed, still standing by the door, shivering.

Shocked rigid at how many bruises were now visible on his arms and chest, she held out the blanket, but didn't comment on them. 'Give me your wet clothes and I'll put them to dry on the fireguard.'

He did that then stood looking at her warily from his place by the door.

'Come closer to the fire and get warm. Would you like a bowl of soup?'

He nodded. 'Yes please, ma'am.'

When Parker came down, she served the meal. The boy was wary, at first eating properly, but then forgetting his table manners as hunger took over.

Suddenly there was a knocking on the front door and a man's voice yelling, 'Charles! I know you're in there. Come home this minute.'

She looked at Parker. 'Don't you dare let that man take him.'

'But he's the father.'

'Stepfather,' the boy said. 'He wants to beat me again. He's hurt my mother badly today, because she burnt the stew. I think she's unconscious because she stopped screaming suddenly.'

'What have *you* done for him to turn on you?' Parker asked.

'I don't know. I never know.'

Alice pulled the edge of the blanket down. 'Look, Parker.' The bruises spoke for themselves.

Parker stared at them in shock and as the knocking began again, he got up and went to the front door.

The boy let his spoon fall into his soup and began to cry soundlessly, tears dripping on to the table. He looked terrified.

She heard the front door open.

Mr Gresham's voice yelled, 'You've got him here. I know you have.'

'Who?' Parker asked.

'My son.'

'Has he run away? Why would he do that?'

Alice reached out to hold the boy's thin claw of a hand, a spark of hope igniting inside her that for once Parker was doing the right thing.

'Are you sure you've not seen him?'

'Certain. He must have run off down the back alley.'

'Hmm. Well, if you do see him, tell him to get straight home.'

Parker shut the front door and she heard him lock it, something he never normally remembered to do. She turned to the boy. 'You're safe here and you can stay the night.'

He nodded, letting out gulping sobs of relief, so that

she had to pull him into her arms and hold him close until the sobbing gradually stopped.

Not until later, after the boy had gone up to sleep on the floor in Louisa's bedroom did Parker say in a low voice, 'That man, Gresham – he had blood on him.'

She looked at him in horror. 'Blood?'

He nodded. 'Yes, definitely. Fresh blood, too. I don't know what to do.'

'I don't think there's anything we can do except keep that boy safe from him.'

12

The following morning Mitchell set off again on his search, feeling more energetic after a better night's sleep. He didn't let his expectations rise too high about this second Mr Gresham, however, because he'd had too many disappointments before.

To his annoyance, the second address proved to be only a few streets away from where he'd said goodbye to Mrs Beaufort and her daughter the day before. If he'd known how close it was, he'd have braved the heavy rain and continued his search. Today was blustery with an occasional light shower, during which he used his new umbrella to good purpose.

When he found the house, he knocked on the front door, but didn't receive an answer. Someone looked out of the window of the next house and then a man came to the door. To his surprise, behind him stood the woman Mitchell had helped the day before.

In common courtesy, he went to greet her and ask how she was. She introduced him to her husband, who seemed a pleasant enough fellow.

'We saw you knocking next door. Are you looking for Mr Gresham?' she asked.

'I'm looking for a Mr Gresham but whether this

man is the one I'm seeking or not, I don't know. The man I want is Humphrey Gresham.'

'That's our neighbour's name.' Mr Beaufort described him.

Excitement rose in Mitchell. It sounded like – was it possible, after all this time? 'That does sound like him. I'll just try the door again.'

But there was still no answer.

'Would you like to come in and wait?' she asked. 'Perhaps a cup of tea?'

'That's very kind of you. It does look like rain again.'

The house reeked of genteel poverty and Mrs Beaufort was clearly very conscious of this, but her husband didn't seem to notice anything. Mitchell soon began to consider him a friendly blockhead.

'Just a minute!' Beaufort went bounding up the stairs and was back a minute later with a piece of paper and some charcoal.

'How's the child?' she asked her husband.

'Hiding under our bed. He's terrified, thought it was his father come to find him.'

'Leave him there.' She turned back to her guest, but offered no explanation for this strange conversation.

Out of politeness, Mitchell didn't ask what they meant.

'I can draw our neighbour's face for you,' Mr Beaufort said. 'I'm an artist and quite good at faces.'

With a few swift lines, he brought to life Humphrey Gresham.

For a moment Mitchell couldn't speak because the sight of the man who'd stolen his wife and son made him feel literally sick with anger. Then he saw them both looking at him and he forced himself to speak calmly. 'That's the Gresham I'm looking for. I've been chasing him all the way from England. He ran away with my wife and though I don't want her back, they took my son with him.'

Mrs Beaufort gasped. 'Charles is *your* son?'

'Yes. Only his real name is Christopher. Have you seen him? Is he all right?'

Before she could answer him, the front door was flung open and someone crashed into the house.

It was Gresham, but looking so strange and wild-eyed, no one moved for a moment in shock.

'You have him here. I know you do.' He produced a knife and brandished it at them. 'Give him to me or you'll be sorry.'

Mrs Beaufort let out a scream. Her husband moved to stand in front of her.

Then Gresham's gaze fixed on Mitchell. 'You! I knew you were following us. But you'll not get her back. I've made sure of that. No one can take her away from me now.'

Mitchell picked up a chair in case he needed to defend himself, because he was certain the man had gone completely mad and that knife had dried blood-stains on it.

Without warning Gresham lunged forward with the knife and Mitchell used the chair to keep him at bay.

'Get out of my house!' Beaufort shouted.

Gresham turned to him and again brandished the knife, which had a thin, sharp blade and looked like a meat boning knife. 'Shut up or you'll be next.'

Mitchell tried to jab him with the chair while he was distracted, in an attempt to make him drop his weapon. Gresham stepped sideways, a move which brought him closer to Beaufort, who reached out to try to disarm him.

'Stay back!' Mitchell shouted, sure this was a way to get injured.

Laughing wildly, Gresham yelled, 'I warned you!' and deliberately thrust the knife into Beaufort's chest.

Mrs Beaufort screamed and tried to pull her husband back, but already he was buckling at the knees, his eyes rolling up.

Still keeping the chair in front of him, Mitchell tried to get round the side of the madman, afraid now for Mrs Beaufort.

Still laughing, Gresham yanked the knife out of Beaufort's chest and turned its dripping blade towards the other man.

Out of the corner of his eye, Mitchell saw Mrs Beaufort push her child under the table and crouch protectively in front of her, but she didn't have the wit to grab a chair to protect herself.

However, her movements distracted Gresham's attention and before he could make another move, Mitchell thrust the chair forward with all his force, trying to knock the knife out of the madman's hands. He didn't succeed but he managed to throw the man off balance and seized the opportunity to grab him from behind.

As the two men struggled for control of the knife, Gresham's foot slipped in the puddle of blood on the floor. With a yell, he went down, pulling Mitchell, who didn't dare let go, on top of him.

For a moment there was silence. Mitchell held on tightly, terrified Gresham would attack again. Then, as the loud tick of the clock continued to be the only sound in the room, he realised the other hadn't moved since he fell. Was he pretending to be hurt, waiting for an opportunity to stab again?

Mrs Beaufort said in a faltering voice, 'He's fallen on the knife. It's sticking out of his chest.'

Very quickly, ready to defend himself again, Mitchell thrust himself upright and stepped quickly backwards. Gresham still didn't stir.

He stepped forward and rolled the madman over with his foot, but although he could see a pulse at Gresham's throat, the other's eyes didn't open and he continued to lie motionless amid the blood and gore, with the knife sticking out of his chest.

'Find a neighbour. Get them to call the police!' Mitchell didn't take his eyes off Gresham.

'My husband—'

'I'm sorry. He's beyond help.' There was no mistaking the look of death on Beaufort's face.

She sobbed as she moved away from him. 'Stay under the table, Louisa. Play hidey.'

'I'll keep an eye on the child,' Mitchell said. He half-expected Mrs Beaufort to have hysterics, but though her face was chalk-white and her clothing stained with her husband's blood, she managed to make her way unsteadily towards the door.

He was left with a dead man and another who was probably dying. The child was playing with a rag doll under the table, murmuring to it, seeming unaware of the horrors around her. And that damned clock was still ticking loudly.

Bile rose in his throat, but he controlled it, as he controlled his desire to leave the room with its stink of blood. He stayed where he was because someone had to keep an eye on Gresham and the child.

Mrs Beaufort came back alone and sagged back against the wall, as if she found it hard to stand on her own. 'A neighbour's gone for help.'

'You might as well wait somewhere else. There's nothing you can do here. It's no sight for a lady's eyes.'

She didn't move. 'This is the Gresham you were seeking?'

'Yes.'

'Then I think we have your son upstairs. He's hiding from this – this . . .'

It was easy to supply the correct word. 'Madman.'

'Yes. Madman. I've never been so terrified in my whole life.' She closed her eyes and sagged even more.

'Don't faint!' he said sharply. 'Think of your daughter.'

'Yes. Yes, I must think of my child.' She looked across the room to where the little girl was hiding under the table. 'Come to Mama, Louisa. Let's go and find your ball.'

The child toddled out, seeming not to notice or at least, not understand that she was passing her dead father.

Mrs Beaufort scooped the child up into her arms and cuddled her close for a moment or two, then said in a stronger voice, 'I'll stay with your son upstairs till help comes. I don't want him to see this.'

When she'd gone someone knocked on the door.

'Come in!' Mitchell yelled.

A man appeared in the doorway. 'Hell fire! What happened?'

'Gresham went mad and stabbed Mr Beaufort then turned on me. We struggled and he fell on the knife. I think he's still alive.'

'And Beaufort?'

'He died instantly.' Mitchell watched the man bend to check.

'Yes, he's definitely dead. That's tragic.' He turned to Gresham. 'This one's dead, too! Saves a hanging, eh?'

'We'd better stay away from the bodies, so that the police can see what happened.' He swallowed another wave of nausea. He didn't go near Gresham because he felt sick at the mere thought of touching him.

The other man went to look at Beaufort and his voice grew gentler. 'Poor fellow. He was a fool, but a kind man, didn't deserve to be murdered.'

It was twenty-six long, slow minutes by the clock on the mantelpiece before the police arrived. There were two of them and they seemed unmoved by the horror and blood.

Mitchell explained again what had happened, then it suddenly occurred to him that they'd forgotten something. 'The Greshams live next door. I'm told no one's seen his wife since yesterday.'

'Would Mrs Beaufort come to the house with us, in case there's trouble, do you think? A woman's presence can be a great comfort to another woman.'

'I'd not ask it of her. She's had a dreadful shock, just seen her husband killed. And anyway, she's looking after two children. They need her more. Besides,' he had to take a deep breath before he could continue and even so his voice wobbled as he added, 'the lady next door isn't really Gresham's wife. She's mine. I've been looking for her for nearly a year, ever since she ran away with him. I've followed her from England to get my son back.'

'Ah.'

'So I'll recognise her and she knows me.' Was Betsy locked in, or were there more horrors waiting for them? After what he'd seen, he suspected it was the latter. He didn't want to go, didn't want to see another body, especially his wife's, but had to make sure.

'I'll stay here, you go with him and check,' the older policeman said to his companion.

Mitchell followed the younger policeman to the next house.

'I'd better go first, sir.' The front door was partly open and the policeman pushed it wider with his foot, calling, 'Hello? Mrs Gresham? Are you there?'

They waited but there was no answer, no sound at all.

The policeman led the way inside.

When the front parlour was shown to be empty and immaculately tidy, Mitchell allowed himself to hope.

But he stopped dead in the kitchen doorway, hope extinguished. Betsy lay on the floor, her face shockingly battered, splatters of blood everywhere.

The policeman bent over her. 'She's been dead for a while.'

'He must have killed her yesterday. The blood's dry.' Suddenly Mitchell could stand it no longer and ran out of the front door, to vomit into the gutter. Whatever her sins, Betsy hadn't deserved this.

He became aware that the policeman was standing beside him, a sympathetic look on his face. Neighbours were gathering, asking what was happening.

The policeman raised his voice, 'Can someone take a message to the police station for me? Tell them we've three people dead and need more help.'

'I'll go!' one lad volunteered eagerly.

'Well, get off with you, then. Remember, give them this address, tell them three people dead, two murdered, and they'll need to send help and the death van.'

Mitchell suddenly remembered that his son was waiting for him next door and made his way inside on unsteady legs. He found the older policeman still standing guard on the bodies.

'Is Mrs Beaufort still upstairs?'

'Yes. Can you just tell us—'

'No. I've not seen my son for over a year. I'm going to him before I talk to anyone.'

The thought of Christopher gave Mitchell the strength to climb the stairs. At the top he called, 'Mrs Beaufort?'

'I'm in here.'

He turned towards the front bedroom and found her sitting on the bed, with a boy sitting on one side of her and her own little girl asleep at the other side. 'Christopher!'

The boy looked at him in disbelief, so he said it again, more loudly, 'Christopher! I've been looking for you for months. Don't you recognise your own father?'

With a sob he stumbled towards his son, who was

still sitting there like a rigid statue, then the statue seemed to melt and Christopher flung himself into his father's arms, sobbing loudly.

Weeping, Mitchell kissed his son and held him close, while the boy continued to weep and cling to him. It was a while before either of them could stop.

Christopher hadn't said a word but he was holding on tightly to his father.

'He's not been well treated,' Mrs Beaufort said, her eyes warning Mitchell not to exclaim or make a fuss over the bruises.

'He'll be well treated and loved from now on, I promise you.' He looked down at his son. 'I'll look after you, Christopher. No one will hurt you again.'

The boy didn't say a word, but pressed against him more closely.

'How did he come to be here?'

'He was hiding from his stepfather. We took him in yesterday, couldn't bear to see him being hurt any more. How's his mother? Is she hurt badly?'

He mouthed the word 'Dead' and then 'Shh' looking down meaningfully at the boy. He didn't want to add a further burden of sadness to him for the moment. She looked at him in shock, but didn't say anything, thank goodness. He held Christopher close, drawing comfort from the one bright thing in this dreadful day.

He'd found his son!

The police couldn't be held at bay for long, but the man who came to question them was older, a sergeant, and he treated them with gentle courtesy. After he'd taken down the details, he asked, 'Where are you going to stay now, sir, madam? We might need to talk to you again.'

Mrs Beaufort looked round unhappily. 'I've got nowhere else to go. I'll have to stay here.'

'And you, sir?'

But Mitchell was looking at her, seeing the shadows of the day's horrors on her face. He wondered if she'd got any money, wondered what she'd do with herself now she'd lost her breadwinner. He owed her a lot, was quite sure that without her help, his son would also have been killed.

'Do you want me to stay here with you tonight?' he offered. 'I'll see if I can find someone to clean up the kitchen and I'll pay them. I can sleep in your front room, if Christopher can sleep up here.' He didn't want to spend money on paying for a room at a boarding house for them. He'd spent a lot on his search and had to husband what was left carefully now.

She burst into tears, muttering broken phrases like 'Thank you,' and 'Frightened'. She'd done little but weep, and left making arrangements to others, so it was hard to remain sympathetic. He exchanged glances with the sergeant, wishing there was a woman to deal with her. But there wasn't, so he'd do the best he could.

When she'd quietened down again, the sergeant said, 'I think that's a good idea, sir, you staying, I mean. I've got all the information I need. Shall I ask one of the neighbours outside if there's someone willing to clean the place up?'

'Thank you. We'd be grateful. I can't leave her alone with this. She saved my son's life.'

'Do you know her?'

'No. I'd never met her before I came to Sydney.'

She was rocking the little girl now, making soothing noises, seeming only half-aware of what they were saying. Christopher hadn't left Mitchell's side or spoken, so he kept one arm round his son's shoulders. It seemed to be what the boy needed.

'We'll let you know when you can bury your wife, sir,' the sergeant said.

Mitchell looked at him in shock. 'I don't want to go near her again. I'm sorry she's dead, and in such a terrible way, but she's caused me more pain than anyone or anything else in my whole life. For a whole year I didn't even know if my son was alive.'

'I can find an undertaker, send him to see you.'

'Thank you. But I can't afford that. I haven't considered her a true wife since she ran away with Gresham. Let her have a pauper's funeral.'

'Are you sure, sir?'

'Yes. Certain.' Although the sergeant looked at him in disapproval, he didn't change his mind. He had only limited money and would rather spend what was left on living people, like his son, for whom he now had to make a new life – a happy one, he hoped.

But he wondered how long it would take to erase the memory of this day from his mind. Or the horrors his son had faced.

And the boy still hadn't spoken.

13

Mitchell slept badly and was already awake when dawn turned the window into a square of grey against the darkness of the room. Noises nearby showed that some people were already going about their business in the narrow street. He heard doors and windows opening, neighbours calling greetings to one another, their voices echoing clearly in the damp air.

It was all so blessedly normal it comforted him. Let him just get through the next few days and he too would lead a normal life.

He lay there on the floor, hard as it was, not wanting to face another harrowing day, but it couldn't be avoided. Wincing, he got his stiff and aching body moving. Beside him his son was still fast asleep. Christopher had refused to go upstairs and clung obstinately to his father.

Every time he looked at the boy he felt soul-sick at the sight of the bruises. They would fade within a few days, but he could only hope a father's love would eventually wipe out the horrific memories his son must have. He wasn't sure anything would ever wipe out his own guilt about this.

Tiptoeing round the sleeping child, he went into the

kitchen, feeling grimy and wishing he had clean clothes to change into. With some difficulty he got the wood stove burning again and put the kettle over the circular hole through which the flames were already sending heat. He didn't let his eyes dwell on the damp, scrubbed patches on the floor where blood had pooled yesterday. Was it only yesterday?

Footsteps approached and he swung round. 'Ah. Good morning, Mrs Beaufort.'

'I heard you moving about, so I came down. I'm thirsty and hungry. I don't think I've eaten since breakfast yesterday.'

'Is there any food in the house?'

She flushed and bit her lip, then admitted, 'A little stale bread and a few potatoes. That's all.'

'I could go to a baker's when they open and buy something for us all.'

'Oh, that'd be such a help. There's a baker two streets away. He'll be selling bread at the back door already. And there's a shop in the same street that will sell you butter. I – don't have much money, I'm afraid.'

'I've enough.'

A sob escaped her and she dabbed at her eyes with a corner of her crumpled pinafore. 'I can't promise to pay you back.'

'You don't have to. You saved my son's life. I'll not leave you until we've thought of some way for you to make a new life.'

She brightened a little. 'You'll help me?'

'For the children's sake.' He didn't want her to think he was interested in her personally.

He peeped in to see Christopher still asleep so didn't wake him as he left the house quietly. It was good to breathe the fresh air. He turned in the direction she'd indicated and found the baker's by following his nose. He bought two loaves and some currant buns. Did anything smell better than freshly baked bread? His mouth watered and he couldn't resist picking off a piece of crust and eating it.

Further along the road he found a little shop and bought butter, jam and eggs. He also asked for milk, but then realised he'd not brought a jug to put it in.

'Are you the gent whose wife got killed?' the shopkeeper asked, staring in fascination at the dried bloodstains on his clothing.

Mitchell nodded.

'I'll lend you a jug, then. We've got to help one another, be Good Samaritans, haven't we? But don't forget to bring the jug back. I'd better lend you a string bag too, or you'll be dropping something.'

Mrs Beaufort should have thought of that, but she didn't seem a very practical woman.

When he got back, Mitchell left the food in her charge and went into the front room. Christopher was just stirring. As he woke up, he jerked his head up enough to look round warily, then saw his father, and seemed to remember the previous day's events. He let his head fall back on the pillow with a whimper of relief.

'It's all right, son. No one's going to hurt you again. You're just in time for breakfast. Are you hungry? I am.'

Christopher opened his eyes again, mouthing, 'Mother'.

Mitchell hesitated, but if he didn't tell him, someone else would, so he said quietly, 'She's dead, I'm afraid. That madman killed her as well as Mr Beaufort. But Gresham's dead now, so he can't hurt you again. Not ever. And I won't let anyone else hurt you, either.'

Christopher didn't say anything else, just stared at him, eyes wide in that pale, bruised face that upset Mitchell every time he saw it.

'Come on, son. We'll have some breakfast and you'll feel better after that. I've bought some fresh bread.'

When the boy didn't get up, Mitchell went across and bent down, trusting his instincts and giving the child a big hug as he lifted him to his feet. 'You'll be living with me from now on, like you used to.' Even this didn't seem to get through, so he repeated, 'No one's going to hit you or hurt you again.'

He looked down at himself then at his son. 'We're both a right old mess, aren't we? We need some clean clothes. Do you have any other clothes next door?'

Mrs Beaufort spoke from behind him. 'I think all his clothes are a bit small for him now.'

'Then we'll buy him some new clothes this morning. Perhaps Mrs Beaufort will help us.'

Christopher stared at him, then at her, then gave the smallest of nods.

'Breakfast,' Mitchell said firmly. No one could think properly with hunger growling in their belly.

And after all, life went on, whatever happened to you. Sometimes that hurt and at other times, like now, it was a great comfort to focus on the details of everyday life.

At least his son ate a decent breakfast, even though he couldn't be coaxed into speaking.

After the meal was over, Alice cleared the table, then looked uncertainly at Mitchell.

'We need to talk,' he said. 'Why don't you sit down?'

She did so, shoulders drooping. He was just about to speak when she did.

'I can't even afford to bury Parker, Mr Nash. I simply don't have the money.'

'Where did he get his money from? Selling paintings?' He'd seen the attic studio and hadn't thought the paintings very good.

'No. No one wanted to buy the paintings. He wasn't very good, was he? He did sketches sometimes. He was better at that, but he hated doing it, said it demeaned him.'

'How did you live, then?'

'Parker was a remittance man. His family in England paid him money as long as he stayed in Australia. The lawyer gave him an allowance every quarter – and Parker spent it before the next payment was due.'

'Ah, so your husband had a lawyer.'

'Yes.'

'We'll go and see him this morning, then, and ask him to pay for the funeral.' She didn't seem happy about that. 'What's wrong?'

'Mr Sherwood isn't very helpful. He said he'd write to Parker's family when we got married, but they said they'd not pay any more, so what use was that? And . . . I don't know if they'll still send me the money. But surely they won't let his child go hungry?' Her eyes went to the little girl, playing some wordless game with a dirty rag doll.

He suppressed an impatient sigh as Mrs Beaufort began to sob. She looked pretty even while weeping, but he wasn't tempted in any way by a foolish woman like her. He'd had his fill of foolish women.

'I only have enough money left for a few days' food. Mr Nash, what am I going to do?'

Mitchell didn't speak ill of the dead, but he guessed Parker Beaufort must have done something bad for his family to send him out to Australia like that – something more than being careless with money. Betsy had been hopeless with money, too. It had been the cause of many quarrels between the two of them. He looked across at his son. Christopher was listening carefully. He'd stayed close to his father ever since he woke, even going to wait outside the privy when need took Mitchell there.

With a sigh Mitchell forced his attention back to her. 'How much money do you have left, Mrs Beaufort?'

'A few coins, that's all, less than two guineas. Parker had done some sketches, but he spent some of the money he was paid for those on paint – and drink. He was good at catching a likeness in charcoal, when he was sober.'

'I saw that. I burned the sketch he made of that madman,' Mitchell said. 'I hope you don't mind.' When she shook her head, he continued, 'I'll not leave Sydney until we've worked out what you can do, then I'm going back to settle in the Swan River Colony. I liked it there and have nothing waiting for me in England now. Where were you living before you came to Sydney?'

He thought for a minute she hadn't heard, then tears welled in her eyes and she whispered, 'Singapore. That's where I met Parker. I lived with my aunt and uncle, and my cousin. But my uncle died and then our life was horrible. I suppose my cousin and aunt are still there. I didn't write to them after I ran away from home. I was too ashamed of myself.'

Now this was more hopeful. Perhaps they'd take her in. The lawyer could surely get the money for her passage there. 'When I was in Fremantle I met some people and the wife had come from Singapore. Maybe she'll know your cousin. She's called Isabella Deagan. She's—'

'Isabella?'

'Yes. She married Bram recently. She'd been living with a Chinese family in Singapore, working for them.'

'There can't be a lot of Isabellas in Singapore. She doesn't have red hair, does she?'

'Yes. And she's quite tall. A very striking woman.'

Mrs Beaufort clapped her hands together in a theatrical gesture. 'It must be her! There weren't any other red-haired women called Isabella in Singapore. And she's married! Oh, I wish I could go to her. She always knew what to do. She'd look after me.'

She burst into tears again. Mitchell felt sorry for her, but he was growing tired of the constant weeping and the way Mrs Beaufort was doing nothing to help herself. However, he summoned up the patience to wait, feeling his son's hand creep into his and giving it a quick squeeze.

'I'm sorry. I can't s-stop crying.' She mopped her eyes again, but another tear escaped almost immediately. 'How is Isabella?'

'She's well. She and her husband are going to open up a shop in Fremantle.' It seemed so obvious that when Mrs Beaufort didn't say it, he did. 'If she's your only surviving relative, you should go to her. She'll help you until you get on your feet again. Perhaps you can get a job as a housekeeper – or something?'

'How can I go there? I've no money to pay the steamer fares.' She looked at him hopefully.

He didn't offer to pay her fare or even to lend her the money. 'We'll go and see your husband's lawyer and tell him about Parker. I'm sure we can persuade him to give you the money to pay for a passage to the Swan River Colony for yourself and your daughter.'

'Do you really think so?'

'Yes, I do,' he said firmly. She was such a weak reed.

He asked a neighbour to tell the police where they were if they came back, then set off with Mrs Beaufort, going to his lodgings first to change into clean clothes. On the way they passed a draper's shop, which sold children's clothes, and he led the way inside to see if there was anything that fitted his son, whose ragged clothing was a disgrace.

To his relief there was suitable clothing available and when the young man serving him stared at the blood on his own clothes, he said curtly, 'His mother was killed in an accident yesterday. My son needs everything new.'

'Yes, sir.' The man became very enthusiastic. 'You'll need drawers, undervests, shirts, nightshirts, a cap, everything.'

'Yes. And I'd be obliged if you'll throw away the things he's wearing.'

'I should think so, sir.'

With Christopher looking more respectable, they left the rest of their parcels to be delivered later and went on to Mitchell's lodging house.

His landlady greeted him very stiffly, staring suspiciously at Mrs Beaufort and the two children. 'You didn't come back last night, Mr Nash.'

When he explained, she threw up her hands in horror. 'I'm sorry, but I can't have such scandal in my house. I'd be obliged if you'd pack your luggage and leave.'

He stared at her narrow, mean face. 'Not until I've had a wash and shave, and then you must give me my money back for the day I've paid you in advance. What's more, as you're a Christian woman, I expect you to find somewhere for Mrs Beaufort to sit and wait for me with her little daughter. Or do you expect a widow and her child to stand out in the rain?'

Mrs Beaufort flourished a handkerchief and sobbed.

'My son will be coming up to the bedroom with me,' he added.

His landlady hesitated then shrugged and said, 'I'll get you your money, sir. Please hurry up so that I can clean that bedroom. You can wait in the hall, Mrs – um.'

'Beaufort.'

She turned to leave them.

'Don't forget the hot water,' he called after the land-lady. 'I can't go out without shaving.'

As they walked on towards the lawyer's rooms, he said to Mrs Beaufort, 'I'd be obliged if you would let me and Christopher sleep in your sitting room until we can make arrangements to leave Sydney. We may be able to find some unstained mattresses next door.'

'Oh, yes. Please stay. I don't know what I'd do without you.'

The lawyer's clerk stared down his nose at them, but when it was disclosed that his master's client had been murdered, he asked them in a hushed voice to please take a seat.

As soon as Mr Sherwood was free, they were shown in.

Again, Louisa played quietly on the floor and Christopher stayed by his father's side. Mitchell waited for Mrs Beaufort to explain, but she turned to look at him, so with a sigh he did it for her.

The news rendered the lawyer speechless. He opened and shut his mouth a few times before he managed to find any words. 'Shocking! Dreadful! I shall of course pay for the funeral. I'm sure my clients will want me to do that for their son. I've no instructions to look after his wife, however. Indeed, my clients haven't mentioned her in their replies to my letters, though I did inform them about his marriage.'

'There's his daughter as well. Don't forget the child.

Mr Beaufort's parents will surely be interested in their granddaughter's welfare? It's not my responsibility to look after her, so I'll have to leave Mrs Beaufort here with you today unless you can find the money for the fares to take her to her relatives.'

She began to sob even more loudly and the lawyer looked at her in irritation.

Mitchell waited but Mr Sherwood said nothing, so he added, 'I'm prepared to escort them to the Swan River Colony, because that's where I'm going now. I know where her relative lives, but I can't afford to pay for the fares for Mrs Beaufort and her daughter.'

The lawyer sighed. 'I suppose I'll have to do that. As you say, the child is my clients' granddaughter. I'll get my clerk to book passage for them on the next steamer.'

'Get him to book another cabin for me and my son while he's at it. As soon as I hear from you, I'll go and pay the shipping company for the cabin my son and I will be using.'

'Where are you staying?'

He hesitated, but couldn't say he'd just been thrown out of his lodgings, or that he was staying with Mrs Beaufort, because it wouldn't look respectable. 'In my late wife's house, which is next door to Mrs Beaufort. I have to clear it out and see her buried.' As he said it, he suddenly decided that if it was at all possible, he'd sleep there tonight. He didn't want anyone thinking he was taking advantage of the widow.

'A very sad business, sir. You have my sympathy. Um – do you have an address in Western Australia?'

'I can give the address of the friends with whom I'll be staying. He's a ship's captain.'

'It'd help for Mrs Beaufort to have a lawyer there. Do you know of one?'

'No. Perhaps one of your colleagues will know someone for you to deal with, since you don't seem to wish to deal directly with the widow.'

'I'm afraid the Beaufort family will only deal through a lawyer.'

'Well, if they're willing to support their son's wife, I'm sure they'll find a way to get money to her there. There are banks in the colony, after all.'

When they got back to the Beaufort house, Mitchell steeled himself to go into the house next door. He found a scowling man with a cap looking round it. 'Who are you?'

'I'm the owner. I heard about what happened and came to check on my property. It's a shocking business, but who's to clear this mess up?'

'You'll have to pay someone to scrub it out but I'll clear my wife's things out or throw away those I can't use.'

'You can pay for the scrubbing too, then.'

He was sick of paying for other people's mistakes and problems, had to conserve his money now for making a new life for Christopher. 'No. I wasn't living here and I didn't rent it. The house is your responsibility. If you don't get it scrubbed, the stain won't be easy to get rid of. My wife left me for the man who went mad, so I'm doing you a favour by even clearing her things out.'

'I'll want the place clear by nightfall.'

'You'll get it clear by the end of the week. I'm sure the rent's been paid till then.' He saw by the man's scowl that he'd guessed correctly. 'This child needs somewhere familiar to sleep after what's happened to him.' He stared back at the man till the other's eyes fell.

'Oh, very well. For the child's sake. But I'll be over every day to make sure you're not damaging anything.'

'Certainly.'

When the landlord had left, Mitchell began to walk round the house, shuddering at the dark brown patch of dried blood in the kitchen and the broken chair lying in the corner. A knock on the front door interrupted his bleak thoughts and with a sigh he went to see who was there.

It was the woman who'd scrubbed out Mrs Beaufort's house.

'I'm Janey Thorpe, sir. I scrubbed out the house next door yesterday. I was wondering if you wanted any scrubbing done here? Only I'd be glad to earn a bit more money because my husband's sick.'

'I'm glad you came. Come in! You can not only scrub out the kitchen for the landlord, you can help me clear out my wife's things and you can take anything I can't sell. Gresham's things, too. You can have all of those. I don't want to touch them.'

She looked at him as if he'd grown a halo. 'Oh, sir! That'll be such a help.'

He went to tell Mrs Beaufort what he was doing and suggest she begin packing her own and her daughter's things.

'What about Parker's things?'

'We can sell them to a second-hand dealer.'

She pulled a face at that and he added sharply, 'You're going to need every penny you can get, so we'll sell everything we can, from your house and mine.'

'You're a hard man.'

'I'm a practical man. I suggest you start going through everything in this house, checking what can be sold. And do it quickly.'

He didn't wait for an answer, but took Christopher next door with him, touched when the boy took hold of his hand as they re-entered the house. He wished the boy would speak, but had decided not to press him to do so.

'Why don't you go up to your bedroom and sort out your old clothes, Christopher? That'd be a big help to me. Pile up any clothes that are too small for you on the floor and Mrs Thorpe will take them away.'

The boy hesitated.

'I won't go away without you, I promise.'

His son stared at him, seemed to find something reassuring in what he saw and ran upstairs.

Mitchell took a deep breath and followed. He started to go through the things in his late wife's room. She hadn't had much and nothing new, that he could see. He handled her clothes with distaste. As for Gresham's things, all he did was shake the pockets. When he found a little money, he had no hesitation in keeping it for himself. He threw the clothes on the ground afterwards.

As he was finishing, Mrs Thorpe came upstairs to say, 'I've done the kitchen, sir, and it's drying nicely. Are you going to sleep here tonight?'

'Yes. The bed was untouched, after all.'

'Then I'll put clean sheets on, shall I?'

'Yes. I'm piling up Gresham's clothes near the door. You can take them all. Sell them, do whatever you want with them. Whatever's left after I go is yours too, if you'll come in every day to cook and clean for us until then.' He was beginning to rethink throwing things away. Pots and pans weren't worth taking, but Gresham had good bedlinen, which wouldn't take up a lot of space and he'd already seen a trunk upstairs in the attic. Maybe the table linen would also be worth keeping. After all, Mitchell would need to set up home in Western Australia, as well as start a new business.

He slept well that night, lying in Gresham's bed with Christopher by his side. And woke to smile at his son's peacefully sleeping face.

Things would get better now. Surely they would?

Mitchell stared at the pile of baggage that Alice had got ready. 'What on earth is all this?'

'You said I could take what I needed.'

'Not that much or we'll have to pay extra to have it shipped. I told you that already.'

'It's all I have in the world, and there are Louisa's things too.'

She began to weep – again – and he gritted his teeth

because he'd already discovered that if he shouted at her, she only wept more loudly.

'How can you ask me to throw any of it away? And how do I know what I'll need in the Swan River Colony?'

'Do you have the money to pay for extra baggage? Because I don't.'

She fell silent, scowling at him like a naughty child who had been reprimanded. Then she brightened up. 'If Isabella's husband has a shop, he'll be able to repay you if you lend me the money.'

'No. He doesn't have much money. He's only just starting up.' Mitchell decided to go through her luggage himself, but the thought of dealing with her under-clothing embarrassed him. 'Stay there and keep an eye on Christopher.'

His son looked at him pleadingly.

'Not this time, son. I have to hurry.'

He walked out of the door and hurried along to where Mrs Thorpe lived. 'I need your help to sort out Mrs Beaufort's luggage. We may have to work all night, but I'll pay you sixpence an hour.'

Her face brightened and she turned to her oldest, a sensible lass who looked just like her mother. 'Get the kids to bed and see to your father. I'll be back by morning.'

As they walked along the street, he said, 'Mrs Beaufort can only take one trunk and two bags on the ship, otherwise she'll have to pay extra. I need a woman to go through her luggage and sort out what's worth taking. You can have anything we have to leave behind. I trust you to make sure she keeps the best of what she owns.'

She gave him an earnest look. 'Thank you, Mr Nash. You've been good to me and I won't try to cheat you.'

'We'll have to be very strict with her.' The words burst out before he could stop them. 'She's such a fool.'

Mrs Thorpe smiled knowingly but didn't comment on that.

It took them four hours to go through Alice's luggage and he was amazed at the ragged items it contained. What it didn't contain, however, was anything painted or drawn by her husband. He went up to the studio and studied the paintings. They were, as she'd said, very amateurish. But there was one which was better than most, plus two sketches of little Louisa which were excellent, and one of Alice which caught her pretty foolishness exactly.

He'd told the lawyer to send someone to pick up the rest of Parker Beaufort's art works in case his family wanted them, but he removed the three sketches and the painting, and took them downstairs again. 'We need to fit these in.'

Mrs Beaufort scowled at them. 'I'm not taking any of his drawings or paintings. It was them that dragged us down.'

'And if his family ever come to see their grand-daughter, how are you going to explain that she has nothing of his? How are you going to explain to *her* when she grows up that you kept nothing of her father's for her?'

She stared at him, biting her lip. 'But I'll have to leave some more of my own clothes behind to fit them in.'

'Then leave them. This is important.'

Behind her, Mrs Thorpe shook her head and continued to go through the clothing, bedding and other items. Alice had at first tried to stop them doing this, but now she simply sat and glowered, refusing to 'throw things away' and leaving all the repacking to Mrs Thorpe and Mitchell.

Dear God, how was he to bite his tongue for another two or three weeks?

14

Bram and Isabella spent a long time on their first advertisement, which they planned to place in the *Perth Gazette* and *Western Australian Times* on the second Friday in September. It took a lot of discussing, arguing and scribbling down of ideas, until in the end they both admitted they could think of no way to improve the advertisement.

They worked hard on preparing the shop itself, arguing over that, too, mostly amicably.

'We need to lay a wooden floor in the shed,' Isabella insisted. 'Ladies won't want to walk on the bare ground, especially when it rains, and it won't make a good impression on better-class customers, those with the most money to spend.'

'Can't we start as we are and do the floor later?' Bram protested. 'We're running through the money so quickly and it's not even our property. It's Conn's.'

'He's too far away to consult about details and besides, he said he had absolute confidence in you.'

'I wish I felt the same.' He stared round. 'So much is depending on this, Isabella. I wake in the night sometimes, worrying. And it's costing more than I'd expected.'

'Whose idea was it to open a Bazaar?'

He shrugged.

'Yours. And it's a very good idea, too.' She took hold of his hands, standing in front of him, smiling slightly. 'I have every confidence in you, Bram.'

He clutched her hands convulsively. 'I couldn't bear it if I let you down. You deserve a better life and—'

She let go and set her hands on her hips. 'Are we back to me being a lady and you a peasant again?'

He could feel himself flushing. 'Well, it's the truth.'

'We're husband and wife, partners in every way, wasn't that what you said to Conn on his last visit? Didn't you mean it?'

'Of course I did.'

'Then stop going on about me being a lady. We must work together, make sure we don't let each other down. Anyway, I've watched you dealing with people who have things to sell. You handle them beautifully, even though some of them have ridiculous ideas about what their goods are worth. I've watched you come up with ideas for how to set out the Bazaar, too, good ideas, things I'd not have thought of. And I'll watch you become rich one day, I'm quite sure of that.'

'Ah, you're a darling, you are.' He grabbed her and gave her a long, lingering kiss, then set her away from him and took a deep breath. 'That'll have to keep me going till tonight.'

She blushed and tried to gather her thoughts. She hadn't expected to feel like this about him. 'Yes, right. Now . . . let's get back to this floor. It's important to make a good first impression. Xiu Mei used to spend a lot of time arranging and re-arranging her silks, so that they'd catch the eye, and I'm sure the beauty of her displays brought people into the shop.'

He threw up his hands. 'Even if we wanted to put in a floor, we haven't got the ship's carpenter to help us now. Dougal's delayed his departure but he'll be leaving in a day or two. There's a shortage of skilled men in the colony. Who's going to make the floor for us? I'm not skilled enough.'

'We'll find someone.'

'In the meantime, thank goodness for the livery stable!' he muttered. 'And for your careful ways. We're living on what it brings in, even with part of the money set aside for Conn. So we'd better—'

There was a knock on the front door.

'I'll get it,' he said. 'You put the kettle on. I'm in desperate need of a cup of tea.'

'When are you not?' She went into the tiny kitchen, intending to get the fire burning up to boil the kettle, but spun round as he shouted, 'Isabella! Come here!'

She went running, only to stop short as she saw who was standing there. '*Alice!* Alice, you're alive!' She burst into tears and her cousin did the same, which made the little girl clinging to Alice's hand sob in fright.

It was a few minutes before they could calm down and by that time, Bram had shepherded them into the parlour, together with their travelling companions. As the mother continued to weep, he picked up the little girl, shushing her and rocking her to and fro, and she was soon smiling shyly at him.

When Isabella had calmed down somewhat, she noticed the man and boy standing behind her husband.

'I'm sorry to ignore you, Mr Nash. I've been so worried about my cousin.'

'It's understandable.'

'Alice, this is my husband, Bram.'

'I'm pleased to meet you. And I haven't introduced my daughter, Louisa. Darling this is your Auntie Isabella and your Uncle Bram.' Alice looked across at him with a frown. 'She doesn't usually go to strangers.'

He smiled. 'I've younger brothers and sisters, and a whole crew of nephews and nieces, so I'm used to children. Please sit down, Mr Nash. How about we all have a cup of tea? I'll go and put the kettle over the heat.'

He gave the child back to her mother, who immediately put her down an the floor and told her to be good. Before he went into the kitchen, he turned to Mitchell. 'No need to ask who this fine boy is – he has your eyes. So you found your son.'

Mitchell smiled at Christopher. 'I did.'

'You all look tired.'

'It's been a . . . trying journey.' The look he gave Alice made Bram glance at her sharply.

'I'll just go and get that water heating up, then you must tell me how you came to find Isabella's cousin.'

He repeated his question when he returned.

'It's a long story, and rather upsetting, I'm afraid,' Mitchell said.

'Tell us anyway,' Isabella said firmly. She listened in horror and reached for Alice's hand as he explained what had happened.

'We're grateful to you, then, for bringing Mrs Beaufort to us,' Bram said. 'I'll see how that kettle's coming on.'

'I'll come with you,' Mitchell said.

It felt strange, sending two men out to make the tea, but Isabella was still trying to comfort her cousin, who was weeping delicately into a sodden handkerchief. Still, the kitchen was close enough for her to hear most of what they were saying.

Mitchell said to Bram in a voice edged with frustration, 'That woman weeps at the drop of a hat, and she hasn't a practical bone in her body. I'm sorry to bring this burden to you just as you're setting up.'

Alice had obviously heard it too and jerked upright. 'That man has no sympathy for another's troubles, none at all.'

'Well, you're here now, so that doesn't matter,' Isabella said soothingly.

Only when the men brought in the tea tray did Alice brighten up. She waited for her cousin to pour her a cup and made no attempt to help her daughter. It was Bram who took the little girl on his knee and helped her drink some milk.

After he'd made sure his son had something to drink, Mitchell went back to sit on the end of the couch, his long limbs sprawled across the rug.

'We're hoping Mr Beaufort's family will send money to support his wife and child. I've given the lawyer the McBrides' address, because I didn't know anywhere else here, but it'll be months before we know anything and in the meantime—'.

'In the meantime I'm penniless! A pauper!' Alice started to cry again. 'Oh, Isabella, if you won't take us in, we'll be thrown into the poorhouse.'

'Of course we'll take you in. Though you and Louisa will have to share a tiny bedroom, I'm afraid. It's all we have.'

'I always shared a bedroom with *you* before.'

Typical Alice remark. 'Well, I'm a married lady now, so you can't do that.' Isabella looked at her husband and gave him a wry smile. She'd known without asking that he'd let Alice stay. He believed very strongly in family helping one another.

Alice sniffed. 'I'm grateful for your help, Mr Deagan, for myself and my poor, fatherless child.'

'Cousin Bram,' Isabella corrected.

Mitchell had had enough of watching the silly woman pity herself so stood up. 'Right then, if that's settled, we've got two lads waiting outside with a cart containing Mrs Beaufort's luggage. Shall we bring it in?'

Bram went outside with him, but when he saw the large trunk and bags, he shook his head. 'There's no room for that trunk upstairs. The rooms here are all tiny. We'll have to store the luggage in the tack room and bring across only what she needs from day to day.'

'She'll throw a fit or start weeping all over you again.'

'Yes, I've noticed she's a wailer.'

'I don't envy you.'

Bram grinned. 'Oh, I dare say we'll work things out. There are worse things than weeping women.'

'I used to think so. I'm not so sure now. Anyway, we'd better go and see the McBrides, find out if they have a room for Christopher and me.'

'Ah. I happen to know they're fully booked at the moment. Flora came to tea with Isabella only yesterday and was telling us what a large family they have staying.'

'Oh dear. My son and I will have to find somewhere else, then.'

'You can bed down in the stables, if you like. That's not as bad as it sounds. There are cubicles upstairs meant for visiting grooms. They're clean enough, if you don't mind straw bales for a bed.'

'And they'll be cheaper than lodgings, I presume?' Mitchell asked.

'We'll not be charging a friend who's helped the family. Come and look at them before you decide.'

Christopher trailed after them and Mitchell said quickly, 'He doesn't like to be separated from me.'

The cubicles were roughly partitioned on the upper floor of the stables, next to the hay store. They were as clean as the rest of the place now, thanks to Les's efforts.

'We can find you some bales of straw to sleep on, but if you want proper beds you'll have to provide them, and I can't afford to pay for doors, because I'm stretching myself a bit far at the moment. I have to buy some suitable wood and find someone to lay a floor in the shop.'

Mitchell brightened. 'Perhaps we can help one another, then. I've got some skill with wood and I need to start earning money. I could do the floor for you.'

'You know about carpentry?'

'Yes. My father owned a timber yard and he left it to me when he died. I had to sell it to pay for my trip to Australia, but I grew up knowing about wood, not only how to buy and sell it, but how to work with it, thanks to my grandfather, who was a very skilled carpenter. I wasn't officially apprenticed to him, but I might as well have been. He taught me everything he knew, which helped greatly when I was running the yard.'

Bram stared at him in astonishment. 'You'll do the floor for us?'

'Yes. And make a good job of it too, I promise you.'

'You're a godsend, so you are. We've not been able to find anyone we trust to do the work and Isabella won't let me open the Bazaar till it has a floor and looks right.' He shrugged. 'She knows more about buying and selling than I do, but it's fretting me to keep the stock piled up unsold when people here are crying out for goods. There's a shortage of skilled men in the colony, too, you know.'

'Then perhaps I've done the right thing in coming back. I'm thinking of staying here permanently, you see. I want to try to make a new life for Christopher and myself, somewhere away from all the scandal that I lived through when Betsy left me and away from Sydney, which has bad memories for us both.' He cast a worried glance at his son.

Bram stuck out his hand. 'Done, then. We'll house you both for as long as you need, if you do the floor. And I'll pay you a fair wage, too.' The two men shook hands solemnly, then he shouted for Les and asked him to get some bales of hay for their visitors to sleep on tonight.

When they got back to the house, Alice was sitting with her feet up while Isabella fussed over her and Louisa was asleep on the rug. Bram studied his new cousin, eyes narrowed. She didn't look worn out to him. Why was his hard-working wife running round after her?

'You were longer than I expected,' Isabella said. 'Have you found somewhere for Alice's things?'

'What? Oh, those. Yes, they can go in the tack room.'

Alice looked at him indignantly. 'But they'll smell all horsy.'

'Better than leaving them out in the rain,' he said cheerfully.

'Couldn't they go in the shop, since it's not open at the moment?' Isabella suggested.

'No, they couldn't. I've just hired a man to do that floor you've been fussing after.'

'Well, what about the sleeping cubicles over the stables?'

'They're going to be occupied too.' Bram grinned at her and flourished one hand towards Mitchell. 'Meet our new carpenter.'

She looked at him and asked coolly, 'My I ask about your experience, Mr Nash?'

He was surprised that she'd interfere in men's business. 'I've satisfied your husband about that.'

'You never said you were a *carpenter*,' Alice said in a patronising tone.

'Didn't I?' Ignoring her remark, he turned to Bram. 'I'll get our things moved into the sleeping area and see to Mrs Beaufort's at the same time. Christopher, I need your help.'

The son had clearly picked up on his father's feelings, because he scowled at Alice before he left.

Isabella frowned at her husband. 'Are you sure about this?'

'I am. I'll tell you the details later.' From his own acquaintance with weepy women like his new cousin,

Bram reckoned anything they said in front of Alice would become public knowledge almost immediately.

Isabella hesitated, then nodded. 'Come upstairs, Alice, and we'll make up the bed.'

'Just a minute,' Bram said. 'You're welcome to the shelter of our roof, Cousin Alice, but I want to say from the start that you're to be responsible for yourself and your daughter, your washing, the cleaning of your room, everything like that. Isabella might not have told anyone yet, but she's expecting a child and I don't want her getting too tired.'

His wife looked at him, flushing. 'You'd guessed?'

He grinned. 'My mammy had nine of us, and me the eldest. I know what it means when women are sick in the mornings.'

'You have everything, don't you, Bella?' Alice said sourly. 'A husband, home and business, and now a child, while I've lost everything.'

'You've still got your child,' Bram said as mildly as he could manage.

'And you've got us,' Isabella said, shooting him a warning glance.

He watched her take her cousin upstairs. You'd think the woman was an invalid, the way she sighed and drooped, instead of a plump woman not yet thirty. He hadn't taken to her at all, and the thought of her sharing their little house upset him. It'd been grand to have Isabella to himself. Now, that woman would be around every minute of the day, and if he wasn't mistaken, would hang round their necks like a millstone.

He didn't think he was mistaken. He prided himself on being a good judge of character.

But he couldn't refuse to house her. She was family.

Sometimes families could be the very devil, though.

Mitchell got the lads with the handcart to help him upstairs with his trunks and various bags. It was a humble place, but it'd do for the moment. What mattered was that he was starting to earn money, instead of just spending it.

And, if he was not mistaken, he'd made a friend in Bram Deagan. Life without friends was very bleak, as he'd found in the past year.

He chatted to Christopher as they worked together to organise the two tiny sleeping spaces.

'You'll have your own room,' he told the boy.

Christopher looked unhappy at that thought.

'These rooms are so tiny, they only fit one narrow bed in them. Anyway, I'll be so close you'll hear me snoring – and I'll hear you.'

The boy smiled.

There were footsteps on the wooden stairs and Les joined them. 'Anything I can get you, sir?'

'My name's Mitchell.'

Les grinned. 'I've worked for gentlemen most of my life and I can tell one when I see one – sir.'

'I'm not a gentleman now. I'm a carpenter, here to do the floor in the new shop.'

'And were you a carpenter back in England, if I might ask?'

'No. I owned a timber yard, not a big one, but it

brought in a steady living. I hope to set one up here, but while I'm looking round, I need to earn our bread and have a roof over my head.'

'There's one for sale a few streets away.'

'There is? I saw a timber yard, but there was no sign on it.'

'Probably fell off. He's a sloppy devil.'

'You must tell me more about it. For now, we need to settle in. Christopher and I are both tired.'

'How do you like Fremantle, lad?'

Christopher stared at him but didn't answer.

'He had some upsetting experiences in Sydney and he's not saying much at the moment,' Mitchell said hastily.

'Well, in that case, let me show you the cooking area, which you'll be sharing with me. Are you a good cook?'

Mitchell shook his head. 'I haven't the slightest idea about cooking, except to fry up a piece of ham or some eggs.'

'I can show you how to do a few things. I'm not a bad hand at cooking these days.'

Mitchell looked at him speculatively. 'I'll pay for food for all three of us if you'll cook it.'

Les stuck out one hand. 'If you don't mind plain food, it's a bargain.'

Someone shouted from below and he hurried off, calling, 'Coming, sir.'

Mitchell listened to Les arranging to look after the horse of a gentleman from the country. Not until that business was concluded, did he take his son down the rough wooden stairs to inspect the cooking facilities.

'If others can learn to cook, so can I,' he said as

Les came back to join them. 'I can't be worse than my wife was.'

'Your wife's dead?'

'Yes.' Mitchell glanced at Christopher and shook his head slightly, pleased when Les had the wit to stop that line of questioning.

Now that they'd stopped travelling, surely the boy would settle down again, start speaking, even playing like other lads?

Flora arrived at the stables in the afternoon to invite the Deagans to a farewell tea with her brother the next day.

Alice was upstairs, supposed to be arranging her possessions in a wooden box Isabella had found for her in lieu of a chest of drawers, but as there were no noises from the smaller bedroom, it seemed more likely she was having a nap. Dear Alice, Isabella thought. She'd always been a bit lazy, but so kind and good-natured that you couldn't help loving her.

She'd have to find a way for her cousin to contribute to the household, though. She'd been surprised at the steely look on Bram's face when he'd said he wasn't having their visitor placing a burden on his wife. And indeed, Isabella didn't feel as full of energy as usual.

'Have you time for a cup of tea?' she asked her guest.

Flora nodded and joined her in the kitchen, listening attentively while she explained about her cousin. 'You'll have to bring her to take tea with us later, once she's settled in. Tomorrow is partly a business meeting, as we agreed, so I won't invite her then.'

'Have you decided to invest some of your money in trade goods with your brother?'

Flora shuddered visibly. 'No. I can't bear to risk it. It's been so hard to put together even that much. I'm hoping to find a house soon where my friend Jeanie and I can take in lodgers. I'll move out of home when Dougal comes home from this voyage. That'll give me time to collect what I need.'

'Have you told your mother yet?'

'No. She'll have hysterics and try to stop me.'

'You won't be able to hide it from her if you're buying things for your house.'

Flora shrugged. 'She won't notice. She's too busy playing the gracious lady with our lodgers and leaving the work to me. My business will be less generous with guests than she is, I can tell you, and I'll make more money from it.'

Her voice sounded so bitter, Isabella shot her a sympathetic glance, but didn't say anything. She felt sorry for Flora.

When Bram went home for the evening meal, he frowned to see his wife doing everything on her own. 'Where's your cousin? Why isn't she helping you?'

'She's very tired.'

'*Tired!* She's done nothing but let others wait on her for the whole journey. What has she to be tired about?'

'Give her time to settle, Bram. She's just lost her husband.'

'And is she grieving for him? She didn't look like a

grieving widow to me, and that's a bright gown for a widow to wear.'

'She can't afford to buy any mourning clothes.'

'Ah. She has no money at all?'

'None.'

He was silent. 'I could wish she'd found another relative to turn to, then, especially now.'

'There isn't anyone but me. Bram, you will let her stay?'

'I'll not turn a member of the family away, but she's to earn her keep, Isabella. And if you won't keep her in line, then I will.' He put his arms round her. 'You're feeling far more tired than usual, aren't you?'

She sighed and leaned against him. 'I am.'

'Sit down and rest.'

She looked at him in surprise. 'I've a meal to prepare.'

'Go up and rouse your cousin first. She can do that. Is she a good cook? Maybe she can take care of that side of our life? It'd be a big help.'

'She was a terrible cook and lets things burn.'

'Well, we'll just have to get used to burnt food, then, till she learns better. And so will she. You'll have enough to do with the shop and so I'll be telling her.'

It said much for his wife's weariness that she didn't argue, he thought. He'd have to keep an eye on her from now on, he decided. Some women bloomed when they were carrying children, others found it uphill going. He'd hoped there wouldn't be a child yet, but there you were. It was the curse of the Deagans that they produced a rich harvest of children. And he did want children of his own.

But whatever the church said, he was going to be a

bit more careful how he spilled his seed in future. He'd heard other men talking. There were ways to prevent children, not infallible, but still, ways to make children come less often.

He heard murmuring upstairs and it was a while before the two women came down. Isabella was still fussing over her damned cousin and the woman was playing on that.

'We'll have to show you how this stove works,' he said brightly to Alice, 'so you can take the cooking off Isabella's hands. There's a trick to keeping it burning steadily.'

'I'm not good with these Australian stoves,' she said sulkily. 'They go out on me. It'd be better for someone else to do the cooking.'

'There is no one else. Isabella and I are busy with the shop. If you want to eat, you'll have to learn how to cook. And if the stove goes out, you can always light it again, can't you? Don't worry. It's myself will be showing you how, and practice makes perfect.'

Isabella opened her mouth, as if to protest at this brisk way of dealing with her cousin, and Bram gave her a look that made her keep quiet, then turned back to Alice. 'I'm sure you'll agree that we have to look after Isabella. I don't want her losing the baby or falling ill on us.'

Alice pressed her lips together and made a sound that could have been agreement.

'Here, let me show you how the stove works.'

He and Isabella had a short, furious argument in whispers when they went up to bed.

'Ah, stop this, my love. We've never quarrelled before,' he said suddenly into the darkness, reaching for her. 'That makes me feel sad, but I'm not giving up with your cousin. You've not seen me at my most stubborn yet, but I think you're about to do so. I want children with you, want them very much, but most of all I want to keep *you* safe and healthy. You come before the children, whatever the church says about that. And I'm not letting your cousin play on your sympathy and get you waiting on her hand and foot. She's a lazy piece, that one. I can tell it already.'

When Isabella didn't contradict him, he knew he was right. If she'd been her usual self, she'd have continued to fight with him about this, so he guessed she felt worse than she was letting on.

'Don't be too harsh on her,' she said at last.

'Have you ever known me be unkind?'

'No.' Silence then. 'I'm glad about our baby, aren't you? I'd meant to tell you when we were alone.'

'As if I'd not notice. And I'm happier than I can say.' He gathered her close and rained kisses on her face. 'We'll have a family of our own, children to love, but not too many of them, like my Ma had. It wears a woman out. I love you, Isabella Deagan. I know we married for practical reasons, but I do love you.'

There was silence. From her deep breathing, she was asleep. But would she have told him she loved him in return if she'd been awake? Had she even heard what he'd said? He sighed and snuggled up to her.

15

The next day, Bram went with Mitchell to buy some wood and check out the timber yard, which Les, who always heard the gossip first, said was for sale. Bram watched his companion reject some pieces out of hand, hum and ha over others, and gradually pile the planks he considered satisfactory to one side.

The man who owned the timber yard grew sulky. 'You're taking all my best pieces. You'll have to have a share of the others.'

'I've no use for them. I'm surprised you even bought that rubbish.' Mitchell pointed to the pile of rejected pieces.

'There's a shortage of dressed wood in the colony. We have to take what we can get. They're sending the good stuff overseas, because they make more money that way.'

'How do you find your wood?'

'People bring it in to me. Men saw their own timber as they clear it and then sell it to make extra money for their farms.'

'You don't go out and search for timber to buy? Visit timber mills?'

'Haven't got time. And who'd look after this place

if I did? You're new to the colony. You'll soon find out it's not like England. There's no hiring help, the roads are poor, if there are any at all, and there are hardly any settlements of a decent size outside Perth.' He looked round sourly. 'I wish I'd never come here, but the wife would join her brother. She's living with him now in the country, living in comfort she is, while I try to sell this yard. Only no one will buy it.'

'There's no For Sale sign.'

'It fell down.'

'Hmm. Do you have a cart you can lend me to take the wood back?' Mitchell asked. He could see the man was about to say no, so added, 'I'll pay extra.'

'I'll get my son to harness the horse.'

Bram looked on in disgust as a poor, weary gelding was brought out and the cart made ready. 'That horse would do better for proper feeding.'

The lad shrugged and leaned against the cart, watching as Bram and Mitchell loaded the planks on it, not offering to help.

'That's enough wood for this trip!' Bram said.

'He can pull more than that,' the lad protested.

'Well, he's not going to do it for me. I'll have no hand in ill-treating animals.'

They came back for the rest of the wood and as Bram bent to pick up a plank, Mitchell snapped, 'Stop!'

'What's wrong?'

'That fellow's changed some of the planks round.' He went striding off and hauled the loudly protesting owner out of the hut from which he conducted business. 'I didn't pay you for this rubbish. Did you think

I wouldn't notice that you'd changed some of the pieces? That's stealing in my book. Where did you put my wood? If I don't get it back, I'm reporting you to the police for stealing.'

When the second load was in place, the man said sulkily, 'You just try to make a living from wood.'

'I've been doing it all my life,' Mitchell snapped.

'Not in Australia, you haven't.'

As they watched the empty cart leave the livery stables for the final time, Bram said something to Mitchell and got no response. When he looked, his companion was staring into space, clearly thinking hard. 'Will I need to offer you a penny for them? Or will it cost me sixpence?'

'What? Oh, sorry. I was just thinking what a pitiful way that is to run a business. Surely there's plenty of wood in the colony? I saw trees everywhere when I was looking for my son.'

'Plenty of trees, yes, but I'd not be knowing about milled wood. I do know that Dougal sometimes carries sandalwood as a cargo, but that's not milled, just the branches and twigs as gathered. It grows wild here, you know.'

'Hmm. Well, I'd better get started on laying your floor.'

'How quickly can you do it?'

'I could do it in half the time if I had a lad to help me.'

'We'll put up a sign saying "Lad wanted" and they'll be queuing up. I'll pay his wages.'

Mitchell talked to the first few lads who turned up

and rejected them. Most were too weak and one or two seemed slow-witted. Where were all the strong lads, the sort he'd had working for him in England? he wondered.

Just as he was finishing for the day, a man turned up.

'Are you still looking for a lad?'

'Yes. Do you know one?'

'No. But I'll work for my food and a lad's wages.'

'Why would you do that?'

The man shrugged. 'I was a convict. It isn't easy to find work, even after you've served your time. If I worked for you for a while, you could maybe write me a paper saying I'm a hard worker? And I am.'

'Do you know about working with wood?'

'No, sir. But lads don't know, either. And you'd not find anyone more willing to learn than me. Please, sir. Give me a chance.'

'What were you transported for?'

'Stealing.'

He knew there were various reasons for committing this crime. 'What did you steal?'

'Anything I could sell for food. I couldn't bear to see my kids starving.'

Mitchell hesitated.

'I'll not steal from you, sir. I've only myself to look after now and if you give me my food and a few pennies, I can always find a corner to sleep in.'

'Have you heard from your family since you got here?'

'No, sir. My wife can't write and even if she could, who's to pay for a letter to be sent all this way? I'm a ticket of leave man now, so I've to stay near Fremantle and report to the magistrate every month.'

'All right. I'll try you out tomorrow. Get here by eight o'clock. What's your name?'

The man's face brightened. 'Tommy Hawton, sir.'

Les, who'd been standing to one side listening, came up to join them and ask, 'Are you hungry?'

Tommy nodded.

'You can share my food tonight. I've plenty.'

Tears started running down the man's cheeks and Les looked at Mitchell, shaking his head pityingly as he said in a low voice, 'They break men in those places, break their spirits and their bodies too. I should know.' He put his arm round the man's shoulders. 'Come with me, Tommy lad. We'll find you something to eat and a corner to sleep in.'

Mitchell was moved by this kindness from one who had so little to one who had nothing.

His son, who never left his side if he could help it, said suddenly, 'That man was hungry. I used to be hungry, but I've not been hungry since you came for me.'

Mitchell wanted to shout for joy to hear his son's voice, but he didn't want to upset the lad, so said simply, 'And if I have my way, you'll never go hungry again.' Nor would anyone he could help along the way.

Once the guests had left after the farewell tea for Dougal, Mrs McBride said a final tearful goodbye to her son, then went looking for her daughter. In the end she heard a noise above her head and puffed her way up to the attic, standing with one hand on the door frame as she caught her breath. She stared in puzzlement at the pieces of furniture set neatly to one side, a chest of drawers leaning to the left because one stumpy leg was broken, two bed heads and the frames which attached to them and on which the mattresses sat. The canvas webbing of the frame was broken and the wood scratched.

Flora stood up from where she was polishing a small table whose only fault was shabbiness. 'Are you looking for something, Mother?'

'You. I didn't know where you'd got to. What are you doing? I thought we'd agreed to get rid of everything up here.'

'Did you want something, Mother?'

'You. You should have been there to say goodbye to our guests this morning. Such bad manners. What will they think?'

'You were there, Mother. It didn't need two of us to see them out. And they weren't *guests* in that sense, they were lodgers, paying to stay with us.'

'I run a superior establishment and I treat the people who stay here as my guests, and so will you while you're under my roof.'

Suddenly Flora's resentment of years boiled over. It had been simmering for days as her mother reverted to her picky, bullying ways now that Dougal was away. And this was typical. The minute she tried to take some time for herself, her mother came looking for her, demanding help for the silliest of tasks and refusing to listen to any excuses, whether her daughter had other plans or not. 'It's Dougal's roof, not yours, actually. And I was busy.'

'I can't see why you're fiddling about with that rubbish. It's just cluttering up the attic. I'm going to have it all carted away this very day.'

'If you try to have these things removed, I'll leave with them,' Flora said sharply.

Mrs McBride gasped. 'How dare you speak to me like that? What on earth use can you have for such broken bits of furniture?'

Still too angry to keep quiet about her plans, Flora said baldly, 'When Dougal comes back, I'm going to move out and open my own lodging house, so I'll need this furniture to help me get started.'

There was dead silence as her words sank in, then, 'You'll do no such thing, my girl! Your brother won't let you and neither will I, because I need you here.'

'He already knows and approves of my plans. And *you* can't prevent me, Mother. Stop treating me like a girl. I'm a woman, thirty years old, for heaven's sake.'

'You're not married though, and an unmarried lady can't live on her own, not unless she wants people gossiping about her. As for taking in lodgers, that means strange men sleeping in your house. It isn't respectable.'

'I shan't be living on my own. A friend will be living with me. We'll be sharing the duties and keeping each other company.'

Mrs McBride immediately burst into tears, but Flora had been caught that way before. Her mother could turn on tears as easily as anyone else turned on a tap. Going back to her polishing, she left her mother to sob artistically by the door.

When she didn't pay any attention, her mother soon stopped crying and tottered downstairs, muttering, 'Talking to me like that. Who does she think she is? I won't *have* it!'

The next day, Flora came home from shopping to find a cart at the door and her precious furniture being carried out of the house. She walked up to the men doing this and said, 'That's my furniture and if you take it away, it'll be stealing.'

They gaped at her for a moment, then one said, 'But the old lady told us—'

Flora tapped her forehead suggestively. 'She gets a bit forgetful. But I'm not having my things stolen.'

They immediately began unloading the cart, but refused to carry the things inside again, just dumped them and drove off.

Fortunately, Mr Nash came past at that moment and Flora hailed him with relief. 'I'm sorry to trouble you, but could you please help me?' She explained what her mother was doing.

'It sounds to me as if she'll only do it again, once you're out of the house.'

'You're right.' Flora thought furiously. 'Do you think Bram would store these things for me in his shed till I can find a house to rent?'

'I'm sure he would. Do you want me to go and ask him while you stay on guard?'

She nodded, feeling closer to tears than she had for a long time. It was one thing to think of defying her mother, a lot harder to actually do it.

Bram and Mr Nash came back within a few minutes, followed soon afterwards by a man with a cart.

'I'm sorry about your troubles, Miss McBride,' Bram said. 'Is this all?'

'No. There are more things upstairs.'

'We'll take this lot back then return for the rest.'

So she waited again. She could see the curtains twitching, but her mother didn't come out.

When the two men returned, she opened the front door, to find her mother standing in the hall.

'Please leave my house, Mr Nash!' she said sharply.

'It's my brother's house, Mr Nash. Come right in.'

But Flora literally had to push her mother out of the way to let them past. While Mrs McBride fell into screaming hysterics, she took the key out of the front door lock and put it in her pocket. The men were looking to her for guidance. 'Don't worry about my mother. She's a very good actress. Go straight up the stairs to the attic. I'll join you in a moment.'

She paused partway up the stairs to watch and as soon as the audience had gone, Mrs McBride subsided into the occasional sob, accompanied by artistic flourishes of a handkerchief. The two women stared at each other.

'Why are you doing this, Mother?'

'It's you who's causing trouble. You'll regret this, you ungrateful wretch!'

With a sigh, Flora followed the men upstairs. She was relieved to be leaving, if truth be told, had run out of patience with her mother.

When the last of the furniture was carried down,

Mrs McBride came out of her sitting room, stared across the hall at her daughter and said in a chill voice, 'You'd better pack your clothes as well, hadn't you? Unless you care to change your mind? No? Well, I'm not having you living under my roof when you defy me like this. Maybe a time with nowhere to call your own will teach you the value of a good home.'

Bram, who'd stayed in the doorway, let out an angry whoosh of sound, then whispered, 'Go and pack your things, Flora. We'll come back for them and you.'

'I don't have anywhere to go tonight. I was going to look for lodgings tomorrow.'

'Isabella and I will find you a place to sleep till you can get a place of your own, if it's only on our sofa.'

Flora hated to hear the front door close behind him.

'You *will* regret it,' her mother repeated sharply.

Flora didn't even try to reply, but continued steadily up the stairs, hiding how desperately upset she was. She hadn't expected her mother to take things to this extreme, but then, she hadn't openly defied her mother before. She'd always preferred to manage her gently and put up with what she couldn't change. She hated rows and fuss.

But she wasn't letting her mother throw away her furniture. And this only meant she could begin to live her own life sooner. Could she do it, though? Earn her living? She could try. You could only try your best when you attempted new things.

She rushed up to the attic and fetched a portmanteau, flinging things into it pell-mell.

When the men came back she let them in and asked them to carry down a trunk from the attic. She emptied everything in the room into it and as an afterthought, made a bundle of her sheets and blankets.

Bram and Mitchell stood waiting outside her bedroom, then silently carried everything out. As she turned to follow them her mother, who hadn't moved from the far end of the hall, called, 'You'll be back. The world isn't as easy as you seem to think, *especially* for an unmarried woman. But you'll apologise to me on your knees before you come into this house again.'

As Flora moved towards the front door, she felt a shove in her back and stumbled through it as the door was slammed hard behind her. She'd have fallen if Mr Nash hadn't caught her.

'Are you all right, Miss McBride?' he asked gently.

She took a minute to pull herself together, then took a deep breath. 'I will be.'

When they got home, Bram opened the front door. 'I told Isabella about your problem when we brought the other things.'

'I'll try not to trouble you for long. I'm so grateful for your kindness.'

'Well, people have been kind to me in the past.'

He stopped at the door, because the smell of burning was strong. 'Wait here!' He left her outside and went into the house, finding Isabella in the kitchen scraping some blackened lumps from a baking tray.

'Where's your cousin? I thought she was doing the cooking?'

'Alice is lying down. She got a bit upset when she burned the scones.'

He took the tray out of her hands and banged it down on the table. 'I shall be the one getting upset if she doesn't learn to clear up her own messes.'

'It doesn't matter.'

'It does to me.' When Isabella stared at him in surprise, he said gently, 'I never say things I don't mean, and this is very important to me. You're the mistress of this house and your cousin's a temporary guest. You're not here to wait on her. If she continues to burn the food, then we'll buy bread and butter, and manage with that until she does learn to cook properly. She mustn't expect others to do the work for her, *especially* not my wife.'

'Alice isn't very practical.'

'She managed to survive for several years without you, and she had a husband and child to look after. I'd guess she cooked then. She's just plain lazy.' His voice grew gentler. 'Darling, this is very important and I won't change my mind about it.' He put his arm round her shoulders and guided her into the front room.

'Now then, let's think how to help poor Flora McBride. Her mother has thrown her out. Who'd have thought the woman could be so vicious? The trouble is, I don't know where to take Flora. She needs to find a house to rent if she's to set up her business and that's not always easy. Then she needs to get her business going, which is even harder. So, my love – what can we do to help her?'

'You're a dear man.' She thought hard for a moment

or two. 'We can't really have her in the cottage with us. Alice is enough. But what about the little room in the stables, next to the tack room? I know Les is sleeping there at the moment, but I'm sure he won't mind moving up to join Mitchell and Christopher, just as a temporary measure. We can fit a lock on the door so that people stabling their horses can't get into it, and Flora can stay there for the time being. There's even a place to cook out there, so she'll be able to look after herself.'

He beamed at her. 'I can always rely on you to come up with an idea. Let's go and tell her what we can offer. And darling . . . she's very upset.'

'I'm sure she is. But we can't take in anyone else after Flora,' she warned. 'No matter how great their need. That's absolutely the last space we have left.'

'Not unless they're desperate.' He grinned. 'We still have the hayloft, you know.'

Isabella didn't argue. She was finding this a new side to Bram, one she admired. 'Where did you put her furniture?'

'In the lean-to next to the Bazaar. We'll need to put a lock on that door, too.'

'It can't stay there for long. The timber's rotten. Anyone could break in.'

'I'm hoping we can help her find somewhere decent to live. If you'd seen Mrs McBride's sour face, heard how viciously she spoke to her daughter . . . Well, I just couldn't leave Flora to live with that. She said her mother was never as bad while Dougal was at home or in front of their lodgers.'

'Perhaps she saves her worst for when he's away.'

'Could be. And some people become more bitter as they grow older. Now, tell your cousin to clear up her own mess, then come and cheer poor Flora up. She's very upset and her problems are much more important than a few scones.'

When he went outside, he found Flora standing by the cart with shoulders slumped, looking pale and upset. 'We've found you somewhere to stay for a few days. It's not grand, but it'll keep the rain off. Isabella will be out in a minute to help you settle in. I need to go and find Les.' He hesitated. 'Will you be all right?'

She nodded. 'Yes. And thank you.'

As he'd expected, Les was happy to sleep in the upstairs cubicles to help out, so Bram helped him to move his few possessions and take the bedding upstairs. 'It'll be straw to sleep on, I'm afraid, this first night.'

Les shrugged. 'I've had harder beds. Poor Miss McBride. She's a nice lady, always has a pleasant word for you.'

Mitchell came out of his cubicle. 'Anything I can do to help?'

'No. We're all right now. Are you going out?'

'Yes.'

'It's going to rain.'

'I'll be all right.' Mitchell brandished the umbrella at him and turned to his son. 'Now, we've agreed that you'll stay with Les for an hour or two.'

Christopher looked at him, pleading mutely to go with him.

'I need to do some things on my own. You know I'll

come back. I came all the way to Australia to find you, after all, so I'm not going to lose you now.'

Les stepped forward and laid one hand on the lad's shoulder. 'I'm hoping he'll help me set up my new room.'

Bram smiled as he went down the narrow wooden stairs. He was pleased at how Les was turning out. Give someone a chance and they'd usually do the right thing by you. And if they didn't, well, you'd tried, hadn't you?

He'd also been touched at the way Les was looking out for Tommy, so was turning a blind eye to the fact that Tommy was still sleeping in a corner of the stables.

Maybe they'd have other jobs for the poor fellow as things got busier.

16

When Bram went out to the stables, Isabella steeled herself to go upstairs and confront Alice. She found her cousin lying on the bed asleep, with the child sleeping by her side, and felt a surge of indignation. It was one thing to be upset, quite another to take a nap and leave the clearing up to someone else. And Alice had simply piled her dirty washing in a corner, making no attempt even to soak the child's garments. Who was supposed to see to that?

Bram was right. She had to be firm with her cousin right from the start. She and her mother had been too soft with her in the past, feeling sorry for her because she'd lost both her parents suddenly. But in those days there had always been native servants to do the work. Here, there was only Isabella, and her first loyalty was to Bram and her unborn child.

She shook her cousin's shoulder. 'Wake up!'

Alice jerked awake and blinked at her. 'Oh. Why did you wake me? I'm tired and so is Louisa.'

'Leave her to have a nap, then, but *you* need to clear up the mess you made in the kitchen, and after that, we still need some scones baking.'

Her cousin sat up, looking shocked. 'But I burnt the

last lot. You can see how useless I am at baking. You'd do them in a trice.'

'I've other things to keep me busy. And until you learn to cook simple things, we'll just have to get accustomed to burnt offerings, shan't we? Everyone has to pull their weight here. Bram and I have no money to spare for servants.' She pulled Alice upright. 'Hurry up. I have to go out.'

'Where are you going? Can't you stay and show me how to do it?'

'It doesn't take two people to bake a few scones and you know perfectly well how to make them. I've got a friend who's been thrown out of her home and desperately needs my help.'

'Well, we can't fit anyone else into my bedroom!'

Isabella stared at her in shock. 'It's our bedroom and our house, not yours. We could put a pallet on the floor if we had to, and it'd be our choice.' She relented, feeling Alice had had enough shocks for today. 'But as it happens, that won't be necessary. Come on. I haven't got all day.'

'You've turned into a hard woman, Isabella Saunders.'

'Isabella Deagan now. And I've had a hard life since you ran away from home and Mother died.'

'You've still got a husband, though. Mine's dead. What am I going to do now? How am I going to provide for my poor fatherless daughter without a breadwinner?'

'We'll think of some way for you to earn a living and—'

'*Earn* a living? But I—'

Isabella walked out, afraid of giving in, because her cousin was right: she could have half-finished the scones by now if she'd done them herself.

But that wasn't the point. Bram was right. They mustn't let their guest become a burden. Isabella stopped on that thought and smiled. More and more, she was turning to him, relying on his strength and his innate decency. *Handsome is as handsome does*, people said – in which case, he was the most handsome man in the whole world.

Outside, Isabella found Flora looking so wan and shocked that her heart went out to her friend. 'Bram told me what happened. I'm so sorry to keep you waiting! We had a little problem in the kitchen.'

'I'm sorry to have to ask for your help.' Flora's voice wobbled and she sniffed away a tear. 'I shouldn't be burdening you with my troubles. I know you're busy and you've got your cousin, too, but I was desperate, had nowhere to go.' Her mother had been relying on that, she was sure.

'Friends should help one another, so I'm glad Bram brought you to us. Let me show you what we can offer you by way of a room. I'm sorry it's not better but it'll maybe do for a few days till you sort yourself out.' She took her to the small room vacated by Les. 'He's left you the bed frame but we need to find you a mattress.'

'I don't have one.' Her voice wobbled again.

'I've got some ticking up and we can stuff it with straw. We've plenty of that, at least. And we've more than enough space to store your things up in the shed. This room won't hold much, so just keep your more valuable things here.' Isabella paused at the entrance to the room, stepping aside and gesturing for her companion to go inside. She waited while Flora turned round on the spot, inspecting the tiny space, which couldn't have been more than eight feet by ten. 'Are you sure you want to do this?'

Flora squared her shoulders. 'Yes, I am. I'm never going back to live under my mother's control. But I'd like to have left home in a less – upsetting way. Only she was horrible. The things she said . . . No, I'll be all right. I will.'

'I'll go and find that ticking, then.'

Bram came clattering down the stable stairs. 'We'll bring your things in now, Flora, and leave you to arrange them as you please. Tell us which bags you want in your room and which can go in the shed.'

When she'd arranged everything, Flora made herself a mattress by sewing up the ticking, pricking her fingers till they bled on the coarse material. And if tears fell on it, well, no one saw them except herself. With Les's help, she stuffed the new mattress cover with straw, then went out and bought some bread and cheese to make herself an evening meal of sorts. She was determined not to be a burden to the Deagans.

After she'd eaten, she sat alone in the overfilled room and eventually blew out the candle and got into bed. Lying in the darkness on the prickly mattress, she couldn't hold back more tears, even though she took care to weep quietly.

What she was doing would make some people reject

her socially, because she was sure her mother wouldn't keep what had happened to herself and would make it sound worse than it was. But people who'd known her for years would understand, surely?

She wasn't even certain that Jeanie would join her in opening a boarding house now, and she knew she couldn't finance this on her own. Her friend was rather timid and Jeanie's aunt was a close friend of Flora's mother.

It wasn't easy to defy the woman who'd dominated her life for thirty years, but Flora knew she had to carry this through. She'd never have had a chance of happiness if she'd stayed, would always have been an unpaid servant, harried and nagged and never left alone for more than a few minutes.

And if she didn't lead the life of a lady from now on, well she'd survive. She was strong physically and capable, she knew that.

She scrubbed her eyes fiercely on the sheet. She wasn't destitute. Lots of people managed with far less than she had. It was just a matter of time before she found a way to earn her living. There was a shortage of servants in the colony. At worst she could find herself a position in the country for a year or two, and save up more money.

After today, she wasn't going to let herself cry again. She was just going to get on with her new life – whatever it was like.

Beside, once Dougal got back, he'd help her, she was sure. He'd been sympathetic when she talked about her plans. He'd not believe her mother's tales without listening to his sister's side of the matter, surely?

No, only utter desperation would make her go back to live with her mother.

Mitchell strode through the streets, not needing his umbrella yet, though the clouds were gathering fast. He stopped outside the small timber yard he'd bought the wood from. It looked deserted, but there was a thread of smoke coming out of the chimney of a small shack to one side.

He didn't tug the rusty iron bell-pull near the small side gate to let them know they had a customer, but began to wander round the yard, disgusted by the chaos he found. Timber had been dumped anyhow, with no attempt to sort it out or stack it off the ground to continue seasoning.

When he'd finished his tour, he went back to the gate and rang the bell. He had to ring again before the door of the shack opened. The owner came out and slouched across to him, not attempting to hurry. His son was nowhere to be seen.

'Oh, it's you again. More wood?' He flung out one arm. 'Help yourself and ring the bell when you're ready to pay.'

Mitchell could smell drink on his breath and took a quick step sideways to avoid it. 'I'm not here for wood. You spoke of selling this place. I might be interested in buying. How much do you want for it?'

Orrin stared at him in shock and it was a minute before he pulled himself together and named a sum.

Mitchell laughed. 'Either name a reasonable price or I'll find somewhere else to set up. Let's start at half what you suggested. That's more like what it's worth.'

'There's the house and the stock, don't forget, as well as the shed for the horse and cart.'

'We both know your stock is mainly rubbish, your cart needs mending, your shed's nearly falling down and your poor animal is on her last legs. I'll have to restock this place completely with decent wood. Show me the house. If it's sound, I might raise my offer a little.'

The man hesitated. 'It's in a bit of a mess at the moment. My wife's gone to live with her brother in the country, you see.'

'The yard's in a mess too. It's the house itself I want to look at, not your ornaments.'

He followed Orrin inside, not saying anything about the sour smell or the filthy conditions. It was tiny, two bedrooms and a living area which was also the kitchen. There wasn't even a proper scullery.

'Let's go outside again. The air is fresher there. What's in that shed?'

Without a word, Orrin led him across to a shed that had slats missing from the sides and looked ready to fall down in the next high wind. Inside were tools, none of them stored properly and a filthy stall from which the mare turned a lacklustre eye on him. It upset Mitchell to see ungreased blades rusting and saws lying on the ground.

'I could sell you the tools as well,' Orrin offered.

Mitchell picked one or two up to study the quality. 'They're not worth much, but I'll pay you ten pounds for the lot.'

They bartered for a while, then agreed to a price. Orrin's pudgy face brightened.

'I'll have my lawyer draw up a contract.'

The other man's smile vanished. 'I usually do business on a handshake.'

'I don't. I'll go and check that you're the owner of the land first, then get a lawyer to draw up a bill of sale.'

'You're a hard man.'

'No, just a careful one. And I checked what's in the yard before I spoke to you, so don't try to take any of the wood away. You must shut your gates to business now and we'll make a list of the tools that you can sign as part of our agreement.' The tools were good enough to give him a start and he'd gradually replace them with better ones.

He hoped he was doing the right thing. The timber yard was run down and he still had to find a timber mill or two outside the town, places which would supply him with decent wood not this rubbishy stuff. But the yard was in a good position with regard to a growing town which had a lot of wooden buildings.

He'd not only visit timber mills in the country, but would see if he could find landowners prepared to sell a few really large trees here and there, to give him bigger pieces of wood that he could set aside to season, then sell separately. He'd have a lot to do.

As long as Orrin proved to be the legal owner, the main problem now was what to do with his son, who still got upset if left for long, even for an hour or two. What was he going to do about Christopher? He needed to go out into the country to find suppliers and would be away for days at a time. He couldn't take the lad with him on a buying trip. Christopher was too little to cope with hard travelling.

Life was like that. Didn't give you easy choices.

Mitchell was now itching to get started, so hurried back to finish the Bazaar floor and tell Bram he'd be away the following morning to go into Perth and check the land he was buying.

A week later Bram surveyed the new floor, which was now varnished. Mitchell had said the planks were made of a hardwood called jarrah, not a wood either of them had seen before coming to Australia. It looked a bit like mahogany, was a pretty dark red colour when varnished and should wear well.

'We might as well use that pile of offcuts on our stove,' he told Mitchell.

'Some of them are worth more than that. Let me have them instead. I'll cart them away and give you half of what I sell them for – well, I will if you can keep them for me for a few days until I take over the timber yard. I'll pay Tommy to help me stack them out of your way for the time being.'

'What can people do with little bits like that?'

Mitchell grinned. 'They need small pieces of wood for all sorts of domestic purposes and I never scorned a few extra pennies.'

'You're a man after my own heart.' Bram walked up and down the Bazaar, admiring the floor. 'You've done this well.'

'I enjoy working with wood.'

'Well, we can get ready to open the shop now, or we can once we've got the stock set out in here. We've been going through our things and planning how to set them out. I'll need to put another advert in the newspaper when we're ready.'

Mitchell hesitated. 'May I make a suggestion?'

'Yes, of course.'

'Don't just open, make it a Grand Opening, with someone cutting a ribbon across the door.'

Bram stared at him open-mouthed, then slowly began to smile. 'Why stop at that? Sure, I'll hire a band and have it march through the town with a banner. People love a show.'

They grinned at one another.

'I wonder what Isabella will say.'

'She'll do whatever you want.'

'Not my Isabella. She has a mind of her own.' Except where her stupid cousin was concerned.

'Will you get other sellers in?'

'I think so. I've had a few enquiries from people who want me to sell their goods, craftsmen of various sorts, or women who sew in their spare time. I'm leaving the women's side of things to Isabella, but we're only taking well-made goods. No shoddy stuff in my Bazaar.'

'The trestle tables are all finished now. I've just waxed the wood, or rather, Tommy has.'

'I'm glad you suggested making them. Till we know how the business goes, we can move them round as needed.' Bram said goodbye and went to find Isabella.

He needed her to come and discuss the counters, help him decide what was needed and when to open.

Mitchell went to ask Tommy if he'd scrub out Orrin's stinking little house. The man's face brightened at the thought of another job. It was touching to see him looking better with each day that passed, standing more proudly, getting colour in his cheeks.

Tommy had said he was a hard worker and he'd told the truth there. Maybe he'd be useful at the yard, too. There was the poor old mare to care for, as well as jobs around the place.

Isabella knew Flora had been to visit her friend Jeanie in order to discuss them opening a boarding house. When she saw her crossing the yard, she went across to see if she'd had any luck. She knocked on the door, but there was no answer. She turned to go away, then decided to risk peeping inside. Something must be wrong.

Flora was sitting on the bed, staring blindly at the wall and didn't seem to have noticed her.

'Are you all right? I did knock.'

'Oh, sorry! I didn't hear you.'

'Something's wrong.'

Flora hesitated, then nodded. 'Jeanie no longer wants to set up a boarding house with me.'

'I'm sorry about that.'

'It seems my mother spoke to her aunt and she said such things! She accused me of being immoral, wept and said how hard she'd tried to keep me on the straight and narrow.'

'I can't believe she'd do that to you!'

'Jeanie's family made such a fuss, threatened to disown her if she associated with me any more, and she daren't go against their wishes. She doesn't even want to speak to me from now on.' Flora blinked her eyes rapidly, but a tear escaped. 'Why is my mother doing this to me?'

'To try to get you back, of course.'

'Well, it's having the opposite effect. I've enough money to last until Dougal comes home. Well, I have as long as you'll let me stay here. He'll help me, I know he will, and he'll tell people my mother's lying.'

'Of course you can stay here, though it's not a very nice place for you to live.'

'It's wonderfully quiet, though.' A horse neighed loudly in the nearby stables just then and she smiled. 'That sort of noise doesn't disturb me. Someone talking nonstop about nothing does.'

'Have you had any luck in finding a house to rent?'

Flora shook her head. 'I thought it'd be easy and there are one or two to let, but I'm a woman on my own, unmarried, not even a widow, so they don't trust me to pay the rent. I have to find a man to guarantee it for me.' She sighed. 'I'm going to look in the newspaper. Maybe there will be a job as a governess, or something I can do till Dougal comes back. I like children.'

There was silence for a minute or two while Isabella tried to think what to say, then Flora said, 'I'm keeping you from your work. I'll be all right, I promise you.'

But Isabella knew her friend wasn't all right.

*   *   *

Mitchell didn't mean to eavesdrop on the two women but he was passing by to go upstairs and couldn't avoid hearing what they were saying. Since the stairs creaked, he waited till they'd finished their conversation to continue. He knew why Flora was staying there and felt sorry for her. Mrs McBride was exactly the sort of woman he detested, fussing over you and yet totally insincere.

No one who had any decency would treat their daughter like that. Fancy saying Flora was immoral! You only had to look at her to see she was decent and honest.

He continued up the stairs, smiling as he heard his son's voice in the distance. Christopher was spending a lot of time with Les and the horses, and he'd started talking to the animals, and to Les.

At the top Mitchell stopped suddenly as a thought struck him. He turned, seeing Mrs Deagan leaving, so walked down and knocked on the half-open door.

Flora came to see who it was.

'Look, I couldn't help overhearing what you were saying as I passed and . . .' He couldn't think of a tactful way to phrase it. 'I know you're looking for somewhere to live and you want to open a boarding house, but in the meantime, I wonder if you would work for me, just temporarily?'

She stared at him blankly for a moment or two, then clapped one shaking hand to her mouth, as if to hold her emotions in. It was a moment before she could speak. 'You're offering me a job?'

'Yes.' He glanced upstairs. 'Could I come into your room, so that we won't be overheard? Voices carry all too clearly up this stairwell.'

It was a small room and she had no chair to offer him, just a creaky old bed.

'I'll stand here by the door. You take the bed, Miss McBride.'

He watched her sit down. She looked weary, her face pale, dark circles under her eyes. A lock of hair had slipped out of the bun at the nape of her neck.

'What is the job?' she asked.

'I don't know what to call it. I'm in desperate need of help with Christopher and it has to be someone who is prepared to be patient with him. I believe you already understand something of what he's gone through during the past year and you've seen how little he speaks.'

'Yes. But he's looking better, even in the few days since you've been back and he's starting to speak. I have no experience as a governess, but I'm willing to try.'

'It'd be good if you could get him reading and writing a little, but what I really need is someone to care for him and play a mother's role while I'm away.'

He explained about buying the run-down timber yard. 'It'd be impossible to take a lad of his age along on a trip scouting for timber. I'd probably be away for a week, perhaps a little longer. I hate the thought of leaving him, but I must start earning money, and if he's with someone I trust, I think he'll be all right.'

'You'd trust me to look after your son?'

'Yes, I would.'

'You hardly know me.'

'I think I know enough about you, and you're a friend of the Deagans, which means a lot. I greatly respect Bram. I thought of asking them to keep an eye on things and help you if necessary.'

'Are you intending to leave him here in the stables?'

'No. I want him to feel he's in his own home, so I'd like to move into the house at the timber yard before I leave. It was in a terrible mess, but I've paid Tommy to clear it out and scrub the walls and floors. Orrin left to join his wife in the country as soon as I'd paid him. I need to find some furniture before we can move in. So . . . I wonder if you could consider living in the house with Christopher while I'm away? I'd pay you a wage and all found.'

She didn't speak, just stared at him with those steady grey eyes, a thoughtful expression on her face.

'You could stay on there afterwards and work as my housekeeper until you find something more suitable. I realise it's quite a menial job, but you'd have your own bedroom, of course. I promise you'd be treated with respect and Christopher and I won't even set foot in your room.'

'You know my mother's spreading gossip about my morals?'

'Yes, but I'd never believe it of you.' He gave her a wry smile. 'You have a very honest face.'

'Thank you for your trust. I'll accept the job willingly, but on one condition.'

'What's that?'

'If Christopher agrees to being left with me. For all I know, he may have taken a dislike to me.'

'I doubt it. But I can ask him. He's helping Les with the horses at the moment.'

'How much would you pay me?'

'I don't know.' He smiled suddenly at how inefficient he was being. 'I've only just thought of offering you the job so haven't given it any consideration.'

'My board and lodgings plus ten shillings a week would be adequate, I think.'

'Is that enough? I'll pay for a scrubbing woman too, of course. I'd not expect you to do that sort of menial work. Or no, Tommy could do that, if you don't mind. He's desperate for any jobs there are.'

They stared at one another and he was the first to speak. 'So, do we have a bargain, Miss McBride?'

'Yes, we do.'

He held out one hand, feeling he needed to do something to mark the occasion, and she shook it.

'Please call me Flora. I'm not very fond of the McBride name at the moment. If Christopher agrees, perhaps you'd take me to see the house? I have some furniture I could use for my room.'

She looked unhappy, not her old brisk self. He hated to see families at war. It hurt so much more when those who should love and care for you acted spitefully and unreasonably.

'I'll go and ask Christopher, but I'm sure he'll be happy about my plans. Then we'll come back and take you to see the house.'

* * *

The boy was dirty but happy, helping Les clean out one of the stalls. When his father called, Christopher ran over to him.

'I helped feed the grey mare, Dad. Les told me what to give her but I did it all by myself.'

'Good. But if you're finished, we'll need to clean you up because I want to show you our new home.'

Some of the boy's sparkle died. 'Are we leaving here?'

'Oh, we're not going far, just to a house of our own a few streets away. You'll still be able to come back and visit Les and the horses.'

He took his son upstairs to wash and change, then they went down and knocked on Flora's door.

She was ready to go, wearing a plain bonnet that didn't flatter her. None of her clothes flattered her, he realised. Was that by her own choice or her mother's?

'I'll tell him about going away when we get to the house,' Mitchell whispered to her as they left the building.

Flora enjoyed the walk, loved to see the boy's eager face as he looked round.

Then they came face to face with her mother and a friend, and had to wait for them to pass before they could turn the corner.

Immediately, Mrs McBride stopped dead, took out a handkerchief and started talking loudly about ungrateful children and the pain of being a mother. The friend put an arm round her and shot an angry glance at Flora. The two older women were still blocking the way.

Flora didn't seem able to move, she felt so humiliated. Then Mitchell took her arm.

'Let me help you past this obstacle, Miss McBride. Christopher, come round this way.' He stepped out into the street and led her round them, ignoring the continuing comments behind them.

As they turned the corner, Flora said, 'Thank you.'

'Are you all right?'

'I was so shocked I couldn't think straight. I didn't think she'd be so unkind in public. I'll cope better next time, I promise you.'

'I'm sure you will. Now, we're nearly there. I told you it wasn't far, Christopher.'

The lad fell in beside them, stealing curious glances at Flora.

Flora decided he was old enough to know the truth, because they were bound to experience such encounters again if she was looking after him. 'The old lady was my mother, Christopher. She doesn't like me.'

'Oh.' In a low voice, he added, 'My stepfather didn't like me. He hit me. Does she hit you?'

'No. But she says unkind things.'

He nodded as if accepting that and didn't ask any more questions.

At the gates of the timber yard, Mitchell stopped to unfasten the padlock. 'It's very run down, but I shall put that right. First I have to acquire stocks of good quality wood. What's here is mostly rubbish.'

He unlocked the gate and led the way across to the cottage.

Inside, Flora looked round. It was certainly clean now, but still damp from the scrubbing. 'You should light a fire to dry it out.'

'I don't like to leave a fire untended.'

'For the price of a meal or two, Tommy will be willing to watch the fire, I'm sure,' she said quietly. 'You do need to dry it thoroughly. He was over-enthusiastic in his use of water.'

'I'll arrange that.' He gestured. 'This would be your room.' Both bedrooms opened out of the kitchen and living area, but this was the smaller one.

She moved across to stare at it then step inside. Not much bigger than the one she had now at the stables, but better finished and with a proper window.

'It's very small, I know, but Christopher and I would need to share the larger one.'

She looked at the boy and then back at Mitchell. 'Why don't you show Christopher round the yard while I work out what we'll need?'

When they'd gone she sighed. Living here would lend fuel to the gossip, but she'd just have to face that. Not many people would be interested in her doings anyway, once the fuss about her leaving home had died down.

She was glad about the job. It'd give her a way of supporting herself until Dougal came home, and she could even save money. That was what mattered most, having money to supply her needs. She couldn't open a boarding house without spending quite a lot.

She must live very frugally from now on.

* * *

Mitchell walked across to the ramshackle shed and said abruptly, 'I have to go away for a few days, son, and I shall need to leave you behind.'

He saw that the boy had that rigid look back on his face and put an arm round him. 'It's just for a few days. Miss McBride has agreed to look after you while I'm away, but only if that's all right with you.'

'I could stay with Les.'

'I'd like us to have our own home now. And Miss McBride's mother has thrown her out of their home, so she has nowhere else to go.'

'Oh.'

He waited a minute, then asked, 'So, will you stay here with her, Christopher? I have to set up our business.'

The boy shrugged.

'Good lad.' He squeezed his son's shoulder and then turned to go back to the house.

Just then a man came through the open gates. 'Have you seen Orrin? I need some rough timber for fencing.'

'I'm the new owner. I'm not really open at the moment, but if you're quick, I'll sell you what you need at a good price. I want to clear out this wood and stock some better quality timber.'

'You're right about the quality. I only come here for fencing and firewood.'

'Come again in a few weeks' time and I think you'll be pleasantly surprised.'

After a short discussion the men agreed to a price, which Mitchell had deliberately made just a little cheaper than what he'd seen elsewhere. He helped load the timber on a cart, then watched the man drive off.

Satisfied customers brought you more business. He hoped the man would indeed come back, if only out of curiosity.

'We need a sign,' he told Christopher. 'Nash's Timber Yard. No, Nash and Son. One day, you'll be able to work here with me, as I did with my father in England.'

Christopher nodded, but the news of his father's trip had reduced him to monosyllables. Damn Gresham! Mitchell hoped he was roasting in hell.

17

Bram and Isabella began the exciting task of setting out the goods in the Bazaar, leaving space for the people who'd responded to their first advertisement and wished to sell their own goods there. They'd agreed that anything they accepted for sale would have to be of high quality, whether the items being sold were large or small, or even if they were second-hand, like the furniture.

'Good quality and good value,' Bram said firmly. 'We don't want the place to look shabby.'

He stared round the refurbished shed. 'We own more things than I'd remembered.' He wished his family could see the piles set out and the boxes still waiting to be unpacked. They'd think he was rich. He turned to look at his wife. He was rich, in the way that mattered most to him.

Isabella smiled and linked her arm in his. 'We must bring our trunks across from the house and lock up the lengths of silk in them, for protection against roof leaks or mice, or spiders or whatever tries to creep into the shed. I love the smell of the sandalwood linings.'

'They're supposed to keep insects away. Do you think they do?'

'I hope so. We'll have a separate area built for the silks once we get going. I'm sure we'll do well with them.'

He soon found she had an instinctive understanding of how to use the space and he let her make the final decisions about where to put things. After the first day she decided to draw up a plan.

When they finished for the day, a sulky Alice served them with another of her scorched offerings for the evening meal, and would have laid the worst piece of burnt meat on Isabella's plate.

Angry, Bram swapped the plates round. 'You burnt it, you eat it.'

Alice burst into tears and would have rushed from the room but he grabbed her by the shoulder. 'Sit down!' he ordered in his loudest voice and she looked at him in shock at this treatment. 'You're not a child. Face up to what you've done and do better next time.'

Little Louisa looked from one to the other, shrinking away from the loud voices, but not crying as he'd expected her to do. That made him wonder how many arguments she'd seen her mother involved in during her short life, how much shouting she'd overheard.

He was worried that Isabella didn't eat much, but left her to decide what she could face. One of his sisters had been very sick when she was expecting and he was sorry that Isabella seemed the same. He ate as much of the unappetising piece of lamb as he could force down, and all the boiled potatoes that accompanied it, then went into the kitchen to get himself a slice of bread and jam.

After the meal, Alice just sat there, sighing and fiddling with a bow on her bodice, so he said sharply, 'You can clear the table now and wash the dishes. I made sure the kettle was on the hob when I went into the kitchen, so the hot water should be ready.'

She looked pleadingly at her cousin, but Isabella stared stonily back, so Alice got up and went into the kitchen. She broke two plates as she was washing up.

Bram went storming into the kitchen. 'I'll be keeping note of how much you owe us for breakages. If you make a habit of it, you'll have to sell some of your things to buy new crockery.'

'Isabella wouldn't do such a thing to me.'

'It's not up to Isabella. I'm master in my own house and since I'm quite sure you broke those plates on purpose, I'm taking steps to stop it happening again. Unfair to your cousin, don't you think, to break her crockery? Does she deserve that?'

She flushed and avoided his eyes, muttering, 'It was an accident. You're cruel to me!'

'It wasn't an accident and I'm not cruel. I can't abide lazy folk who expect others to wait on them. And I'm not having *my wife*, who is carrying my child and working hard to set up our Bazaar, waiting on you as well.'

Alice began to sob and would have rushed up the stairs but he barred the way to the stairs. 'Didn't I just tell you that you're not to be running away every time I pull you up about something?' He waited a moment, then said more quietly, 'Finish clearing up and make sure everything's tidy in here.'

'I need to put Louisa to bed.'

'She can wait.'

When he went back into the sitting room, he found the child curled up on the rug in front of the fire and Isabella sitting on the sofa. She looked at him in awe. 'I've never seen you like that, Bram. I didn't know you could be so . . . so masterful.'

'I can do anything that's needed to look after you and my home.'

She stretched out her hand to him and for a moment they simply smiled at one another, not needing words. Then she pulled the hand away. 'I need to work on the plans for the Bazaar. I've been thinking about how we should use the space for a while, but it's the details that need working out now the room itself is ready.'

He sat down opposite her and after fiddling with his newspaper said, 'Do you think it's going to be all right?'

'I'm sure it is.' She looked at him in surprise. 'Do you doubt it?'

'Not in the morning when the sun is shining, but sometimes at night I lie awake and worry. Everything depends on it, you see, and it's the biggest thing I've ever done in my life – bigger than anything I used to hope for in my wildest dreams.' He gave her one of his gentle smiles as he added, 'And you're the best part of it all. What I'm doing is for you and our children, even more than for myself.'

In the kitchen Alice heard every word they said and tears filled her eyes. Why couldn't she have found a husband like Bram Deagan? She was prettier than Isabella. It wasn't fair.

But she didn't dare break any more crockery.

When he went up to the Bazaar early the following morning, before he'd even had breakfast, Bram saw footprints in the damp earth. He frowned. They must have been made during the night because they were on top of his own footprints from when he'd locked up yesterday. One of his boots had a small chip out of the heel which made his prints easy to recognise. The person who'd made these marks had larger feet and was wearing heavy boots. He didn't wear boots like that, nor did Les and Tommy, so who could it have been?

He went to the door and found it had been wrenched open, the padlock hasp torn out of the door frame. He should have heard that. When had it been done? While he was shouting at Alice? Why had Les not heard it? It must be too far away from where both of them slept, that was the only answer.

Sick with dread, he went inside, terrified that someone would have destroyed his beautiful new floor or the trestle tables.

But there were just the muddy footprints, tracking to and fro, and the things they'd unpacked had been disturbed but not damaged. Nor did he think any had been stolen. He had a pretty good memory for the piles and boxes.

Had someone broken in purely to have a look round? Why would they do that?

He went back to the stables and found Les already up and at work. 'Did you go up to the Bazaar last night?'

'No, sir. I'd enough to do down here, with those two horses that came in late.'

Tommy came out from a corner to join them and Bram repeated his question.

'No, sir.'

'It was raining last night, so I let him sleep in a corner,' Les said, his eyes pleading for understanding.

'That's all right. He can sleep there whenever he wants.'

'Did someone go up to the Bazaar?' Les asked.

'Yes. And broke the padlock on the door. I don't think anything's been stolen but they had a good look round. They might come back and take something next time, so I intend to put in better locks. Is Mr Nash up yet?'

'Up and gone out, sir, him and the lad both. They're getting their house ready, building shelves today, I think he said.'

'Would you take a message to him for me, Tommy? Tell him about the break-in and ask if he'd help me make the place more secure. I know he's busy, but we don't want people just walking into the Bazaar any old time they fancy, so it's an urgent job.'

Mitchell came back within the half hour, studied the double doors that formed the main entrance. 'We'd better get a locksmith in.' He went inside and checked the other doors that led out of various parts of the Bazaar. 'We should put in large bolts on the inside of these other doors, top and bottom, maybe even one in the middle as well. The doors are good and strong, except for this one, which should be replaced. It's too flimsy, could easily be kicked in. Once we've done that, you can go round last thing at night and check that all the bolts have been shot, then the front door will be the only entrance you need to lock as you come out. Though there are always windows. People can break those.'

'It makes more noise breaking a window, though.' Bram frowned. 'I think what I really need is a night watchman. Perhaps Tommy could do it.'

Mitchell said 'Ah!' very softly, then, 'I've already offered him a job at my timber yard and a corner of my shed to live in. I hope you don't mind. I thought I'd teach him about wood.'

Bram would never stand in the way of a man bettering himself. 'I'm glad for him. I'll find someone else to do the job.'

'Ask Les. He has a lot of friends now that he's settled. He'll find you someone.'

'When are you and Miss McBride moving into the timber yard?'

'As soon as I can get the place furnished.'

Bram grinned. 'I happen to have some second-hand furniture for sale . . .'

He went into breakfast delighted to have sold some pieces of furniture already. Mitchell hadn't hesitated, but had picked out two beds, a chest of drawers and a table, four chairs that didn't match it but would do. Flora had her own furniture, stored in the other shed.

'And Flora is to choose a few more pieces,' Bram told his wife happily, 'if she thinks they're needed, that is. Les knows someone with a cart who can take everything across for them today.'

Alice dumped a plate in the middle of the table and flounced out to the kitchen again.

He stared at the fried eggs on it. 'These are overcooked. Thank goodness we buy our bread from the baker's!'

'Shh.'

Alice came back to join them carrying the butter dish and a loaf on a board, complete with bread knife. Louisa was clinging to her skirts and she snapped at the child and sat her down hard on a chair. 'Just stay there, will you!'

The child began to cry and Alice yelled, 'Be quiet!'

'Have an egg,' Bram said quietly to his wife.

'No, thank you.'

'Don't you like eggs?'

She looked at him ruefully and glanced at her cousin.

'No, I don't like overcooked eggs, either.' He scowled at Alice and she scowled back.

He forced an egg down but couldn't face a second one. 'I must buy you an egg timer, because what I really like for breakfast, when I can get them, is soft boiled eggs. I'll teach you to do them just so. Now, where's the jam?'

'In the kitchen.'

'Then go and fetch it, please. You should have put it on the table in the first place.'

She breathed deeply, got up and came back with

a dish of jam, which she plonked down in front of him.

He held it out to Isabella. 'I'm sure this will make that bread and butter of yours more appetising. We must buy a lot of jam. We're clearly going to need it.'

Alice began to weep.

Raising his voice, he asked Isabella about the sellers' area and continued talking about that till their guest had stopped weeping. Only then did he turn to her. 'When you've done the shopping, Alice, you can come up and help us unpack our goods in the Bazaar.'

She scowled at him. 'Am I a shopman now, as well?'

'Shop woman, surely?'

'Women don't usually work in general stores, only in shops selling ladies' clothing.'

'They work in markets all the time, and our Bazaar will be like a better-class market.'

Isabella, who was spreading jam on a piece of bread, intervened quickly. 'I shall be working in the shop too, Alice. I thought you'd want to help. You'll meet people that way and I'm sure Louisa will play quietly in a corner while you work. She's not a troublesome child.' When her cousin didn't answer, she said with a slight edge to her voice, 'If the Bazaar doesn't make a success, we'll not be able to support you.'

Bram was glad to see his wife following his lead and being stricter with her cousin. He watched Alice frown and hoped she was thinking things over. Perhaps she was, because after a few moments, she said in a quieter voice that she'd come up to join them later.

He looked at his wife as she hiccupped and covered

her mouth with one hand. 'Are you feeling sick again, Isabella?'

'A bit. It'll pass.'

She never complained, but he'd keep an eye on her and make sure she didn't overdo things. 'I'll give the rest of these eggs to Tommy and Les, then, shall I? Only cook eggs for me next time, Alice. Two eggs, soft-boiled. Oh, and one for yourself if you like eggs.'

She sniffed and said nothing, slathering jam on her bread as if it cost nothing.

What a stupid woman she was! Bram thought. Fancy treating the people who were feeding and housing you to such displays of laziness and sulky bad temper. He didn't think he could face having her in his house for much longer if she didn't change her attitude.

When he'd finished eating, he went round to kiss his wife's cheek. 'I'll be in the Bazaar. Don't come up till you feel better.'

When he'd gone, Isabella turned on her cousin. 'Alice, I'm ashamed of you! Why are you so reluctant to help out?'

Alice burst into tears. 'I don't know. I don't mean to be, but when I see you and Bram so happy together, see all you have, it upsets me.'

'You've been married. Surely you were happy?'

'Not for long. I fell for a baby straight away, and that's no pleasure, as you'll find out. Sickness in the mornings is only the start. You get backaches as you get bigger, then you grow fatter and fatter till you think you'll burst. I hated it. And anyway . . . Parker was useless as a provider. We had a lot of quarrels about money. If his family hadn't sent him some every quarter, we'd have starved. I didn't know that when I married him, but I'd have married him anyway, to escape from the – the situation I was in.'

'Why didn't you tell me that?'

'Because I was ashamed. First I went off with that horrible Renington, believed his lies.' She shuddered visibly as she said his name. 'Then I married a fool. And look at you – you've married a clever man, who'll probably make you a fortune, even if he isn't a gentleman.'

'And he'll share it with you, too. He's generous to a fault, my Bram is. Help us make the Bazaar work, Alice. Just . . . help us in every way you can, and we'll make sure you never want.'

So Alice cried some more, then started to clear the table and do the washing up without being told. By the time she came back to ask what they needed from the shops today, Isabella was feeling much better. It seemed she needed to rest in the mornings, not start work early, and then the sickness went away for the rest of the day.

Any other woman than her cousin would have taken over the kitchen and organised the shopping herself, without having to ask about every detail. Not Alice, Isabella thought with a sigh. Her cousin didn't seem to be able to organise anything, either herself or the house.

The best thing would be for her to find another husband, one with enough money to hire servants to look after her. They were supposed to be short of women in the colony, so perhaps the men here wouldn't be as choosy. And Alice was still pretty, or would be if her eyes weren't reddened from weeping and she made more effort.

Isabella drank another cup of weak tea, sipping it slowly then got ready to go up to the Bazaar. Alice wasn't in the kitchen, neither was her niece, so she went up the stairs. She found Alice giving Louisa some liquid on a spoon, with a small blue bottle standing nearby.

'What are you doing?'

Alice jumped as if she'd been shot. 'Look what you've made me do! I've spilled it now and there's not much left.'

'What is it?'

'Medicine.'

'What for?' She stared at the bottle. She'd seen bottles like that before, when her mother was ill, to dull the pain. 'That's Godfrey's Cordial, isn't it?'

Alice flushed.

'Why are you giving the child laudanum? That stuff is made from opium.' Her father had got addicted to opium and she hated the stuff.

'To keep her quiet. Children can be so noisy they make your head ache.'

Isabella looked at her in horror. 'That's why she eats so little, why she's so lethargic. Alice, it's wrong to give her that, very wrong.'

'Everyone uses it.'

'I never would. And everyone doesn't use it.'

'A lot of people do. Some of my neighbours did in Sydney. That's how I found out about it.' Alice made a huffing sound. 'What do you know about it anyway?'

'Someone tried to get Bram to sell something like Godfrey's Cordial in the Bazaar, a mixture the man had made up himself. But Bram knew what was in it and refused point-blank. I agreed with him.'

'Well, it's all right for you to talk. You've got a husband to help out. I need to keep Louisa quiet or I get the most dreadful headaches.' She turned back to the bottle and began to pour some more into the spoon.

Isabella slapped the spoon out of her hand, sending the sticky liquid scattering over the bedcovers. She snatched the bottle from her cousin. 'You're not using that horrible stuff in my house.'

'Give it back to me this minute.'

'No.'

'You've changed and I blame it on that dreadful husband of yours. You were never like this before.'

'My mother and I were too soft with you before. Don't bring any more of that horrible cordial into my house again.'

She waited but her cousin said nothing else. There was a look in Alice's eyes, though, that of a defiant child. If little Louisa continued to be so lethargic, she'd get Bram to search Isabella's things.

In fact, she'd tell him about this when she went up to the Bazaar. That poor child! What a horrible life she was leading. How must it feel to be drugged all the time? No wonder Louisa was so quiet.

Mitchell rubbed soap on the end of the screw and turned it slowly into the wood with his screwdriver. This wood was very hard and he'd had to use the hand drill to make a hole first. But wood like this would last well, he was sure, and the shelves he'd been making would hold their crockery and foodstuffs.

He turned as someone came in and smiled to see Flora standing there with Christopher beside her.

'They're bringing my furniture soon,' she said. 'We walked ahead to make sure everything was ready.'

'As ready as I can make it for the moment.' He looked round. 'It's not what you're used to.'

'I don't mind it being small. I shall be able to do things my own way and to have quietness when I want.'

He grinned and ruffled his son's hair. 'With this one around?'

Christopher shuffled his feet, but a grin peeped out and with it a stronger resemblance to his father.

'I wondered . . .' She hesitated.

'What?'

'Whether Christopher would like to go to school. He'd make friends of his own age, then.'

Mitchell looked at his son. 'Do you want to go to school?'

The lad shrugged.

'You can read and write well for your age,' Flora said. 'I've been surprised by how good you are.'

He didn't manage to hide a proud expression and managed the longest sentence he'd yet said in her hearing. 'Mother taught me – when *he* wasn't there.'

'She did it well, then.'

Christopher nodded.

Mitchell let the silence ebb around them for a minute or two, then asked, 'Is there a school nearby, Flora?'

'There's the Fremantle Boys' School, but I was thinking of a smaller school for younger children that I know of, run by a lady I'm acquainted with. Christopher isn't used to the rough and tumble of a boys' school. There would be fees to pay, but she's very good with children and if I explain . . . Shall I take Christopher along to meet her?'

Both father and son nodded, then the men arrived with Flora's furniture.

After they'd gone she began to sort out her smaller possessions and Mitchell turned to his son. 'Remember! That room is Miss McBride's private room. You're not to go in there, and I shan't either.'

He nodded.

Flora came to the door of her bedroom, smiling. 'I found this and thought Christopher would like to look at it. It's a book I used to read when I was a child.'

The boy smiled as he took it and managed a 'Thank you'.

The following day, she set off with an excited Christopher, who alternately walked, hopped or skipped beside her. He'd said several things this morning, which had made her and Mitchell exchange pleased glances.

She'd made sure he was neatly dressed, his unruly hair slicked down with water. They stopped outside the house used as a little school, listening to the sounds of children chanting their lengths and measures for a moment, then she knocked on the door.

A maid opened the door and when Flora asked to speak to Miss Marley, showed them into the hall to wait.

Miss Marley came out of the door at the end, gasped at the sight of her visitor and flushed a bright red, taking an involuntary step backwards.

Flora stared at her in surprise. 'I've brought Christopher Nash to meet you. He's just arrived from Sydney and needs to go to school.'

'I – we – don't have any vacancies.' Miss Marley made no attempt to come closer.

Flora knew this wasn't true, because she'd heard the teacher say more than once she could always fit another child in. She nearly turned and left, then pulled herself together. She had to start speaking out for herself. 'Why?'

Miss Marley hesitated, then said, 'Perhaps the boy can wait outside?'

When Christopher had left, Flora said firmly, 'Tell me what's wrong. I'd thought we were friends.'

There was dead silence then, 'You weren't living with Mr Nash then.'

'I'm his housekeeper and nothing more. I'm taking care of Christopher while his father goes to the country on business. The boy's just lost his mother, you see.'

Miss Marley stared at her, looking near to tears. 'She's died recently?'

'Yes. About a month ago.'

'I'm sorry to hear that, but . . . I still can't take him.'

'Who's spreading these lies about me? Other women work as housekeepers. People don't ostracise them.'

'It's – your mother.'

It was a moment before Flora could speak. She couldn't believe her own mother would spread lies about her. 'How can you believe that of me? How *can* you? You've known me for years.'

Miss Marley bowed her head for a moment or two, then looked up and said quietly, 'I don't believe it. But it seems others do – your own mother saying it, you see – and it'd ruin my business if I let you place him here. Other people might – *would* take their children away. I'm sorry, truly sorry.'

'That's not good enough. You call yourself a Christian!' Flora said scornfully. 'Well, next time you're sharing gossip, tell them what I swore on the Bible,' she slapped her hand down hard on the big Bible that always stood on the hall table, making its owner jump. 'I swear by Almighty God that I'm no more than the housekeeper to Mr Nash.'

Without waiting for an answer she left.

'Why didn't she want me to go to the school?' Christopher asked as they walked away from the little school.

'Because my mother has been telling lies about me, saying I'm – not a nice person.'

'Oh.' He looked longingly back at the school, then said so quietly she could barely hear him. 'Mr Gresham said that about me when he hit me.'

'He was wrong. I think you're very nice indeed.'

She put her arm round his shoulders, so furious she couldn't think straight, not only angry at her mother, but at the man who had so hurt this little boy.

As they walked home, she found a new cause to worry. People she'd known all her life passed her with eyes averted and no attempt at a greeting. Some even crossed the street to avoid her. On the way here, she'd thought one acquaintance simply hadn't seen her, but now she couldn't deny the evidence of her own eyes. They were definitely avoiding her.

She kept her head high until they entered the gates of the timber yard, then she couldn't hold back the tears any longer.

Mitchell saw them coming and as they got closer, dropped the piece of wood he was holding and ran across to them. 'What's the matter? Are you hurt?'

As she let out an inarticulate sound and made a dash for the house, he followed. Once inside she covered her face with her hands and sobbed aloud.

'What's wrong?' He tried to take her in his arms and she pushed him away.

'Don't touch me! Don't ever touch me.' She turned her back on him, shoulders shaking.

He looked at Christopher, who had followed them in and was also upset. 'What happened, son?'

'The lady at the school said I couldn't go there. Miss McBride said her mother had been telling lies about her.'

There was a pregnant silence, then Mitchell said harshly, 'I'm sorry, Flora. I didn't think, didn't mean to – but it seems I've ruined your reputation.'

Flora made a huge effort, mopping her eyes and clutching the damp ball of her handkerchief. 'You've done nothing wrong. It's my mother who's ruined me.'

'But living here – that adds fuel to the fire. I shouldn't have asked you to do it.'

'Other housekeepers live in. It's her lies that have

tipped the scales. She wants me back as her unpaid servant, wants me afraid to leave home again. I know how her mind works. But after this, I'd rather *die* than go back. I'm sorry. I need to be alone for a few minutes.'

She went into her bedroom and closed the door quietly then sat down on the bed, not knowing how to cope.

Christopher was frowning. 'Dad – why did people turn away from Miss McBride in the street?'

Mitchell looked at him, aghast. 'They did that?'

'Yes. She pretended not to notice but I saw them. Two old ladies crossed the road when they saw us.'

He knew then that this was even more serious than he'd thought. That mother of Flora's should be taken out and shot like a mad dog, and when the captain came back, Mitchell intended to go and have a serious word with him. But the *Bonny Mary* wasn't due back for a couple of weeks.

In the meantime, the eggs were broken and you couldn't put them back into the shell, so if Flora agreed, he'd still go off on his first buying trip. But he'd make sure he was back within a week and then he'd wait for her brother and demand he control his mother's wickedness.

It was only as he started making a list that it suddenly occurred to him that Christopher was speaking more. At least that was good news.

Later, when Flora came out of her room to prepare their evening meal, she was composed but pale.

Before she started cooking, Mitchell gestured round them. 'If you can manage with the place as it is, I'll leave the day after tomorrow. I need to buy in some decent stocks of wood and find regular suppliers. I don't have unlimited money now that I've bought this place and must start earning as soon as I can.'

She nodded. 'Don't worry. I'll be all right. What else can my mother do to me, after all?'

'Your brother will set things right once he returns.'

'Mud clings,' she said tiredly.

Unfortunately she was right. He decided to have a word with Bram and Isabella before he left. Someone had to keep an eye on her until the captain came back.

18

Les came back to the stables after saying he might know where to find a night watchman for Mr Deagan. He hurried up to the old shed, beaming with pride at being able to help. No, the Bazaar. He must remember to call it that. He stopped in the doorway, amazed at how different it looked now.

Bram looked up from where he was setting out some small bowls and blue and white crockery. 'Did you find me someone?'

'I did, sir. He's coming here in an hour's time so that you can meet him and see if he'll suit. Sim Hollins, he's called. He was a pensioner guard on the ship coming to Australia, and he's a decent sort, not like some. He says he doesn't need much sleep anyway, so the job would suit him just fine.'

'Thank you, Les. What would I do without you?'

Les felt warm inside. It was good to feel needed, to have regular employment and hope for the future. He nearly left it at that, not wanting to spoil the happy mood, but his conscience wouldn't let him. 'Sir . . .'

'Yes?'

'I saw Miss McBride. I think she must have been trying to get Christopher into that little school of Miss

Marley's, but she came away looking upset. Near to tears she was, sir. And . . .'

'Tell me.'

'People were avoiding her, not saying good day, people who must know her because when they saw her, they crossed the street.'

Bram was shocked by this. 'Why would they do that?'

'It's that old besom of a mother of hers, begging your pardon, sir, but she *is* an old besom. She's been spreading rumours about Miss McBride and Mr Nash, bad rumours about the two of them. Even I've heard them.'

'Damn the woman!'

'Nothing we can do about it, sir. It's too late now. No one can stop a rumour once it's started.'

Les left it at that, shaking his head at the ways of the gentry. As if a decent, respectable lady like Miss McBride would behave immorally! He might only be an ex-convict, not even able to read properly, but he knew a lady when he met one and he could recognise a loose woman, too.

That thought brought to mind an image of Mrs Beaufort, who was staying with Mr Deagan. If the rumours had been about her, well, he might have believed them. She had a way of looking at the men when she was doing the shopping in town and she had what a friend of his called 'lay-me-down eyes'.

He was sorry to think like that about a relative of Mrs Deagan, but he'd seen the way Mrs Beaufort behaved for himself.

* * *

Bram went back to the Bazaar to join Isabella, stopping in the doorway to admire yet again how it was looking. People were stopping him in the street now to ask when it would be opening. Well, the advertisement would go into the newspaper shortly and the big sign for over the entrance would be ready tomorrow.

Sellers were turning up, some with goods he gently refused, others with attractive items he was glad to sell on consignment. He'd take ten per cent of the prices he sold their goods for. That seemed fair. He wasn't sure what would sell and what wouldn't. If people's items didn't sell, after a while he'd suggest they try elsewhere, but at least they'd not be out of pocket from paying stall fees. He knew what it was like to be poor, by hell he did, to be scratching for every farthing, however respectable you were.

He nodded to a woman who was setting out her goods in one corner. She'd made some exquisite aprons, lace-edged cuffs and collars, handkerchiefs with embroidered corners, all sorts of small feminine items. Isabella was helping her write the prices on little pieces of card, chatting quietly as they worked.

The poor woman looked tired and hungry, a widow, he'd guess, having difficulty making ends meet. There was a small child standing behind her, thumb in its mouth. He couldn't tell whether it was a boy or girl, only that it didn't have a rosy face because it wasn't getting enough to eat. He knew that look, had seen it in the village back in Ireland. Enough to survive but not enough to thrive, people said. He did hope the woman's needlework would sell.

He'd not tell his wife about Flora's troubles till they went home for the evening. Perhaps they'd be able to think of a way to help her.

A man further along was pulling wooden items out of a wheelbarrow: turned bowls and platters, wooden spoons. What made them special was the carving on them, all done by the seller's father, who was a cripple.

It was surprising what clever people there were, if you looked beyond the end of your nose.

When he turned, he saw Mundy standing in the doorway and wished the fellow would stop hovering round.

'I come to look what you're doing,' he said by way of greeting.

Bram didn't want him hanging round. The former owner was looking even more scruffy, his body giving off a sour, unwashed smell, and a faint aroma of booze – and it not yet noon! Mundy didn't look like a man who had made a decent sum of money from selling his business. 'We're not open yet.'

'You will be soon. Got any jobs going?'

'Why would you need a job? You said you were going back to England.'

'Changed me mind. Don't fancy the snow and cold.'

'Well, I'm sorry, but my wife and I will be doing the selling.'

'They said you needed a night watchman.'

'I've already hired someone.' He hadn't, but he'd rather have kept watch himself than employ a man like this.

Mundy didn't move.

'I'll see you out,' Bram said firmly and started walking towards the door.

After a moment's hesitation, Mundy followed him, hands thrust deep into his pockets, scowling. He walked away without a word of farewell, muttering to himself.

Bram didn't go back inside till the man was out of sight, then he went to ask Les, 'Has Mundy been hanging around?'

'I seen him a few times, standing across the road, staring, but he never come in afore, not that I saw, anyway.'

'Don't let him into the stables. Call me if he won't go away. I don't want him on the premises.'

'I'll keep my eyes open, sir. Ah, here's the man I told you about. Sim, this is Mr Deagan. Mr Deagan, this is Sim Hollins.'

Bram studied the man, who was grey-haired but sturdy, with a good-humoured look to his face. He asked a few questions then took him round the Bazaar.

Sim studied everything carefully, asking about this and that, nodding approval. 'You've made something special of the old sheds, sir.'

'Sure, I hope so.'

'Just one thing, sir. You've not got anything for sounding the alarm, a big bell or a metal triangle, something for the watchman to make a loud noise with.'

'Do you think that's necessary? I thought someone being here would – you know – keep people away.'

'Not always. My older brother did this job back in England and he had a fair few problems with intruders. That's how I know you need to be able to call for help.

And there's another thing. Who would come to help if there was trouble?' He cocked his head and waited for an answer.

'I would. And Les.'

'Better warn the town watch, too, and the constables. The neighbours as well.'

'I'll do that.' Bram was already sure the man was going to be a good employee. He wasn't at all subservient, but was courteous and confident. 'Look, I'm happy to employ you if you're happy to take the job.' He smiled and stuck his hand out.

They shook, then Hollins looked round. 'If your good wife needs any help around the shop, my wife's a sensible soul and would be happy to earn a few shillings here and there. She's clever with money. No need to fear she'd give the wrong change or not add up properly.'

'Send her up to speak to Mrs Deagan. I'm not promising anything, but if things go well, there's definitely a chance that we'll be hiring extra help.'

'Good. Do you want me to start tonight?'

'Definitely. I'll find you something to sound the alarm with before then.'

'In case you can't, I'll bring my bugle for the time being. I think a bell would be best, though, either a handbell or one hung from the rafters – if you can find one, sir.'

'I'll find one.' Bram stuck out his hand and the two men shook on their bargain.

As Sim walked away, it occurred to Bram that he now had two men working for him. That thought made him catch his breath in wonder. But they were good men, and it wouldn't be hard dealing with them. He wouldn't treat them as he'd been treated back in Ireland. He'd never treat anyone that badly.

After Bram had walked Sim to the gate, it occurred to him that there had been no sign of Alice for a while, though she was supposed to be helping up at the Bazaar. He found her sitting inside the house with a pot of tea on the table in front of her – a big pot, half-full still, though when he felt it, the pot was cold. What a waste of tea to make so much for one person! Had no one ever taught her to be careful?

He grabbed the pot and poured the liquid into a saucepan, setting it over the hob. Might as well have a quick cup before he went back to work. Then he turned to deal with her. 'What are you doing sitting round like this, Alice?'

'I was just having a rest. I'm not used to such hard work.'

'Hard work! We have a scrubbing woman coming in twice a week and the washing goes out to be done, so you've not got all that much housework to tire you out. I know you finished the shopping some time ago because I saw you coming back with the basket. Isabella needs your help up at the Bazaar. Go up there now and never mind cooking tea tonight. We'll buy a pie from the baker's.' He'd send Les to buy it, too. Les could get there and back in a quarter of the time Alice took.

He ignored the dirty look she gave him and waited. 'Well?'

She heaved a sigh and got slowly to her feet. 'Louisa

will only get in the way up there. It's not the place for a small child.'

'She's one of the quietest children I've ever seen, even now you've stopped giving her that nasty stuff. And she never seems really hungry.' He stared at Alice. Was it his imagination or did she look faintly guilty? Surely she wasn't still giving the child Godfrey's Cordial. 'Hurry up! We've a lot to do. I'll join you after I've had my cup of tea.'

When she'd gone, he hesitated, feeling guilty about what he was about to do. Going up to her room, he searched it carefully. There was no sign of a blue bottle.

But just as he was about to leave, the sun shone on something, causing a quick flash of colour. He turned back, moving slowly and there the flash was again. It was coming from the top of the rough beam that ran along the upper edge of one wall. He reached up and brought down a bottle, feeling sickened that Alice was still giving this poison to her own child.

What to do? He didn't want her to cause a fuss just before the opening. Then he smiled. Taking the bottle downstairs, he rinsed it out and filled it with a mixture of water and treacle till it looked about the right colour, then set it back where he'd found it.

He finished his cup of tea quickly then went back to the Bazaar. Alice was standing part way along it, with her back to the door, talking earnestly to Isabella. The child was sitting in a corner, looking drowsy.

'Not started work yet, Alice?' he called loudly.

She jumped in shock and turned to scowl at him. 'Can I not chat to my own cousin now?'

'Not when I need you to work,' he said firmly. He didn't wait for an answer, but set her to polishing with beeswax the shelves that now lined one wall. 'Take care. You'll pay for anything you break,' he warned.

She breathed deeply but didn't respond.

He went to unpack more of his Singapore purchases, taking out the tea bowls and smiling at them. He had a fancy to keep a few of them for his own use, so called his wife over. 'Which ones will we keep, Isabella? I've a fancy to drink my tea sometimes like Mr Lee and his family do.'

She reached out to touch one bowl gently. 'These bring back memories, don't they? I miss Xiu Mei and Mr Lee. I even miss Ah Yee snapping out commands.' She picked a bowl up, studied it, then looked at the others, finally choosing some blue and white ones. 'Could I take a couple of the bigger dishes as well? We don't have a lot of crockery.'

'And some of that got broken.'

She chuckled. 'Alice is terrified of you. You should see how carefully she washes the dishes now.'

'Good. So she should be.'

She leaned closer to whisper, 'You and I both know you'd never hurt anyone.'

'Don't tell her that or I'll never be able to keep her in order. As for the dishes, yes, of course you can take what you need.'

He couldn't resist putting his arm round her waist and giving her a quick hug. He looked up in time to catch a wistful look on Alice's face as she watched them. It suddenly occurred to him that what that young woman needed was a man to keep her in order and make her happy. She simply wasn't the sort to live on her own. And it'd better be a man with enough money to hire a servant or two, because Alice was bone idle and you'd never change that.

When she was quiet, she had such an unhappy look on her face. Even though she was a nuisance, he didn't like to see that look on anyone. Only, how did you set about finding someone a husband? He'd have to think about that, and think hard too. If they didn't find someone for her, he'd be lumbered with her and let alone she was the helpless, useless sort, he wanted his wife to himself. Isabella's voice brought him back to the present.

'What were you thinking of, Bram? You suddenly looked very stern.'

'Your damned cousin.'

'I'm sorry. But I couldn't turn her away.'

'That's not your fault. Every family has them, black sheep I mean. Now, put what you want into this basket and I'll carry it down to the house for you.'

He got there just as a man was bringing in a mare for stabling. Good. The proceeds of the livery stable were not quite enough to live on with Alice and the child to feed and provide for, and Conn's share to put aside, so every bit extra helped.

The man came out again, looking up the slope at the refurbished sheds and the new path. 'What's going on up there?'

Bram explained. 'The Bazaar isn't open yet, though. Come back on Saturday to the Grand Opening and you'll be able to buy all sorts of curious and interesting things.'

'I might just do that. My sister's getting married and I need to find her a present.'

'It's the wives who usually choose wedding presents.'

'I've been too busy making my fortune to get married. Have you got a woman up there to advise me?'

Bram took a sudden decision. 'I have. My wife and her cousin are setting out the goods now. Tell you what. I'll show you the Bazaar if you've got a few minutes to spare. It'll be good to get an outsider's view of how we're doing things and if there's anything you want to buy, you can take it now. Just let me put this basket in my house. I'm Bram Deagan, by the way, the owner.'

'Leonard Chawton. I have a farm near York.'

'That's in the country on the other side of Perth, isn't it?'

'Yes. Better land than round here.'

They walked up to the Bazaar together and Bram noticed that Alice perked up when she saw a man come in, then he frowned as he saw the sort of looks she was casting this one's way. He'd never seen that sort of look on her face before. If it meant what he thought it did, then she needed a man sooner than he'd thought.

Bram stopped near to where she was polishing, pretending to admire the dishes set out on the shelves, and saw the two of them looking at each other.

That's the way to do it, he thought. *I'll introduce every blessed man I meet to her, whether he's young or old, starting with this one. She'll do the flirting. Surely one of them will want her? She's pretty enough.*

Aloud he said, 'This is my wife's cousin, Mrs

Beaufort. She's a widow. That's her little daughter over there.'

'We're only just setting out the goods, Mr Chawton,' Alice said, looking up at the newcomer in a languishing way.

Bram felt sickened by her air of blatant invitation. Did she act like this with every eligible stranger?

After he'd seen the Bazaar, Chawton promised to come back and buy his sister's wedding present when the goods were set out, if Alice would help him, then Bram walked him down to the gate.

'I hope you get what you want,' Bram said politely.

'I'm going to speak frankly. What I'm really here for is to find a wife, preferably one who's a good breeder. There aren't a lot of women to choose from in the colony, let alone ladies, and it'd take a long time to get my family in England to send one out, with no guarantee about what she'd be like. Is Mrs Beaufort a grieving widow?'

'Not very. Her husband was – rather a weak fellow, not a good provider.'

Chawton looked him in the eyes. 'I've two other ladies to meet, friends of my new brother-in-law. But I like the looks of your cousin.'

Bram blinked in shock. 'Do you now?'

'Yes. I'm a man who likes his women willing and friendly.'

Bram made a non-committal sound and watched the other stroll off down the street, whistling. He'd never have believed this if he hadn't heard it with his own ears. He knew there were ten men to every woman in the colony, so he supposed this frankness about searching for a wife was the result.

From inside the stables came a low murmur: Les talking to the new horse. He had a way with horses, Les did, treated them more like pets.

Then Bram forgot about Les as he quickly unloaded the dishes and platters from the basket, then walked back up the new crushed limestone path. The thing now was how to make the opening of the Bazaar special, so that people would come out of sheer curiosity. He was looking forward to seeing the big sign he'd ordered go up.

He hoped Dougal would have a quicker trip this time and bring back plenty of trading goods. He'd ordered some more, but not as many as he'd have liked because they were going to be short of money till they started selling goods. All the more reason to get Alice off their backs.

It wasn't till they were getting ready for bed that Bram remembered to mention Flora's troubles.

Isabella stopped getting undressed to stare at him in shock. 'That's terrible! How can a mother do that to her own child?'

'I don't know. The old besom is as selfish as they come. Perhaps she thinks if Flora loses her reputation, she'll not dare do anything but stay close to the house and do as her mother tells her for as long as she's needed.'

'What can we do to help Flora?'

'Not much till Dougal comes back, except deny the rumours, say we don't believe them.'

'Will people believe us?'

He shrugged. 'I don't know. Some won't. We can only do our best.' He stretched and yawned.

'You look tired,' she said. 'You're working too hard.'

'It'll be better once the Bazaar opens. And you're working pretty hard yourself.'

His yawn was infectious and she found herself yawning too. 'I get more tired than usual at the moment.'

'Come and rest, then. We'll just chat quietly till you fall asleep.'

But she was asleep within a minute of lying down beside him. He stared at her in the moonlight, smiling at the way her hand was curled under one cheek. He didn't mind how hard he worked. He wanted to make a good life for Isabella and their children.

Fortune seemed to be smiling on him. He'd not take things for granted, though. Fortune usually needed helping along with a lot of hard work, and that was fine by him.

19

The alarm bell from the Bazaar rang in the middle of the night, carrying clearly through the still air. Bram jerked awake, taking only a few seconds to realise what it was. He rolled out of bed, shrugging into his dressing gown and thrusting his bare feet into his boots. Without waiting to light a lantern, he rushed straight up to the Bazaar, his feet crunching on the path. Its lighter colour guided him through the darkness.

He banged on the entrance door, realising he'd forgotten his key. It was flung open almost immediately by Sim, who had a lantern in his hand.

'What's happened?'

Sim stepped back to let him in, picking up a cudgel leaning against the wall. 'Someone threw a chunk of rock through one of the back windows.'

Bram turned to lock the front door and they hurried to the rear of the Bazaar, where Sim held the lantern to show a mess of broken glass on the ground.

'I saw someone out here, a big man. But the moon hadn't risen yet, so I couldn't make out his face.'

'Light another lantern. I'll go out and check that all's secure.'

'Take my cudgel, sir. I'll use one of these wooden

walking sticks if anyone tries to get in while you're gone.
They've got nice solid handles, with all that carving.'

Bram hesitated. He hated weapons of any sort, but
still, he wasn't a big man and maybe it was sensible to
have something to protect himself with.

He walked round the building, shining the lantern
ahead of him and taking care not to step on the footprints
that were clearly marked in the moist sandy earth.
Someone had moved along one side of the building, had
stood still at one point, judging by the way the footprints
piled up on one another there. He must have been edging
to and fro while he waited. These were similar to the
previous footprints, again made by heavy boots.

He'd guess the intruder had gone first to the main
door, seen Sim inside and moved quietly round the
side. It occurred to Bram that if he had a crushed
limestone or gravel path made all round the building,
no one would be able to approach any part of it silently.

Why had the intruder come again? He hadn't stolen
anything last time, so what was he looking for? Why
had he decided to damage the place?

There was no sign of anyone nearby, so Bram went
back to help Sim finish clearing up. He fetched some
boards out of a rough lean-to shed at the rear of the
building. It was out of sight of the main entrance and
in poor condition, so he was only using it for storage
of unimportant items. Together he and Sim nailed the
boards over the broken window.

All the time his mind picked at the problem. Who
was making a nuisance of himself? Who wished him
harm? The only one who came to mind was Mundy.

'Excuse me, sir. This must have come in with the chunk of rock. I've only just seen it.'

He turned to see Sim holding out a piece of crumpled paper and took it. On it, in capital letters, crudely printed with what looked like a child's wax crayon, were the words:

PAY ME 100 PUND AND YORE SHOP IS SAFE
WOOD BUILDINS BURN EASY

Bram felt sick at the sight of it, and so angry his vision blurred for a few seconds. Money. That's what the person wanted. He saw Sim watching him anxiously. 'You did well, stopped him getting inside.'

'Didn't stop him breaking the window, though.'

'We'll get that mended.'

'Glass isn't easy to find or cheap.'

'I've got some window glass. I was going to sell it, but I'll have to use some of it for the repairs now.'

'Better put wire mesh across the outside, Mr Deagan, in case he tries to chuck more rocks through.'

'Good idea.' More expense, though.

As Bram went back to the house, he saw Les standing in the doorway of the stables, holding a pitchfork. He'd been told to stay there and keep an eye on things, unless they called for help, and he'd done that, thank goodness. They didn't want to leave the stables open to thieves, not with other people's horses in their keeping. Now that Tommy was sleeping at the timber yard, there was only Les there, but luckily he was a light sleeper.

'What's happened, sir?'

'Someone threw a rock through the window – with this wrapped round it.' He held out the message.

Les didn't take the piece of paper. 'I'm not so good with reading. What does it say?'

Bram read out the message without commenting on the need to do that.

Les looked thoughtful. 'Could we maybe put a booby trap or two out at the back each night?'

'I'll see. And of course, I'll inform the town constables.'

His employee made a scoffing sound. 'Them lot. Too busy chatting to people, they are. Never around when you need them. They'd not notice anything unless it hit them between the eyes. We have to depend on ourselves, sir. Only ourselves.'

'It's a bit hard to defend yourself when you don't know who's attacking you.'

Les hesitated, half-opened his mouth then shut it again.

'Are you guessing the same as me? Mundy?'

'I heard his lady friend had run off with most of his money, took the steamer to Sydney. He's a fool, that one.'

'He's a big man, and Sim says the intruder was big. Keep your ear to the ground and let me know if you hear anything else.'

Bram hesitated, because he hated the thought of spending more money, but it had to be done. 'I'll ask Sim if he has a friend who can come and help him, just till the big opening's over. I'd not like anything to spoil that.'

'Better set out some buckets of water and sand, too, just in case.'

Bram made a mental note to buy some buckets then went back to bed. He told Isabella what had happened and they settled down again. He heard her fall asleep but couldn't seem to switch his mind off. He kept going over and over what had happened, trying to work out what to do to protect his property. He wasn't going to let anyone spoil his dream.

He dozed on and off but didn't sleep properly and when dawn began to lighten the room, he got up, leaving Isabella slumbering peacefully.

He turned at the door to look at her fondly. She wasn't only his support in this venture, she was his inspiration.

Flora decided not to be a coward. She wasn't going to cower in the little house in the timber yard for fear of being ostracised. But she didn't want Christopher upsetting again, so left him in Tommy's company. The two seemed to get on well and Tommy was looking a lot better now that he was eating regularly. He was touchingly eager to please them and keep this job.

'Don't let him out of your sight,' she said quietly. 'And don't take the chains off the big gate. We don't want anyone trying to steal Mr Nash's wood.'

'I won't. Will you be all right, Miss?'

She saw the pitying look in his eyes and realised he understood what was going on, so straightened her shoulders. 'Yes, I will. I'm not giving in to this.'

But it was hard to keep a serene expression on your

face when people you'd known for years walked past you as if you didn't exist. Very hard.

She turned the corner on to High Street with a sinking feeling, sure she'd meet even more rejections on this busy shopping street. Almost immediately, she met one of Dougal's fellow captains and his wife. Feeling sick with apprehension, she watched them come closer, expecting them to walk past her . . . But they didn't! They stopped and smiled at her.

'How are you today, Miss McBride?' the man said.

The woman hesitated but her husband nudged her and she said, 'Good morning, Miss McBride. How are you?' But her voice was toneless, as if she was reciting something learned by heart.

Flora decided on utter honesty. 'I'm having a difficult time. Someone is spreading rumours about me, *rumours that are not true*, and I'm being ostracised.' She saw the other woman blush and added, 'I can see you've heard them.'

It was the captain who spoke. 'I must admit I was – surprised. Do you know who's started all this? Your mother says she has no idea but—'

'But what?'

'She did confirm that you'd left home to live with a man.'

At that further proof, Flora decided not to protect her mother any longer. 'I know for a fact that it's she who started the rumours.' They gasped in shock, but she went on doggedly, 'I wanted to leave home and start a boarding house with a friend. My mother wanted me to stay and continue to act as her unpaid servant.

Dougal was quite happy for me to make a life of my own, but he's away at the moment and when we had a quarrel, she threw me out. I went to stay with Mr and Mrs Deagan at first then I took a job as housekeeper to put a roof over my head. That's not the same as leaving home to live with a man.'

'Oh.' The woman relaxed a little.

The captain smiled at her. 'You stick to what you want to do, Miss McBride. My cousin is an absolute martyr to her elderly mother. She's had a miserable life and I'd not wish that on anyone. Besides, your mother isn't all that old and she's certainly not infirm.'

As they were walking away, their voices carried clearly and Flora heard him say to his wife, 'I told you so.'

'Did you believe her?'

'Yes, I did. Absolutely. Didn't you?'

'I think I did. She's never been the flighty type.'

Flora had to stop to calm herself down, because this unexpected support and kindness were as hard to bear as the unkindness had been. As she moved on, she saw Alice Beaufort coming towards her and stopped to say, 'Good morning, Mrs Beaufort.'

Alice hesitated then walked on.

Flora felt indignant. She'd put together enough snatches of conversation she'd overheard when she was staying the livery stables to work out that Alice Beaufort had once run away from home with a man to whom she wasn't married. She turned abruptly on her heel and hurried after the woman.

'Don't you dare treat me like that, Mrs Beaufort, or I'll tell people about *your* background – and what I know about you is the truth. The rumours about me aren't.'

Alice's mouth fell open in an O, and she glanced hastily from side to side. 'I was just – lost in thought. I wasn't avoiding speaking to you.'

'You'd better not.' Flora went on with her shopping then strolled slowly back to the timber yard. She felt weary now, tired of fighting against shadows.

Christopher was hanging over the gate, watching for her, while Tommy was going through the pieces on another of the untidy heaps of sawn wood, sorting them methodically into piles.

'Can we go and see the Bazaar now, Miss McBride? You said we could.' The boy looked at her pleadingly.

'Give me time to put my shopping away and have a cup of tea, then we'll go. You're making good progress on sorting out the wood, Tommy.'

'Mr Nash said I could use some of the warped planks to fill the holes in my hut. Me and that poor old horse get the wind whistling round something terrible.'

'Good idea, though the weather's getting much warmer now. Soon be spring, then we won't get as much rain. And in summer we won't get any. Are you enjoying working here?'

He beamed at her. 'Yes, I am. Mr Nash says he'll teach me about timber if I'm a good worker.'

'Well, you couldn't find anyone who knows as much as he does about wood, so you couldn't get a better teacher.' She was surprised that Mitchell had made that offer. But then, she'd also been surprised at the way Bram had got the best out of Les, who looked a different person to the haggard man who'd been hiding in the stables.

Perhaps Bram and Mitchell could recognise potential – or perhaps it was simple kindness that worked wonders with men who weren't used to being gently treated.

She liked and respected Bram and Mitchell, but neither of them stirred romantic feelings in her. No man had done that since she was nineteen. She put that memory resolutely out of her mind. Her mother had quickly put an end to that budding romance and Flora had wept herself to sleep for weeks. If he'd asked her, she'd have defied her mother and run away with him.

She realised Tommy was looking at her expectantly. 'Oh, sorry. What did you say?'

'I said, I have to go and report to the magistrate today, Miss. I'll do it whenever is most convenient to you.'

'Why not go now? I'll stay here till you get back, then Christopher and I will have our little outing.' She needed a rest before she summoned up her courage to face the world again.

Tommy raised his ragged cap to her, and was off at once, calling over his shoulder, 'I'll be as quick as I can, Miss.'

Isabella studied the new wall shelves and trestle tables, on which all sorts of goods were now set out. She was really pleased with it, with all she and Bram were doing, in fact.

She glanced across to the other side of the room and saw her cousin standing staring into space instead of working. 'Alice! Haven't you finished that polishing yet?'

Her cousin threw her an angry glance. 'You're getting as bad as *him*, nagging me.'

'What do you expect from us? Luxury? Leisure? We can't afford that.'

She turned to look for the child and saw that she'd snuggled down again on a pile of sacking. 'I'm going down to get something ready for luncheon. I'll take Louisa with me, then you won't have to worry about her, so you'll be able to get on with your work.'

Alice shrugged.

Isabella gently roused the little girl and took her down to the cottage, surprised Louisa was still so sleepy all the time.

Bram came in as she was preparing the food.

'Hello, darlin'.' He plonked a kiss on her cheek. 'I've been to see the town constables and let them know about our intruder. Is there some food for me? I'm ravenous.'

'You always are. You've got hollow legs, you have.' She set out bread, butter and cheese, but had to rouse the child again and sit her at the table. Then she went to brew a pot of tea. 'I'm worried about Louisa. She's still sleepy.'

'No wonder.' Bram walked across to tell her in a low voice about finding more of the cordial in Alice's room.

'Oh, no! How terrible. Bram, what are we going to do about my cousin? I've worried about her all these years, but now . . . I don't even like her. She's changed so much.'

'Ah, forget about her for a few moments. Let's eat our food together and take her something to eat up there later. We'll feed the child too.'

'If we can keep her awake long enough.'

'Should we consult a doctor, do you think?'

'Let's see how we go. Alice must have some money of her own if she can buy more bottles of that horrible Godfrey's Cordial. I'll never give it to our children.' She laid one hand on her stomach and he put his hand over hers.

'I wonder if it's a boy or girl.'

'Girl,' she said at once.

He grinned. 'And here was I thinking it was a boy. What'll we call him? Or her?'

They discussed names as they ate, persuading Louisa to eat something, both of them enjoying the time away from Alice.

There was the sound of someone walking up the path and Alice jerked to her feet from the pile of sacking, where she'd been taking a rest, thoughts of the intruder making her suddenly wish Bram or Isabella was here.

A man stopped in the doorway, a tall, burly man, outlined against the sun. Who was he? Her heart began to thud.

He stepped inside and to her relief, once she was able to see his face, she recognised Mr Chawton. He was very-strong and masculine looking. He was neatly, but not fashionably dressed and had his hat in his hand now that he was indoors. Good manners, that. Not a handsome man, though not ugly either.

Well, Renington and Parker had both been good looking and what had that done for her? She should have looked for a strong man like this, a man who could look after her. If she ever married again, that's what she'd do.

Her pulse speeded up as he came closer. It had been a long time since a man had touched her and she missed it. He stopped a short distance away to eye her up and down, smiling as if he liked what he saw. She patted her hair, hoping he did. Finding another husband was the only way she could see out of this slavery.

'Is Mr Deagan here?' he asked.

She smoothed down her skirts, moving in a way that showed off her figure, of which she was still proud, in spite of having borne a child. 'He'll be back soon if you care to wait, Mr Chawton.'

'I'd be delighted to wait in such pleasant company. Perhaps you can show me round in the meantime? I'm looking for a wedding present for my sister.'

She hesitated, unable to prevent herself from scowling round. 'I'm not the best person to do that, Mr Chawton.'

'Oh? Why not?'

He held out his arm to her and she took it, liking the solid strength of him. 'I don't think I was born to be a shopkeeper.'

'What were you born to be?'

'A wife.'

'Not a mother?'

She didn't tell him she found being a mother boring, just smiled and said, 'Doesn't the one follow on from the other? I do have a little daughter.'

'So Mr Deagan said.'

'Louisa's with my cousin Isabella at the moment, but they'll be back soon.'

He patted her hand as it lay on his arm. 'Let's walk round the displays together, then, and you can pretend you're going shopping instead of trying to sell me something. If you see anything that might make a good wedding present for my sister, point it out.'

She stopped at the trunk of silks, which was nearby. 'There are some beautiful bolts of silk in there, which is why it's kept locked. I'm afraid I don't have a key to open it. My cousin Isabella brought them back from Singapore. I'm sure your sister would love a dress length. Any woman would. Does she look like you, have your colouring?'

'Dark hair? Yes. But I prefer red-gold hair, like yours.' He reached out to touch it with one fingertip.

She caught her breath and looked at him. The way he was smiling at her made her feel warm inside. Was it possible? Could he be interested in her? He'd said he was from the country. Was he staying long enough for them to get to know one another?

Letting him do most of the commenting on the various goods offered for sale, she continued to walk by his side, murmuring agreement with what he said, occasionally pointing out something she thought pretty. But he seemed to spend as much time looking at her as at the goods on display, and the looks he continued to give her brought a blush to her cheeks. Those looks had a language of their own, different from the words he was using.

She didn't know whether to be glad or sorry when Isabella and Bram returned, each holding one of Louisa's hands. 'Ah, there you are. Mr Chawton has come to choose a present for his sister and I've been—' She tried to pull away, but he kept hold of her arm by simply grasping her hand tightly with his free hand and she looked at him in surprise.

'Mrs Beaufort has kindly been showing me round, but we haven't yet found a suitable present. Perhaps we could continue and then join you to discuss . . . what we've found?'

Alice saw Isabella throw a puzzled look at Bram. She knew she was blushing even more hotly so avoided her cousin's eyes.

Bram smiled and said, 'Take your time. Isabella and I have a few things to discuss and we'll keep an eye on Louisa for you.'

'Perhaps you should talk to Bram about the present,' Alice murmured to her companion.

'But I'm enjoying talking to you.'

'You are?'

'I'd not have stayed here otherwise. I'm a busy man.'

'What exactly do you do, Mr Chawton?'

'I have a property near York. A farm, you might call it. Are you really interested in cows and sheep?'

She smiled and shook her head.

'I have a large house, servants and a man to manage the farm. My sister has been keeping house for me for the past three years, but she's getting married shortly, so I've come here to find—' he hesitated, then continued, 'a present for her and a wife for myself.'

'Oh. Then we must definitely find you this – present.'

'Yes, I've come to the right place for that. But I'm more interested in finding a wife.'

She felt disappointed. For a few moments she'd hoped he was attracted to her. But he sounded as if he already had a wife in mind. He'd probably want her to help him choose a present for his betrothed, too. She sighed.

He stopped walking. 'Is something wrong?'

'Why do you ask?'

'Because you sighed, Mrs Beaufort. It sounded sad.'

She took a chance. 'I was envying the woman you marry.'

'Don't. There's no need to.' He moved on again, not explaining that remark.

Near the front entrance he stopped again. 'Let's step outside into the sunlight.'

She was puzzled but didn't want to stop talking to him. And anyway, Bram would probably make her scrub the floor once she was free again.

Outside, Mr Chawton pulled her to one side and into his arms in one swift movement. Before she knew what was happening, he'd started kissing her, smothering her squeak of surprise with his lips. She should have pulled away, but his lips were warm, and it had been so very long since anyone had kissed her, so she didn't. She'd always enjoyed kissing.

It was a while before she realised he'd stopped and was smiling down at her.

'You – shouldn't have done that!' she managed, trying and failing to sound outraged.

'How else would I find out if you liked kissing me? Or I liked kissing you? Do you enjoy it when a man beds you, too?'

She felt mesmerised by him, couldn't look away, could only nod at this shocking remark.

'I thought so. Well, Mrs Beaufort, I'm going to be blunt. I'm here to look for a wife and I don't have long to find one, as I have to get back to York. Are you looking for a husband yet or are you still grieving?'

That brought her mind fully alive again. It didn't take more than a minute for her to decide what to say. 'Yes. I am looking for a husband. But I'm penniless.'

He waved one hand. 'I'm not. Will you marry me, then?'

She stared at him in astonishment, unable to say a word.

'Well?'

'Do you – mean that?'

'Oh, yes. I always mean what I say.'

'Are you – comfortably circumstanced? I don't wish to sound mercenary but I hate being poor.'

He threw back his head and laughed. 'Yes. I'm very comfortably circumstanced. And I'm glad you've got the sense to ask me.'

'Then yes, I will marry you.' She smiled. 'But only if you stop calling me Mrs Beaufort and call me Alice.'

'Alice. A pretty name.' He threaded her arm through his and turned round. 'We'd better tell your family, then I'll go and see the local magistrate about getting married quickly.' He looked down at her, frowning now. 'Do you have any better clothes than that?'

She shook her head. 'Not really. Well, only a little better.'

'Then we'll have to get you some other garments made up quickly. I like my wife to look elegant.' He grinned. 'That made your eyes sparkle.'

'I love pretty clothes.'

'I love pretty women.' He gave her a push. 'Go and talk to your cousin while I talk to Deagan.'

Looking flushed, girlish and extremely pretty, Alice walked past Bram, saying, 'Mr Chawton wants to have a word with you.'

He turned to find Chawton standing watching Alice and grinning.

'You cousin and I have decided to get married.'

Bram struggled to find his voice but could only gape at the man in shock.

'I looked at the other two prospects and they were ugly. Not a patch on your cousin.'

'But you don't know her.'

Chawton's smile broadened. 'For what I want from a woman, I don't need to know her well.'

'She has no money and she has a daughter. Are you prepared to take on the child?'

'Not straight away. I want to enjoy my new wife a little first. I wondered if you and your wife would look after the child. Newly-weds should have some time together, don't you think?'

Bram wasn't prepared to answer for Isabella. 'You'll have to ask my wife about looking after Louisa. She'd be the one doing most of it.'

'I'll make it worth your while. I'm not short of money.'

'It's not a question of payment but of time and energy.'

'I'll pay for a maid to help you, then.'

'You sound determined.'

'I am. I'm a man who enjoys a woman in my bed and I'd rather not wait to have a wife shipped out from England.'

'What have you been doing until now?'

Chawton winked. 'I found a willing lady nearby, but she's got herself married again, and I don't want to use whores. Too much risk of disease.'

'Is that sort of need any basis for a marriage?' Bram asked, not pleased by Chawton's attitude.

'It's *my* basis for a marriage.'

'And children?'

'She's proved she's fertile, which puts her a step ahead of a virgin bride, don't you think?'

'From what she's said, she didn't enjoy carrying a child.'

'Once we're married, she'll do as she's told.'

Bram looked at him suspiciously.

'I don't beat or ill-treat women. I can usually get my own way by soft words and presents.' Chawton waited and when Bram said nothing, he added, 'Alice doesn't really need your permission to marry, but I would prefer it to be an amicable arrangement and for you to look after the child for a while.'

'Well, then, we'll ask Isabella if she'll have Louisa for a few weeks.'

'Thanks. And as I said, I'll pay for a maid.'

　　　　　*   *   *

When the engaged couple had gone for a walk, Isabella looked at Bram. 'I can't believe this is happening.'

'No. And with any other woman, I'd be asking them to wait, but quite frankly, my love, your cousin is making both our lives miserable. And anyway, this is the same way she behaved with her other two men. She's impulsive in that way. If it's not Chawton, it'll be someone else. I'd rather she was married than have her getting into trouble without a wedding ring or a breadwinner.'

Isabella shuddered. 'I'd never thought of that.'

'Are you sure about looking after Louisa, though?'

'Oh, yes. And if Mr Chawton is paying for a maid, I even know a girl who'll do it. Sim's granddaughter lives with them. She's thirteen and helps a neighbour sometimes with her children. But Sim's fussy about who he'll let Sally work for. I'm sure he'd be happy for her to come here, though.'

'So we've got a very busy weekend ahead of us. The opening of the Bazaar *and* a wedding.'

20

OPENING SOON

Deagan's Oriental Bazaar

14 Clover Street

Fremantle

A selection of goods will shortly be offered for sale at this new Bazaar. More than a shop, a miniature market full of exciting new goods and also high-quality second-hand furniture and other goods.

Sellers may leave items with us on consignment, or rent space for stalls in our Bazaar.

Discerning buyers will be delighted by our exquisite Oriental goods, arriving regularly from Singapore. These include crockery, perfumes, quilts, table linen, and exclusive dress silks from Mr Lee.

The next day Conn turned up unexpectedly. 'I thought I should be present at the opening of the Bazaar,' he said as he swung off his horse. 'I came a day or two early because I want to have a good look round Fremantle, see whether we might like to live here for part of the time.'

Bram smiled at his old friend. 'You're looking well, and I'm glad you've come. Letters just aren't the same as being here. Besides, the Bazaar is your investment, too.'

'I've only contributed money. It's you who've put in the hard work, you who're the trader. You've also found the goods. No, Bram, you've put in far more than I have and our agreement will reflect that.'

'Are you leaving your horse here?'

'Of course. And I'll stay at the McBrides', as usual, I hope.'

'Ah.'

Conn looked at him, eyes narrowed. 'What does that mean?'

'There's a problem.' He explained about Flora.

'I'll not be staying there, then,' Conn said at once. 'As if Flora would behave like that! I never did like her fussy old mother and it always upsets me when someone is falsely accused.'

They were both silent for a moment or two at that reminder of what had happened to Conn.

'Luckily Dougal will be back soon,' Bram said as the silence went on for too long. 'Then I hope he can sort out Flora's problems once and for all.'

'It's difficult to stop spiteful gossip. It has a way of growing of its own accord, adding lie upon lie.'

'Well, we can only do our best. Look, if you don't mind rough accommodation, you could stay here. Les hasn't bothered to move back to the little room beside the tack store. I'm sure we can find you some suitable bedding, but it'll have to be a straw mattress, I'm afraid.'

'I've had worse. I'm a sound sleeper, so that'll be fine.'

'You'll eat with us, of course.'

'Thank you.'

'And attend Alice's wedding?'

Conn looked at him in surprise. 'Alice is getting married again?'

'Yes.' Bram explained.

Conn gave him a quizzical look. 'Dear me, she's a rather impulsive lady.'

'Yes, very impulsive. She's run away with two men already, and not made good choices at all. But we're hoping it'll be third time lucky. Chawton seems a decent enough sort, with plenty of money, but he runs his life by his physical needs. I wouldn't say it's a love match for him, just a convenience and a way of getting sons. Anyway, that's enough about her. Come and look at our Bazaar.'

Conn walked part way up the slope and stood looking at the Bazaar. 'You've worked wonders with a mess of ramshackle sheds. If this is a sample of what you can do with almost nothing, I'd guess you'll be rich one day.'

Bram couldn't see that. 'I doubt I'll be getting *rich*, but comfortable would be nice. I could bring my family out from Ireland to Australia then and give them a better chance in life.'

Conn smiled. 'You Deagans. You always did stick together, even when you were children. I can ask my brother Kieran about your family next time I write, if you like.'

'I'd be grateful. I worry about them and though I've written to them, I only got a stiff little note from my sister saying they were all well and glad to have your brother at the big house.'

Conn stared up. 'The sign looks good, nice and big: Deagan's Bazaar.'

'Did you want your name on it as well? I can still have it changed, if you like.'

'Good heavens, no. I'm a sleeping partner here.' As they went inside he stopped in amazement. 'It looks ready to open. Look at the shining floor and those shelves and tables full of goods. How did you find so much in such a short time?'

Isabella, who was arranging some of the second-hand items, with the help of Sim's wife, looked up and smiled at Conn. 'Were we supposed to know you were coming, Mr Largan?'

'Call me Conn. Bram and I are such old friends. And no, you didn't know I was coming. When I got Bram's letter, I took a fancy to be here for the opening and Maia said I should come. She thinks Karsten is too young to travel.'

Bram looked round. 'Where's Alice?'

Isabella's expression grew cool. 'Who knows? She went out with Mr Chawton and I've not seen her since.'

'I see she left Louisa with you.' He looked down to

the far end, where the little girl was playing on a blanket with her few toys. 'She seems a bit livelier today.'

'She's not falling asleep all the time, anyway. Do you want me to show you round, Conn, or do you just want to wander?'

'I'd like a tour. I'm surprised at how many goods you've gathered.'

The conversation turned to business, and it was as well, Bram thought. It was so unfair of Alice to leave her child with Isabella, who had enough on her plate.

Later that afternoon, someone told Bram that Dougal's ship had just arrived back at Fremantle. He went to tell Isabella.

'Do you think Flora knows he's back?'

'She may, but I don't think she's going out a lot, so we'd better make sure she knows, hadn't we?' Bram suppressed a sigh. As if he hadn't got enough to do, with the wedding the next day and the Grand Opening two days after that. 'If you can deal with whatever crisis Alice thinks up next, I'll nip over to see Flora.'

Isabella pulled him back to give him a quick hug. 'Tell her if there's anything we can do, she mustn't hesitate to ask.'

'I will, so. Don't work too hard.'

'I've got excellent help now. Thank goodness for Mrs Hollins! I don't know what I'd do without her.'

'At least we haven't had any more intruders.'

'Perhaps us having a night watchman has made him give up.'

'Perhaps.' But Bram had one of his feelings about that and had engaged a friend of Sim's to keep watch in the grounds around the Bazaar as well. He hadn't got second sight, or anything like that, but he did occasionally sense when something bad was going to happen. And he felt that chill sense of unease in his belly right now.

He kept starting awake during the night, to listen for the alarm bell or for footsteps – he didn't know what he was expecting, but the one thing he was certain of was that he definitely didn't intend to be blackmailed into paying out good money. The nights were getting warmer as spring began to fulfil its promise. He wished it was still cold and pouring with rain, then the intruder might not have troubled them as much.

Banishing those thoughts, he walked briskly through the streets to the timber yard, pleased to see the difference Tommy had made there. The whole place now looked neater, giving a better impression to passers-by, and there was now plenty of space for new wood.

He opened the gate and walked across to the cottage, knocking on the door.

Flora opened it. 'Bram! Do come in.'

'Better not,' he said. 'Gossips would have a feast if someone saw you receiving men on your own. I came to tell you that Dougal's ship's just come in.'

She closed her eyes and let out a long, shuddering breath. 'Thank goodness! Has he come ashore yet?'

'I don't think so, but I don't know for certain.'

'I'll go down and see what's happening at the quay. Christopher! Let's go and look at the ships. I think my brother's just come back.'

'Can I go on his ship, Miss McBride?'

'I'm sure he'll let you go on it later, once he's unloaded his cargo, but not today. Go and wait for me at the gate.'

'He's starting to speak normally now,' Bram said.

'Yes. I'm doing one thing right, at least.'

'You've done nothing wrong,' Bram said firmly.

She looked at him steadily. 'I know. But that doesn't stop people thinking the worst, does it?'

'Not your friends.' Bram stepped back. 'I'll leave you to it, then.' He tipped his hat to her and walked away. He had a thousand things to do today.

She stood there for a moment staring into space, then sighed and went to get ready.

Flora made sure Christopher looked tidy and then they walked along to the quay together, the boy making the occasional remark and looking happy to be out.

The *Bonny Mary* was sitting out in Gage Roads with lighters beside her, waiting to unload the goods. There might not be any passengers this trip. Dougal only ever took a few.

She shaded her eyes and squinted, but couldn't see any sign of her brother on deck. She was annoyed with herself for not thinking to write a note to send out to him, mentioning what had been happening. But how could you put such nastiness down on paper? What if it got into the wrong hands?

'No use waiting around,' she told the little boy. 'My brother will be a while yet before he comes ashore.'

'Can we go and buy some cakes for tea?'

'Why not?'

But a further surprise was waiting for them at home. Mitchell had just arrived back and was standing talking to Tommy.

He turned round as the boy yelled, 'Dad!' and started running towards him. Beaming, he picked his son up and swung him round.

'You look well, son.' He looked across the boy's head at Flora and frowned. 'You look strained. Something's wrong.'

She hesitated, then said, 'Not now,' with a meaningful look at the boy.

After they'd had a cup of tea and the cake had been reduced to a few crumbs, Mitchell said to his son, 'Go and play outside now. I want to talk to Miss McBride. Don't leave the yard.' Then he turned to Flora with a determined look on his face. 'What's happened? Is there something I don't know about Christopher? He looks well enough.'

'It's not him.' She was silent for a moment or two, then decided Mitchell would find out the truth as soon as he started talking to people, so told him exactly what her mother had been doing to her.

He stared at her, aghast. 'I can't believe what I'm hearing! How could your own mother destroy your reputation like that? Has she gone mad?'

'No. She's just selfish, always has been, sees only her own needs and never thinks what others may want or that they may be h-hurt.' Her voice wavered, and she looked down at her clasped hands, struggling not to weep.

'Would it do any good if I went to see her?'

'I doubt it.'

'I'll definitely go and see your brother, though.' Silence fell for a few moments, then he said thoughtfully, 'Look, I was thinking while I was away. Perhaps you and I should get married? That'd certainly settle the gossip.'

She looked at him in shock. 'Get married!'

'Why not? My life would be a lot easier if I had a wife. Christopher needs a mother and you need a home. All in all, it seems a very sensible solution to me.'

Flora didn't answer, trying to think whether it would be the right thing to do. Then something he'd said echoed in her mind: *a* wife, *a* mother. Not 'I'd like to marry *you*.' Or even, 'We could build a good life together.' Just *sensible* to get married. Well, she was tired of being sensible.

And besides, she'd never forgotten what it felt like when a man loved you, wanted you and only you. She'd experienced that once and knew Joss would never have looked for simply *a* wife. She tried to find the words to refuse tactfully. 'I'm grateful for the honour you do me in asking, Mitchell, but you don't really want to marry me, any more than I want to marry you. I'm sure we can remain good friends, but I can't see us as lovers. You're not attracted to me and I'm not attracted to you, not in that way. Without love, it'd be an empty relationship.'

His gaze was kind, but not at all lover like. 'You don't think we could make a pleasant life together? You don't think that'd be enough?'

'No. Definitely not. I loved a man once and my mother drove him away, told him lies, told *me* lies. But she couldn't wipe away my memories. I know what it's like to be deeply loved, and it's spoiled me for anything less.'

He sighed and stared blindly through the window for a moment or two. 'You may be right. I've got to confess that I've never felt such a passionate attraction to anyone. Perhaps I don't have it in me.'

'I think we all have it in us, if we meet the right person.'

There was silence. She could hear Christopher shouting and laughing outside, could hear her own soft breaths, and couldn't think what to say next to end the awkwardness, so changed the subject completely. 'Christopher is much improved, starting to talk and behave like a lad again.'

Mitchell smiled. 'Yes. I'd noticed. Thank you for your care of him.'

'Thank Tommy, too. He's good with children.'

'He's a good worker, convict or not. Well, I'll go and check the yard now.'

'I didn't ask if your journey was successful.'

'It was excellent. I've got my first load of timber being delivered in two days' time, so Tommy and I have to get the rest of this cheap rubbish moved to one side.'

'He's worked hard, sorting it out.'

'I can see that. He's done more than I'd expected.'

'Are you going to keep him on? He's desperate to know.'

'Yes, I am. I'd rather train a man to my own ways than have someone who thinks they know everything.' He gave her a wry smile. 'I'm a bit of a fusspot where my timber is concerned.'

As he turned to leave, she realised she'd not told him about the weekend. 'Wait! I nearly forgot. The Bazaar is opening on Saturday and we're all invited to be present at the Grand Opening. And my brother's ship has just arrived. I don't think he's come ashore yet, or at least, only on ship business. I expect he'll be coming here once he's seen my mother.'

'Do you think he'll believe the gossip?'

'No. Definitely not. Dougal knows my mother too well. And he knows me.' Plain, ordinary Flora. What man would ever want to sweep her away?

It was well into the evening and nearly dark before Dougal had sorted all his ship business out. He left the *Bonny Mary* in his mate's charge, knowing the weather was likely to stay calm and the ship would be beyond the reach of thieves, anchored out in the Gage Roads and with a crew member keeping watch on deck. He strolled slowly through the streets to his home, not hurrying because he was tired now. All he wanted was a quick meal then bed. Flora would understand and keep his mother at bay for a while. She always did.

The minute he walked through the door, however, he heard his mother weeping hysterically in her room. What the hell had upset her now? He stood in the hall for a moment or two, hoping Flora would calm her down. He wasn't usually greeted with tears.

But there was no sound of Flora's voice, nothing except his mother weeping loudly. And no maid came running to take his coat or bid him welcome. What had happened? Surely Flora couldn't have been hurt . . . or worse? He didn't think he could bear that.

Dropping his bag, he hurried along to his mother's sitting room. The door was half-open and he saw her lying weeping on the chaise longue.

'I'm back.'

Her only answer was to glance quickly towards him, then bury her face in her handkerchief and let out another loud wail.

He went to kneel beside her. 'What's the matter? Mother? Tell me. Has Flora been hurt?'

'If it were only that. Oh, the shame of it! The shame! I can no longer hold my head up in public because of your sister.'

'Flora? What do you mean? Where is she?'

'She's gone! Run off with a man. Living with him in sin.'

For a moment he felt as if the room had shivered round him, then he shook off his shock and moved forward. He knew how his mother exaggerated, so said crisply, 'Sit up!' using his captain's tone. 'Now, don't say another word until you've stopped crying.'

She sat up, using her handkerchief, muttering phrases like, 'Such a comfort.' And 'You won't bring shame on us.'

What on earth was going on? He waited impatiently for her to quieten. When she'd wiped her eyes for the final time, she looked at him uncertainly. He knew that look. It meant she'd done something he wasn't going to like. 'Tell me about Flora. Where is she?'

'Gone. Your sister left home, just a few days after you'd left. She's living with that Mr Nash who stayed with us, the one who was looking for his wife and went to Sydney after her. He came back and I wish he hadn't. Flora's *alone* with him now in that small house! I never would have thought it of her. I'm so ashamed.'

She began weeping again and he had trouble not shouting at her. But it never did any good, so he asked, 'Where exactly is she?' He had to repeat the question before she answered.

'That Nash person has bought the old timber yard in Fairley Street and they're living there together.'

Even his mother couldn't have made this up. Could she?

Perhaps Flora had got married? No, his mother kept talking about *shame*. 'I'd better go and see my sister, then, find out what's happened.'

'I've *told* you what's happened. She left her home, left *me*, and went to live with him. You shouldn't associate with her now. You shouldn't even speak to her.'

'Don't be ridiculous. She's my sister. Have you seen her since she left? Remonstrated with her?'

'Certainly not! I'm never speaking to her again unless she apologises to me on bended knee.'

'She won't do that and I won't ask her to. But I do need to know exactly what's happening.'

'You can't go out again tonight. It's dark and you're tired. Surely it can wait till the morning?'

'If my sister is in trouble, it definitely can't wait.'

She grasped his wrist tightly. 'Don't go, Dougal. She's done it before and this time she must learn her lesson. Remember that horrible young man who was trying to get her to run away from home? I saved her from herself then, but this time she wouldn't listen to me. I think she's desperate for a man, because of being unmarried and—'

He pried her fingers loose and stood up but she seized hold of his jacket.

'Dougal, it's too late! Everyone knows about her sinful ways. The only thing to do is ignore her.'

He jerked out of her grip. '*Ignore her*? How can you suggest such a thing? She's your daughter, my sister. I'd never abandon her, whatever she did.' And he'd never take his mother's word for something as important as this, knowing how she exaggerated. He walked towards the door.

'Dougal, come back! Dougal, I need you more than she does. *Dougal!*'

He ignored her screams and left the house, walking at a furious rate towards the old timber yard. Flora had said she would be leaving home, but how could it have happened like this? If she'd gone to this man, then their mother had driven her to it, he was sure.

But he couldn't leave her living in sin. At the very least, this Nash fellow must be brought to marry her.

Chawton didn't bring Alice back until late, by which time Conn had gone to bed and the Deagans were considering it, too.

Alice looked like a cat that had swallowed a dish of cream and to Bram's eyes she had the air of a woman well bedded. Surely they hadn't—! He broke off that thought. If they had done anything like that, it was their own business. All he cared about was getting her married and out of their lives.

She was carrying packages, which she dropped on the floor to one side of the doorway.

'Unless you want your things trampling on,' Isabella said tartly, 'you'd better move them out of the way.'

Alice sighed. 'I'm so tired.'

With a grin Chawton moved the packages for her and nodded to Isabella and Bram. 'The wedding is to be at ten o'clock tomorrow morning at St John's Church. I have a special licence.' He patted his pocket. 'Did you ask about that girl to help you look after Louisa?'

'Yes. Sally's starting work tomorrow.'

'How much are you paying her? Right.' He fumbled in his pocket and brought out a coin purse, carelessly dumping enough sovereigns to cover Sally's wages for a good many weeks on the table. 'Let me know when that runs out.'

Bram gathered up the money, jiggling the coins in his hand. 'By that time, you'll be wanting Louisa back, surely, Alice? And my wife will be too near her time to look after someone else's child.'

Again it was Chawton who answered. 'Oh, yes. Wasn't thinking. Still, you'll need some new clothes for her as well.' Five more sovereigns joined the others.

It sickened Bram to see the lack of interest in her

daughter on Alice's face. Did she even care about Chawton, or was this just about her own comforts? Well, one thing she didn't seem to understand was the sheer determination of the fellow. He'd bet that Chawton made sure she did exactly as he wanted, especially when it came to bearing him children. She was probably in for quite a few shocks, and serve her right.

Just as he was about to show Chawton out, something thudded against the front door. When he opened it, no one was in sight, but there was a rock on the floor and a scratch mark in the door. He bent to pick up the paper that had been tied round the rock, and read a message similar to the previous one. It ended: *LEVE MONEY BEHIND STABL. NO TRICKS. DRY TIMBR BURNS EASY. THIS IS FINAL WARNIN.*

'Trouble?' Chawton asked.

Bram handed him the message, telling him what had happened and what they suspected.

'Count me in.'

'What?'

'You said you were thinking of setting a trap. Count me in.'

'But you're getting married tomorrow.'

'Dammit, so I am. Pity. I like a good scrap almost as much as—' He broke off with a glance at the ladies, and winked at Bram instead. 'You *are* still going to set a trap, aren't you?'

'I'm thinking of it.' He sniffed suddenly. 'Do I smell burning?'

They all sniffed the air.

'Hell, it is, too!' Chawton said. 'Where?'

Bram looked up at the Bazaar but could see no signs of flames there. Then a voice shouted from the stables and Les came pounding outside in his nightshirt.

'Fire! Fire! Out at the back.'

21

Dougal strode along the dark streets, torn between annoyance that he couldn't get the food and rest he needed, and anxiety for his sister. He encountered a couple of men he knew, nodding, not wanting to stop, just get this over with. But as he passed them he couldn't help seeing the wariness on their faces.

Were things that bad, then?

One thing was certain: Flora must come home with him immediately. This very night. He'd make sure their mother treated her with respect, but he wasn't having her staying in Nash's house, whatever she was doing there.

He saw the ramshackle house – more like a hut! he thought indignantly – some distance from the gates of the timber yard. No wonder people were talking. It was tiny.

But the big gates that let in carts and the small side gate for people on foot were all padlocked. He could see a lantern glowing inside the house so someone was still up. There was no easy way of attracting their attention. If he yelled or rang the bell, he might attract attention or cause a scene, and that was the last thing he needed.

In the end he climbed over the gate, cursing as something sharp caught on his trousers and tore them.

As he started moving towards the cottage, a man hurtled out from behind a pile of timber and knocked him flying, yelling at the same time.

'Mr Nash. Come quickly. We've got a thief.'

Dougal tried to get free of his assailant but though the man was thin, he held on like a limpet. 'Will you let go!' he roared. 'I'm not a thief!' With a mighty effort, he threw the fellow off, but at that moment someone else grabbed him and twisted his arm behind him.

'Don't struggle or I'll hurt you.'

Other footsteps came running and the third person was carrying a lantern. He couldn't see her face, only a woman's outline, but he guessed it was Flora.

'Mitchell, let him go. It's my brother.'

The grip on him slackened and the man pushed him quickly away.

Dougal resisted the urge to punch him in the face. 'I was only coming to see my sister, but I didn't want to attract attention.'

'Come into the house,' Flora said in a cool voice. 'We don't want to discuss this in public.'

He stared at her retreating back in shock. What sort of greeting was that?

'Are you coming, McBride?' Nash asked. 'You're not hurt, are you?'

'I ripped my trousers on your damned gate, and got a few bruises when that wild idiot leaped on me.'

'I thought he was a burglar, sir,' the man said.

'And you did just the right thing. You're not hurt, are you, Tommy? Good, then you go back to bed and we'll see to Captain McBride.'

Dougal followed Nash to the cottage, whose door was open to light their way. Inside it, Flora was standing by the fireplace, hands clasped tightly in front of her, looking stiff and nervous.

A boy was standing by an open door on the other side of the room. 'I heard noises, Dad.'

'Captain McBride fell over in the darkness. You go back to sleep now, son. I'm not coming to bed for a while.'

Once the boy had gone back inside the bedroom, Dougal said, 'I've come here to try to sort out what's going on.' He looked across the room, seeing how upset his sister was, even though she was trying to hide it. 'Don't you have a hug for your brother now, Flora?'

She hesitated, so he walked across and pulled her into his arms. 'I don't know what's been happening, but you're still my sister and always will be.'

She gave a sob and seemed to collapse against him, sobbing as if her heart would break.

He patted her shoulders and made shushing noises, but she went on sobbing.

Nash pushed a chair forward. 'Here, get her to sit down and I'll make us all a cup of tea.'

'Have you nothing stronger?'

The other gave him a rueful smile. 'I'm afraid not. And I'm sorry about the black eye.'

'Oh, hell!' Dougal settled Flora on the chair and glanced in the mirror above the mantelpiece. 'That'll really get people talking.'

Every smile vanished from the room.

'They're talking already,' she said dully. 'Your black

eye will only add fuel to the fire.' And she began weeping again.

He looked across at Nash. 'I can't get a word of sense from my mother, who won't stop wailing. She says Flora left home to come and live with you.'

His sister blew her nose and said indistinctly, 'That's not true. As usual, she's twisting the truth to suit herself.'

'Then suppose you tell me what really happened.'

She nodded and against the homely noises of Nash making a pot of tea, she told him the bare bones of the tale.

'Are you sure it's that bad?'

'Oh, yes. She's convinced all her friends and acquaintances that I'm living in sin with Mitchell.'

'*She*'s the one spreading rumours? Surely not?'

'Who else could it be?'

'But why would she do that?'

'So that I'll have to go home and never leave her again. People I know cross the street to avoid me now, Dougal. And though Miss Marley, who runs that little school for younger children, believed me when I said I wasn't living in sin, she still didn't dare allow Christopher to attend. She thought other parents would object . . . because I'm living here.'

'We'll have to tell people the truth.'

She tried to laugh but it turned into a sob. 'What, admit she's been telling lies? Mother will never do it. She'll just take to her bed and weep, then tell more lies.'

'But the Deagans can prove you went straight to them.'

'Yes, but afterwards I came here . . . to look after Christopher and to be Mitchell's housekeeper, nothing more.' She went across to fling a door open. 'Here's my bedroom. See if you can find any sign of him sharing it with me.'

He was shocked. 'You don't need to prove that to me, Flora. If you tell me something's true, I believe you. Sit down again, please. We have to work out a plan. Um . . .' He glanced at Nash. 'The obvious thing would be for you two to marry and you look as if you get on well enough.'

'I asked her, but she refused.'

Dougal looked at his sister in puzzlement. 'Nash seems a decent enough fellow. It'd solve both your problems and give you a home of your own.'

'But I don't love him.'

'You seem on good terms with him, though.'

'I know what love is like, the sort of love that makes you want to marry and share a bed. I've seen it recently in Bram and Isabella – and I knew it once with Joss. I'd have defied Mother and run away with him, only she intercepted our letters and wrote to him to say I didn't want to see him again. He mustn't have cared enough, because *I* never heard from him again.'

'Just a minute!' Dougal looked at her in puzzlement. 'I remember her telling me he'd been pestering you and you didn't want to marry him. And you never seemed sad . . . or anything.'

'I was too proud to wear my heart on my sleeve. But if he'd not left the colony, or if he'd ever come back, I'd have gone with him in an instant, even if you did refuse to speak to me again.'

'Why should I do that? I liked him and he seemed to make you happy.'

She looked at him in bewilderment then her face crumpled again. 'So every bit of it was lies. She said you didn't approve, wouldn't have anything to do with him or me, if we married. And you were away for months, by which time Joss was long gone.'

'But why did she do it? No, don't answer. To keep you by her side. Devoted daughter, looking after mother. Marrying a sailor might have taken you away. She wanted a safe husband for you, one she could use, or none at all.' He felt sick to think of Flora being separated from the man she loved by their mother's tricks. 'I'm sorry. She fooled me completely.'

'She fools most people.'

Mitchell brought some brimming cups across and they each took one, sipping in silence.

'What do you want to do, then?' Dougal asked after he'd drained his cup.

'I'm going to leave the colony as soon as Mitchell and Christopher don't need me any more, start afresh somewhere else.'

'No, don't do that. Please don't. I don't want to lose you,' said Dougal.

'What else can I do? Mud clings.'

'We'll think of something.' Dougal stretched out his hand to his sister and she took it. 'I can't bear it if you move away. Family should stick together. I *will* think of something.' As she continued to look doubtful, he pleaded, 'At least let's try.'

She nodded, but the frown was still there, and the doubt, and the sadness.

* * *

'Get some horse rugs from the tack room!' Bram called. 'Maybe we can beat out the flames.'

Conn's voice carried through the darkness. 'I'll get them.'

Bram set off running, still yelling, 'Water buckets. Isabella, fetch the kitchen bucket.'

Alice began to scream hysterically.

'Quiet!' her fiancé called sharply and the noise stopped abruptly.

The fire was soon out, because they weren't short of willing helpers, what with the new night watchman as well as Chawton and Conn, but Bram's blood ran cold at the thought of what might have happened if the flames had really taken hold.

'I'm not going to pay that fellow blackmail money, whatever he does,' he said as they stood round afterwards, drinking cups of tea that Isabella had brought out to them.

'What *are* you going to do?' Conn asked.

'I don't know yet. I'll have a good long think before I go to sleep. Maybe something will come to me. He probably thinks he has more leverage before the Grand Opening.'

When everyone separated to go to bed, Bram waited till he was alone with his wife to murmur, 'Whatever next?'

'Whatever it is, we'll deal with it.'

'Are you all right?'

'I am as long as you're safe, Bram darling.'

She slipped into his arms and laid her head on his shoulder, a way of cuddling that now seemed the most natural action on earth. He stroked her hair absent-mindedly. He knew if he'd been on his own, she'd have been there with him, hauling buckets, beating at the flames. She hadn't been needed in that way, thanks to his friends, but she'd provided drinks afterwards to take away the acrid taste of smoke and soften the harsh feel of their throats, while Alice kept out of the way.

How could they go to a wedding tomorrow and leave the yard unprotected?

Dougal walked home from the timber yard with a heavy heart. Poor Flora had suffered enough. It was time to end the situation, and though he had a duty to support his mother, this whole affair sickened him. He didn't want her living in his house any longer, not when she played tricks like that.

What he really needed was a wife. Silly time to realise that. But he didn't intend to bring one home while his mother was there or a marriage would have no chance of success. And he didn't intend to marry unless he met someone he really liked, as Bram liked Isabella.

He stopped to look up at the stars for comfort, as he sometimes did on the ship. They were constants in his life and he loved their cool, sparkling beauty, knew all the main constellations like old friends. But nothing could replace the people you loved.

If he didn't act quickly, his sister would leave the colony. He and Flora had lived together for thirty years and had rarely disagreed, let alone quarrelled, even as children.

When he got back to the house, it was dark, except for a lamp shining in the hall.

There was a note propped up against it, a message from his mother. 'Gone to bed. Have taken a sleeping draught.'

Good. He wasn't ready to speak to her yet.

He picked up the lamp and went through to the kitchen, which was dark, with everything put away. As he stood wondering what to eat, there was the sound of a door opening and Linny came in from the maids' room behind it, still fully dressed.

'I thought you might need something to eat, sir, so I told Mary to go to bed and I waited up.'

'Thank you. I'm absolutely ravenous. Anything will do, just something quick.'

She bustled around, getting him some cold meat, bread, butter and a pot of jam, together with a big slice of cake.

'That'll be fine. You get to bed now.'

She looked at him doubtfully, then asked, 'Did you see Miss McBride?'

'Yes.'

'Is she all right?'

'Not exactly. You know what's been going on?'

'Yes, sir. I can't help overhearing things. Miss Flora had taken a lot of trouble with those things in the attic. It wasn't fair for your mother to give them away.'

In between mouthfuls he questioned her and got further details of what had started the dispute, feeling anger at his mother's callousness rising again.

'Miss Flora told me she wanted to run her own boarding house and I said I'd like to work for her.'

'You wouldn't like to go with my mother, if I found

her a small house somewhere? I'd raise your wages and hire someone to do the rough work.'

She shook her head violently. 'No, sir. Meaning no disrespect, but it's very hard to work for your mother without Miss Flora to keep the peace and organise things.'

'Hmm. I'll have to find someone else to look after my mother, then.'

'She'll not leave here, sir. She loves this house.'

'She'll have to leave. I'm bringing my sister back and Flora can run it for me till I marry.'

Linny's face brightened. 'That'll be good, sir. Only . . . how will you persuade people those stories were just lies? All the servants I know are talking about it, too, asking me . . . But I don't say anything except Miss Flora would never do anything wrong.'

'Thank you for your loyalty. I'll tell everyone I know that she's innocent, and I'll say it again and again till they have to believe me. Anyone who doesn't will not be welcome in my house. And perhaps you'd do the same with the servants?'

'Yes, sir. I'll do my best.'

But he could see by her expression that she didn't believe this would work. Only what else could he do?

Bram crept down the stairs and left the house before dawn, even though he'd only had a few hours' sleep. He had a word with the night watchman patrolling the grounds and then went to see Sim up at the Bazaar.

'Any other disturbances?'

Sim shook his head. 'It was very quiet the rest of the night.'

'Good. What I want is . . .'

He smiled as he walked back down to the house later. In two days' time, they'd have the Grand Opening and he was determined nothing should spoil that, whatever it cost him.

Today they'd have a wedding and try to catch a thief.

For once, Alice didn't need rousing in the morning. She woke early and lay in bed for a while, beaming at the ceiling, glad Louisa was still asleep, glad to be leaving all her cares behind. She felt a bit guilty that she'd be leaving Louisa, because she did love the child, but Leonard said it was best to start their marriage with just the two of them, and he was right.

A shiver ran through her as she thought about how strong and masterful he was, how well he could pleasure a woman. It had been scandalous for him to hire a room in the daytime and take her there, but she hadn't cared. She knew she'd at last found a man who'd take care of her and she'd do anything for him, absolutely anything.

She got up and had an all-over wash in cold water since there was nowhere to have a bath. She'd washed her hair the night before and she admired it in the mirror, proud of the way it was shining again. When she'd been short of food and short of fuel to heat water, it had become very dull.

Her daughter stirred and she stiffened, praying Louisa would stay asleep. But the child opened her eyes. 'Hello, darling. Not time to get up yet.'

'Want to wee-wee.'

With a sigh, Alice abandoned her own needs to help the child use the chamber pot, then sent her to wait downstairs. She didn't dare give Louisa any cordial this morning, in case Bram noticed and got angry. She didn't want to give him any excuse for refusing to keep Louisa for a while.

There were sounds of people stirring in the other bedroom, so Alice slipped on her dressing gown and went downstairs to heat the kettle. She needed a drink of tea and something to eat. She'd make a big pot for them all. That'd keep Bram in a good mood.

Strange how wide awake she felt and it wasn't yet seven o'clock. Still, the wedding was at ten, so the time would pass very quickly in getting ready because she wanted to look her best. They were going up to Perth after the wedding, from where they'd start their journey to Leonard's home tomorrow. She'd miss the Grand Opening of the Bazaar, but who cared about that?

She was looking forward to seeing the capital of the colony. She'd been stuck in Fremantle ever since the ship arrived, with nothing but work, work, work. What sort of life was that? Not the one she wanted. Dear Leonard said he had maids to do the hard work, and a housekeeper, too.

'Good morning. Did you sleep well?'

Alice turned to smile at her cousin. 'Oh, yes. Once the fire at the stables was out I soon fell asleep. Where's Bram?'

'He got up early to do a few jobs.'

'Doesn't he ever think of anything but work? You two never have any fun together.'

Isabella looked surprised. 'Fun? What does that matter? We're building a life for ourselves and our children. That's what gives us both the most satisfaction.'

Alice didn't argue. She didn't want to leave any bad feelings behind. She suddenly remembered Leonard's instructions. 'Um, I just want to thank you and Bram for having me and for looking after Louisa for a while. I'm very grateful.'

'Who else would you turn to but your relatives?' She hesitated. 'Alice, are you really sure about this? You hardly know Mr Chawton.'

'Conn told Bram he knew of the Chawtons and Leonard was telling the truth about his situation, so what can be the problem?'

'But what if you don't like living with him?'

Alice laughed. 'He has a big house and maids, he's going to buy me lots of clothes and he's good in bed. What on earth more do I need from a husband?'

'Good in bed! How do you know that?'

Alice felt her cheeks grow warm. 'We, um, hired a room yesterday.'

Isabella opened her mouth then snapped it shut, shaking her head and looking disapproving.

Best get on with making the pot of tea, Alice told herself. Some people were very stuffy. And it was important to enjoy making love together. Very important. To her, at least. And to dear Leonard, too. What a fine man he was!

Alice was fussing so much about her hair and clothes that Isabella got Louisa ready for the wedding. She hadn't realised that the child had no best clothes, because she'd been too worried about the threats to the Bazaar. And anyway, the child had a mother. Surely her cousin could have taken an interest in her daughter's clothes?

'I'm ready,' Alice said.

Isabella turned round, still holding Louisa's hand. 'You look beautiful! I didn't realise you had a dress like that.'

'I didn't until yesterday. Leonard bought it for me and paid extra to have it put together quickly. They had a few bodices and skirts nearly finished, you see.' She studied her cousin. 'Your dress is beautiful too. I've never seen silk as beautiful as that before.'

'Mr Lee and his family sold silks and material of all sorts. We're going to sell silks in the Bazaar. I could get you some lengths if Mr Chawton agrees. They gave me this one before I left.'

'Oh, I'm sure he'll agree.' She came across to finger the heavy silk. 'They must be rich to give you this. Perhaps you should have stayed with them. You might have found someone to marry who didn't make you work so hard.'

No use arguing, Isabella told herself and just said quietly, 'Even though the Lees were rich, they didn't live in a lavish manner or entertain Europeans much.' She sighed. She still missed them, especially Xiu Mei. 'I couldn't find anything better than this for Louisa to wear, I'm afraid.'

Alice studied her daughter but made no attempt to go across to her. 'No. I forgot about her. Leonard's left you some money for new clothes. Can you get some made? She's growing fast.'

'Yes. I'll see to that.' But there was no answer, because Alice had already turned away to primp in front of the mirror as she put on one of the new Empire bonnets, a small tight bonnet, with broad ribbons tied under the chin and artificial flowers under the front of the tiny brim. Where had she got that from in such a short time with Mr Chawton?

The wedding party walked to the church, enjoying the sunny spring day. They were to meet the bride-groom there. Isabella held Louisa's hand because Alice didn't want her dress dirtying or crumpling. When the child couldn't keep up, Bram scooped her into his arms and carried her, making her laugh. Isabella realised in shock that it was the first time they'd heard her sound like a happy little child.

Mr Chawton was waiting for them outside St John's Church, which was a large stone building with a tower and a dome.

'Not bad, for a Protestant church,' Bram whispered to his wife, making her chuckle, 'but the Catholic church is prettier.'

It was, too. She couldn't argue.

Chawton behaved very politely to everyone, but the lust in his eyes as they rested on Alice was indecent, Isabella thought indignantly.

'Just look at him!' she whispered to Bram.

He grinned. 'He's welcome to her.'

'I wish she wasn't marrying him, if that's all he wants from her.'

His smile vanished. 'Don't say that. I'm delighted we're getting rid of her. I'm tired of having to bully her into doing anything to earn her keep, and I'm looking forward to your cooking again.'

'We'll still have Louisa.'

'Sally will help you look after her from now on.'

'Yes, and she'll be teaching me, too.' She gave him a rueful smile. 'I've not had much to do with babies and small children. Mrs Hollins is going to help us as well.'

'Ready, everyone?' Chawton called and led the way inside without waiting for an answer. He greeted the clergyman who was waiting for them, then went to stand at the altar.

Bram handed Louisa to his wife and held out his arm to Alice, escorting her down the aisle, leaving Conn to follow them with Isabella and the child.

The five of them were the only people in the church at that time of day. Isabella felt a little sad about that but Alice didn't seem to care. She beamed at Chawton throughout the whole service, hardly seeming aware of the solemnity of the promises she was making.

When the groom kissed the bride it went on for so long that the clergyman had to clear his throat to remind them of where they were.

As they came out of the church, Isabella saw a man standing in the shade across the road, staring at them. 'Isn't that Mundy?' she asked her husband.

'So it is.' Bram looked suddenly angry and his Irish accent was more pronounced. 'Sure, I'd hoped . . .' He let the words trail away.

Mundy gave them a triumphant smile and wave, then walked off whistling.

'What had you hoped?'

'I set a trap for him early this morning, had the men in place and everything. I thought he might try to do something while we were at church.'

'Oh.'

'Damn the man! How could he know about it? There was no one around. That's why he came here today, to rub it in. If I had the slightest shred of proof that he's behind our troubles, I'd have him locked away.' He grew thoughtful. 'I wonder where he's living. Perhaps one of Sim's pensioner guard friends could find out.'

Isabella was worried about what Mundy might do next, but Bram had made her promise to stay out of things if there was trouble. And she intended to keep that promise, because neither of them wanted to jeopardise their unborn baby.

She realised someone had spoken. 'Sorry. What was that, Alice?'

'Leonard wants us to go straight home and change our clothes. He's arranged for a cake to be delivered there, and a bottle of wine. We can have a toast and then we really must set off.'

'Of course. Do you want to carry Louisa for a bit? She can't walk very fast.'

'And crumple my new dress? No, I don't. She can walk perfectly well if she has to.'

So Bram, tight-faced, picked up the child again and carried her back, walking behind the newly-weds and talking softly to Louisa, making her laugh several times.

He seemed to understand instinctively that his wife didn't feel like talking just now.

Isabella was both glad and sad that Alice was leaving. She'd felt so alone when she had no close relatives to turn to, and Alice had been more like a sister than a cousin.

She'd forgotten how irritating Alice could be, and how lazy. And yet, she didn't want to lose her cousin again. She wished they'd be living closer to one another, within visiting distance at least, so that she could be sure Alice was all right and be able to see her sometimes.

Well, if she had her wish, she'd make up for that lack in her life by having several children, making her own family. She wished there wasn't this threat hanging over them. She wanted her life to get back to normal, wanted time with Bram just to sit quietly and enjoy each other's company.

When they got home, she tried not to show how tired she was. Expecting a baby did make a difference to your energy, she was finding.

She sipped the wine Leonard Chawton had provided, swapping her nearly full glass for Bram's nearly empty one, which made him grin. 'It's a lovely cake,' she told Leonard.

He nodded. 'Another slice?'

'No, thank you.'

As he helped himself to another large piece of cake, she turned to Alice, who was fiddling with the crumbs on her plate. 'I'll look after Louisa carefully.'

'I know you will.' In a rare moment of honesty, Alice

added, 'Better than I ever could. I'm not . . . practical like you. Isabella—'

'Alice—'

They both spoke together, stopped and smiled at one another.

'Thank you,' Alice said, moving to give Isabella a hug.

'I'm going to miss you.'

Alice shook her head. 'Not really. I'm not much use and I was only a burden on you. I'll be better off with Leonard.'

'I hope you'll be happy.'

'Oh, I shall. He's got plenty of money and he's a fine bed partner.'

'Alice!'

Her cousin smiled. 'We're both married women. We know that's important.'

Leonard came back to stand beside his wife. He gave Isabella such a shrewd look she felt sure he'd been listening to their conversation. 'I'll look after her,' he said. 'And you must come and visit us. Plenty of space for visitors – or there will be once Alice has furnished the empty rooms.' He put one arm round his new wife. 'Time to go, my love.'

'Yes, Leonard.' She turned, hesitated, then went back to throw her arms round her cousin for one final hug.

As Alice moved away, Bram came up to Isabella. 'She'd have driven you mad if she'd stayed.'

'I know, but . . . she is my cousin . . . my only relative.'

'Well, I've got brothers and sisters, not to mention cousins galore. You can share them.'

It wasn't the same, but she didn't say that.

They went to wave the newly-weds goodbye and Isabella stood by the gate for a few moments after their vehicle had disappeared from view. As the last drifts of fine sand blew softly across her shoes, she told herself not to mope and turned to her husband. 'You go up to the Bazaar, darling. I'll just have a little rest and wait for Sally.'

'Are you all right?'

'A bit tired, that's all.'

'Shall I take Louisa with me?'

'No, she's no trouble. She's been playing quietly in that corner for a while. She loves that doll of hers. And anyway, Sally will be here soon to look after her. That girl is going to be a big help to me, I'm sure.'

She watched him walk up to the Bazaar, then went to sit down with a sigh of relief, feeling exhausted, both physically and emotionally.

Alice would be all right with Mr Chawton. She was as sure of that as you ever could be.

She just needed a few minutes' rest and she'd be fine. Bram was right. Alice would have driven them mad. But still . . . this was her only cousin.

22

That same morning Dougal's mother sent him word yet again that she wasn't feeling well. He looked at Linny, who'd delivered the message in a monotone. 'How did she look? Tell me the truth.'

The maid didn't hesitate. 'Just as she does normally. And she ate a good breakfast.'

'Go back up and make sure she's decent, then I'll go and see her.'

He waited outside the bedroom till Linny came out and gave him a nod, then he opened the door and walked in.

His mother let out a wail. 'Dougal! You shouldn't be here. I'm not feeling well. I need to rest.'

'You can rest as much as you want after I've spoken to you.'

She pulled the covers up to her chin, staring at him over them like an animal caught in a trap.

'I'm very angry with you for spreading all those rumours about Flora.'

'I didn't.'

'*Don't lie to me, Mother!*'

She began to weep, but he ignored that, continuing to speak loudly and slowly over her sobs. 'I'm going to look for a cottage for you and find you a maid, then you're moving out of this house.'

Her mouth fell open and for a moment she could only stare at him as if he'd suddenly spoken gibberish, then she said in a husky whisper, 'But this is my *home*.'

'It's my house and I don't intend to bring a wife back to face the same troubles with you that Flora's had.'

'*Wife?* You're getting married?'

'I'm starting to think about it seriously. I've not met anyone yet, but when I do, I'll be bringing her back here to live and we won't be taking paying guests any longer.' He paused then added, 'not unless she wants to do it, that is. I was grateful when you and Flora helped out financially while I was establishing myself, but I've been wondering for a while if we should continue to do it, only *you* said you enjoyed it.'

'I could stop taking paying guests. I can't manage that without Flora, anyway. She was wrong to abandon me. It was her duty to stay.'

'Flora will not be coming back here until you've left. I hope her presence will show people in this town that I'm not ashamed of her.'

'She's made you believe her lies. You believe her over your own mother.'

Her voice was shrill and her expression different from usual, not at all amiable. Was this how she looked at Flora and spoke to her when he was away?

He remembered suddenly the quarrels there used to be between her and his father, the lies she'd told her husband regularly. As a lad he'd noticed the lies, of course he had, but hadn't dared say anything. He'd forgotten about that after his father died, because he'd been so busy, but now it all came back to him. 'I do believe Flora because I've seen you tell lies before.'

'When?'

'To Father.'

She flushed and let out a sniff. 'That fool!'

'Father wasn't a fool, just a kindly, gentle man who could never seem to please you.'

'He was a fool with money.'

'He left me enough to buy my ship and take care of you, which doesn't seem all that foolish to me. Anyway, that's neither here nor there. I've made up my mind about you leaving and I shan't change it. I'll keep you in comfort but not here.'

'I won't go. *This* is my home.'

'You'll go if I have to carry you out of here myself.'

She stared at him, more tears welling in her eyes and rolling down her plump cheeks. This time the tears didn't make him feel sorry for her. There was too much anger inside him at the way she'd twice destroyed her only daughter's life.

'I mean what I say.' He left the room ignoring her cries to wait. He was determined to start looking for a house for her immediately, and he'd need to hire a maid, whom he'd no doubt have to pay extra to put up with her.

Bram strolled across to the stables and paid off the men who'd been hidden there while they were at church in case anyone tried to damage the Bazaar.

'Not a sign of him, or anyone else, sir,' one of them said. 'They didn't even walk past.'

That surprised him. 'I wonder if you could find out for me where Mundy is living?'

'I could try, sir.'

'Don't let anyone see you looking.' He felt in his pocket and handed over a couple of coins. 'Maybe you'll hear something in the alehouse.'

Les was just finishing grooming a horse that had been brought in while they were away. 'Did the wedding go all right, Mr Deagan?'

'Yes. It was quick and painless. There's some cake left at the house. I'll keep an eye on this handsome fellow while you nip across to sample it. Tell my wife I said you deserved a piece.'

Les beamed at him. He always seemed hungry but he never put on an ounce of fat. A bit like his master, Bram thought with a smile.

When he was on his own in the stables, he stood near the front door studying the buildings opposite. Businesses, mainly, and not the sorts of place where a scruffy man like Mundy would be welcome, either.

He went up to the sleeping cubicles and stared out of the tiny single-paned windows there, first those over-looking the overgrown, empty lot at the side, which provided an easy way for someone to get into the grounds at night, but offered nowhere to hide during the day. The other windows overlooked the short street at the rear of his block of land, where a few modest weatherboard houses alternated with small empty blocks. A couple of the houses were looking rather shabby.

Could Mundy be hiding in one of those?

When Les returned to the stables, smiling, with a couple of crumbs on his chin, Bram left him to work and strolled up to the Bazaar. He looked round with great pride at what he and Isabella had accomplished. 'No trouble, Mrs Hollins?'

'No, sir. Nothing's happened at all today. I hope it's all right, but my Sim's having a nap in the storage area at the back. He'd have come running if I'd needed him because he's a light sleeper. Did the wedding go well? I watched everyone come back. She made a lovely bride.'

'Yes, I suppose so. It was very quick, anyway.' And Alice was someone else's responsibility now. Oh, the relief of that! 'I'll just take a walk round outside.'

He strolled along the crushed limestone path that now surrounded the irregular building, trying to think things through. You'd hear if someone walked over this, surely? His own feet were making a crunching sound and the dust was whitening his boots. He tried not to show how carefully he was studying the houses opposite as he walked along to the end of the shop.

He stopped and pretended to examine a window frame. The hair prickled at the back of his neck and he had a strong feeling that he was being observed. Was he being fanciful? Or was someone indeed spying on him?

He went back into the Bazaar and shook Sim awake. 'Sorry to wake you, but could you watch out of that back window after I've left? Keep your eye on those houses. I felt as if someone was watching me all the time I was at the back of the Bazaar.'

Sim got up from the makeshift bed of sacking and gave his head a shake, as if he'd just come out of water. 'We used to feel like that when we were on patrol sometimes. It's well to pay heed to such feelings.'

'The thing is, if Mundy's watching from there, he'll need to see me walk back to our cottage or he won't come out again. But you can watch out for him from one of the back windows. Don't get too close to the glass or he'll see you. You can send Mrs Hollins to me if you have anything to report.'

Sim grinned. 'Yessir.'

'Good.' Bram looked at him very solemnly. 'And look, Hollins. If you see everything through and stick with me, I'll make sure you never want again.' He knew old soldiers sometimes worried about that as their strength failed.

He stuck out his hand and Sim shook it.

'You can count on me, sir. You've treated me and Mrs Hollins more than fairly.'

Bram sauntered out and down to the cottage to report to Isabella. But she was busy with Sally and Louisa, discussing what the maid's duties were, so he went to sit in the living room and indulged himself in a quiet hour with the *Fremantle Herald*, a newspaper he bought occasionally for a treat.

How things had changed! He hadn't been allowed to read the family's old newspapers when he was a groom in Ireland, even though the papers were lying around and being used to keep things clean. It was considered unnecessary and presumptuous for him even to think of reading them.

He looked round the comfortable room. No one was going to take this away from him, or hurt his wife and unborn child. Whatever he had to do to keep them safe, he would.

Mitchell walked along High Street, lost in thought, surprised when a man he knew only by sight stopped him.

'It's not liked, you know, Nash.'

'I beg your pardon?'

'You've not dealt fairly with Miss McBride and it's not liked. I'm telling you frankly, if you're starting up in business in this town, you should take care not to offend your customers. The least you can do now that you've ruined Miss McBride is marry her.'

The man would have moved on then, but Mitchell grabbed his arm. 'I've not done anything that would offend people's morals. The lady in question is my housekeeper and she looks after my son, whose mother was killed recently. Miss McBride stepped into the breach to care for him until I can make more permanent arrangements, and I'm deeply grateful to her for doing so.'

He let that sink in, then added, 'Since you've been blunt with me, I'll be equally blunt in return. She and I do not share a bad and never have done, so there is no reason for us to marry. Furthermore, she's a highly respectable lady, and I'll thank *you* to remember that when speaking about her in future.'

'That's not what her mother told my wife and she says it was pitiful how poor old Mrs McBride wept as she said it. A mother wouldn't say something like that about her own daughter unless it was true.'

The old harridan! Mitchell hoped he didn't meet her in the street, because he'd never manage to be civil. 'I suggest you speak to Captain McBride, then, and find out the truth of the matter. He's very angry at his mother for her spiteful words – and that's all they are, spiteful words because her daughter dared to leave home. The captain came to visit us yesterday evening and is perfectly happy that his sister is being accorded every respect while she's under my roof.'

'He did?' The man frowned. 'But surely – I mean, her own mother . . .'

'Sometimes people who are getting on in years begin to behave irrationally. I shall say no more on that head because *I* don't go round maligning people.' With a nod, Mitchell stepped back and allowed the other to pass.

A few paces away the man stopped to turn and stare at him, then shook his head and walked on again.

Mitchell hoped his words had sown some seeds of truth to counteract the gossip. It upset him to hear Miss McBride's name blackened, and now there was the added worry that this scandal might harm his business, too.

But what else could he have done except find someone to look after Christopher? He'd have no business if he hadn't found timber suppliers.

Mrs Hollins came down to the cottage with a message for Bram. 'My Sim saw a man go into that house on the right at the back, sir. A few minutes later Mundy came storming out. Sim said he looked furious. The other man looked respectable and Sim thinks he's the one who owns the house. When he came out again, he stood looking at the house and shaking his head, as if he was upset. I can't help hoping he's thrown Mundy out. The place is a disgrace.'

'I wonder where Mundy was going.'

She smiled. 'We'll soon find out. My Sim hailed a lad who was passing by, promised him sixpence if he'd follow Mundy and find out where he went.'

'Your husband is a treasure, Mrs Hollins, a real treasure.'

She beamed at him. 'He's a good man, sir, I do know that.'

He fumbled in his pocket. 'Here's sixpence to pay the lad. Perhaps when you go back to the Bazaar, Sally should walk part way up the path with you, so that it'll look as if you were visiting her, not me. Just in case Mundy has come back.'

'I'd like that anyway, sir. Me and Sim have brought that girl up since our daughter died, and we love her as if we were her parents, not grandparents.'

Bram went upstairs, where he could hear the young maid talking softly to Louisa. Sally looked up and put one finger to her lips, gesturing to the other bedroom. He peeped in and saw Isabella fast asleep on the bed, her glorious hair spread out on the pillow.

He beckoned to the girl. 'Bring Louisa downstairs. I thought you'd like to have a word with your grandmother, who came to see how you were going. After that, you could take the child out for a walk. It's a shame to sit indoors on a lovely day like this.' They got sunny days here nearly all year round, but people said it was best in spring, before it got too hot. He still didn't take sunshine for granted, not after growing up with the Irish mist and rain.

He watched the three of them walk up the path, then Mrs Hollins went back to the Bazaar and Sally held out her hand to the child. Louisa took hold of it trustingly and the two of them walked off in the direction of High Street. Even as he looked, Louisa gave a skip of sheer happiness which brought a lump to his throat. That child had been badly treated, but perhaps they could make it up to her a bit now.

When he went into the house, he heard the bed creaking upstairs and went to check on Isabella.

She was yawning and stretching, but not really awake. Almost immediately she turned over and went to sleep again. He went downstairs and settled on the sofa. He'd grant himself the luxury of a nap as well. He'd had quite a few disturbed nights, and who knew what would happen tonight?

After all Conn wouldn't be back from his day in Perth yet, and there was nothing else Bram could do to get ready for the Grand Opening.

'The lull before the storm,' he murmured as he drifted off to sleep.

In between dealing with various business matters and seeing his ship's holds cleared out and cleaned, Dougal put out word that he was looking for a small house for his mother to live in, as well as a maid to look after her.

The house was far easier to find than the maid, and he was quickly told of two places he could see that very day.

He sent a message to his sister, asking her to help him inspect the houses that evening and she sent word back that she'd be happy to do so.

They met outside St John's Church on High Street and strolled to the first address he'd been given. But it was in a poor situation and looked ready to fall down in the next high wind, so they moved on to the second house.

To their surprise, this was right behind the Bazaar. He stopped to study it and decided it was probably in good condition, structurally, though it needed smartening up and something doing about the garden, which was a tangle of weeds.

The owner was waiting for them on the front veranda, looking distressed. 'I'm so sorry, Captain, but the woman I asked to scrub it out this afternoon didn't turn up and the interior's still in a dreadful mess. And though I threw the other tenant out, he hasn't picked up his things yet. Perhaps you could come back in a day or two and I'll have it ready for you to inspect?'

Flora didn't wait for Dougal to speak. 'Let us have a quick look at it now. If it's not suitable, it won't matter what you do to it. But if it is suitable, we can perhaps come to some agreement about refurbishing it.'

'Well . . . if you're sure.'

The place smelled of stale cooking and sweat. Dougal

hesitated in the hall. 'You shouldn't be in a place like this, Flora.'

She laughed. 'I've seen worse when I was visiting the poor for the church.'

'I didn't know you were involved in that. Mother never said.'

'She didn't approve, so she told me not to tell people.' Flora moved ahead of him as she began to check the inside of the house. It was quite roomy, with six rooms and a very nice veranda at the back. This looked out on to a garden, another overgrown mess after the winter rains.

Flora walked back round the house a second time, looking thoughtful, so Dougal simply followed her, letting her come to her own conclusions while he worked out what he felt.

She turned first to the owner. 'I think it could be made very nice, but it needs cleaning and some rooms need painting.'

'That would cost a lot.'

'But if we took it on a two-year lease, your rents would be secure, would they not, and it'd pay you to do it?'

His expression brightened. 'Three years?'

She nodded. 'All right, three. Rent payable in advance, monthly.'

Amused at how businesslike she was, Dougal kept out of it. All he had to do was nod when the owner agreed to what his sister asked for.

'We'd like to move our mother in next week,' she said firmly. 'Can you have it ready for then?' As he nodded, she turned to Dougal. 'I think you should let Mother decide what furniture she wants to bring from home. She'll probably take far more than she needs, but it's a small price to pay. Don't let her into my old room, though, or the room I used as an office. I'm quite attached to some of the bits and pieces there that I had to leave behind.'

As they walked away, they met someone whose face he recognised. The woman hesitated, as if unsure how to treat them, and he raised his hat, saying loudly, 'Mrs Porter, how delightful to see you. I've just been taking the air with my dear sister. A lovely day, is it not?'

'Oh, um, yes. Good morning, Captain, Miss McBride.' She didn't linger, but at least she'd acknowledged Flora.

'We can overcome this gossip,' he said firmly as he heard Flora sigh. 'I'm not setting sail again until my mother has been moved and you're being treated as you deserve.'

She looked at him, eyes brimming with tears. 'You're the best of brothers.'

He patted her hand, as it lay on his arm, and kept his hand on it as they continued to walk. Twice he saw ladies he knew cross the street to avoid them, and he felt Flora's hand quiver beneath his. Once they met a lady at a corner before she had time to escape. She didn't respond to his greeting by more than an elevation of her nose and a quickening of her pace. He heard Flora's quick intake of breath.

He would remember that insult the next time the

lady's husband wanted to do business with him, he decided grimly.

After he'd taken Flora home, Dougal went back to deal with his mother, who was sitting downstairs, her hands idle, an unhappy expression on her face.

'Shall I ring for tea, dear?' she said at once.

'Yes. That would be nice. I need to talk to you.'

When Linny had left to prepare a tea tray, he said bluntly, 'I've found you a house. We'll move you in there next week.'

Her face turned so white he was afraid for a moment that the shock had been too severe, then she went bright red and the vicious, angry look reappeared. 'I told you: this is my home. After all I've done for you, I have the right to stay here. I can't believe you'd be so heartless as to turn your own mother out.'

'I still can't believe how cruelly *you* treated Flora. And to save further disputes, let me assure you now that I shall not change my mind about you moving, not for any reason.'

She seemed to shrivel and grow older before his eyes and he felt sad that it had come to this, but he'd only to remember the way people had avoided his sister today to stick to what he'd decided.

'When the house has been cleaned out, I'll take you there to see it, then you can choose which furniture you'd like to take with you from here.'

'What does that matter when you're sending me to a hovel?'

She forced a sob. He ignored it because he could tell it wasn't genuine. 'It's not a hovel, but a six-roomed house, just a short walk from High Street, a very convenient position. You'll be near your friends and the shops. We'll find you a maid, a scrubbing woman and someone to do the garden. I'm sure you'll be perfectly comfortable there. But if I ever hear that you've said *one word* to blacken my sister's name again, or even dropped a hint, then I will indeed throw you out on the street and cut off your money. You'd find it very difficult to manage on your godmother's legacy.'

She didn't say another word as Linny carried in the tea tray, didn't thank the maid and seemed uncertain what to do with the paraphernalia. Finally, she said, 'Tea?' in a tight, thin voice.

He nodded and accepted the cup she poured, drank it and forced down a piece of cake, then left.

Sometimes you had to do things that weren't easy, that made you feel uncomfortable.

But Flora needed his support now and for the fore-seeable future. And what more visible support was there than to install her in her old home again once he'd moved his mother out?

She could run the place as a boarding house, if she wished, or simply live there and keep house for him. That was up to her. She said she didn't want to live with him after he married, but it would take him time to find someone suitable, no doubt.

Sim came down to the cottage to report on what he'd seen, rightly judging it to be important.

'Captain McBride and his sister were looking round the house Mundy came out of. After they'd gone, the man who'd showed them round brought in some women to scrub it out – they're there now, sir, three of them – so what I want to know is, where's Mundy gone? He only went to the alehouse last time and stayed there, getting drunk.'

'Where indeed? And who's the house for, I wonder? Is Flora going to move in? If so, we must offer her all the help we can.'

Sim grinned. 'My wife strolled across to talk to one of the cleaning women, who lives in our street. She said the house was for Captain McBride's mother and that Mundy had left it in such a filthy state, they were having to scrub the whole place out.'

'Thank your wife, Sim. I don't know what we'd do without you two.'

When he'd gone, Bram let out a low whistle. 'For his mother! That *will* throw the cat among the pigeons.'

'But maybe it'll help Flora clear her name,' Isabella said softly. 'I do hope so.'

23

After a quiet supper, Bram and Isabella left Sally sitting in the kitchen with his newspaper, which she was thrilled to be able to borrow in the evenings, after he'd finished with it.

'How did it go with Louisa today?' he asked his wife.

'Very well. She's much livelier now she's not drugged and Sally is very good with her. I think the girl's a hard worker, too. Well, she would be, brought up by Mrs Hollins.' Isabella yawned. 'I'm so sleepy. I think I'll go up to bed early. I can't seem to stay awake these days.'

'Some women are like that when they're expecting.' He hesitated, not wanting to spoil her happy mood. 'Look, I think Mundy will be trying something on tonight. He'll want to spoil the opening if he can.' He saw her spread one hand across her chest in an instinctive reaction and didn't tell her of the latest written threat he'd received, this time asking for only fifty pounds. He'd shown it to Sim and Conn but no one else. 'I'm going to stay up and keep watch with the men.'

'Mundy must know you're taking precautions. Surely he won't be so stupid as to try anything else?'

'I don't think he is stupid. Cunning is the word I'd use. The trouble is, with over an acre of land, we can't watch every bit of the fences and of course he grew up here, knows every inch of the grounds and buildings. It's a pity the clouds blew in this afternoon. It's only a quarter moon so with the cloud cover, it'll be a dark night.'

'You'll be careful?'

'Of course. And I'll not be alone. I have four men helping me, as well as Les. There's only one of him. If anything happens, please stay inside the house. I don't want you tripping . . . or anything.'

'Carrying a baby makes me feel so helpless,' she complained. 'I want to help you, be by your side.'

'Ah, my darling, there's nothing you can do that'll please me more than providing me with a family.' He grinned. 'That's something I can't do myself, after all.'

She tried to smile at him but it was a poor effort. 'Well, the baby won't stop me developing the sales of silk and other materials as my contribution to the Bazaar. Mei Xiu and I discussed it before I left and we're going to work together on that. We have all sorts of ideas that will benefit us both. She has a wonderful eye for colour, and knows her silks.'

'That'll be good. It's not an area I understand anyway, but I gather ladies sometimes find it difficult to get good materials, especially as it's often feast or famine with goods for sale in this colony. In between shipments some items can be difficult to find.'

'You don't mind?'

'Mind what?'

'Me planning to work in the Bazaar? Some husbands wouldn't allow their wives to work in their businesses at all.'

'I'm not some husbands, and I want you with me as much as possible.' He pulled her close and held her against him, breathing in the soft, womanly smell of her. 'Your Mr Lee did me the best favour in the world, suggesting I marry you.'

'I feel the same,' she echoed. 'He's a very shrewd man.'

Always aware that someone could be watching the cottage, Bram waited till it was dark to slip out of the back door and lock it carefully behind him. Stifling a curse as he tangled with a washing line on the way across, he climbed the wooden rear fence of the small garden. He was wearing dark clothes and took care to move slowly and carefully, avoiding the noisy limestone path and making for the fence that adjoined the empty block of land.

There was one part where you could lift a section slightly to make a gap. He hadn't had it changed, because he felt sure this was where Mundy would cross. But where the man would go next was anyone's guess. Would anger at Bram's refusal to be blackmailed make him try once again to burn down the stables or the Bazaar? If so, he'd find it difficult. They were on the watch for that.

As well as having men guarding the place, Bram had had Les fill all the buckets he could find with water, and set them out at strategic intervals once it was dark. But the group of joined buildings that made up the Bazaar had been extended a few times, and not always to the same width, so the walls had angles and crannies where a man could hide. The task of keeping watch at night wasn't going to be easy.

He'd already told the guards where to find him, but

he detoured first to speak quietly to the one patrolling the perimeters, asking him to let the other men know he was now in place.

Time seemed to hang heavily and Bram was filled with a sense of dread. If anything went wrong with this venture, if his Bazaar was destroyed, he didn't know what he'd do. As a mere groom, he could never earn enough to keep Isabella in the manner she deserved. Only as a trader could he do that. And though he knew she'd never complain, it'd upset him greatly to make her live in poverty.

Worse still, if anything happened to her, he'd never forgive himself.

No, surely with all these men in place they could keep one villain at bay?

The watcher crouching in a hollow on the other side of the fence smiled as his eyes grew used to the dark. Little by little he marked out the men guarding the place and noted where each was patrolling. Fools! They kept following the same paths as they made their rounds, so once they'd passed he had time to move forward.

He'd not patrol so sloppily. He was cleverer than them, as he'd already proved.

The only one he couldn't see tonight was that scrawny Irish sod, who now seemed to be a part-owner of the livery stables. Him and Largan had paid too little for it, and it was only right that they make that up to a fair price now.

Somewhere in the distance there were footsteps and drunken laughter. Mundy smiled. It was starting and it'd work. It had to. He'd been a fool twice. He'd accepted less than his property was worth and he'd let that lying bitch steal most of his money.

But he'd not be a fool this time. He'd planned it all carefully, even how to disappear after he'd got his money. Oh, yes. It was going to work just fine.

Bram craned his ears as he heard something, then relaxed a little as he realised it was only drunken revellers going home past the stables, something that happened every now and then. He wondered what time it was but had left his pocket watch behind to keep it safe. He couldn't have seen it clearly even if he'd still had it on him. It must be earlier than he'd thought, though, if people were still around.

The men's voices and laughter came closer, several of them by the sounds of it. He caught the word 'birthday' and smiled in the darkness. Someone might be celebrating today, but they'd have a sore head tomorrow.

As they came to the stables, one of them stopped. 'Thass where Mundy used to live.'

'Damned Irish! They sneak in ev'rywhere,' another called.

Someone picked up a rock and hurled it at the stables, then suddenly the whole group started throwing things and yelling insults.

Bram moved forward, stumbling on a piece of rock, then stopped again, leaving it to the guards he'd employed to stop the group from causing any damage. He still listened carefully to the shouts and yells, though, in case it got out of hand.

Suddenly he heard something behind him, but as he turned, the world exploded in pain.

Mundy smiled down at the motionless figure. 'See how you like that, Irish.' Then he slipped away through the night, while his friends continued to jeer and yell, providing the distraction he needed.

At the cottage he slipped round to the back. He had no trouble climbing the fence, had done it many times as a youth to avoid his father's wrath when he'd been out drinking. The kitchen door was locked but his key still worked. Fools should have changed all the locks! Grinning, he edged inside, stopping for a moment to check where the furniture was, then feeling his way carefully across the back room.

He knew which stairs creaked and which didn't, so he made it up to the top without betraying his presence. It was quiet up here, not like the alehouse where he now lived and had to share a room with several other men and their night noises.

Mrs Irish would be alone in the house, now that her fancy friend had gone away.

Grinning in the darkness, he entered the front bedroom and crept forward to stand by the bed, fumbling in his pocket for the rope. He could see the shape of her, soft and womanly, and wished he had time to do more than snatch her, but he had to be out of the house and away before anyone realised he was there.

Isabella jerked awake with a muffled shriek when a clammy hand clamped itself across her mouth. Before she could fight him off, the intruder stuffed a gag in her mouth and tied a piece of rag round her face to keep it in place. Then he flipped her over to tie her hands behind her back.

She was terrified for her baby as well as herself, but was helpless to resist when he picked her up and carried her down the stairs.

Mundy. It had to be. She tried to struggle and he muttered, 'If you make any noise, I'll knock you out, missus. See how you like that.'

She stopped fighting, biding her time.

In the other bedroom, Sally was woken by the muffled shriek. She stayed perfectly still, wondering what the noise had been, then she heard a man speaking, threatening her mistress. She knew they were patrolling the grounds that night, because her granddad had warned her to stay indoors. How had the man got inside?

She didn't run to help, because her grandfather had taught her that only fools rush into something they aren't sure about. Praying that Louisa wouldn't wake up, she crept across to hide behind the door and listen more carefully.

When the intruder passed her doorway, carrying her mistress over his shoulder, she could see his outline and knew he was big. She could do nothing against a man like that so held back.

She heard the back door open and close again, knew the sound of it already, and let out her breath in a soft whoosh of relief. He hadn't seen her!

Only then did she creep down the stairs and turn

the big key in the front door lock. *Please don't let him hear me!*

Before she moved out of the house, she glanced round but couldn't see any sign of him. Run, she told herself. Run faster than you ever have before.

She flew across to the stables, where a group of men was taunting Les and the watchers. They sounded drunk. They didn't seem to notice her, thank goodness, so she got past them without any trouble.

Grabbing Les's arm, she said, 'It's me, Sally.'

'What are you doing out here, lass?'

'A man broke into the cottage and he's carried Mrs Deagan away. He'll still be in the grounds.'

Les was instantly alert and tugged the arm of the man next to him. 'That fellow's got past us, damn him, and captured Mrs Deagan. The lass thinks he may still be in the grounds. Fetch the master quick.'

The guard ran round to the rear of the stables, to the place where he'd last seen Mr Deagan. He heard someone groaning and that led him a short distance away, to a figure sitting on the ground, one hand to its head.

Quickly he explained what had happened and watched as Mr Deagan came suddenly alert and leaped to his feet.

'Fetch Sim from the Bazaar. And lanterns, as many as you can get. If the fellow's still in the grounds, he'll not get far.'

After a moment's thought, he yelled, 'Mundy! We've got you surrounded. You'll not get away with this.'

A sound from further along the fence made him spin round. Scooping up the rock that had hit him on the head, he began to run in that direction, yelling, 'This way. This way, men.'

Mundy stopped dead in his tracks as he heard the Irishman calling his name. Damnation, the little sod had recovered quickly. He should have finished him off, only he couldn't kill a man in cold blood, just couldn't do it.

'Don't come near me!' he yelled. 'I've got your wife here, Irish. If you come too close, I'll hurt her.'

Bram's heart began to thud with fear and anger combined. 'Let her go and we'll let you go, as well.'

'I need that money. Isn't your wife worth that much?'

'I haven't got fifty pounds. I'm telling you the truth, dammit!'

'How much have you got?'

'About twenty pounds.'

Silence, then Mundy said, 'Bring that. I'll let her go once I'm away from here.'

'I'm not handing over the money till after you've let her go.'

'You'll have to if you value her life.'

'Give me a minute to think.' Bram nearly jumped out of his skin as someone touched his shoulder. He turned to see Conn crouching behind him.

'Shh,' Conn whispered. 'He doesn't know I'm here. Make as much noise as you can while you walk to the house, and I'll try to sneak up on him.'

Bram hesitated. Conn was bigger than he was, but he doubted Conn would have learned to fight dirty, as Bram had had to. 'No, you go to the house.' He raised his voice and yelled, 'All right. But it's in the house. I'll have to go and fetch it.'

'Don't try to trick me.'

'I daren't. It's my wife and unborn child you're holding there.'

'Oh, hell! A baby!' Mundy muttered, the words carrying clearly in the quiet air.

'Go on,' Bram whispered.

Conn set off, making a lot of noise, and Bram crouched down, moving like a crab across the space that separated him from Mundy and Isabella. He circled them cautiously, trying to get out of Mundy's line of sight.

As he got closer, he realised Mundy had started moving towards the empty block of land. The liar! He didn't mean to keep his promise at all.

That made the anger suddenly burn white hot.

Isabella was still slung over Mundy's shoulder with her head dangling down his back and her arms tied, a horribly uncomfortable position. She could feel the tension emanating from her captor and was sure the slightest thing would make him explode into violence. She'd been listening to the exchanges carefully and knew Bram was near, or had been near. He'd gone to get some money now, though.

Her head was aching from hanging down and she hated being so helpless, but what was the point in wriggling? Mundy had meant what he said when he threatened to knock her senseless if she struggled, she was quite sure of that. But she raised her head slightly to ease the discomfort and peer around.

Suddenly she saw a patch of darkness behind Mundy move. She raised her head and strained her eyes. Someone was definitely there.

But then Mundy started moving away from the stables towards the empty land, walking quietly. Was he going back on his word, trying to escape, not waiting for the money? Her blood ran cold. What did he intend to do with her, then?'

The patch of darkness turned into a man-shape that continued to follow them through the muddy-coloured night. But whoever it was didn't manage to gain much ground and she began to worry that Mundy would get away and take her with him. He must have made some arrangements to escape, after all. What if he killed her first?

She tried to raise her head still further and Mundy growled, 'Stay still, you, or you'll be in trouble.'

So she lowered her head and waited a minute, but the only way she could see of slowing Mundy down and allowing the man she hoped was coming to rescue her to get closer was to make a fuss. She drew a deep breath and began to buck up and down, trying to drum her feet against Mundy's chest.

'You stupid bitch! Be still or you'll be sorry.'

She lay motionless for a moment and could feel him relax. But the man following them had come closer while they struggled, and she was almost sure it was Bram. She waited a few moments more then used every last bit of her strength to try to roll off his shoulder, kicking out at Mundy again.

With a roar of rage, he flung her down, knocking the

breath out of her. He swung back his foot to kick her and she tried to roll away, but only partly succeeded and the heavy boot connected with her shoulder. If it hadn't been for the gag, she'd have screamed with the sudden pain.

As he swung back his foot to kick her again, Bram hurtled out of the darkness behind him, arm raised, and thumped him on the head, thumping him again as he roared in pain, then a third time, which made Mundy slump to the ground.

'To me! I've got him!' Bram yelled at the top of his voice.

Footsteps came towards them. Someone cursed, someone else surged out of the darkness and suddenly they were surrounded by a group of men.

'Make sure he doesn't escape.' Bram threw himself to the ground beside her, unfastening the gag. 'Are you all right, my darling?'

'I am now.'

'Thank God! Let me unfasten this rope.' He turned her gently over. She winced and cried out as his touched the shoulder that had been kicked. He cursed as he had trouble unfastening the thin rope that bound her hands, then said, 'Aah!' and she felt her hands come free. She couldn't help groaning as she began to move then and they tingled painfully.

Bram gathered her close, covering her face with kisses, leaving Mundy to the other men.

Sim's voice got their attention briefly. 'I'll take that rope, sir. I'll tie him up good and tight, then we'll send for the constables.' He turned away.

Conn came to crouch beside them. 'Is she all right?'

Isabella answered for herself. 'Just a little bruised.'

'Now if I were a real hero,' Bram said softly, 'I'd carry you back to the cottage. But I'm not big enough to do that. Conn, could you be lending me a hand here?'

'Of course. You take her head and I'll take her feet.'

Isabella tried not to wince as she was carried across the bumpy ground, with some stumbles on the way.

Nothing had ever felt as soft as her bed. Someone lit a candle and brought it up. She closed her eyes for a moment or two at the relief of being back safely, then looked at her husband.

'You *are* a real hero,' she said.

Bram smiled at her and looked across the bed at his friend. 'Thanks, Conn.'

'I'm glad to be of help. Shall I go and supervise the handing over of our captive?'

'Oh, yes, please.' He turned back to his wife. 'I have someone much more important to look after.'

When Conn had left, Bram gathered her gently in his arms, burying his face in her hair for a moment or two. 'If anything had happened to you, I think I'd have lost my reason. Let me hold you, just for a moment or two.'

After a final kiss, he sat upright, still keeping her hand in his. 'I'll send someone to fetch the doctor.'

'There's no need. It's just a bruised shoulder.'

'And our child?'

'I'm sure the baby will be all right. Mundy kicked my shoulder, not my stomach.'

'We'll make certain of that. Ah, Sally! Come in. Can you keep an eye on Mrs Deagan for me.' He turned to Isabella. 'This clever lass saw Mundy take you and had the wit to stay hidden. When he'd gone, she came running for help. You did well tonight, Sally, really well.'

The maid beamed at them and set down the lamp she'd brought. 'I'm glad you're safe, Mrs Deagan.'

'How's Louisa?'

'I can't believe it, but she slept right through all that noise. Shall I make you a cup of tea? My Gran says tea's the best medicine there is.'

'I'd love one. And some water to wash in. I feel gritty. Bram, go and see that everything's all right. Sally will look after me.'

When he'd gone she let her head fall back on the pillow and gingerly felt her shoulder. It hurt more than she'd admitted, but she didn't want the fuss of a doctor. She just wanted her normal life back and no more upsets or threats.

Bram came back half an hour later and found her propped against pillows, her face rosy and clean now, sharing a second pot of tea with Sally. 'You look a lot better.'

'Have the constables taken him away?'

'Yes. And he'll not get out of prison for a long time, Conn reckons. He went with them to make sure everything was done properly. Mundy's friends, who pretended to be drunk to distract our attention, couldn't get away fast enough once he'd been caught. A guard managed to capture one of them, though, so he'll be facing the law too.'

'That's good.'

'I'll take the tea things down now,' Sally said.

They didn't answer, were too busy holding hands and smiling at one another.

Then Isabella gasped as something occurred to her. 'Bram! It's the opening of the Bazaar tomorrow, and we've had no sleep.'

'You're not going to the opening now. You need to stay in bed and rest, make sure the baby's all right.'

'The only way you'll keep me away from the opening is by tying me up and sitting on me.'

'But Isabella—'

'I mean it, Bram. I'm not going to be left out.'

'Are you sure you're all right?' He laid one hand gently on her belly.

She covered that hand with hers. 'I don't feel any pains or twinges. I'll not overstretch myself, but you'll not keep me away from the opening of my own Bazaar.'

He smiled ruefully. 'You're the perfect trader's wife. Well, you'd better get what sleep you can. I'll make sure it's all locked up downstairs and send Sally up to bed.'

He laughed as he walked towards the stairs. 'One day we're catching villains, and the next we'll be catching pennies. And I know which I prefer.'

EPILOGUE

The small band Bram had hired, marched slowly up and down High Street, playing a rousing march. Two men on either side of them carried posters on poles announcing

DEAGAN'S BAZAAR
GRAND OPENING TODAY
TEN O'CLOCK
BARGAINS FOR EVERYONE

He stood and watched them start their parade, pride filling him, then hurried back to the Bazaar. At ten o'clock Dougal had agreed to cut a ribbon stretched across the shop doorway. He was bringing his sister to the opening, but not his mother. No one had seen Mrs McBride since the day the captain returned from his voyage.

Isabella was sitting on a chair just inside the shop door, her arm in a sling, her face pale, with a couple of bruises showing along her jaw. Every time he saw them Bram wanted to punch Mundy.

Conn was standing opposite them, immaculately clad, looking elegant as only he could. Near him were other dignitaries of the town.

As ten o'clock approached, Bram went to offer his wife his arm and they moved to the ribbon, ready for the small ceremony. People were walking up the path already and more of a crowd had gathered than he'd expected.

'Are you all right?' he asked her.

'I'm fine. I keep telling you, it's just the shoulder that hurts. The rest of me is all right.'

'Then stand beside me. It's *our* Bazaar, not just mine. I couldn't have done it without you.'

Proudly she took her place and Sim stepped forward, calling for silence in the loud voice he'd developed as a sergeant in the Army.

When the crowd had stilled, he continued, his voice carrying clearly down the slope to the latecomers. 'I call upon Captain McBride to say a few words, then open Deagan's Bazaar.' He began to clap his hands and everyone joined in.

Dougal stepped forward to the ribbon. 'I'm not going to make a long speech—'

Someone shouted 'Hurrah for that!'

Smiling, he continued, 'But I do want to say that Fremantle is lucky to have a man like Bram Deagan setting up business here, providing a service like no other, trading in goods and items made by skilled craftsmen and women, and oriental specialities. I had the pleasure of walking round the Bazaar earlier and enjoying the sight not only of things everyone needs, but of the sort of goods that you don't often see in the Swan River Colony.'

The crowd broke into loud hurrahs, led by Sim's carefully placed men.

Bram's hand tightened on his wife's and he had to swallow a big lump in his throat.

'So as I'm sure you're all eager to look inside, without more ado, I'll declare Deagan's Emporium well and truly open.' He took the scissors and carefully cut the ribbon.

Bram stepped forward. 'Thank you, Captain McBride. And now, I'd like to welcome you all and invite you to come inside. The Bazaar is open for business.'

People moved forward eagerly and he tugged Isabella to one side to let them pass.

'I'll sit behind this table near the door and take money,' she said firmly. 'I'm not being left out.'

When the Bazaar was crowded, Dougal went to fetch his sister, who had been standing nervously out of sight.

'Are you sure this is the right thing to do?' Flora asked him.

'Certain. I've spread word that my mother will be moving out, that it's all been a big mistake caused by her being muddled, and I'm going to show the world that I'm proud to be your brother. Nash is going to follow us in a few minutes and we'll chat happily to him to show I'm not angry at him.'

He could feel the tension in the arm she laid on his but he ignored that, moving steadily forward with her, smiling as if he hadn't a care in the world.

Some people turned aside from them still, trying to do so unobtrusively, but many didn't and he began to relax a little. It'd take time, but his plan was working.

*   *   *

When Mitchell went into the Bazaar with his son, he looked round and spotted Dougal. Telling the boy to go and find something to buy as a celebration of this day, he moved forward, weaving through the crowd until he got close to the captain.

As they greeted one another amicably and stood chatting, the noise around them died down a little as people craned their ears.

Instead of hearing what they were saying, people were startled to hear a boy's voice raised in protest from across the room. 'My Dad does *not* share Miss McBride's bedroom! He shares with me and we never go in there. It's a lady's room.'

Heads turned to see two boys glaring at one another.

'And if you ever say that again, I'll punch you in the face,' Christopher added, looking so fierce as he took a step forward that the other boy fell back.

'You tell 'em, lad!' a man called out, and that broke the tension. People laughed and the voices started again.

Mitchell rolled his eyes at Dougal. 'I'm sorry. He always says exactly what he thinks, and now that he's started talking again, you have a hard job stopping him. That's thanks in part to your sister.'

'I think it was probably a good thing he said that. It just shows how far the poison had spread if children are saying things.'

Mitchell turned to Flora. 'Are you all right, Miss McBride?'

'Yes, of course I am.' She smiled. 'I don't think I've ever had such a passionate defender.'

After that, she noticed more people were smiling at

her and as their paths crossed, Miss Marley from the school stopped to say quietly, 'I'm so glad it's all been sorted out. Do bring Christopher to school on Monday.'

When all the fuss had died down and there was only the watchman's light showing in the Bazaar, Bram and Isabella settled down to count their money.

'I can't believe how much we've made today,' he said as they totalled up the last column of figures.

'It's a wonderful start. And the things from Mr Lee sold well. I hope Dougal is going to Singapore again next trip. We need to send for more goods.'

'Let's put the money away now and go to bed. You've done more than enough for one day.'

She smiled at him. 'I'm stronger than you think.'

'You're perfect in every way, but let me spoil you from time to time. It makes a man happy to look after his wife.'

'And you make me happy just by being . . . yourself.' She moved to take his hand. 'I love you, Bram Deagan. Surely you know that?'

He clutched her hand tightly and his voice was gruff with emotion. 'In spite of the differences between us.'

She pulled him towards her and put her arms round his neck. 'Don't say that, my darling. Don't ever say that again. The differences are what make us strong, what link us together and make our life richer. I can't imagine any man, gentleman or not, suiting me as you do.'

'Ah, Isabella, I don't think I've ever been as happy in my whole life.' He kissed her, then held her close. And the way they stood said as much about how they felt about one another as the words they offered each other.

She yawned suddenly and pulled away with a soft laugh. 'We've years for the loving, but I must admit, I'll be glad to seek my bed now. I'm tired. Aren't you?'

'I am, yes. You go up first and I'll just make sure everything's safe.'

As she climbed the stairs, she listened to him checking that everything was locked up below, including the new bolt on the back door, even though he'd shot the bolt himself earlier.

Like Bram, she hadn't felt as happy as this since she was a carefree, giddy child. It was a source of wonder to her that she'd met him, and in Singapore of all places. How had the Lees known he'd make such a good husband? She must write and tell them how happy she was. She smiled. They'd think it more important that she and Bram were working profitably together.

'Are you not in bed yet?' His voice was soft in her ear, and his lips were even softer on hers.

The trader's wife sighed happily and got ready for bed, lying next to the man she loved and staying awake for at least two minutes longer.

Bram lay smiling in the darkness, still holding her in his arms. Tomorrow was another day. And with Isabella beside him, sharing his life, loving him almost as much as he loved her, who knew what the future held? He had more now than he'd aspired to in his wildest dreams, but he'd continue to work hard: for her, for his children to come, for his family back in Ireland, too. But most of all, for her.

ABOUT THE AUTHOR

Anna Jacobs grew up in Lancashire and emigrated to Australia, but she returns each year to the UK to see her family and do research, something she loves. She is addicted to writing and she figures she'll have to live to be 120 at least to tell all the stories that keep popping up in her imagination and nagging her to write them down. She's also addicted to her own hero, to whom she's been happily married for many years.